Praise for *The Sea Before Us*

Sunrise at Normandy #1

"Sundin displays her usual knack for weaving historical detail into a rousing war drama in this enjoyable launch of the Sunrise at Normandy series. Sundin's lively book combines heart-pounding war action with inspirational romance to great effect."

Publishers Weekly

"The author of *When Tides Turn* kicks off a new wartime series, mixing her usual excellent historical research with fast-paced, breathtaking suspense."

Library Journal

"With a commanding grasp of naval history, Sundin spotlights women in the war effort and immerses readers in the ups and downs of naval missions and military exercises as she leads up to a riveting climax in the waters off Omaha Beach."

Booklist

"*The Sea Before Us* is another deftly crafted gem of a novel by Sarah Sundin and showcases her genuine flair for creating a simply riveting and entertaining read from beginning to end."

Midwest Book Reviews

"Sundin's research is fantastic and her historical research is second to none."

RT Book Reviews

"With a pitch-perfect balance between history and the fine-tuned elements of story, *The Sea Before Us* stands out as superior in WWII fiction. Faith anchors the narrative with realism and sensitivity, while Sundin's meticulous attention to historical research around the massive D-day invasion shines to the level of a master storyteller. It's at once engaging, emotional, and a strong series debut. I couldn't put it down—and when it came to the last page, I didn't want to."

Kristy Cambron, bestselling author of The Lost Castle and the Hidden Masterpiece series

"Once again Sarah Sundin delivers a powerful World War II story in *The Sea Before Us*. History comes to life through Sundin's characters, who cope with the trials and dangers not only on the fields of combat but also in their personal lives. This great combination of dramatic history and likeable characters will keep you turning pages to find out what happens next."

Ann H. Gabhart, author of These Healing Hills

Books by Sarah Sundin

SUNRISE AT NORMANDY SERIES

The Sea Before Us
The Sky Above Us

WINGS OF GLORY SERIES

A Distant Melody
A Memory Between Us
Blue Skies Tomorrow

WINGS OF THE NIGHTINGALE SERIES

With Every Letter
On Distant Shores
In Perfect Time

WAVES OF FREEDOM SERIES

Through Waters Deep
Anchor in the Storm
When Tides Turn

SUNRISE *at* NORMANDY

TWO

The

SKY ABOVE US

SARAH SUNDIN

Revell

a division of Baker Publishing Group
Grand Rapids, Michigan

© 2019 by Sarah Sundin

Published by Revell
a division of Baker Publishing Group
PO Box 6287, Grand Rapids, MI 49516-6287
www.revellbooks.com

Printed in the United States of America

Library of Congress Cataloging-in-Publication Data
Names: Sundin, Sarah, author
Title: The sky above us / Sarah Sundin.
Description: Grand Rapids, MI : Revell, 2019. | Series: Sunrise at Normandy ; 2
Identifiers: LCCN 2018026551 | ISBN 9780800727987 (pbk. : alk. paper)
Subjects: LCSH: World War, 1939-1945—Fiction. | GSAFD: Historical fiction. |
    Christian fiction.
Classification: LCC PS3619.U5626 S59 2019 | DDC 813/.6—dc23
LC record available at https://lccn.loc.gov/2018026551

19 20 21 22 23 24 25   7 6 5 4 3 2 1

Supreme Headquarters, Allied Expeditionary Force

6 June 1944

Soldiers, Sailors and Airmen of the Allied Expeditionary Force!

You are about to embark upon the Great Crusade, toward which we have striven these many months. The eyes of the world are upon you. The hopes and prayers of liberty-loving people everywhere march with you. In company with our brave Allies and brothers-in-arms on other Fronts, you will bring about the destruction of the German war machine, the elimination of Nazi tyranny over the oppressed peoples of Europe, and security for ourselves in a free world.

Your task will not be an easy one. Your enemy is well trained, well equipped and battle-hardened. He will fight savagely.

But this is the year 1944! . . . Our air offensive has seriously reduced their strength in the air and their capacity to wage war on the ground. . . . The tide has turned! The free men of the world are marching together to Victory! . . .

Good luck! And let us all beseech the blessing of Almighty God upon this great and noble undertaking.

General Dwight D. Eisenhower

1

OFF SAN FRANCISCO BAY, CALIFORNIA
SATURDAY, OCTOBER 2, 1943

Wars weren't won with caution, and aces weren't made in straight and level flight.

Lt. Adler Paxton tipped his P-39 Airacobra to the right and peeled away from the poky formation.

"Paxton? Where're you going? We're not in position."

Adler ignored Lt. Stan Mulroney's voice in his headphones and thrust the stick forward.

Five hundred feet below, Lt. Luis Camacho's flight of four P-39s grazed the top of the fog bank moseying toward the Golden Gate Bridge. By the time Mulroney found a position he liked, Cam would spot him and dive away into the fog.

Adler wouldn't wait that long. He lined up his tail with the afternoon sun, the engine thrumming in its strange position behind his seat. Most of the pilots in the 357th Fighter Group didn't like the Airacobra, but Adler had taken to it. They had an understanding.

The fighter plane screeched down to its prey at one o'clock below. Adler pulled out of his dive and aimed his nose just forward of Cam's nose. If he'd had any bullets, Cam would've flown right into them. Maybe the wreckage of his plane would've hurtled out of control and taken out another Airacobra or two like bowling pins. A pilot could dream.

He spoke into the radio. "Howdy, Cammie. Got you. Perfect deflection shot."

"What?" The wings waggled below. "Paxton? Where'd you come from?"

"Out of the sun and into your nightmares." Mama would scold him for cockiness, but it was part of the game. Besides, he'd never see Mama again.

He tightened his chest muscles against the pain, then sent Cam a salute and wheeled away.

Good-natured curses peppered the radio waves, but Camacho would pull the same move on Adler, given half a chance.

Alone again in the sky, Adler got his bearings and headed for base. The twin orange towers of the Golden Gate Bridge tempted him as always.

He'd beaten the fog, and the air and waters were calm for once, so he succumbed.

"Come on, darlin'. This may be our last time." In a few days the 357th was transferring to bases in the Midwest, and soon they'd head overseas. Into combat. Finally Adler could do some good.

He eased the plane into a shallow turning dive, aiming for the center of the bridge between the towers.

Down he went to seventy-five feet, his prop wash whitening the wave tops. Plenty of clearance, but the folks on the bridge wouldn't know that. He shot a glance to the pedestrians pointing and gawking, and he chuckled. Folks needed entertainment with the war on.

The girders rushed by over his clear canopy. He whooped, pulled back the stick, swung over Alcatraz, and did a neat roll over Treasure Island and the Bay Bridge.

Nice day for flying. Strange thing about the San Francisco Bay— autumn was warmer and clearer than summer.

Even though Adler had spent the better part of two years in

California, he still hadn't gotten used to the hills in summer, toasted to tan. Not like the green of the Texas Hill Country.

A cheek muscle twitched. Nothing there for him anymore anyway.

Adler contacted the control tower at the Hayward Army Airfield and made a smooth landing. After he and the crew chief finished the postflight check, Adler pulled off his flight helmet and life vest, slung his parachute pack over his shoulder, and strolled toward the equipment shed.

Major Morty Shapiro, the squadron commander, ambled toward him, tall and lean and angular. "Good flight? Heard you bounced Cam."

"Sure as shooting."

"Mulroney's not happy with you."

"Neither's Camacho." Adler sent him half a smile.

Shapiro didn't send even a quarter back.

"All right." Adler dipped his head to the side. "But I saw an opportunity and took it. Got in a great deflection shot."

"Your specialty." Shapiro's eyes narrowed. "Pull a muscle?"

"Hmm?"

Shapiro pointed to Adler's chest.

He paused, his right hand caressing his left breast pocket as if he'd indeed pulled a muscle. Yes, the scrap remained pinned inside, the fabric that had torn from his fiancée's dress when she'd fallen to her death.

Adler rolled his left shoulder. "Reckon I shouldn't have done those extra forty push-ups in calisthenics this morning."

Shapiro glanced behind him toward two men in dress uniform crossing the field. "There he is. Paxton, I want you to meet our newest pilot."

"Want me to show him the ropes?"

Shapiro's gaze slid back to Adler. "Actually, he's an ace. Nick Westin. He flew a tour in the Pacific."

The competition, then. Adler studied the two men. Westin was a big man, his chin high, a swagger to his step, a plume of cigarette smoke trailing behind him.

Adler had no intention of coming in second again, not that being first would be easy with all the hotshot pilots in the 357th. "Who's the other fellow?"

"New staff officer. Fenelli's the name."

Little guy, clipped step, soft about the face. The squadron needed pencil pushers to keep the planes in the air, and Adler would greet him as warmly as the ace.

"Capt. Nick Westin, I'd like you to meet Lt. Adler Paxton."

The little guy stuck out his hand.

Adler blinked, recovered, and returned the handshake. "Nice to meet you."

The man must have stood on tiptoes to meet the five-foot-four minimum height for fighter pilots, just as Adler had slouched to meet the six-foot maximum.

Westin's smile was soft too, but his handshake was good and firm. "Adler? That's an interesting name."

"Means *eagle*." Not only was it true, but it was easier than saying it was his mother's maiden name, given to appease her parents when she died birthing her second son.

Westin's dark eyes crinkled around the edges. "Born to fly, huh?"

"Sure was."

"Good trait in a wingman."

Wingman? Adler's heart stilled. But jostling for position was part of the game.

Wasn't it?

It wasn't. Shapiro nodded. "You'll be Westin's wingman. Figured he'd be the right man to teach you to work as a team."

A punch to the gut. Wingmen didn't make ace. They were sidekicks. Second class. Never first.

Adler threw on a smile. Nothing to be gained from pouting, and he could learn a few tricks from the veteran. "Looking forward to it. The major says you made a name for yourself in the Pacific. Reckon you have some stories."

"Sure do."

After Shapiro introduced Fenelli, the big, swaggering desk jockey, Adler excused himself to return his flight gear to the equipment shed.

Westin fell in beside him. "Where are you from? Down South?"

"Texas. And you?" The man's accent pegged him as a Yankee.

"Indiana. Prettiest land you've ever seen." Westin waxed on about the farms and the small town where his family ran a feedlot. Three sisters, two brothers, the prettiest wife, and the prettiest baby girl.

Fighter pilots loved to talk, and Adler loved to encourage them. He'd tell flying stories of his own to entertain, then toss out questions before things got personal.

"How about you?" Westin snugged his cap farther down over his dark hair. "Come from a big family too?"

Out of the sun and into his nightmares. He hadn't talked about his family in over two years, and he wasn't about to start now. Tell people he'd tried to kill his older brother Wyatt for accidentally causing Oralee's death? Tell people his younger brother Clay had tried to kill Adler later that same night? Not in a million years.

Instead he raised a rueful smile and snatched his set answer from the shelf. "Not all families are happy."

Westin's eyelids rose, then settled low in compassion. "So what do you think of the P-39? I flew the P-40 out of New Guinea. Got any pointers? Heard she's dangerous in a stall."

Adler liked the man already. "She can be. We've lost four pilots in stalls. You've got to keep a cool head."

Yes, the deflection shot was Adler's specialty.

11

NEW YORK CITY, NEW YORK
TUESDAY, NOVEMBER 23, 1943

This wasn't how Violet Lindstrom had dreamed of sailing overseas.

On the pier in New York Harbor, Violet tried not to lose sight of her fellow Red Cross workers among the thousands of soldiers, but her eyes were drawn to the HMT *Queen Elizabeth*.

Designed to be the most luxurious ocean liner in the world, she had never fulfilled her purpose. Instead, she'd been painted a dull gray and outfitted to pack in over twelve thousand troops.

Violet sighed, her unfulfilled longing echoing that of the great ship.

"Are you all right, Violet?"

She smiled down at her new friend, Kitty Kelly. "I couldn't be happier."

"Liar." Kitty winked a pretty brown eye. "I know homesickness when I see it."

Violet tightened her grip on her suitcase. How could she already be homesick? She who dreamed of being a missionary in Africa?

Kitty's teasing gaze wouldn't let up.

So Violet chuckled. "I'll be fine when we get to work in England."

"I can't wait to find out where the Red Cross assigns us."

"Me too." Violet latched on to her friend's eagerness. With her teaching experience, surely she'd be assigned to work with refugee children or orphans. What a lovely way to serve the Lord.

Winnie Nolan glanced back at Violet and Kitty. "I'm hoping for an Aeroclub. Sure wouldn't mind meeting a bunch of dashing pilots." She nodded toward a dozen men in olive drab overcoats and the misshapen "crush caps" favored by airmen.

"I'd rather work at one of the service clubs." Jo Radley adjusted her steel helmet. "Can you imagine living in London? How thrilling."

Violet refrained from wrinkling her nose. Entertaining the able-bodied wasn't serving.

"Lookie here." One of the flyboys, a dark-haired man in need of a shave, worked his way through the crowd. "The Red Cross is here to see us off. Where are the donuts, girls?"

"On the other side of the Atlantic," Jo said with a wink.

"How about a kiss instead?"

"You're more likely to get a donut, pal." Kitty spread an empty hand and a saucy smile. "And as you can see—no donuts."

His buddies crowded around, and Violet eased back, glad girls like Kitty could banter.

The pilot slapped a hand over his chest. "Aw, have a heart. We're going to war. We might not come home."

Kitty gave Violet a nudge and a mock pout. "Wouldn't that be a shame?"

"Come on. A fellow needs something to remember the good old US of A." His gaze drifted up to Violet. "Say, I've never kissed an Amazon."

And he never would. She ignored the sting of the familiar barb and opened her mouth to tell him . . . something.

He grabbed her head, yanked her down, and slammed a kiss onto her mouth. Wet, warm, awful.

She pushed against his chest, but he wouldn't budge. Masculine laughter and feminine protests filled her ears, and everything inside her recoiled. Where was the Red Cross chaperone when she needed him?

Someone wrenched the man away. "What on earth are you doing, Riggs?"

Violet hunched over and wiped her mouth with the back of her sleeve.

"Just getting a good-bye kiss."

"Not by force, you numbskull." Her rescuer had a Texas drawl. "Whatever made you think a pretty girl like her would want to kiss your ugly mug?"

Violet kept scrubbing at her mouth as if she could scrub away the humiliation.

"Here, sweetie." Kitty handed her a handkerchief. "You'll ruin your coat."

Oh no. Red lipstick smeared the sleeve of her charcoal gray Red Cross topcoat. How would she get it out?

"Listen up, boys." The Texan had to be their commanding officer. "These ladies are going overseas too. They're serving their country. Y'all will treat them with respect, first as ladies and second for wearing a uniform. Is that clear?"

The men grumbled their agreement.

"Apologize to her, Riggs."

Violet kept her head bent, the handkerchief over her mouth, her eyes scrunched shut.

"Sorry, miss."

"Apology accepted," she mumbled.

"Now, y'all get along," the Texan said.

Footsteps shuffled away.

"They're gone now." Kitty massaged Violet's lower back.

"Are you all right, miss?" A big hand rested on her shoulder. The Texan? Hadn't he left with the others?

Violet dragged her gaze from his brown oxfords up his olive drab overcoat to sky blue eyes right at her level. "I—I'm fine."

A smile twitched on his handsome face. "You will be. Any woman strong enough to meet Red Cross standards can handle one unwelcome kiss."

She tried to return his smile. "Thank you, sir. I appreciate your help."

"Anytime, miss. They give you any more trouble, send for me."

It would be handy to know a high-ranking officer. "Your name, sir?"

He swept off his cap and bowed his head, revealing sunny blond hair. "Lt. Adler Paxton, at your service."

A lieutenant? Yes, only one silver bar on the shoulder straps of his overcoat. He held the same rank as the others. Why had they listened to him? "You must be a married man."

His head jerked up. "Why—why would you say that?"

She held herself straighter, her dignity returning. "I've found married men are more chivalrous. Your wife is blessed."

"I'm not . . ." His eyelids sagged, clouding the blue. "Was engaged once."

Was? Her mouth drifted open, full of questions.

Then he flashed a grin. "Pleasure meeting you, miss." And he was gone.

Gone before she could tell him her name.

And she wanted to tell him, wanted to tell him she'd been engaged once too.

"Well, he's a looker," Kitty said.

Yes, he was. More importantly, he was a gentleman, like the cowboy heroes in her favorite movies.

"Remember the Red Cross guidelines," Jo said in a singsong. "We're here to offer mercy, a listening ear, and wholesome fun."

Winnie laughed. "If Violet wants to offer it to a handsome pilot, so be it."

"Not on your life, girls." Violet put on a playful smile and held up Kitty's soiled hankie. "I've had enough of flyboys to last a lifetime."

They all laughed.

And yet, Violet searched the sea of olive drab for the tall man with the intriguing blend of chivalry and mystery.

Something told her Adler Paxton needed that listening ear.

2

HMT *Queen Elizabeth*
NORTH ATLANTIC
THURSDAY, NOVEMBER 25, 1943

In the officers' mess on the *Queen Elizabeth*, Adler carved grooves for gravy in the mashed potatoes he wouldn't eat. Lately, he hated holidays.

"I've had better Thanksgiving dinners." Nick Westin inspected the greasy pork chop on his plate. "My wife makes the moistest turkey you've ever tasted."

Luis Camacho poked at limp green beans. "Gringo food. You should taste my mama's tamales. Those are something to give thanks for."

Adler's stomach wrenched. Nothing could beat his own mama's tamales. Daddy always said he'd married Lupe Ramirez for her cooking, but anyone who saw the way he looked at her knew he was only joking.

Memories. The reason Adler hated holidays. He shoved his chair back. "See y'all later."

"What's the matter? Seasick?" Willard Riggs stretched his face long in mock sympathy.

"Stomach of iron." Adler slapped Riggs on the back. "Unlike some pilots."

The other boys hooted, joshing Riggs for how he'd fed the fish their first night at sea.

Adler grabbed his cap, overcoat, and life belt.

Fresh air and a vigorous walk to clear his mind, then he'd fill the empty space with something else—a book, a magazine, whatever it took.

Five flights of stairs up to the sundeck, past officers sitting on the steps with their helmets between their knees. The seas were calmer today, but some men couldn't take it.

The *Queen Elizabeth* hadn't been fully fitted out before being commandeered as a troopship, but the stairways did boast Art Deco woodwork and brass banisters. Completely wasted on the green-faced men.

Adler returned the salute of the military policeman guarding the door to the sundeck, and he swung the door open. Cold air slapped him in the face. "Hoo-ey!"

He yanked on his gloves, turned up his coat collar, and strode toward the stern of the ship, the wind to his back.

Sundeck? It might have been partly sunny, but it sure as shooting wasn't warm.

Far below, gray waves spread to the horizon. And nothing but waves. The *Queen Elizabeth* sailed alone. Since she made thirty knots, she could outrun any German U-boat—and not many escort ships could keep up with her.

The cold air and the holiday had swept the deck pretty much clean of men. Most fellows were eating pork, sleeping it off, or revisiting it.

Four Army officers strolled on the swaying deck about twenty feet ahead of him, and a woman passed them, a tall pretty blonde with a red scarf over her hair.

Adler stopped. The girl Riggs had kissed on the pier.

He'd better reverse course.

She brightened and waved. "Lieutenant Paxton?"

Too late. He returned her smile. "Yes, ma'am. And I apologize. I can't recall your name."

She laughed and stopped a few feet away, her cheeks pink. "That's because I never told you. I'm Violet Lindstrom." Her voice had a gentle lilt, not quite Southern, not quite Yankee.

"A right pretty name." She wasn't any shorter than he. Just like Oralee.

"Thank you. It's my great-aunt's name, and I love it. She's my heroine."

Someone else's stories might keep his at bay—and she shouldn't mosey around alone. "May I join you? Reckon you could use a bodyguard."

She ducked her head, and the pinkness spread to her forehead. "Maybe. I just had to get some fresh air."

"Seasick?" He headed toward the bow of the ship.

She sighed. "Homesick. The girls are reminiscing, and all I can think about is the Lindstrom clan at home in Kansas, eating and laughing and telling stories."

To his left, the portholes in the gray superstructure had been painted over to block out all light. "I always say, 'If it hurts, don't think about it.'"

She turned startled blue eyes to him. "Don't think about it? Is that even possible?"

He shrugged. "Ponder something else. How about that Great-Aunt Violet of yours? Or would that make you think of Kansas?"

"Nope." Her smile rose. "She's in Africa."

"Africa?"

"She and Great-Uncle Gus are missionaries in Kenya. That's why she's my heroine."

"Great." He stiffened and shoved his hands into his coat pockets. A missionary. Maybe Great-Aunt Violet wasn't the best topic after all.

"She's an incredible woman." Violet's face lit up. "She came home when I was ten and asked if I loved Jesus. 'Oh yes,' I told her. She said I should be willing to make any sacrifice to serve him. And what could be a greater sacrifice than leaving my family for the mission field?"

Adler glanced to the lifeboats on their racks overhead as if they could whisk him away from the church talk.

"Want to see?" She reached into her coat pocket and pulled out a tiny wooden elephant. "Great-Aunt Violet gave this to me. It's ironwood from Africa."

"Cute." But not as cute as her girlish smile and the way she stroked the elephant's trunk.

"I named him Eliezer, but my youngest brother broke off the tusks. I renamed her Elsa."

Adler laughed. "Boys destroy."

"Yes, they do." Her face darkened, and her gloved fingers coiled around the elephant. "I keep her close to remind me of my dream."

She was awful far from Africa. "How'd you end up in the Red Cross?"

Violet tucked away the elephant. "As you said, boys destroy."

"The war?"

She brushed her hand along the wooden railing. "You could say that. I became a teacher instead, and I put every spare minute into our Red Cross chapter. I had to wait until I turned twenty-five to serve overseas, so on my birthday I applied."

So she was his age.

The path narrowed as it curved around the bridge area, and the wind swirled in a new direction, biting cold. Adler fell in behind Violet and slapped one hand on his cap. "Why twenty-five?"

"The Red Cross knows we might see difficult things, so they want ladies who are more mature."

"Makes sense."

"And—well, I'm hoping to work with refugee children or

orphans, but most of the girls will work with servicemen. The Red Cross wants the boys to see us as big sisters rather than sweethearts."

They rounded the corner to the port side of the ocean liner, and the wind dropped off. Adler released his grip on his cap. "You ladies aren't allowed to date? Not that y'all have to worry about advances from me."

"No. We—we're allowed to." She lowered her face and re-arranged her red scarf. "But that isn't our purpose."

Swell. He'd embarrassed her and started a topic he always avoided. He'd better find a reason to break away. Where was a door back inside?

"Is it too fresh?" Concern crimped one corner of her mouth.

Adler blinked. "Fresh?"

"Too soon?"

They were both speaking English, but she might as well have been speaking Swahili. "Huh?"

"Your engagement." Red rushed up her face. "I'm sorry. When you said we had nothing to worry about from you—well, in New York you said you'd been engaged, and you sounded so sad. I assume it must have been recent."

Too cold to breathe.

"I'm sorry." She pressed her fingertips over her mouth. "What a horribly personal question. I shouldn't have—"

"It's okay." He forced air in and out. He'd asked her some fairly personal questions too. Besides, he made a point of letting people know about Oralee so they wouldn't pester him about going out. And he wouldn't see Violet in Britain, so it was harmless to talk to her. "My fiancée—she died."

"Oh no. I'm sorry. Was she sick?"

Breathe in. Breathe out. "We were hiking. She fell, hit her head."

He could still hear himself coaxing her to cross the footbridge, sweet-talking, manipulating. He could still hear his older brother

Wyatt. *"Stop forcing her to do something she doesn't want to. Protect her for a change."* He could still hear Oralee pleading with them to stop fighting, that she'd go, that she could take care of herself.

And he could still hear her scream.

A touch to his arm. "Adler? I mean, Lieutenant?"

The tall blonde swam into focus, compassion and worry etched into her features.

He swallowed, wet his lips, found part of a smile. "Reckon you can call me Adler now."

Her face softened. "Would you like to talk about something else? Flying perhaps?"

"Yeah. Yeah." He headed toward the stern, under the lifeboat racks. "Flying is good."

Violet let out a low laugh. "I'd expect a pilot to think so. Do you fly fighters or bombers or . . . ?"

"Fighters. I'm in the 357th Fighter Group. We've been assigned to the Ninth Air Force in England, the tactical force. The Eighth Air Force is strategic."

"What's the difference?"

The cracks in his control filled in again. "Think of it this way. Tactical is for today. Strategic is for tomorrow."

"All right." She nodded, head tilted.

"A tactical air force usually supports ground troops, shooting up airfields and trucks and gun positions, meeting today's needs. A strategic air force knocks out the enemy's war machine—the factories he needs to keep fighting tomorrow. In the Eighth Air Force, the fighter aircraft escort the bombers."

"I understand now. So, are you an ace?"

That hit another sore spot. "Haven't seen combat. And they made me a wingman, so I might never make ace."

"A wingman supports the other pilot, right?"

"The leader. Yeah."

"That sounds important, protecting and guarding."

Adler's hands clenched in his pockets. "Second class. It's a second-class job."

Her smile widened. "As Jesus said, 'The last shall be first, and the first last.' You're in a wonderful position indeed."

He knew better than to argue with a woman quoting Scripture. "Yeah."

But if that were true, he would have been first long ago.

The wind curled around the stern end of the superstructure, and Adler charged into it.

"Paxton!"

Adler followed the sound of the voice over the railing to the decks below, which dropped off like steps at the stern of the ship.

"Paxton! D'you hear me?" someone barked on the promenade deck right below. But that area was for enlisted men, and no enlisted man in the 357th would talk to Adler like that.

"Yes, Sergeant. Sorry, Sergeant."

Adler sucked in a breath. He knew that voice.

A soldier turned from the railing below. A dark-haired soldier with a familiar tan complexion and a familiar stocky build.

"No." Adler's voice huffed out. Clay? It couldn't be. Clay was in Texas, in college, studying to be a physician.

"Get your tail in here," the sergeant barked.

"Yes, Sergeant." That gait. No mistaking it.

Adler darted back from the railing, out of his younger brother's line of vision.

"Daddy and Mama can't protect you forever," Clay had said that night, his eyes black with rage. "If you ever come back home, I'll kill you."

He would. He'd finish the job he'd started. Adler didn't intend to give him the chance.

"Adler?"

Violet.

She stood there, staring at him.

He forced calm onto his face, then pointed over his shoulder with his thumb. "Remembered something I've got to do. See you later."

Adler marched away from Violet, away from Clay, away from his memories.

If only he could get away from what he'd done.

3

HMT *Queen Elizabeth*
GREENOCK, SCOTLAND
WEDNESDAY, DECEMBER 1, 1943

Violet closed her suitcase and patted her overcoat pocket to make sure Elsa was safe.

In their stateroom, Kitty and Jo and Winnie chattered. "Scotland! I hope we see men in kilts." "Do you think we'll meet the king?" "The air raids are over, aren't they?" "I brought *Pride and Prejudice*. Imagine reading Jane Austen in England."

Violet kept her face toward the bunk, put her helmet over her Red Cross cap, and blinked away the moisture in her eyes.

"You're quiet, Violet," Jo said.

"Making sure I packed everything." She was supposed to be excited, not homesick. This was what she'd worked for, the closest she could get to being a missionary with the war on.

If only Dennis Reeves hadn't abandoned the dream of missions that had led to their engagement. Then they would have been serving abroad well before the United States entered the war. As Adler had said, "Boys destroy."

A rap on the open stateroom door. "Ready, ladies?"

Kitty pulled her helmet over her brown curls and saluted the Red

Cross chaperone. "Yes, sir! Mr. Porter, sir! Private Kelly reporting for duty, sir."

Long-suffering Mr. Porter shook his gray head. "The Nazis are quaking in fear."

Even Violet laughed.

"Come along, ladies." Mr. Porter motioned them into the passageway.

Violet slung her purse and musette bag and gas mask across her chest and picked up her suitcase. She peeked under the bunks, but nothing had been left behind.

In the passageway two dozen Red Cross volunteers tramped along, looking for all the world like GIs, if not for skirts, curls, and lipstick.

Violet stroked the polished wood paneling as she walked. Her brother Karl would love to get his woodworking tools on bird's-eye maple like this.

Her throat swelled. Maybe she should follow Adler's advice—if it hurts, don't think about it. But why would she want to stop thinking about the people she loved?

Someone bumped her and apologized, and Violet said, "That's all right." And it was. She'd be all right.

The throng of officers and Red Cross girls climbed the broad elegant staircase in the middle of the ship. The ladies had been billeted on the deck that would have housed first-class passengers in peacetime.

She scanned for Adler once again. She hadn't seen him since Thanksgiving. Hardly surprising given the quantity of troops aboard, but disappointing.

Most men stretched taller when they talked to her, stood on steps, lifted their chins. But Adler looked her straight in the eye, unfazed by her six feet of height.

And that sad air of mystery about him.

Why had he left so abruptly, ashen faced?

Violet shook herself and climbed the final steps onto the promenade deck. She'd never see him again anyway.

"Stay together, ladies." In the crowd of GIs, Mr. Porter waved his hand overhead. "If you get separated and catch different ferries to shore, meet at the Red Cross booth on the pier."

Violet made her way along the covered promenade deck with its banks of long painted-over windows. Cool air flowed through the opening for the gangway, relieving the stuffiness.

Mr. Porter paused at the top of the gangway. "Let this group pass so we can stay together."

"A gal could get claustrophobic in here." Tiny Jo looked pale, walled in by the crowd.

Violet didn't have that problem, but she offered Jo a reassuring smile. "We'll be on our way soon. Take deep breaths."

From the other direction, a group of men filed onto the gangway. They wore pilot's caps.

Violet's gaze flew over the men. She recognized a few faces from New York, including that horrid Riggs, who was busy joking with a friend, thank goodness.

There was Adler. He had his head down and his collar up, as if he didn't want to be seen.

"Adler," she called.

His gaze jerked up. After a bewildering long pause, a smile twitched and he worked his way over to her. "Hi, Violet. Good to see you again."

"Good to see you too." Why did she feel like an awkward schoolgirl all of a sudden?

"Listen, I apologize for how I ran off the other day." He gave her a sheepish look and adjusted the duffel bag over his shoulder.

"It's all right. I understand." Although she didn't.

"Thanks." He flashed that great grin. "You and Elsa have a good time in jolly old England, you hear?"

"We will." She smiled, longing to wish him so much more than a good time—to pray for his healing and joy and safety and success. "I'll be praying for you."

"Thanks." He tipped his cap to her. "Bye, now."

"Good-bye." He didn't say he'd pray for her too. Not that she selfishly wanted his prayers, but only a hint that he might know the Lord. *God, please be with that man.*

"Follow me, ladies." Mr. Porter led the way.

Violet stepped outside and had her first glimpse of a foreign country. Across the gray waters of the Firth of Clyde, heavy dark clouds pressed low over flat green hills. It was pretty in a brooding sort of way, but it wasn't . . . home.

For the first time since she was a child, Violet felt very small.

RAYDON ARMY AIRFIELD, SUFFOLK, ENGLAND
THURSDAY, DECEMBER 2, 1943

So this would be home. Adler peered over Nick Westin's shoulder out the back of the canvas-covered Army truck.

Through the drizzle, gray-green forms rose from the mud, hangars and huts and utility buildings.

"Notice what's missing?" Luis Camacho said from the bench across from Adler.

Riggs leaned out the back and swore. "Where are the airplanes?"

"Airplanes for pilots?" Lt. Tony Rosario slapped his hands to his thin cheeks, making his ears stick out even more. "What'll you want next? Guns for soldiers? Boats for sailors? You keep talking crazy like that, and they'll lock you up."

Adler joined the men's laughter.

"Don't worry, boys," Nick said. "We'll have planes before you know it."

Riggs waved away Nick's words. "Baloney. They left us here to rot in the mud."

Adler chose the middle road between cheerleading and whining. "You know the Army Air Force. Hurry and wait. Hurry and wait."

"Adler's right." Nick gave him a warm smile. "While we wait, we'll have plenty to do."

Camacho chuckled. "Leave it to Saint Nick to find that silver lining."

The nickname had sprung from Nick's easy way of talking about God.

Adler's grip tightened around the duffel bag between his knees. Violet talked that way too. So did Mama and Daddy. So did Oralee and Wyatt and Clay.

Clay.

His chest tightened. After he'd seen his brother on the *Queen Elizabeth*, Adler had stayed in his stateroom except for meals in the officers' mess.

When Adler fled Texas in June 1941, Wyatt had just graduated from college to take his place in Paxton Trucking, freeing Clay to start college. After Pearl Harbor, the universities had converted to three-year programs, so Clay should have been about done with his bachelor's degree, ready for medical school. The US desperately needed physicians, so medical students were deferred from the draft.

How on earth had Clay Paxton ended up in an Army uniform on a troopship? And how far was he stationed from Raydon Army Airfield?

A bump in the road jolted Adler. No way of finding the answer, so no use pondering.

The truck stopped in front of a Nissen hut. The building looked as if a giant had pressed a tin can sideways into the mud with only half showing.

Adler hopped out and shielded his eyes from the cold mist. He'd lived in better places, but he'd also lived in worse.

The pilots stepped through a door in the brick end of the tin can, lugging their duffel bags. Cots ran down both sides of the hut, and two coal-burning stoves sat in the aisle.

Nick threw his gear on the cot at the far end, farthest from the stove, and Adler took the one next to it.

Rosario pressed his cap over his heart and sang "Home, Sweet Home" in a warbling falsetto.

The last place Adler wanted to think about, but Rosie's antics kept the men laughing.

Adler hung up his overcoat on a long rack that ran above the cots and set his cap on the rack. Then he unpacked his uniforms and underwear, and stacked his books on a wooden crate beside his cot—well-worn Zane Grey novels he'd bought in a secondhand store in Los Angeles.

Next to the books, Nick set out framed photographs.

Adler picked one up. Nick and a pretty light-haired woman on their wedding day. "Can't believe you found a woman willing to put up with you."

"Neither can I." Nick handed him another photo. "Here's Peggy with little Gail."

"Beautiful." The baby sat on her mother's lap, one plump hand stretching for the camera as if waving at Daddy.

If Oralee had lived, they'd have been married by now, might have had a baby.

"Do you have any photos?" Nick asked.

"No." Adler set down the frames. "I told you I'm estranged from my family."

Nick sat on the cot. "Your former fiancée?"

Adler stuffed his empty duffel under his cot. "Her picture's in my wallet."

He'd escaped that night with his wallet in his trousers and the scrap from Oralee's dress in his shirt pocket. And he'd barely had time to fetch his trousers and shirt.

Pain ripped through him. He would *not* think of that.

29

"Want to hear my theory?" Riggs rummaged inside his duffel. "Paxton's a wanted criminal. No mementoes, no pictures, no mail."

"Better watch your back." Adler cocked one finger at him like a gunslinger and dropped an exaggerated wink.

Theo Christopher jumped in front of Adler and planted his fists on his hips. "I'll protect you, Riggs. I'm your wingman."

Adler patted the kid on the shoulder. "We'll all sleep better."

Riggs kissed a stack of envelopes. "I get letters from dozens of dames."

"Good thing you've got so many women," Adler said. "Once they get to know you, they scram."

Riggs laughed. "Shows what you know. Then we've got Baby-Face Theo. Bet he's never even kissed a girl."

Theo whirled around. "That's a lie. I kissed a girl once."

The men all roared with laughter.

Adler grinned and reclined on his lumpy cot. Thank goodness for the joking. The boys had dug too deep, too close.

When he'd talked to Violet, he should have stopped after he told her Oralee had died. Why had he let more details escape? Every detail poked a hole in his shell, begging more details to follow.

That would destroy him.

4

Violet, Winnie, and Jo shielded Kitty as she huddled under the eaves with the map. Mist feathered the back of Violet's raincoat.

"This is Grosvenor Square." Kitty pointed over Jo's shoulder. "So that's Headquarters."

Violet peeked under the brim of her rain hat. Through the mist, bare trees filled the square, bounded by solid buildings in brick and gray.

"Let's go." Kitty tucked the map into her coat pocket and hooked her arm through Violet's. "If this meeting doesn't take long, what sights should we see this afternoon?"

Winnie strolled behind them. "Over the weekend we saw Buckingham Palace and Westminster Abbey and Big Ben and Harrods."

"How about the Tower of London?" Jo said.

Kitty winked at Violet. "Wasn't it nice of the English to put all their tourist attractions so close together?"

Violet laughed. It was exciting to be in London, if disorienting. She'd spent a month in Washington for Red Cross training and a few days in New York City before they shipped out, but she wasn't used to traveling on subways and the crush of people and buildings.

31

Where would the refugee children be? The children had been evacuated from London during the Blitz in 1940, but Violet had seen plenty of little ones in town. If only she could serve in one of the charming villages she'd seen from the train. That would feel more like home.

They passed four American naval officers, and the men tipped their caps to the ladies. Mr. Porter had said several US military commands had headquarters in Grosvenor Square.

So did the American Red Cross, a tall brick building with the American flag and the Red Cross flag over the door.

In the coatroom they shed damp raincoats and smoothed their gray-blue uniforms. Violet loved the single-breasted jacket and knee-length skirt, the white blouse closed at the neck with the enamel Red Cross pin, the garrison cap, and the black oxford shoes—with flat heels, thank goodness.

A matronly Red Cross worker led them to the Field Service Director's office, where eight more girls from their ship waited.

Mr. Charles Abrams met them, a trim gentleman with wavy salt-and-pepper hair. "Welcome. Please make yourselves comfortable. I'm sorry I don't have enough chairs."

Kitty perched on the arm of a chair, and Violet leaned against the back wall.

Mr. Abrams sat behind a big wooden desk. "We're glad you ladies are here. The troopships bring tens of thousands of our boys each month. Someday soon we'll invade the continent and drive out Hitler and his gang. In the meantime, the boys need the services of the Red Cross."

Violet raised a benign smile. That might be why the other girls were here, but not her.

"This month alone we're opening two service clubs, seven Aeroclubs, and two clubmobiles. You may have your choice among these three assignments."

An emptiness formed in Violet's chest. "Excuse me, sir? What about those of us who are here to work with children?"

"Children?" He frowned around a cigar.

"Yes, sir. I'm a teacher. I'm here to work with refugee children or orphans or—"

"The British Red Cross takes care of those needs. The American Red Cross is here for our servicemen." He tilted his head toward a poster that showed a GI raising a tin cup of coffee, with the slogan "Your Red Cross is at his side."

The emptiness spread to her belly. "I was told I could work with—"

"You misunderstood. What's your name?"

"Violet Lindstrom." She took deep breaths as he shuffled papers. There had to be a mistake. Had to be.

"Lindstrom . . . yes, you were selected for your administrative skills. You ran your local chapter with distinction and helped organize other chapters."

She nodded, but the hollowing carved out her last hopes.

"Service club, Aeroclub, or clubmobile?" Mr. Abrams grinned at the ladies.

Winnie leaned forward. "What's a clubmobile?"

The director chuckled. "We're proud of that innovation. The clubmobile is a van that contains a kitchen, serving counter, and a reading room. Two girls drive it to airfields and serve coffee and donuts to airmen returning from missions. It even has a phonograph and speakers so the girls can dance with the boys."

"What fun." Winnie nudged the girl beside her. "I wanted to work in an Aeroclub, but this sounds better. Sign me up."

Three more hands shot up, and Mr. Abrams took down their names.

Violet pressed her shoulder bag tight over her rebelling stomach. A clubmobile required perky girls who could wisecrack and jitterbug. Not someone like her.

Jo thrust her hand in the air. "I want to work in a service club."

"Like where we're staying here in London?" the girl beside her asked.

"Isn't it wonderful?" Jo said. "The club gives our boys a hot meal and a comfortable room when they're on leave, organizes tours and activities, and assists them."

Violet's mind reeled. She hadn't come across the Atlantic to serve coffee. *Lord, what should I do?*

More hands popped up, volunteering to work at clubs in cities throughout Britain.

"Sir, I'd like to work in an Aeroclub," Kitty said.

Mr. Abrams's brows settled lower. "Aeroclubs are considered our most dangerous work. The ladies serve on air bases in the country. Conditions are rustic, and the bases are legitimate targets for German air raids."

"Yes, sir. That's what I want. I'm Kathleen Kelly." Kitty looked over her shoulder, her brown eyes large and pleading. "Violet, come with me, please."

"Good idea," Mr. Abrams said. "Each Aeroclub needs a director and a staff assistant."

Violet could barely think. At least Aeroclubs were in the country rather than the city. Danger and rustic conditions appealed to the missionary in her. And she'd be with Kitty. "Yes, I'd like that."

Kitty grinned and hunched her shoulders. "We'll have so much fun."

She wrangled up a smile, but then a new shock rattled her. An Aeroclub. Airfield. Airmen. What had she done?

"Miss Lindstrom, with your administrative skills, you'll be the director. Miss Kelly, the staff assistant." Mr. Abrams made notes. "You'll be at a new Eighth Air Force field."

Eighth . . . Hadn't Adler said he was with the Ninth Air Force?

Now her smile felt somewhat genuine. At least she wouldn't be with that horrible Riggs or the overly intriguing Adler Paxton.

"That's all of you." Mr. Abrams set aside his pen. "My secretary will see to your travel arrangements."

Violet joined the chattering women as they left, but she didn't belong with them, didn't belong in England.

If only Dennis hadn't let money lure him away from missions. Because he'd broken his promises to her and to God, Violet was in England instead of serving the needy in Kenya or China or Brazil.

Not only was she far from home, but now she was even further from her dream.

RAYDON ARMY AIRFIELD
FRIDAY, DECEMBER 10, 1943

Mutton, brussels sprouts, and mashed potatoes. Adler swallowed a nasty mouthful.

"Can you believe it?" From the other side of the table in the officers' mess, Willard Riggs swore at a brussels sprout. "Lousy food, shoveling lousy mud, lousy ground school as if we were only cadets, and still no planes."

With an air war raging over Europe, Adler shared Riggs's frustrations. But bad morale could shoot down the group before the Luftwaffe fired a single bullet. "I reckon they're stalling. They're letting those other fighter groups get in a few licks while they can, 'cause once the 357th hits the skies, it's all over."

Nick Westin laughed. "We'll single-handedly defeat the Luftwaffe, huh?"

Theo Christopher's big eyes lit up. "We'll knock out the entire German army."

"Now y'all are talking." Adler shook pepper on his mutton, as if it'd help.

Riggs jutted out his scruffy chin. "Let me loose, and it'll be over by Christmas."

Adler pointed the pepper shaker at the man. "If nothing else, you can pummel them with your gigantic ego."

"Say, fellows," Nick said. "Now that we've almost won the war, we'd better make postwar plans. What do you want to do, Theo?"

Adler smiled at Nick even though the mutton was as tasty as warm, wet wool. When it came to ending the whining, Nick played a good wingman to Adler.

"Back to Oregon." Theo scooped mashed potatoes onto his fork. "I want to teach junior high English."

Riggs snorted. "No money in that. My old man's a stockbroker on Wall Street. I'm joining his firm. How about you, Santa? Back to the North Pole?"

With Christmas on the way, the nickname "Saint Nick" had changed to "Santa." "The missus and I plan on having a whole brood of elves, turning the feedlot into a toy factory."

Three sets of eyes turned to Adler.

Unlike them, he could never go home, never go into the family business as he'd always wanted. He sure didn't want to go back to college. The only reason he'd gone was because Wyatt had. Whatever Wyatt did, Adler had to do and better, making up for Wyatt's advantage of birth.

How pointless that seemed now.

"Paxton's going back to robbing banks," Riggs said.

Adler cracked a smile. Might as well test his idea. "I'm going to start an air shipping company."

"Hmm," Nick said. "Sounds interesting."

It did. It combined his knowledge of moving freight with his love of flying. "After the war, a lot of pilots will be looking for work. And moving cargo by air is faster than by truck or rail. It's the future."

"I like it." Theo flashed his boyish smile.

"I even have a name—ACES." Adler brushed his hand over the imaginary logo on the tail of his plane. "Air Cargo Express Shipping. I'll hire ace pilots. That'll be my hook: 'First in war—first in freight.'"

Riggs raised one thick eyebrow. "You have to be an ace yourself to make that stick."

"Obviously."

"Hard to do as a wingman."

"So it'll mean even more." Adler took a casual swig of coffee. "Every one of my victories will be like three of yours."

Nick held up one hand. "Remember, this flight is a team, the four of us working together."

"We sure are." Adler flicked a smile to Riggs as if to say, "Beat you in *that* one."

After the men finished their meals, they filed out of the mess, between rows of tables filled with men in olive drab.

And two women in gray-blue—the Red Cross workers who'd arrived that morning.

"What have we here?" Riggs let out a wolf whistle. "Dessert is served."

Adler punched him in the shoulder. "Leave 'em alone, or you won't get any donuts."

"Are you kidding?" Riggs set his hands on the ladies' shoulders. "Once you dolls get a taste of me, I'll be rolling in donuts."

The petite brunette on the left shrugged off Riggs's hand and wrinkled her freckled nose. "One taste of you, buster, and we'll lose our appetite."

Adler howled in laughter, joined by Nick and Theo. These ladies could handle themselves. Still, he was glad the women's quarters were off-limits—and that Violet Lindstrom was nowhere near Raydon Airfield.

The men headed outside into the darkness. An almost-full moon defied the blackout.

Then the air raid siren broke the stillness.

Adler tensed and searched the sky in vain.

Riggs swore.

Adler let out a curse of his own, but it only triggered a string of angry Spanish in his mother's voice in his head. An echo from his first summer home from college. The first time, the only time, he'd cussed in front of her.

"Where are they?" Nick's voice was tight and hard.

The sound of airplane engines competed with the siren.

Adler's fists clenched. They ought to go down to the shelter, but warriors didn't hide. "Four planes. Give us four planes, and we'd sweep them from the sky."

A chain of yellow fireballs rose about a mile away, followed by low rumbles and vibrations.

"They missed," Theo said.

"Stupid Krauts." Riggs shook his fist at the sky. "No lousy planes to hit anyway."

"Soon enough," Nick said. "Soon enough."

Adler glared into the darkness. Not soon enough for him.

5

The jeep bounced along the narrow lane, and Violet clamped one hand over the suitcases beside her in the backseat and the other on her hat.

In the front seat, Kitty held on to her own hat. "It's so flat here. I thought England would be all rolling hills."

"I like it." Violet inhaled the rich smell of farmland and feasted on the wide open spaces. "It reminds me of home."

"Flat land is ideal for airfields." Mr. Rufus Tate, their Red Cross Field Director, turned onto an even narrower lane. "Now that you've arrived, I can give you the details. You two will set up the Aeroclub at Leiston Army Airfield, home of the 358th Fighter Group. They fly P-47s."

The 358th? Off by one digit. Violet's smile grew.

"P-47 Thunderbolts," Kitty said. "My brother flew one."

Violet had heard Kitty mention two brothers in the Army, a brother in the Marines, and two sisters working in factories, but not a fighter pilot.

"Where did he serve?" Mr. Tate said.

"The Mediterranean. He was killed over Sicily."

Violet gasped.

"That's why I requested an Aeroclub." Kitty's voice didn't even quiver.

"I'm so sorry," Violet said. Sicily—that was only this past summer. "You never mentioned—"

"I had two choices. I could sit around and cry, or I could do something. I chose to do something."

"That's the spirit we like to see in our girls." He stopped at a gate.

The guard burst into a giant smile. "The Red Cross is here? A sight for sore eyes."

Mr. Tate showed his card. "Miss Kelly and Miss Lindstrom are here to set up the Aeroclub."

"I'll be first in line." The guard waved them through.

Mr. Tate drove down a street lined with utilitarian gray-green buildings, some square and some semicylindrical.

And men. So many men. Gawking, whistling, tripping over their feet, calling, "Hiya, Red Cross!"

Heat rose in Violet's cheeks, and she tried to shrink down in the seat. "I thought we were taking our luggage to our quarters in the village before we saw the Aeroclub."

"Village?" Mr. Tate shot a frown over his shoulder. "Aeroclub girls are billeted on the bases."

Violet couldn't breathe. On the air base?

"Are there other women here?" Kitty asked. "Is that even proper?"

"Just the Red Cross girls." Mr. Tate slowed as a group of men passed by on bicycles. "We've never had problems. The ladies' quarters are strictly off-limits."

Violet cringed at the thought of telling her parents.

"The boys will treat you girls right." Mr. Tate turned onto another road. "The 358th has been here almost two weeks. The officers and noncommissioned officers have their clubs, but the enlisted men have nothing."

At least the pilots were officers, so Violet wouldn't have to deal with them. They seemed to be the worst of the lot.

"The officers' mess." He pointed to a nondescript rectangular building. "That's where you'll eat. The Army has granted you many of the rights and privileges of an officer."

Violet sighed. She'd have to deal with pilots after all.

"Here's the Aeroclub." Mr. Tate stopped the jeep in front of a large semicylindrical building with a brick façade. "Your quarters are inside."

Violet climbed out of the jeep, but before she could grab her suitcase, half a dozen men in olive drab had gathered around and hauled out the luggage.

"Boy, are we glad you're here." A long-faced man gave her a toothy grin. He had stripes on his sleeve, which made him an enlisted man. "A fellow needs a place to relax at the end of a long day, you know."

She smiled back. Maybe this wouldn't be so bad after all. "We're glad to be here."

Mr. Tate led them through the front door. "The ladies' quarters are in the back, boys."

"Yes, sir." The men traipsed through, carrying only one item each.

Kitty snickered and leaned closer to Violet. "I like that big fellow carrying my little shoulder bag."

"I guess they want a peek inside the club." But there wasn't much to see.

Corrugated steel arched over a bare concrete floor. The building stretched a long way, with only lumber frames indicating where rooms would be. A few lightbulbs dangled from the ceiling, sending sparse light into the chilly space.

Mr. Tate strode along. "They've started construction on the kitchen. You'll need to set up the snack bar, the library, the game room, the music room, the lounge."

Violet stared at the expanse. "The airmen are constructing everything?"

"Heavens, no. They have duties. You may find some volunteers, but you'll hire local workers for construction and ladies to cook, serve food, and clean."

Two enlisted men sawed lumber in what had to be the kitchen, judging by the giant stove.

"How do we find workers?" Kitty asked.

"Talk to the local Minister of Labour. They have rules about whom you can hire—war needs come first, of course. For construction material and furniture, you'll go to the Minister of Works. You may be able to sweet-talk some materials from the fighter group."

Violet pressed her hand over her stomach. Sweet talk wasn't her specialty.

"Order your recreational equipment from the Red Cross." Mr. Tate stepped over a pile of sawdust. "The Red Cross also supplies your coffee and donut ingredients. All other food will be purchased in town. The Minister of Food will supply ration books."

Kitty stared hard at Violet and crossed her eyes.

Violet would have laughed if she weren't overwhelmed. How could two of them do all that?

"The boys are excited to have their own Aeroclub," Mr. Tate said. "Just in time for a big Christmas party."

"Christmas?" Violet almost choked. "That's only two weeks away."

He waved a hand over his shoulder. "Plenty of time. Here are your quarters."

The six men stood by a closed door with the ladies' luggage, grinning as if they hadn't seen a woman in months. Maybe they hadn't.

Violet gave them her most big-sisterly smile. "Thank you, gentlemen."

The men left, grinning and waving.

Mr. Tate unlocked the door, then handed them their keys. "Here's your room. We also have a larger adjoining room for any ladies who visit—USO groups or Hollywood starlets."

"Wouldn't that be exciting?" Kitty said.

"It would." Violet's voice sounded weak. She'd come to England armed with dozens of children's activities and crafts. Back in Salina, Kansas, her mother and sister were gathering art supplies and games from the community to send over.

What did Violet know about starlets? About hiring and construction and government officials?

The room was outfitted with two cots, a wardrobe, and a pot-bellied coal stove.

"I apologize for your quarters," Mr. Tate said. "Not very comfortable."

Kitty plopped her shoulder bag on a cot. "If it's good enough for our boys, it's good enough for us."

"We have everything we need." Violet set her suitcase on the other cot. Great-Aunt Violet had told her about huts with dirt floors and dangers from weather, disease, insects, wild animals, and natives.

Why, this was luxurious.

"Very good," the field director said. "I'll come back on Monday to introduce you to the important people on base and in town."

"We can't wait to get started." Kitty closed the door after he left.

Violet opened her suitcase and found her family portraits bundled in lingerie. Dad and Mom, Alma and Karl and Nels. The photograph was taken seven years ago, before Alma and Karl married their sweethearts and added three babies to the family.

Her insides ached. In Washington she'd been able to make occasional short phone calls to hear their sweet voices, and letters arrived quickly. Not so here.

She harrumphed and set Elsa the Elephant next to the photo. How was this any different from being in Africa or China or

Brazil? It was wrong to feel homesick. Surely Great-Aunt Violet never felt this way.

She folded her underthings and set them in a wardrobe drawer. Then again, her great-aunt was doing the work she was created to do, meaningful work. Violet wasn't.

Thanks to Dennis's decision to abandon their shared dream, Violet was serving coffee.

And still she was in over her head.

6

"Thank you, Santa!" Tony Rosario skipped up to Nick—yes, skipped like a little girl—grabbed him, and smacked a kiss on his cheek. "This is the very best Christmas gift ever."

Nick laughed, shoved him away, and wiped his cheek.

Adler joined in the men's laughter. "Too bad you didn't bring planes for all of us."

For now, one plane would have to do. Even if she was a war-weary RAF Mustang, she was still gorgeous, sunbathing under the blue sky in front of the control tower, sleek and lean, her RAF roundel still visible under a coat of olive drab paint.

"How about me, Santa?" Riggs said. "Do I get one too?"

"Nah." Nick scowled and waved his arm dismissively. "You've been bad boys. Coal for the lot of you."

"Coal? Did you say coal?" Rosario fell to his knees in front of Nick and threw his arms wide. "I've been bad. I've been very bad indeed. Give me a big, heaping pile of coal."

Adler sauntered closer to the plane. They never had enough coal for the puny stoves in their Nissen huts, and the men were all freezing their tails off.

"Watch out, boys," Nick called out over the clamor for coal in stockings. "Paxton's going to take that P-51 for himself."

"Not a P-51, a Mustang III." Adler stroked the wing, hearing the roar and clank of factory equipment in his mind. "The Mustang III has a Rolls-Royce Merlin engine built here in England. The P-51B—the plane we'll fly—has a Merlin built by Packard in the US."

Luis Camacho slapped Adler on the back. "How'd you get a pilot's manual?"

"Didn't. Used to build these beauties. Well, the Mustang I and II, the P-51A. This model didn't go into production until after I enlisted." Working in the factory was the only good part of the darkest year of his life. As the repetitive work pounded the memories into submission, he helped these beautiful birds come into being. Life from death, structure from chaos.

"You worked at North American Aviation?" Nick asked.

"Inglewood, California. The assembly line."

"I didn't know that."

Adler's eye twitched. He'd ripped another hole, hadn't he?

"Don't worry, fellows." Maj. Morty Shapiro caressed the Mustang's white nose. "Colonel Chickering says more of these birds are coming. We'll all get flight time, starting with the senior officers."

Adler's hand clamped around the aileron flap. As a wingman, he'd be relegated to the bottom half of the fighter group, although he was easily in the top quarter.

The seventy-five pilots of the 357th began to disperse. A lot of potential aces. Nick and Shapiro, of course, as well as "Kit" Carson, "Bud" Anderson, Tommy Hayes, Don Bochkay, Chuck Yeager, Jim Browning, Bob Becker, and several others. Strong competition.

"Ready to return to quarters?" Nick asked.

"Sure." He grabbed a bicycle from the stack against the control tower, and he and Nick pedaled through the technical site, past workshops and offices.

"Interesting that you worked the assembly line."

"Good work." Adler swerved to avoid a sergeant pedaling the other way.

"Unusual for a man with a college degree."

"I don't have a degree."

"Oh? I thought you'd mentioned college."

Adler checked for potholes in the road and in his story. "Two years at the University of Texas was enough for me."

Nick turned onto a tree-lined road toward their living site. "How long were you at North American?"

"Almost a year. Then I decided I'd rather fly planes than build them." Time to deflect. "What made you join up?"

Nick studied the tree branches. "Saw how things were going with Hitler in Germany, with the Japanese. I wanted to be ready. I joined in 1940, the day after college graduation."

"Surprised your wife let you."

Nick chuckled. "I wasn't married. Met her at training school."

"She's a pilot too?" Adler dropped a wink.

"Met her at church in town." Nick shook his head and grinned. "As for being a pilot, don't put it past her. If it weren't for the baby, Peggy might have joined the WASPs."

"Sounds like quite a woman."

"She is." Nick slowed down for a line of bicycles turning onto the road to the mess site. "I'm surprised you don't have a girl."

Prickles rose. "I told you about my fiancée."

"How long ago?"

"Two and a half years." He winced. Those prickles poked a second hole, a dangerous one.

"Hmm. The way you talk, I thought it was more recent."

"If Peggy died, how long would it take to get over her?" That came out sharper than intended.

Nick's face grew pensive. "Don't know if I ever would."

"Exactly."

"How long were you together?"

Something about Nick's voice made Adler soften, made him want to remember the woman he'd loved. She wasn't responsible for everything that happened. "Seven years."

"Seven!" Nick's front wheel wobbled. "That's a long time to date."

"No kidding. Her daddy didn't trust me. Thought I was a cocky young fool—not that he was wrong."

His friend chuckled. "Made you wait, huh?"

"Three years for us to finish high school. Another two years while I worked for my dad—to prove I could support her. Another two years while I was away at college—to prove I could stay faithful. We were supposed to get married that summer." His vision clouded. She'd died wearing his ring. Was she buried with it? He'd fled before her funeral. His heart seized.

"You earned her father's trust. That must mean a lot to you."

Adler swallowed hard and focused on the road. "Yeah." He'd been faithful to her.

Until . . .

No! He tried to shove that memory back through the holes, but there it was—heated, fumbling, foggy kisses.

No, that didn't count. That was after Oralee died.

Only hours after she died.

His brother Clay's rage roared through the pinpricks in his shell.

Yes, it counted. It counted very much.

"Seven years."

Adler looked up, panting, his upper lip tingling. "Huh?"

"Seven years." Nick turned onto the path to their living site. "Like Jacob working for Rachel in the Bible."

"Only I never got my Rachel." His voice ground out hard, and he pedaled harder, right up to their Nissen hut. He let the bike clatter to the ground and stomped inside.

"Mail came." Riggs, the only man in the hut, sorted envelopes by his cot. "Package for Santa from Mrs. Claus. Nothing for Paxton again."

Adler grabbed a Zane Grey from the crate by his cot. "Want to make something of it?"

"Lay off him, Riggs," Nick said.

"Fine." Riggs sauntered out. "I'm getting a drink at the officers' club before dinner."

Adler sat on the cot, leaned back against the iron headboard, and drew up his knees. Zane Grey would help. In his free time in Inglewood, Adler had watched Westerns, read Westerns, and numbed the memories.

Nick pulled stuff out of the box. He tossed something onto Adler's cot. "For you."

A long flat box wrapped in green paper. "For me?"

"From my wife. I told her you were estranged from your family."

Adler couldn't stop staring. He hadn't received a gift for . . .

"How long has it been?"

"Two and a half years." A third hole, too close to the others.

"About the same time your fiancée died." Nick's dark eyes narrowed in thought. "About the same time you left college and went to California."

Adler's life shred open in a long gash between the three holes. Connected. Connected forever, and Nick saw it. No deflection shot would do the job this time.

His breath came faster, harder. "My brothers and I—we had a big blowup that night, the night Oralee died. I had to leave."

A blowup? Two blowups.

Through the gash a scene flashed. Wyatt crouching by the ravine where Oralee had fallen, blood trickling down his cheek from the rock Adler had hurled at him. Adler towering over him with a bigger rock, ready to bash Wyatt's brains in.

Then a second scene, hazier, murkier, darker. Adler crouching on the cold garage floor. Clay towering over him with a tire iron, ready to bash Adler's brains in.

"What happened?" Nick asked.

Adler bolted to his feet. The book and package thumped to the floor. He held up one hand to Nick and marched out of the hut.

Outside, he kept marching, sucking in cold air, but it wasn't cold enough to freeze the memories, to numb the pain.

Where had he gone wrong?

The flow of cold air reminded him. The *Queen Elizabeth*. Violet Lindstrom's soft blue eyes. Her innocent questions. He'd told himself it was harmless to talk to her.

How wrong he was.

7

Violet didn't mind a cappella Christmas carols. The Aeroclub hadn't received a piano yet, and it could have been reminiscent of caroling. She didn't mind off-key voices. After all, not one Lindstrom had a good singing voice, but their Christmas songfests were the sweetest memories.

But she cringed at the precious tunes bellowed out in drunken, slurring, guffawing voices. Somehow she kept her Red Cross smile in place as she pushed her cart of empty cups and glasses from the lounge to the kitchen.

Through the mass of men in olive drab and the local girls in their best dresses, Mr. Rufus Tate weaved down the hallway toward Violet.

A frown accentuated the Red Cross field director's heavy jowls. "This is disappointing."

"I'll say." Violet glanced back at the drunken carolers.

"I hoped you'd throw a better Christmas party, especially for the grand opening."

Violet clenched the cart handle. "Sir, we've only been here fourteen days. The Minister of Labour has only allowed us to hire half a dozen women so far. If the local church ladies hadn't volunteered, we couldn't have thrown a party at all."

He gestured into the barren lounge. "Construction is incomplete, there's hardly any furniture, and where are the womanly touches? The boys deserve a homey atmosphere."

Although she bristled, Violet kept her expression soft. "Sir, we're a low priority with the base supply officer and with the Minister of Works. They've given us a bookshelf here, a table there, a few chairs. And we're still waiting on our recreational equipment from the Red Cross."

Mr. Tate straightened the lapels of his gray uniform jacket. "The other Aeroclubs manage."

"In time, we will too."

"At least you brought in enough girls for dancing." In the game room couples jitterbugged to tunes on a phonograph Kitty had borrowed from the officers' club. Since almost every young woman in Suffolk wanted to meet the Yanks, recruitment had been easy.

"I expect to see an improvement when I return after the holidays." Mr. Tate wished her a merry Christmas and departed.

His meaning was clear. He'd take the holidays off, but Violet and Kitty wouldn't. Granted, the men of the 358th Fighter Group didn't get days off either.

She continued on her way. On the phonograph Bing Crosby crooned "I'll Be Home for Christmas," and Violet's jaw quivered.

Nonsense. The men wouldn't be home for Christmas either. How selfish to feel homesick in time of war.

The group had flown four missions so far. They hadn't earned any victories, but they hadn't taken any losses either. They had a right to a party. They had a right to dance.

A sergeant danced with an English girl, his hand far below the girl's waist. He didn't have a right to that. If Violet let the men carry on, the villagers wouldn't let their daughters come to dances. It was her job to foster good relations between the Americans and the British.

Violet left her cart in the hall and tapped the man on the shoulder. "Sir, please behave like a gentleman."

He snapped his gaze up to her, and his eyebrows sprang.

Once again, Violet felt her height. "These ladies are our guests, and we're guests in their country. Please treat them with respect."

"Yes, ma'am." He shifted his hand up to the girl's waist.

But the girl gave Violet a saucy look. "I can handle myself."

"If you let men handle you, you'll soon find you can no longer handle them." She sounded just like Mom.

"Yes, ma'am." The girl flushed and glanced away.

Violet returned to her cart. Now she felt washed-up as well as gigantic.

She passed what would be the library when they actually received books. Men milled around, chatting, smoking, and drinking.

"Next weekend, I'm going down to London," a man said to his buddy. "Heard the girls in Piccadilly will give you everything for a buck."

Violet clamped her hand over her mouth.

"Yeah?" his buddy said. "They'll give you VD—that's what they'll give you."

Head down, face flaming, Violet dashed toward the kitchen. Knowing such coarseness existed and seeing it firsthand were two separate things.

What would her friends from college think? The college where she and Dennis Reeves had run the mission society.

They'd met there. They worked together so well that they decided to turn their partnership into a lifetime commitment. Until Dennis and Preston became roommates. Preston with his fancy car and wads of cash. Preston with the job offer for Dennis from his father. Dennis took it without even informing Violet beforehand.

So she broke their engagement.

The mission agency had refused to send Violet overseas without a husband.

"Boys destroy indeed," she muttered.

In the kitchen, Violet unloaded the dirty dishes into the sink.

"Thank you." Sylvia Haywood brushed a wisp of pale hair from her face, gave Violet a wry smile, and dipped her hands into the dishwater. As a mother of schoolchildren, she was exempt from war work. Her husband's British army salary was so low, she'd taken the Red Cross job to make ends meet.

The beginnings of a headache throbbed behind Violet's eyes, and she groaned.

"What's the matter?" Kitty stirred a bowl of donut mixture.

Violet leaned back against the icebox and pressed her palms to her forehead. "It's Christmas Eve, and these men are drinking and cussing and groping the girls and talking about prostitutes and venereal disease."

Kitty chuckled. "Not much like Christmas with the Kellys."

"Or the Lindstroms. These men are brutes." Why couldn't there be a man like Adler Paxton at Leiston?

"Now, now. Don't focus on the bad eggs. There are some fine men in this group."

"I suppose so." Good people did tend to be overshadowed.

Kitty whirled around, set one fist on her hip, and winked at her. "Besides, I thought you wanted to be a missionary. There you go. The biggest pack of heathens you'll ever meet."

Violet laughed for Kitty's sake. "Thanks, but spreading the gospel isn't part of the Red Cross's mission."

"Mercy, a listening ear, and wholesome fun." Kitty's trilling falsetto mimicked Mrs. Farnsworth, one of their instructors at Washington headquarters.

A burst of raucous laughter invaded the kitchen. Nothing wholesome about it.

8

No doubt about it, the P-51 was the sweetest airplane Adler had ever flown—sleek, fast, and light on the controls. His half-hour training flight was almost up, but he had time for a loop.

With his right hand on the stick and his left on the throttle, he eased the stick forward into a shallow dive to gain speed. At 395 miles per hour, he pulled the stick back. After the P-51 began to climb, he pushed the throttle forward to gain power. Up he went, his stomach pressed to his backbone. He threw his head back and watched the horizon through the canopy.

Pull the nose well over the top of the loop, he'd been told, and that's what he did, his weight straining the shoulder harness. When the plane nosed downward and the green patchwork appeared below him, he eased off the throttle.

The horizon came back into view, the cloudy sky. His stomach made contact with his throat, and he whooped. After he came out of the loop, he turned back for Raydon.

Half an hour wasn't enough, but the 357th had only fifteen Mustangs, so everyone took turns when the weather cooperated. Adler had only had two flights, but the P-51 was easy to fly.

After Adler spotted the control tower for Raydon, he pushed the microphone button on top of the throttle knob to get permission to land.

He adjusted the fuel mixture controls and propeller speed, and then entered the rectangular landing pattern around the airfield.

Three runways intersected, with the perimeter track in a rough circle around them. A couple of aircraft sat on the perimeter track, waiting to take off, but the main runway was clear. Another Mustang circled to the east waiting to land, probably Theo Christopher.

Adler made his first turn. When his speed fell below 170, he pushed down the landing gear lever to his left. The gear snapped down into position, and he set the safety lock.

His controls and instruments looked fine. One of the boys had made a spectacularly bad landing the other day by coming down with his brakes locked. The plane rode up onto her nose, shearing off the propeller. The pilot was lucky to be alive.

Adler made the final turn and lowered the flaps. Speed down to 115, nose lined up with the runway, wings level, altitude dropping. Right before he reached the runway, he eased the stick back for the roundout, lifting the nose so the plane would land on all three wheels at once.

And she did, smooth and silky. He savored the rush and rumble down the runway and the knowledge that he'd added another perfect landing to his record.

At the end of the runway, he turned onto the perimeter track. Adler unlocked his side windows and slid them open so he could see around his nose for taxiing. Cool, damp air replaced the fumy air in the cockpit.

A ground crewman hopped onto Adler's wing to help. Adler lifted his hand in greeting, even though he could manage by taxiing in an S pattern with his head out the window.

When they reached the hardstand, the plane's crew chief motioned him onto the spoon-shaped parking place.

Adler turned off the engines, and the noise and vibrations died. He set the parking brake, locked the controls, and turned off the generator, battery, and radio. After unlocking the canopy, he flopped the left section out and down and the overhead panel up and to the right.

The crew chief hoisted himself onto the left wing and leaned over the cockpit. Gray-streaked hair peeked under his cap, and a smile sent wrinkles fanning out around his eyes. "How was she?"

Adler unplugged his headset and unfastened his lap belt and shoulder harness. "Sweeter than honey washed down with molasses."

"She is, isn't she?" He helped Adler climb out of the cramped cockpit.

Once on the ground, Adler flipped his goggles on top of his flight helmet and shook the crew chief's hand. "I'm Adler Paxton. I didn't catch your name before takeoff."

"Bill Beckenbauer. Call me Beck."

Unusual last name. Like the famous ace from the First World War, now a general high up in the US Eighth Air Force. "Beckenbauer? No relation, I reckon."

Beck chuckled. "You reckon wrong. He's my older brother."

Adler felt the slam of it in his chest. The older brother—lauded and high ranking. The younger brother—anonymous and overlooked.

Oralee had always said, "Adler's never met a silence he can't fill." Well, not right now.

"That's how I got my start." Beck circled the P-51 for his postflight check. "I was his mechanic in the last war."

And he was still a mechanic while his brother was a general.

"Right nice to meet you." Adler ducked his head to remove his flight equipment and to spare the crew chief from seeing his stunned expression.

He kept his head down as he walked back to squadron headquarters. Wasn't that always the way? Firstborn sons got everything, even in America, where merit was supposed to mean more than birth.

Even when the firstborn despised his birthright. Esau selling his rights to Jacob for a bowl of lentil stew. Wyatt paying Adler to meet with the truckers so he could stay in the office with his beloved account books.

Adler would have been the better brother to run Paxton Trucking, but that job would be Wyatt's. Just as well, since Adler could never show his face in Kerrville again.

He set his jaw against the pain and set his mind on Raydon Airfield. Before Christmas, he'd allowed Nick's questions to poke up memories that slashed open his soul. He'd had to do a lot of welding to seal it shut again.

"Hola, Águila!" Luis Camacho jogged over.

"Howdy, Cam." The first time Camacho called him *Águila*, Adler had pretended not to know it meant *eagle* in Spanish, same as *Adler* meant *eagle* in German.

"Shapiro called a squadron meeting at 1600." Cam jogged on past. "Got to find Theo."

"Think he was landing right after me."

It was hard to feign ignorance when Camacho muttered things in Spanish—funny things. He couldn't reveal that he was fluent in Spanish, or he'd hear more of it. And the sound recalled the savory smell of tamales and the tang of jalapeño on the tongue. Rollicking mariachi music and the cool feel of the trumpet on his lips, the tunes welling up from his belly and out to the heavens. And Wyatt and Clay beside him on the guitar and violin.

Adler grunted. The welds were frail, and he didn't dare push up against them.

In the locker room, Adler turned in his flight gear. Then he entered the squadron pilots' room. A dozen men lounged before the fireplace, reading magazines and chatting.

Adler joined Nick on a sofa. "Good flight?" Nick asked.

"The best."

Cam and Theo and Shapiro entered the room, Cam and Theo looking winded.

"How'd it go, Shappy?" Riggs called out.

Shapiro gave him a razor-sharp look to kill the nickname. "Escorted bombers, mixed it up with the Luftwaffe."

Murmurs circled the room, and Adler exchanged a glance with Nick. Wouldn't that have been something? For the second time, senior officers from the 357th had flown with the 354th Fighter Group to gain experience.

The 354th had flown the first American mission with Mustangs on December 1 and the first long-range escort into Germany later that month. One of their pilots had downed eight Messerschmitt Me 110s in a single day—and only five victories were required to make ace.

Major Shapiro stood by the fireplace and raised a hand to silence the chatter. "I'm afraid we lost Captain Giltner, but someone saw a parachute. Let's hope for the best."

Adler's cheeks puffed full of air. The group had lost over a dozen men in training accidents back in the US, but this was their first combat loss.

Shapiro tapped a cigarette into an ashtray on the mantel. "We've learned a lot of lessons from the men of the 354th. Lessons they learned the hard way. I'll tell you all about it, but first I want to relay the latest orders from the Army Air Force."

Adler crossed his arms over his A-2 leather flight jacket. Orders meant change. Could be good. Could be bad.

"As you know, the heavy bombers of the Eighth Air Force took appalling losses on the missions to Regensburg and Schweinfurt last summer and fall—sixty bombers on each mission, ten men in each plane. They can't take on the Luftwaffe without fighter escort."

"We're in the Ninth Air Force," Stan Mulroney said.

Adler managed to avoid rolling his eyes. Leave it to Mulroney to state the obvious.

"The Eighth only has P-38s and P-47s," Shapiro said. "The

Lightnings have mechanical problems at high altitude, and the Thunderbolts don't have the legs for missions deep into Germany."

But the Mustang had both lungs and legs.

"The Eighth will send some of its P-47 groups to the Ninth. The P-47 is more rugged than the P-51 and better suited for ground attack. In exchange, the Ninth will send P-51 groups to the Eighth. Including us."

Adler frowned. Would they encounter more enemy aircraft on escort missions or fewer?

"What's that mean for us?" Theo asked. "Besides new patches."

Adler glanced down to the winged "9" on the left shoulder of his flight jacket—soon to be a winged "8."

"I'll tell you what it means," Riggs said. "Means we'll be baby-sitting a bunch of big, fat, slow bombers. We'll be tied down like old married men, can't chase the girls."

Adler's shoulders tensed. That was what he feared.

"First, your analogy stinks," Shapiro said. "Unless you shoot down the girls you chase. In your case, it's more likely they shoot you down."

All tension faded away. Adler roared in laughter, and he wasn't alone.

Shapiro held up his hands until the laughter died. "A month ago, you would have been right in principle. The fighters were required to stick with the bombers at all cost. But things have changed. General Jimmy Doolittle took command of the Eighth Air Force this month. He has orders to destroy the Luftwaffe in the factory, in the air, and on the ground. We'll still be responsible for protecting the bombers, but we'll have more freedom to engage the enemy."

"Good," Adler muttered.

"We do have to put our desire for personal victory beneath the needs of the bombers." Shapiro took off his cap and ruffled his wavy black hair. "The Germans have been known to send up a handful of fighters to draw off the escort, then send in the main force to decimate the bombers. We must not let that happen."

It wasn't so good after all, and Adler's fingers dug into the sleeves of his jacket. Now he was shackled twofold—to the bombers and as a wingman. Not just second place. Last place.

What was that Bible verse Violet Lindstrom had quoted? She'd spoken with such serene conviction, the cold Atlantic air twirling blonde hairs that had escaped her red scarf. *"The last shall be first, and the first last."*

If only there was truth in that Scripture.

9

Mr. Edwards, the Minister of Food in Leiston, flipped through Violet's paperwork with his right hand—his empty left sleeve was pinned up. Had he lost his arm in World War I? "All in order," he said.

"Thank you, sir." Obtaining ration books was Kitty's job, but she was in bed with an awful cold, so Violet was helping. "I apologize for taking food from the British when rationing is so tight here and our men are fed well at the mess."

"Nonsense, young lady." Mr. Edwards fixed a crinkly-eyed smile on her. "Remember, a great amount of our food comes from the States through your Lend-Lease program. Without you Yanks, we might be starving."

Violet clutched her shoulder bag in her lap. "Still, it doesn't seem right."

"Keep those boys fat and happy so they can knock down the Nasties and put an end to this beastly war. Few of us begrudge you. Those who do must answer to me."

"Thank you." Perhaps the best way to help the British was to help the flyboys end the war. If that meant filling them with donuts and swing tunes, so be it.

Yesterday she'd received another reason to embrace her job. Great-Aunt Violet had replied to her announcement that she was going overseas. She said if Violet excelled in the Red Cross, after the war a mission agency might be impressed enough to accept a single woman.

Her new hope and dream.

Mr. Edwards handed her some papers. "When the new group arrives, have the commander sign these forms. Since the number of men won't change, this is a mere formality, but a necessary one. Do bring this back straightaway."

"Thank you. I will." She shook the man's hand and left the office.

No one could give her specifics, but soon the 358th Fighter Group was going to switch airfields with another group.

She descended the stairs to High Street. Would that be Adler Paxton's group? It would be nice to have another gentleman on the base.

Since Christmas, she'd made a point of looking at the men more objectively. Yes, there were some brutes, but most were polite and kind.

On High Street, Violet savored the scene. Brick buildings lined the narrow road, some painted gray, white, or cream. Shops filled the ground floors of the two-story buildings. Down the block stood the darling half-timbered Leiston Picture House.

Across the street, three of the local ladies hired by the American Red Cross loaded food from Banister's Grocery into a GI truck from the air base motor pool.

Sylvia Haywood waved her thin hand. "Hallo, Miss Lindstrom."

"Hello, Mrs. Haywood. Did you find what we needed?"

"I'll say." Rosalind Weaver flipped back her ginger hair and hefted a box into the truck. "We bought a load of sausage meat for those Yankee hamburgers."

"Wonderful." Violet inspected paper-wrapped bundles in the box. "Hamburger" was a euphemistic term for sausage made of oatmeal and meat of questionable origin, served on coarse National Wheatmeal bread, but the airmen gobbled them down.

"Mustard and pickles too." Millie Clark held up a tin of dry mustard. The sixteen-year-old had finished school but was too young to be required to take a war job, so the Red Cross snatched her up.

The Minister of Labour had been less accommodating than sweet Mr. Edwards. The Red Cross could only hire British women too young or too old to be conscripted for war work, or mothers of young children—like Sylvia and Rosalind.

A band of children chased each other down the street. School must have let out.

Two blond children peeled off from the herd and ran to Sylvia—a boy of about ten and a girl about eight. "Hallo, Mummy!"

Sylvia smoothed her daughter's hair and introduced Violet to her children, Jimmy and Margie. "I told you two not to play with those ruffians."

Jimmy's eyes widened. "They're from London. I think they're brilliant."

"Evacuees." Sylvia wrinkled her nose.

Margie lifted her little chin. "I *told* Jimmy not to play with them. They're dirty."

Sylvia cupped her hand to Violet's ear. "Some came from London without knickers. Some had lice. And none of them had ever seen a cow."

"Poor things." Violet watched the kids playing tag in the street.

"I feel sorry for the little blighters," Rosalind said. "Their fathers at war or worse. Their mums in London, if they even survived the Blitz."

"Well, I don't think they're a good influence." Sylvia put her arm around Jimmy's shoulders and tugged him close. "But we all have to do our bit."

"Where do they stay?" Violet asked.

"My mum took one in." Millie twirled a light brown curl around her finger. "He's a nice little chap, helps with the chores."

Violet's heart went out to the waifs. Some were in caring homes, but some weren't. And all were away from home and family at a young age.

Here was the real need—with the lonely and forgotten. Not with healthy, strapping young men.

Three of those men strutted down the street with their crush caps at rakish angles.

The children cheered and ran to the pilots.

Laughing, the Americans pulled out candy and gum and a baseball.

Violet's jaw drifted open, and an idea molded in her mind. She could serve the truly needy while serving the airmen and fulfilling her duty to the Red Cross.

It was perfect.

10

Leiston looked about the same as Raydon. Hangars, Nissen huts, and mud. Adler sat in the uncovered back of a truck crammed with men from his squadron.

The group's fifteen P-51s had been flown here, but the seventeen hundred men and all the equipment arrived in a long line of Army GMC trucks, clogging the base roads.

The layout of each field was different, but the basics remained— a technical site, a headquarters site, a communal site, and several living sites dispersed around the airfield.

Riggs groaned. "We could walk faster than this."

"I would sincerely hope so," Tony Rosario said in a deadpan.

Adler laughed. Since the truck had been idling for five minutes, even the mud moved faster.

"Say, fellas!" The truck driver leaned out the window and addressed the pilots. "That's the communal site. Go explore. I'll drop your bags at your hut if we ever get in motion."

"You shouldn't have to do that," Nick said.

The driver snorted. "Beats listening to the whining."

"I'll take that as an order." Adler vaulted out the back and shook out his stiff legs. "Come on, boys. Unless y'all like eating exhaust fumes."

The men followed, stretching and grumbling. They'd sat in that truck for three hours.

"Speaking of eating, boy, am I hungry." Theo rubbed his belly.

Nick glanced at his watch. "Too late for lunch, but we could buy candy bars at the PX."

"Let's go." Adler led the way. Trucks were backed up to the buildings, and men hauled boxes inside. Moving a fighter group was no small feat.

At the officers' mess, Rosario rattled the doorknob in vain. "Feed me! Please? Please? Have mercy."

"Come on, Rosie." Camacho pulled him away. "We'll find you a Mars Bar."

Rosario pointed ahead. "Even better . . . a woman!"

A brunette pushed a cart down the road. She wore the gray-blue jacket and skirt of the Red Cross.

Adler's breath caught, but Violet Lindstrom was somewhere else, helping children.

"Red Cross!" Rosario staggered toward her, one arm stretched out. "Please . . . help . . . starving . . ."

The girl laughed, then surveyed the squadron. "Say, didn't you fellows come over on the *Queen Elizabeth* with us?"

Yeah, she looked familiar, the girl who'd stayed by Violet's side.

Riggs sauntered up. "You wouldn't give us donuts."

She looked right through him and smiled at the others. "Didn't we say the donuts were on the other side of the Atlantic?" She whipped a napkin off a tray of—

"Donuts!"

She held the tray out to Adler. "Gentlemen first. I remember you."

"Thank you, ma'am." He'd argue with being called a gentleman, but not with a donut at stake.

She passed the tray around, then addressed Riggs. "Since the Red Cross is neutral, we give aid to our enemies as well as our friends. You'll get a donut, but after the others have had their fill."

Adler took a bite of fried heaven and rolled it slowly in his mouth. "I don't know about y'all, but I'm going to take my sweet time."

Camacho closed his eyes and moaned. "This is the best donut ever."

The men murmured, sighed, and waved their donuts in Riggs's face.

Riggs cussed and turned away.

"Profanity will cost you another five minutes." The Red Cross girl raised a smug smile. "So, would you like to see the Aeroclub?"

"We're officers, ma'am," Nick said. "The Aeroclub is a haven for enlisted men."

She gave him an appreciative nod. "Yes, because you have your officers' club. But the Aeroclub is officially open to all. The only rule—leave your rank at the door. Come see."

"Come on, boys." Adler slipped around her and held open the door to a large Nissen hut.

"My name's Kitty Kelly. I'm the staff assistant." She pushed her cart past Adler. "Violet! We have company."

Violet? Adler snapped his gaze inside. Not Violet Lindstrom!

But yes. She stood at a snack bar, gazing over her shoulder at the men.

What on earth? She'd said she was going to work with refugees. Or orphans.

Not at an Aeroclub. Not on his air base. Not looking statuesque and willowy and gorgeous. When he'd seen her before, she'd been bundled up in an overcoat. Not now.

Her gaze drifted over the airmen, landed on Adler, and she smiled, shy and sweet.

His heart dropped as if he'd pulled a P-51 into a steep climb.

Why hadn't the 357th stayed at Raydon? And was it too late to learn to fly a P-47?

"Welcome to our club," Violet said. "Lieutenant Paxton, why don't you shut the door before all the warm air goes out?"

He closed his jaw and the door. "Yes, ma'am."

"This is Violet Lindstrom, our club director." Kitty shot an amused smile at Adler. "Some of you already know her."

"Yes, ma'am." He pulled himself together.

Kitty swept her arm to the left. "Here's our snack bar, where we serve sandwiches, coffee, donuts, and something vaguely resembling a hamburger. Kitchen right behind it."

To the right sat a dozen tables with yellow-checkered tablecloths. The walls were painted sky blue, and yellow-checkered curtains framed the windows.

"We're finally putting this place together." Violet strolled down a hallway at the end of the dining area. Her light blonde hair fluffed in curls below her garrison cap.

Adler took care to stay at the end of the line.

"Man alive," Rosario muttered. "That's one tall broad."

"Yeah?" Riggs hefted his chin. "I've climbed that ladder."

Everything inside Adler constricted. He grabbed a fistful of Riggs's flight jacket. "You touch these ladies again, and I'll—"

"Lay off me, Paxton." Riggs shrugged him off. "I can behave myself."

"To your right . . ." Violet said in a low voice that still carried. "That'll be the library if we ever receive books."

At least she hadn't heard Riggs. Adler uncoiled his fists and peeked inside. Deep green paint, stuffed armchairs, brown curtains, and empty dark wooden bookcases. Manly and inviting.

"This is the writing room." Kitty pointed to the room just beyond, painted in cream with tables and chairs and red-striped curtains. "The Red Cross provides writing paper and envelopes to anyone who wants them."

"The game room." Violet's sigh reached back to Adler. "Or it will be when we receive recreational equipment."

A big long room to the left, also painted cream, but with dark brown bands so the room resembled a half-timbered English pub.

Kitty kept walking. "We rounded up checkers and chess sets and a dartboard in town, and I brought a pack of cards from home. That'll have to do for now."

"Very nice," Nick said. "I'm sure the men appreciate it."

"Thank you." Violet gestured to the right. "The lounge."

Stuffed chairs, deep red walls, magazines and newspapers on a low table, and an actual fireplace. Adler wouldn't mind spending time in there. Except he'd never set foot in the club again.

"This will be the music room if we ever receive instruments." Kitty opened the last door on the left, which led to an empty room with light yellow walls.

"We still have work to do, but it's coming together." Violet led the group down a short hallway to the right—the exit, thank goodness.

She and Kitty lingered outside by the door.

"For you." Kitty faced Riggs and dangled a donut between two fingers as if it were rotten.

"Yes, ma'am. Thank you, ma'am. I've learned my lesson, ma'am." Riggs managed to sound sarcastic and apologetic all at once.

Violet gazed over Riggs's maggoty head and smiled at Adler. "Lieutenant Paxton, may I steal a minute of your time?"

Luis Camacho grinned at Adler and mimicked whistling.

Adler fought off a wince. He ought to join the men moseying down the road. He'd kept his distance from women since Oralee's death, and that policy served him well.

But Violet's hopeful expression drifted down to disappointment, embarrassment.

What was wrong with him? He raised a smile. "Sure."

"Oh, thank you."

Kitty slipped inside, leaving them alone.

He stuffed his hands in his trouser pockets. "Say, I thought you were going to work with—"

"Children." She heaved a sigh. "I was mistaken, but I'm making the best of it."

"I can see. Looks nice in there."

"Thank you, and I'm glad you're here. You're an answer to prayer."

"Me?" He almost choked. He'd never been anyone's answer to prayer.

Violet laughed, her face glowing. "You see, I had the best idea, but I need help and you're just the man."

That choking changed to a strangled feeling.

"Let me explain." A light laugh curved her eyes into crescents. Mighty cute. "My job is to provide wholesome fun for the men, but the fun they want? It's anything but wholesome." She wrinkled her nose. Also mighty cute.

Adler's throat loosened, and a smile twitched up. "True."

"But the men seem to love children, and the children in town adore the Americans. You're like movie stars to them. I want to organize crafts and games and parties, maybe some outings—the airmen and the local children. Activities that would be good for the men's character and morale. The children would love it. Their lives are so difficult with rationing and shortages and air raids, and some are evacuees from London, far from home and family. And—" She took a deep breath. "Listen to me. I never go on like this."

She ought to do it more often. Her eyes sparkled, and her hands made pretty little gestures. "Sounds like a right good plan." A plan he needed to avoid.

"I thought so. It'll endear you boys to the British. Will you help?"

Adler's brain and tongue froze. He swallowed. "Baseball."

"Hmm?"

He was never tongue-tied. "I could play baseball with the kids."

"That would be wonderful, but I really need your help with your commanding officer."

"Colonel Chickering? Why?"

"I need his approval, and it would help if someone of influence came with me."

Adler grimaced. "I'm not important around here."

"I don't believe that for one minute." Her blue eyes rounded. "You have such authority with the men. I've seen how they listen to you, how they respect you."

He felt that old bending inside. Flattery was his weakness—both giving and receiving. "My mama always said, 'Flattery gets you nowhere,' but my daddy always said, 'You catch more flies with honey than with vinegar.'"

"Battling proverbs?" She laughed. "Which is winning?"

Why did she have to look so doggone hopeful?

He dropped a wink. "Flattery, honey."

Violet flushed and grinned. "Thank you. I'll set up the meeting."

Flirting? What on earth was he doing?

"Bye." He strode away. He had no business flirting, no business meeting with beautiful blondes, no business getting involved with any woman, anywhere, ever again.

Especially Violet Lindstrom.

A lowdown stinking sinner and a missionary. As farfetched as a skunk at a church picnic.

11

Violet sang "Stand Up, Stand Up for Jesus," but she couldn't concentrate. She'd left the aisle seat open for a latecomer, she'd told herself, but she'd told herself a lie.

She'd saved the spot for Adler Paxton. He wasn't there.

How many times had she scanned the bland military building that doubled as theater and chapel? Now she felt foolish as well as self-conscious. As the only woman present, her off-key voice rose high above the tenors and basses, with no sopranos or altos to conceal it.

Maybe Adler was under the weather or flying a training mission, or maybe he attended the Catholic services. She'd ask Kitty if she'd seen him there.

No, she wouldn't.

For all his fine qualities, Adler wasn't a churchgoer and most certainly not a future missionary.

The chaplain announced the next hymn, "God of Our Fathers."

Why was Violet drawn to Adler? It was more than his gentlemanly nature, although that appealed to her. In Colonel Chickering's office, he'd backed her plan, not taking control of the meeting but merely lending the weight of his approval. Chivalry without condescension. Oh my.

His appeal ran beyond his good looks. Beyond his winking "Flattery, honey" that turned every bone to gelatin.

Something else pricked her heart. The way he fled. On the pier in New York. On the *Queen Elizabeth*. After he winked and grinned. After the meeting with Chickering.

Perhaps she should have read those incidents as slights, but instead she wanted to follow him, to reach out, to . . . to what?

The sad mystery. The sense of pain, as if he were retreating to lick unseen wounds. Those pulled her more strongly than any wink.

And he had a fine wink.

Violet huffed and focused on the lyrics. She couldn't let herself fall for a man who didn't share her faith, who couldn't share her dream.

But why worry? As an officer, he had no need for the Aeroclub. She wouldn't see him in chapel. She might see him in the mess or if he helped with the children, but he'd been evasive when she'd tried to pin him down with details.

"Please be seated," the chaplain said. "Good morning to all you 'Yoxford Boys.'"

Chuckles swept the chapel as everyone sat on the wooden benches. The men had picked up the "Germany Calling" Nazi propaganda program on the radio. The infamous host, "Lord Haw Haw," had greeted the men of the 357th Fighter Group and christened them the Yoxford Boys. Except his intelligence was off by a few miles. The base was nearer Leiston than Yoxford, but the airmen thought it a hoot and adopted the nickname.

"I'm glad to see so many of you in attendance. Please open your Bibles to Matthew 25."

Violet flipped pages. Yes, attendance was high, as it had been with the 358th as well. There were far more good men in the Army Air Forces than brutes.

She stifled a giggle remembering how Kitty had put that awful Lieutenant Riggs in his place. If only she had some of her friend's spunk.

The chaplain read the Scripture, culminating in one of Violet's favorite passages: "'Then shall the righteous answer him, saying, Lord, when saw we thee an hungred, and fed thee? or thirsty, and gave thee drink? When saw we thee a stranger, and took thee in? or naked, and clothed thee? Or when saw we thee sick, or in prison, and came unto thee? And the King shall answer and say unto them, Verily I say unto you, Inasmuch as ye have done it unto one of the least of these my brethren, ye have done it unto me.'"

That old passion stirred inside, tainted by sadness. That's what she longed to do—to aid the lonely, the oppressed, and the mourning. So why had the Lord placed her among men who were healthy, well paid, and well fed?

At least she had her plan to help the children—the "least of these." Colonel Chickering thought the programs would have a stabilizing effect on the men and be excellent for morale. Violet agreed, but she was more interested in the benefits for the children.

Every word of the sermon resonated with Violet's soul, reinforcing all she believed. Energy welled within her, and ideas scurried around her head. She itched to write them down, to make them come to pass, to watch little faces shine with joy.

The chaplain closed in prayer. "Lord, please comfort my brothers here, lonely in their separation from family and loved ones, oppressed by the enemy, and mourning the fallen."

Violet's eyes and mind snapped open in unison.

With bowed heads, the men murmured and nodded, eyes squeezed shut.

They were far from home. They hadn't seen combat, but they soon would. They'd already lost friends in accidents. How many more would they lose in battle? How many men here would die? How many would become prisoners of war?

Violet's throat swelled shut. They were indeed lonely, oppressed, and mourning. And these men had faith to comfort them.

What about those who didn't? Why should she be shocked that they turned to liquor and women for comfort?

Were these men also not "the least of these"? All of them, from the most gentlemanly on down? Didn't they deserve more than a donut and a forced smile? Didn't they deserve true compassion, as if for Jesus himself?

Oh, Lord. Her insides contracted, pulling her head low. *Forgive me. You love these men, all of them. You placed me here for a reason. Help me serve these men with mercy and kindness. Help me see them through your eyes.*

The chaplain dismissed the congregation, and Violet stood, her legs shaky.

As she waited to enter the aisle, she met each man's gaze with a true sisterly smile.

A dark-haired man in Adler's squadron approached and extended his hand. "Good morning, Miss Lindstrom. It's good to see you again. I'm Nick Westin."

She analyzed the insignia on his jacket—two silver bars. "Good morning, Captain Westin."

"Please call me Nick." Although he only came up to her chin, he looked her fully in the eye, unashamed of his height. "You're Adler's friend."

Friend? "Well, we met on the ship."

"He mentioned meeting with you and Colonel Chickering about a program for children. Please sign me up. My baby girl is growing up without knowing her father, and I'd like to help other children."

"Thank you so much." Her smile warmed. "I appreciate it."

"That's a well-worn Bible."

She clutched it to her stomach. "Thank you."

Nick's gaze intensified. "Pray for him."

"For—for Adler? Why?"

"I don't know, but the Lord does."

So Nick had seen it too, the sadness, the fleeing. "I—I will."

Violet followed the stream of men outside. Puffs of clouds decorated the blue sky, and cool sunlight brightened the buildings and trees and men.

Her mission had broadened and deepened, and for the first time, she was truly glad to be in England.

12

Technical Sergeant Bill Beckenbauer leaned over the cockpit of Adler's new P-51B, *Texas Eagle*. "You don't look like a man about to fly his first mission."

Adler plugged in his radio headset cord. "What do you reckon I should look like?"

"Scared." Beck ran his chamois over the windscreen for the hundredth time. "Granted, that looks different for every man."

Adler had seen it all in his Nissen hut. Riggs spouting even more bravado than usual, Theo too bright-eyed, Mulroney fidgety, Camacho irritable, and Rosie cracking fifty jokes a minute.

Nick was the one Adler studied, the only man in their section with combat experience. He'd been quiet but calm.

To Adler the day felt like any other, a bit better because he was doing something worthwhile. "Everything looks fine."

"All right." The older man's gray eyes narrowed, but he helped Adler snap the oxygen mask to his leather flight helmet and flipped the goggles down.

The smell and taste of rubber filled his nose and mouth, but he'd need oxygen to survive at twenty-five thousand feet. The radio microphone was built into the mask, so he didn't have to wear the annoying throat microphone.

"Be careful with my baby. Watch where you're driving, and don't scratch her up." Beck flopped the top section of the canopy into place over Adler's head, then raised the left panel.

Adler locked the canopy and continued his cockpit check. From left to right, he swept over the controls and instruments. Flaps up, carburetor air control normal, trim tabs set, and so on. When he finished, he gave Beck a thumbs-up, honored to have the veteran mechanic as the crew chief for *Texas Eagle*.

Beck hopped off the wing, and soon he signaled Adler to start engines.

He set the fuel selector valve to the auxiliary fuselage tank, turned on the magnetos, primed the engine, and hit the starter switch.

With a cough, the Merlin engine came to life. Adler advanced the throttle and mixture control, then let her idle until the oil temperature rose and the oil pressure was steady. Vibrations rumbled through the plane and his body as one.

Ahead of him, P-51s taxied along the perimeter track. When Nick's *Santa's Sleigh* approached, Adler signaled Beck to remove the wheel chocks.

Texas Eagle rolled forward, and Adler stuck his head outside to watch where he was going. Barely above freezing, the air tingled the tiny spots of his face not covered by goggles, mask, or helmet.

He turned in behind Nick and weaved down the perimeter track. At the head of the main runway, he pulled around so Nick was on the left side of the pavement and Adler on the right.

Nick gave him a thumbs-up. Adler returned the gesture then closed his windows.

As wingman, he had to stick to Nick's side and resist the urge to attack the enemy. Any German planes spotted by their flight belonged to Nick.

Frustration churned, but he tamped it down. Before he could be first in this outfit, he had to excel at being second.

The tower cleared the two planes for takeoff. Nick rolled forward, and Adler did likewise a few seconds later.

With the stick back to keep the tail on the ground, he pushed the throttle forward. Speed built, and trees and buildings rushed past in his peripheral vision.

Eagle wanted to soar, but Adler kept her grounded. He maintained a circular watch on the runway and the instruments. *Santa's Sleigh* rose into the air ahead of him.

Manifold pressure high enough, speed high enough, and Adler eased the stick forward. The tail floated off the ground and the nose followed.

Adler tucked up the landing gear and locked it. As the plane swooped up, he throttled down, adjusted the propeller, and trimmed the ship.

He made a climbing turn away from the airfield. Thirty seconds later, Riggs and Theo joined them. They pulled into the "finger four" formation, with Nick in the lead, Adler behind him to the right, Riggs behind Nick to the left, and Theo behind Riggs to his left.

As the landscape shrank below, the flight climbed into position beside Shapiro's flight with Camacho, Mulroney, and Rosario. A few minutes later, their section of eight would join another to complete the squadron. Then all three squadrons would head for enemy territory.

Forty-seven P-51s of the 357th were being led today by Maj. James Howard of the 354th Fighter Group, the man who'd downed eight German fighters in a single day.

This was meant to be an orientation mission and an easy one, a "milk run." They would sweep ahead of B-24 Liberator heavy bombers as they unloaded goods on a special military installation at Siracourt in Nazi-occupied France.

Adler's gaze roamed between the formation and the instruments as England rolled by.

Perhaps he should be scared as Beck said, but he wasn't. Almost three years of numbing himself helped as did a life framed by death. He'd killed his own mother in childbirth. He'd as good as killed Oralee. He'd tried to kill Wyatt. And he'd seen his own death in Clay's eyes.

Perhaps he should fear what would happen after death. He'd ignored every altar call growing up, and now after what he'd done, no altar call would pry open those pearly gates. Whether he died today or fifty years from now, he'd sealed his fate. No use fretting.

Most men worried about their families, but Adler was already dead to the Paxtons. No use fretting about that either.

Adler checked his breathing. Even and regular. Because he was free. Free of worry and fear. Free to fly over Nazi territory as easily as he'd flown over California.

So why did freedom feel as oppressive as his oxygen mask?

"What a great first mission." Nick strolled beside Adler in the cold night air. "Not a single loss."

"Not a single victory either." The 357th had taken a leisurely cruise over Normandy and the Pas de Calais, marred only by light and inaccurate flak lobbed up by German antiaircraft gunners on the ground.

"Don't be too eager to see the enemy."

Adler adjusted his uniform jacket. Couldn't make ace unless he did, and he couldn't start his ACES company without that title.

Nick opened the door to the officers' club, and a scratchy version of "Bugle Call Rag" greeted them from the phonograph. Dozens of officers jitterbugged with local ladies, and dozens more crowded the bar. Some of the girls gave Adler the eye, but he ignored them. Thank goodness Nick didn't drink or chase skirts.

A small table stood alone and unloved beside the bar. "There's the coffee."

Nick followed him. "You're a mystery."

"How's that?" The muscles at the back of his neck tensed in anticipation.

But Nick looked thoughtful rather than prying. "You strike me as the kind of man who'd drink to forget."

If only he could. Drinking just made him remember. He shrugged and poured coffee.

"Hi, Adler. Hi, Nick." Violet Lindstrom pushed over a cart, her cheeks pink from the cold.

Adler almost missed the cup. "Hi, Miss—Violet."

"Miss Violet? How very Texan of you." She laughed and shifted a tray of donuts from the cart to the table. "The donuts are going quickly. Wish I could say the same of the coffee."

"We're doing our part." Nick poured a cup.

"You're drinking coffee?" Violet stared into Adler's cup, and her smile grew.

Apparently she'd pegged him as the drinking kind too. "I like coffee."

She raised her gaze, and her lips parted.

Before she could ask if he also liked dancing, he gave her a grin. "I'll let you get back to work. Say, Nick, let's find a game of darts." He charged into the crowd, only slowing when Violet wheeled her empty cart out the main door.

"You should've asked her to dance," Nick said from behind him.

"Nope."

"Too tall for you?"

Her height was one of her most attractive features, and she had many. "Hardly. She's too . . . She wants to be a missionary."

Nick barked out a laugh. "You don't even go to church."

"Nope." He'd almost said, "Not for almost three years," but Nick didn't need another piece of the puzzle.

Rosario stumbled over, his dark eyes bleary, a shot glass in each hand. "Santa! Paxton! Good to see you, old pals."

"Good to see you too, buddy." Adler patted him on the shoulder.

"What's that?" Rosie stared into Adler's cup as Violet had, but with a frown. "Coffee? Can't have that." He lifted a shot glass.

"No!" Adler covered the cup with his free hand.

Whiskey sloshed over his hand and onto the floor.

The smell assaulted him.

Nick put his arm around Rosie's shoulder. "Thanks for the offer, but someone's got to keep his wits about him tonight."

"Glad it's not me." Rosie ambled away.

Alcohol fumes snaked into Adler's brain, seeking memories in the darkest corners.

That summer night in Texas. Ellen standing in the door of the garage. Dr. Hill's daughter. Clay's girlfriend.

Ellen had held up a bottle of whiskey. "Daddy says you should have a good stiff drink. It'll help you through."

Adler snatched the bottle and downed a good quarter of it, practiced and steady, and Ellen gave him an appreciative smile. Too appreciative.

Before that, Adler had confined his drinking to campus. Never in Kerrville.

Ellen sat beside him while Adler tried to pick the lock to the truck door so he could hunt down Wyatt, cursing Clay for preventing him from killing Wyatt earlier.

Of all the vices he'd accumulated, why hadn't he learned to pick locks? The contents of the bottle had inched lower, and Ellen's skirt had inched higher.

"Adler?"

His breath hitched, and his eyes fought to focus. Nick. The officers' club.

"You still want to play darts?" Nick's brow crinkled.

"Yeah. Yeah." Adler shook the booze off his hand. If only he had a rag. Didn't dare wipe that stink onto his uniform.

On the far side of the room, a couple of men played darts where the crowd was thin, and Adler worked his way over.

"Stop!" A feminine voice broke through the music and chatter.

An officer had a redhead pinned to the wall, his hands too high, his mouth on her neck. She pushed against his chest, but he didn't let up.

Something hot burned and baked and broiled every muscle. Adler grabbed the man by the collar and yanked him back. "Riggs. Should've known."

"What the—"

Adler slammed him into the wall.

Riggs shrieked, and something crashed on the floor.

The coffee. He'd spilled it down Riggs's front. Good. "See how you like it, pinned against the wall, can't move."

Riggs cursed him, his face distorted. "What's wrong with you?"

"What's wrong with *you*?" Adler shoved him harder against the wall. "You can't just grab a girl, touch her, take what you want."

"Break it up, boys." A hand clamped on Adler's shoulder. Major Shapiro. "What are you doing, Paxton?"

"He's protecting me from him." The redhead pointed at Riggs, her face mottled.

Protecting? Protecting? Adler protecting a woman?

"Is that right, Riggs?" Shapiro set his other hand on Riggs's shoulder.

Riggs shoved at Adler in vain. "I was just having fun."

"He had his hands all over me." The redhead straightened her dress. "I'm not that kind of girl."

Shapiro sniffed Riggs's breath. "Go sleep it off. We'll discuss your punishment in the morning."

Adler released the weasel. Riggs stumbled away through a gaping crowd, rubbing the back of his head.

"As for you, Paxton," Shapiro said.

Adler's breath chuffed out, his vision doubled.

"He hasn't had a drop," Nick said. "He did what any gentleman would do. Come on, Adler. Let's get out of here."

"Good idea," Shapiro said. "Go calm down, Paxton."

Calm down. Calm down. That was what Daddy had told him when they took Oralee's body from the ravine, when they returned to the house to find Wyatt had fled with Mama and Daddy's approval, when Daddy locked the truck doors and refused to give him the key.

Calm down. Calm down. He'd gone to the garage, determined not to take that advice.

Nick had his hand on Adler's upper back, guiding him past the curious faces to the door.

Cold air. Darkness. They failed. Failed to numb the pain. Failed to hide the secrets.

"What happened in there?" Nick asked.

Adler strode down the path. "You saw. You saw what Riggs did."

"Yeah. Then I saw you fly into a murderous rage."

"You can't treat a woman like that, like I—" That wasn't entirely true. He hadn't forced himself on Ellen. She was willing, very willing, cooing that she'd only dated Clay to please her daddy, that Adler was the one she loved.

She'd offered, and he'd taken—taken what he really wanted—revenge on his younger brother for spoiling his revenge on his older brother.

"Like you what?" Nick said, too calm, too firm.

"Nothing." He walked faster, fists pumping by his side. "Lay off me."

"How long are you going to keep lying to yourself?"

"I said, lay off."

"You're lying, you know, saying it's nothing, when it's definitely something."

Adler glared at him. "I'll tell you what it is—it's none of your doggone business."

Nick matched his pace and his glare. "Except it is my business when I have to fly with you. If you're not careful, someday you'll blow up and it'll be a lot messier than a broken coffee cup and a knot on Riggs's noggin."

Adler let out a choice word and wheeled on him. "You want to know?"

Nick stared him down. "Yes, I do."

A sharp laugh. "No, you don't. Trust me."

"Try me."

Adler shook his head, fast and hard, and he marched away.

"Fine. If you won't tell me, tell God."

Another laugh, even sharper. "Don't you think he already knows?"

"Yes, so stop avoiding him. You're due for a wrestling match."

"A what?" Adler turned on his heel. Nick made no sense at all.

But he was nodding as if he did, the corners of his mouth turning up. "You seem to know the story of Jacob and Rachel. I'm guessing you went to church at some time."

"What of it?"

"Like Jacob, you ran away from home. Like Jacob, you don't want anything to do with God."

"Trust me, the feeling's mutual."

More of that infuriating nodding. "Jacob was a lying, cheating, manipulative thief, and God chose him to be the father of his people, the leader of the faith."

A squirming sensation, as if someone had dropped ants into his shirt. "That's where the similarity ends."

Nick shrugged. "All I know is God likes wrestling matches, and I have a hunch you're itching for one."

The last time he'd wrestled was with Clay at the ravine while Wyatt escaped. He'd lost that day, and he didn't intend to lose again.

Adler stepped closer to Nick and raised one finger. "Listen. The only thing I'm itching for is peace and quiet. I'd suggest you give it to me."

Nick held up both hands. "I'll lay off, but I'm not the one who can give you peace."

One last glare, and Adler stormed off into the night.

Despite what Nick thought, no one could give him peace.

13

Rufus Tate strode into the Aeroclub kitchen. "Hurry up, ladies. The planes will land in less than an hour."

Violet gave him a sweet smile as she set out the coffee urns. "We'll be ready, sir."

Not that it would be easy. The Aeroclub was already busy, plus she had to prepare refreshments for the returning pilots on short notice. Tomorrow she'd talk to the flying control officer and request at least two hours' notice before the planes were scheduled to land.

Sylvia Haywood fried donuts, her hair tied up in a red kerchief. Kitty laid cooled donuts on trays. Rosalind Weaver made sandwiches for the snack bar, and young Millie Clark swished into the kitchen and out with a tray of sandwiches.

And Rufus Tate was in the way.

Violet edged past him and opened a cupboard. Where was it? "Kitty, did you move the coffee?"

"No, it's right—it was there last night. We had three sacks."

"You ran out of coffee?" Mr. Tate's mustache twitched. "You need to be careful."

Kitty opened and shut cupboards, her mouth tight. "I keep

careful inventory, sir. We had more than enough to last until our next shipment."

The field director harrumphed.

"Maybe someone stole it." Sylvia rubbed sweat off her cheek with her sleeve.

"Stole it? Why?" Kitty said. "The men get plenty of coffee in the mess and the clubs."

Rosalind chuckled. "Ever hear of the black market? And this station isn't quite secure."

Violet frowned. "But the English drink tea, not coffee."

"Some like coffee." Rosalind set another sandwich on the tray. "And it's frightfully dear, frightfully scarce."

"Never mind all that," Mr. Tate said. "The boys will be here soon, cold and tired. They need coffee."

"I'll see if I can borrow some from the mess." Kitty dashed out the side door.

Violet flung open more cupboards. They had plenty of tea. Why hadn't the thief taken that instead? "Tea will have to do."

Mr. Tate peered around her shoulder. "Our boys don't drink tea."

She squeezed around him to the coffee urn. "At least it's hot and invigorating."

"Just when I thought this club was shaping up." He marched out the door.

Violet set her teeth and got to work making three urns of tea. She and Kitty had done their best. They'd ordered books and recreational equipment but had only received dribs and drabs. They'd begged and bought and borrowed a mishmash of furniture. They'd painted the walls and hung curtains. But it still wasn't enough for Mr. Tate.

Kitty slammed the door. "The mess won't help. Not one lousy bean."

"Oh dear."

Kitty jutted out her jaw and mimicked a muscular man crossing fisted arms. "Sorry, lady. The mess gives the boys coffee before the mission. You dolls give it to 'em afterward."

"Well, thanks for trying."

The ladies loaded three carts with urns, donuts, sugar, and milk to make the tea more palatable for the tea-teetotalers.

Violet took off her apron and put on her jacket. Then she, Kitty, and Sylvia each wheeled a cart out the side door and headed for the three squadron pilots' rooms.

She shivered in the cold, but she didn't have time to grab her overcoat. It was four thirty, and P-51s already circled in the clear sky. They were such pretty little planes, long and slim, unlike the P-47s with their cute, squat, round noses.

If only they'd painted the planes in colors other than olive drab above and dull gray below. But the Eighth Air Force was more concerned with camouflage than beauty.

Had they lost anyone today? The group hadn't suffered losses on their first two missions, but they hadn't achieved victories either. Apparently those went hand in hand.

She tried not to think of anyone shooting at a tall blue-eyed Texan.

Yesterday evening Violet had held a meeting about the children's programs. Adler hadn't come. Few men had, and they had no interest in activities other than baseball, even after she'd shown them the boxes of craft materials her mother had mailed, donated by the ladies of Salina.

Only Nick Westin had taken her side.

Violet entered Adler's squadron headquarters building. Already four pilots in leather jackets were being interrogated by four staff officers in olive drab dress uniforms.

At a table in the back, Violet set out the refreshments.

Four more pilots strolled in and made a beeline for the table, yanking off gloves.

A sandy-haired pilot grabbed a cup and opened the spigot on the urn. "Coffee! You're a lifesaver, Miss Lindstrom."

"Actually, we're—"

"What the—" He stared into the cup. "Miss, I think this needed to brew longer."

"Dimwit." His buddy jabbed him in the side. "That's tea. Wrong pot."

"Where's the other one?"

"I'm sorry." Violet clasped her hands in front of her squirming stomach. "We're out of coffee."

Another four pilots crowded around, including Adler.

"What do you mean, you're out?" That awful Riggs.

Violet kept her expression sympathetic and apologetic. "I'm sorry. I made tea instead."

"Tea?" One man made a face as if she'd offered pickle juice. "I've been sitting on my . . . on my tail for over three hours in the freezing cold over enemy territory, and you're out of coffee?"

"Leave her alone, boys." Adler's voice was a welcome tonic. "Drink your tea and stop fussing."

"Tea's a sissy drink," Riggs said.

Nick Westin poured himself a cup. "Tea helped the RAF win the Battle of Britain. If it's good enough for them, it's good enough for us."

"Yeah?" The sandy-haired pilot frowned at his half-full cup. "Just think what they could've done with coffee in their veins. Come on, Red Cross."

Violet pressed her lips together so they wouldn't quiver. She'd done her best.

"Leave her alone." Adler's voice went hard. "She said she's out."

"And if I don't leave her alone, what're you going to do?" Sandy-Hair turned right into Adler's face. "Rough me up like you roughed up Riggs?"

The room fell silent, and Violet held her breath. She'd heard about that dustup.

Adler's face darkened until it was unrecognizable. "Don't try me."

Violet's emotions hovered between fear and gratitude. He was a dangerous man. But like her cowboy heroes, he was only dangerous to bullies.

"Righto, chaps." A man with curly dark hair spoke with an affected English accent. "Shall we all have a smashing good cup of tea, what what?"

The men chuckled and stocked up on refreshments.

"Thank you." Violet relaxed and smiled at the men, particularly Nick and Adler.

Adler helped himself last, but he gave her only a brief nod, his gaze flat and disconnected and still dark.

Something was wrong, and her breathing stilled. "Adler, are you all right?"

His eyes flew open wide. "What? Yeah. Of course."

She gave him a smile. "We missed you at the meeting yesterday."

"Yeah." He studied his donut, and his forehead scrunched up. "I won't be able to help after all."

"All right." But her heart sank. Something told her he wasn't all right at all.

14

Swivel-headed. That's what a fighter pilot had to be to do his job. To survive.

Adler checked the blue sky in all directions. Checked his instruments and controls. Checked the American aircraft silhouetted against the snow twenty-five thousand feet below.

Finally a mission into Germany. The Luftwaffe often ignored Allied sweeps over France, but they wouldn't ignore a thousand heavy bombers and eight hundred fighters knifing deep into the Third Reich.

Adler's flight of four made another turn in its pattern a thousand feet above the B-17 Flying Fortresses of the 1st Bombardment Division. The P-51s had to weave to keep pace with the poky bombers.

He smiled under his oxygen mask. The Nazis would definitely fight if they knew the plans of the RAF and the US Army Air Forces this week—"Big Week," they'd dubbed it. Before the Allies could invade western Europe, they needed air superiority.

Big Week was an all-out attack on the German aircraft industry, destroying planes before they could hit the sky and luring Luftwaffe fighters up so the Allies could shoot them down. Today the B-17s were going to bomb a plant in Leipzig that assembled Junkers Ju 88 bombers.

Adler's fingers burned for the trigger on the control stick, but the sky remained clear and the radio waves silent.

Besides, shooting was Nick's job. Adler's job was to be a second set of eyes for Nick.

Maybe things would change under the new group commanding officer. Three days earlier, Eighth Fighter Command had shuttled Colonel Chickering to headquarters and replaced him with Col. Henry Spicer.

Spicer was Adler's kind of CO—hard-driving and charismatic. Already Adler sensed more confidence and daring among the men.

Violet's worried face flashed in his mind. The other day she'd approached Adler in the mess and asked if she should get permission from Spicer for her children's programs.

Adler had told her to proceed as before unless stopped. Fine advice, but he mainly wanted to avoid another meeting with her. He couldn't risk more damage to the flimsy network of welds and electrical tape and chewing gum that held his pathetic soul together.

If Violet Lindstrom knew what was good for her, she'd keep her distance too.

Adler stomped his feet to keep the blood circulating and shifted his seat on the foam rubber pad Beck had laid on top of the rock-hard dinghy pack. They'd be in the air four and a half hours, a long time to sit in a cramped position.

Through his tinted goggles, he gazed toward the sun and caught sight of something dark in the outer rays.

Six dark somethings.

Adler pushed the "A" button on the radio box to speak to his squadron, then depressed the microphone button on top of the throttle. "Judson leader? Six bogeys at two o'clock high."

"Judson leader here." Morty Shapiro's voice came over the channel. "Roger. Let them come closer."

"Yellow one to yellow two," Nick said to Adler. "Patience."

Patience? This was no time for patience.

Let them come closer? Why? So they could rip through the bombers and blast them to bits? So more of their kin could join the attack?

Adler could get up there, start racking up victories. Wasn't that what the brass had ordered—to destroy the Luftwaffe?

"Sick and tired of this." Tired of being wingman. Tired of being second to Nick. Second to Wyatt. Second, second, second.

"Enough." He gritted his teeth. The only way to make ace was to be first.

Adler pushed the red button on top of his stick and dropped the empty auxiliary fuel tanks under his wings—they'd slow him down. Then he flipped on his gun and camera switches, and he shoved the stick down and to the right.

"Yellow two!" Nick called. "What're you doing?"

"Driving off the 109s before they knock down our Forts."

"Judson yellow two, get back in formation." A direct order from Shapiro.

Too late. With his throttle open and his airspeed up to four hundred, he pulled the stick back to climb and to surprise the Germans with his deflection shot.

The enemy came into sight clearly now without the sun to camouflage them. Six Messerschmitt Me 109s, their slender airframes and square wingtips dangerously similar to the P-51. But ugly iron crosses on the fuselage gave them away.

They broke, peeling off in all directions.

Shapiro barked out orders for the squadron to maintain position.

Adler singled out a bogey crossing his path. He aimed his nose ahead of the Nazi's and fired a burst, the machine-gun fire rattling the Mustang. But he was too far away.

The German rolled onto his back and dove—he was going into a "split S" to change directions and come up behind Adler.

He assumed Adler would hold still. No such luck.

Adler tipped *Texas Eagle* onto her back and whooped as blood rushed to his head. Then he dove, circling until he was level again.

There was the German at ten o'clock low, and Adler gave *Eagle* more throttle.

The 109 zigged and zagged, but Adler gained on him. He fired another burst, but the tracers dripped down the sky. Too far away.

He met each of the German's moves, a deadly dance.

Shapiro finally gave the order to attack. Adler would get reprimanded when he returned to base, but first he'd get a victory, maybe two. Shapiro might like Nick's caution, but he had a hunch Spicer would prefer Adler's aggression.

The Messerschmitt dove to the right toward a bank of clouds. "Yellow-bellied coward." Adler couldn't let Jerry hide.

He squeezed the trigger. *Eagle* nosed a bit to the right, and only three streams of tracers arced toward the German, his aim off.

Great. One of his four guns had jammed.

Worse. The 109 slipped into the clouds.

So did Adler. He leveled off as his quarry would be doing too. Blinded, he flew on instruments alone, a skill he was good at but didn't like. No one did.

He peered into the gray murk, but no flash of color revealed the German's position. Adler emerged below the clouds. No sign of the 109. Back up into the clouds, then above.

Adler rammed his fist on his thigh. He'd lost him.

He wheeled *Texas Eagle* up and to the east. If he didn't find his group in twenty minutes, he'd return to Leiston. But at nineteen minutes, a long dark stream came into view. Soon he picked out the "combat box" of bombers the 357th had been assigned to protect.

Flashes of light and zipping fighters, and Adler opened his throttle to rejoin the battle.

A P-51 raced on the tail of a 109—but another 109 dove in, about to bounce him.

Poor fellow didn't have a wingman to watch his back.

Like Nick.

Despite the cockpit heater, a chill ripped through him.

The pursuing Messerschmitt fired a burst, hit the P-51's wing.

Adler cussed. The code on the P-51's fuselage. It was Nick.

Santa's Sleigh slipped and slid, but the German stayed on his tail.

"No, no, no." Adler turned onto the Messerschmitt's tail. He couldn't take a chance with a deflection shot, not with Nick's life at stake.

The German fired again, missed.

Adler had to get closer. Had to. He couldn't—couldn't let Nick die.

A few more feet, and he squeezed the trigger. Tracers fell below the right wing, and Adler eased his nose up, drawing the tracers higher.

A big chunk of the tail flicked off. The 109 wobbled, rolled over, and the pilot bailed out.

Adler pulled back the stick to clear the wreckage. "Nick! Nick! Are you all right?"

"Yellow two? High time you showed up. You almost got me killed with your stunt." Anger laced Nick's voice.

Never once had Adler heard Nick angry. His mouth flopped open, but an apology stuck in his craw. What could he say? Nothing. Nothing he could say would make it better. "Yellow one, can you—can you make it back?"

"I think so." Hard. Chilly.

Adler eased *Eagle* down into the wingman position he never should have abandoned. The tip of the *Sleigh*'s wing was missing. A few holes punctured the forward fuselage. Where the engine was. And the delicate coolant system. "I—I'll stick by you."

"That would be refreshing." Cold as the North Pole, and Adler deserved it. "Judson leader, this is yellow one. Damaged, heading home. Yellow two is with me."

"Fat lot of good he'll do you."

Adler cringed. "I won't leave him."

Nick didn't respond, just laid in a course due west.

Glued to the wingman slot. Head swiveling, eyes straining, and the rivets on his soul popped open like machine-gun fire.

He'd almost gotten Nick killed. Just as he'd gotten Oralee killed.

Adler beat his fist on his thigh and cried out. Unless he pushed the microphone button, no one would hear him.

Oralee had died because Adler was selfish and manipulative, determined to have his way.

He'd wanted to cross that ravine with his brothers to get the best view of the sunset. Oralee just needed some gumption, and she'd cross that footbridge just fine.

Then Wyatt interfered. Of course he had. He loved Oralee too. Wyatt thought he kept his feelings secret, but Adler knew.

So the brothers fought like two stallions over a filly. Oralee hated it when they fought, hated it enough to cross that bridge just to make them stop.

Wyatt was right. Adler was wrong. And Oralee was dead.

With a roar, Adler pummeled his fist against the cockpit canopy.

Now Nick. A good man. A good pilot. A husband and father. He could've died because Adler wanted his own way. Wanted to be ace, to be first.

"God!" he screamed to the heavens. "I'm a no-good, rotten heel."

It hurt. It hurt like blazes, but he needed to hurt, deserved to hurt, same as he hurt everyone else.

Adler had tried to murder Wyatt for having the guts to stand up to him. And Clay? How did Adler reward his younger brother for stopping that murder and keeping Adler out of the electric chair?

"God! What's wrong with me?"

Drunk with grief, anger, and whiskey, he'd slept with Clay's girlfriend. What kind of villain was he?

And Ellen? It didn't matter that she'd thrown herself at him. He'd used her shamelessly.

He screamed, pounded that canopy, but nothing helped.

That night he'd ripped apart his family. His selfishness stirred up a hurricane of death and revenge and betrayal that destroyed everyone he loved.

He scanned the skies, the instruments, Nick's plane. Not for his sake, for Nick's.

It was happening again. His selfishness could destroy a friend, his whole squadron if he kept up his ways.

"God! I'm no good. No good at all. One, two, three strikes—I'm out!"

Despite the cold, he was sweating. He couldn't take off his helmet or jacket, so he ripped off his gloves.

"Why don't you just kill me, God? Huh? Why don't you? Take me before I hurt anyone else."

He rammed his fist up into the canopy. His knuckles snagged on the riveted metal frame. He cried out and swore.

Who cared if he cussed? Or got drunk? Or lied? What was one more offense on top of the giant, stinking manure pile of his sins?

He tipped his head back and spouted every foul word he knew and made up some of his own. What did it matter? Nothing—nothing could take away his sin.

Wet warmth coated the back of his hand, and he stared at it. Red rivulets ran from his shredded knuckles and dripped onto his coveralls.

Blood.

Oralee's sweet voice flooded his memory, singing her favorite hymn.

What could take away his sin?

Nothing but the blood of Jesus.

15

Violet tucked the book inside her raincoat and headed from the officers' mess to the Aeroclub.

Despite the light rain pattering on her hood, she couldn't imagine a brighter day. After having surveyed airmen, locals, and other Aeroclubs, she and Kitty had put together a calendar of events to benefit Americans and British alike. That morning, they'd met with Mr. Tate, Colonel Spicer, and officials from surrounding towns. The colonel and the officials had approved, and Mr. Tate looked proud and pleased.

"Slow down there, Miss Lindstrom," a man called behind her. "You're moving faster than a Messerschmitt with a Mustang on her tail."

Adler? She spun around. Yes, Adler Paxton jogging to her. With a smile. "If I'd known I had a Mustang pilot on my tail, I'd have moved even faster."

He laughed, and she felt double pleasure—for actually having a cute comeback and at hearing him laugh.

Adler fell in beside her. "You're in an awful hurry."

Violet resumed her pace. "It's raining."

"Oh? So that's why they didn't let us fly today." He frowned at the gray sky.

Had she ever seen him in such good spirits?

He tugged his crush cap lower. "I tried to catch your eye in the mess, but you had your nose buried in a book. What're you reading?"

She pressed the book closer to her chest. Since it belonged to the Red Cross, she had to take even better care of it. "Just a book."

"Strange title." One corner of his mouth twitched. "Don't tell me you're reading something scandalous."

"No, of course not. It's just . . . it's not the sort of book ladies read."

Blond eyebrows inched up. She wasn't helping her case.

Violet sighed. "It's a Zane Grey, all right?"

"Is that so? He's my favorite author."

"Mine too. All the other Red Cross girls read Jane Austen, but I love Westerns."

Adler nodded at the theater building. "They show Westerns. You should go sometime."

You should, not *we* should. Whatever the reason for his sudden friendliness, it wasn't romantic interest. "I should."

"Why Westerns? The adventure?"

"Oh yes. But what I like best are the cowboy heroes. So noble and brave."

"Mm-hmm. That's why I like this fighter group. Like cowboys."

On the far side of the theater building, wind gusted, and she angled her face away from the rain. "I don't see the similarity."

"Sure. Most every day we mount our trusty Mustangs and head off into adventure, six-shooters by our sides." He pointed a finger gun at her, far too much like a handsome gunslinger.

She smiled. "At least you have the right accent."

Adler holstered his hand in his pocket, and his face sobered. "It's more than that. Cowboys look like they ride alone, but they work together, need each other. So do fighter pilots—a lesson I learned the hard way the other day."

"Oh?"

Instead of explaining, he grinned. "And at the end of the day, both cowboys and pilots sit around campfires telling tall tales."

"That's true." Her smile dissolved. "If only the airmen were as noble. But they're so . . . coarse. The language, the drinking, the women."

Adler stepped over a puddle on the walkway. "Real cowboys are plenty coarse. Just because a man is rough on the outside doesn't mean he can't be noble inside."

She'd have to ponder that. She stopped in front of the Aeroclub. "Well, it was good seeing you."

"May I come in?"

Very strange, but she opened the door. "Of course. The Aeroclub is open to all. Not many men here this time of day."

Young Millie Clark sat at a table, sipping coffee with Tom Griffith, a skinny, curly-headed corporal from the motor pool. He'd become very helpful around the club since he met Millie.

Violet pushed back her hood and waved Adler to the tables with their cheery yellow gingham tablecloths. "Make yourself comfortable."

He gripped his crush cap in his hands—one of which was bandaged. "Actually, I'm here to make myself uncomfortable."

Whatever did he mean? She stuffed her gloves in her pocket.

Adler glanced away. "Listen, I don't want to interfere with your work. Any way I can help?"

Violet unbuttoned her raincoat, careful not to drop *The Lone Star Ranger*. "I was shelving our new books—before the Zane Greys distracted me. You could help if you'd like."

"Great. That'll give me something to do while I apologize to you."

"Apologize?"

Adler gestured down the hall. "Books?"

"Sure. Let me take care of my coat." She hung it up in the office and shifted Elsa the Elephant from her coat pocket to the desk.

In the library, boxes and books and a pilot awaited her. "We received our shipment of books and games yesterday. Would you believe we now have a thousand books? All from donations to the Victory Book Campaign back home."

Adler whistled and hung his leather jacket and his cap on a coatrack.

"Fiction on the left in alphabetical order by author. Nonfiction on the right by topic. I don't know the Dewey Decimal System, so I'm making it up. Why don't you work on the fiction? That pile is ready to be shelved."

"Yes, ma'am." He picked up some books and examined the spines. "I owe you an apology. I promised to help with the kids' programs, then I broke my word."

Violet surveyed her nonfiction stacks. "It's all right. I know you're busy."

"No, it's not all right. A wingman doesn't abandon his leader, and a cowboy doesn't abandon his herd."

She'd never been compared to a pilot or a cow, but his apology warmed her. "Thank you."

"I won't abandon you again—or those kids." Adler slipped a book onto a shelf. "Anything you want, I'll do. Even cut hearts out of paper doilies."

"Valentine's Day is over. You're safe." She removed an armful from a box. "But Easter's coming. Maybe we'll dress you up as the Easter Bunny."

He laughed. "That'd serve me right."

Violet set philosophy, geography, and calculus books in stacks—someone had emptied their home of college textbooks. "Why the change of heart?"

Only the sound of volumes swishing into place. "I was wrestling with something."

Vague again. She studied his back—the olive drab shirt tucked into olive drab trousers, but all that olive drab remained silent. "You men have been flying a lot. What are they calling it? Big Week?"

"Yes, ma'am." He grabbed another dozen novels. "The Eighth Air Force put up huge forces three days in a row. We'll do so again if the weather clears. Our bombers are turning German aircraft factories into rubble, and our fighters are picking off Nazi fighters like prairie dogs. The 357th already has ten victories this week."

She set down two automotive repair manuals. "Any for you?"

He frowned at the book in his bandaged hand. "One, but I shouldn't have."

"What do you mean?"

"I abandoned Nick, seeking my own glory." He thudded a book into place. "Almost got him killed. The 109 I shot down was on his tail. If I'd been in position, the enemy never would've gotten that close."

"Oh." That must have prompted his change of heart. She pulled the last group of books from the box—all biographies.

"I'll never leave Nick's side again. He got his own victory yesterday, so he forgave me. Actually he forgave me long before that."

Violet shelved the biographies. "I'm not surprised. He seems like a very sweet man."

"And a married one." He wagged a finger at her with a mock glare. "Don't get any ideas about him, missy."

"I won't." She laughed and wrapped her arms around the top box on the stack by the door.

"Let me." Adler nudged her aside and carted the box to a low round table nestled among armchairs. Four red spots appeared on the bandage around his hand.

"Adler, you're bleeding." She reached for his hand but stopped herself.

"Rats." He twisted his wrist to see. "That's the problem with scabs on knuckles."

"Come with me. We have a first aid kit in the kitchen." She led the way.

"The Red Cross—prepared for any disaster."

No one was in the kitchen. Kitty was meeting with the Minister of Food, and Sylvia and Rosalind would arrive in an hour to prepare for the evening rush.

Violet opened a drawer and found the first aid kit. But where was the flashlight? She opened another few drawers. "Bother. I hope our thief didn't strike again."

"Thief?"

She nodded to the sink. "Take off the old bandage and wash with soap and water."

"Yes, ma'am." He obeyed her. "A thief?"

"Do you remember that day we couldn't serve coffee after your mission? We think someone stole our supply." She removed gauze, scissors, and iodine swabs from the kit. "Since then we've lost a sack of flour, several pounds of sugar, and now our flashlight."

"One of our boys?"

"Why would they want flour? Unless they're selling it on the black market. It's most likely one of our workers or volunteers, or locals sneaking in."

He dried his hands with a rag and returned to her. "I'll keep my eyes and ears open."

"Thank you." She took his fingers to inspect the damage. All four knuckles were badly scraped, but the bleeding had stopped. "How did this happen?"

His fingers tensed in hers. "A wrestling match."

"Oh." She released her grip and opened an iodine swab, worrying her lower lip between her teeth. She'd heard about Adler and Riggs's fight in the officers' club. "Do you . . . get in fights often?"

"Reckon I have that reputation." He tucked in his chin. "I've only gotten in one fight here. Riggs was getting fresh with a girl."

Always chivalrous. She took his hand and dabbed on iodine. "So this . . . ?"

"This I got wrestling with God."

"With God?" She snapped up her gaze into eyes too blue and too close.

One of those eyes twitched. "Would you hurry up with that iodine? No time to be poky." He managed to look both pained and amused.

She painted manly knuckles brown. "You're the most cryptic man. Wrestling with God?"

"Sure. Like Jacob in the Bible. Only God and I had our match at twenty-five thousand feet. This is what happens when you punch a cockpit canopy without gloves."

Violet's mind tumbled. "Who won?"

"Nick asked me that same question. I told him God won. Reckon that means I won too."

Did that mean what she thought it did? She blew on the brown spots to dry them, then let go so she could cut gauze.

He studied his painted knuckles. "I grew up going to church, but the preaching glanced right off me. It wasn't hard to pretend though, make my family happy. Remember how Jacob talked about the God of Abraham and Isaac? That was me. He was the God of my father, my mother, my brothers. Not mine."

Violet wrapped the gauze around his hand. She couldn't imagine hearing and not believing, but it was common enough.

"I think Oralee suspected the truth. Why that woman loved me, I'll never know." Sadness washed across his face, but without the pain she'd seen before.

"Your fiancée?" She worked her fingers under the bandage in his warm palm and secured the loose end with a safety pin. "She must have been a lovely lady."

"She was." He turned his hand back and forth. "You did a right fine job. Slower than molasses in January, but right fine."

"Thank you." She gave him a sarcastic smile.

"I know a good bandaging job. There were three of us Paxton boys, always getting into scrapes. Mama could bandage faster than any doctor and pray faster than any preacher."

Violet laughed and headed back to the library. "I imagine so. And I imagine she'd order you not to use that hand for the rest of the day and not to lift any more boxes."

"Fixin' to order me around?"

"Would it work?" She glanced at him over her shoulder.

A slow smile grew. "Maybe."

Her pulse raced, but she ordered her emotions not to follow. Not yet.

In the library, she emptied the box on the table, separating fiction from nonfiction. "After Jacob wrestled with God, he called him *his* God."

"Wrestling with the Almighty will do that to a man."

"I'm glad to hear it." Her heart warmed all the way through. "Your parents will be glad too."

"Can't tell them." His voice lowered. "We're—I'm estranged from my family."

"Estranged?" She straightened up. "How can that be? How long?"

Adler rubbed the back of his neck with his good hand. "Almost three years. The night Oralee died. Let's just say I took out my grief and anger on both brothers, and I'm no longer welcome in Kerrville, Texas."

Violet sank into an armchair. "I—I can't imagine. I'm such a homebody. My family—why, I've only been away four months, and it aches. But three years? No calls? No letters?"

"They don't know where I am." He plopped into a chair across from her. "Clay almost found out."

"Clay?"

"My younger brother. I saw him on the *Queen Elizabeth* when you and I were on the sundeck. I saw him on the deck below us, heard his voice, no mistaking it. That's why I fled."

"Oh my goodness." What this man had gone through—the loss of his fiancée and his family—no wonder he was so sad and mysterious. But for some wonderful reason, he'd told her.

"Well." His face tightened, and he scooted forward and braced his hands on the armrests. "Thanks for the fine bandage, but—"

"Don't flee again." She gasped at her own boldness.

Adler halted, halfway to standing, and he raised startled eyes.

Somehow the boldness felt right, coming from outside herself, and she held his gaze. "Please stay. Shelve books. Tell me about flying, about your favorite Zane Grey, anything you'd like."

He stretched to his full height, his expression inscrutable.

Oh dear. She'd pushed too hard, hadn't she?

Then one corner of his mouth edged up. "How 'bout instead you tell me about Kansas, about how a self-proclaimed homebody wants to be a missionary to Africa."

"All right then." She smiled, stood, and gathered up the nonfiction stack. "But I don't care where I go—Africa, China, Brazil, wherever the Lord wants."

As she shelved books, she talked about her goal, reminding herself not to let a cowboy-pilot distract her. He might share her faith now, but that didn't mean he'd come to share her dream.

That would be too good to be true.

16

"Berlin!" In the squadron equipment room, Theo pulled his flight coveralls over his olive drabs. "Can you imagine?"

Riggs closed his locker. "If they don't recall us again."

"Sure hope not." Adler zipped up his coveralls. The day before, the entire Eighth Air Force had been briefed to hit Berlin for the first time but had been recalled due to worsening weather. One group of P-38 Lightnings missed the recall message and flew over Berlin alone. "We ought to be the first fighters to actually escort bombers over Hitler's house."

Nick laughed and strapped on the shoulder holster for his Colt .45 pistol. "Unless Hitler's taken up residence at the Bosch electrical works, he's safe."

Rosario flipped one end of his silk scarf over his shoulder and struck a pose. "If we killed Hitler, then this war would be over. There would go all our fun."

Adler didn't join the men's laughter, but Rosie had a point. The bomber boys dreaded missions deep into Germany, sitting ducks that they were, but the fighter jocks loved them—more Messerschmitts, more victories, and a whole lot more fun.

The 357th Fighter Group had flown eleven missions and had racked up twenty-four victories, but the men itched for more.

After Adler put on his holster, flight jacket, and scarf, he turned in his wallet to the squadron intelligence officer. He hated parting with his only photo of Oralee, but no one could take away the scrap in his pocket. Besides, if he were shot down, what could the Gestapo learn from a bit of yellow fabric?

With three little white daisies.

His chest seized, and he didn't fight it. Strange, but the more he'd allowed himself to feel pain over the past two weeks, the less it hurt.

With his flight gear in his kit bag, Adler filed outside with his squadron and frowned at the sky. Cloudier than when they'd left the briefing. If only the weather would hold until they got this mission off the ground. Hitting the enemy's capital would do wonders for morale.

The men piled into and onto a jeep. Adler perched over the left rear wheel and held on to a bracket sticking out between his knees.

The jeep bounced down the lane toward the perimeter track.

Rosario lounged on the hood on the passenger side. "Say, Paxton, don't forget to kiss your Red Cross girl good-bye." He made a kissy face.

Adler kept his expression impassive, the best way to halt teasing. "I'm just helping with the kids' programs, as y'all should be doing too. There's a meeting tomorrow night. Be there."

"Yeah," Camacho said, scrunched in the backseat. "Great way to meet dames."

Adler suppressed a smile. Cam talked tough, but on Sunday afternoon Adler had seen him helping little kids with scissors and paste, patiently explaining that he wasn't Indian but Mexican and he'd never set foot in a tepee.

Wind ruffled Theo's blond hair. "Maybe I'll go."

"Great." Nick flicked a knowing smile at Adler.

Yeah, Adler had deflected talk about Violet, and Nick saw right through him.

How good it felt to be known and forgiven. How strange it felt.

After his wrestling match, bruised and disoriented and reeling, Adler had told Nick every detail of his life story. Every single stinking detail.

Nick hadn't rejected him. He'd stayed by Adler's side, and Adler was determined to pay him back tenfold.

The jeep reached the perimeter track and waited for other vehicles to pass.

"Not too late, Paxton." Rosie blew a kiss toward the Aeroclub.

Adler flapped a hand. "What would a nice girl like that want with the likes of me?"

Cam laughed. "You got that right, *amigo.*"

What would a girl like that want with him indeed?

Nick said Adler was a new man, washed clean, but he didn't feel clean. Definitely not clean enough for Miss Violet Lindstrom.

Too bad. She had all of Oralee's thoughtful sweetness, but with a dash of gumption and drive. Always busy, that woman, always planning and doing. When she'd bandaged his hand, he'd wanted her to be even pokier, stinging iodine or not. And when she'd told him not to flee—insightful, compassionate, unbending.

That woman could be his undoing.

He hauled in a lungful of frigid air. Every fiber in his being wanted to run, but he'd keep his word. He just had to remind himself—missionary, missionary, missionary.

Thank goodness he'd asked her to talk about that. She loved God so much she was willing to give up everything she loved in order to do something that didn't seem to suit her.

The jeep made a lurching turn onto the perimeter track, and Adler gripped the bracket. One of the reasons he'd avoided God so long. Bad enough the Lord told you not to do things you liked, but then he told you to do things you didn't like.

At least God had only asked Adler to keep his promises and do his duty. Fair enough. But after what the Lord had done for him—he still couldn't comprehend it—he ought to be willing to do a whole lot more.

The jeep slowed as they reached the hardstands. Cam hopped out and headed for his P-51, named *El Mesteño*, the Mexican-Spanish word that *mustang* had been derived from.

Adler jumped to the ground and strolled to his plane. She looked magnificent. José Flores, the assistant crew chief, had painted "Texas Eagle" on the left side of the nose, in white script edged in black. On the right side, he'd painted an eagle, wings spread wide. One wing was emblazoned with the American flag, the other with the flag of Texas.

Beck shook his hand and pointed to the single swastika painted below the cockpit. "You're going to get another one today, aren't you?"

Adler hefted his kit bag onto *Eagle*'s wing. "Only if I'm protecting Nick."

Another jeep pulled up, and an officer in dress uniform climbed out. "Say, buddy, you look like a future ace."

Adler frowned and looped his Mae West life preserver over his head. "Time to get your eyes checked."

The officer laughed and stuck out his hand. "A humble one too. Great. That'll play well in the papers. Walt Schumacher, group public relations officer."

"Adler Paxton." He sized up Schumacher—tall, slight build, narrow-set eyes in a wide face.

"From Texas, I see." Schumacher pulled a notepad from inside his jacket. "What town?"

Adler stiffened. "Why do you want to know?"

"Getting background on our top pilots. When you make ace, I can whip out an article lickety-split. Think how proud your ma and pa will be to see your name in the hometown paper."

"No!"

Schumacher drew back. "No?"

Adler stepped closer and stared the man down. "No articles about me ever. Even if I die. Understood?"

His gaze skittered away. "Uh, sure, buddy."

There he went, bolstering his hot-tempered reputation. He worked up a smile. "Besides, I'm a wingman, not an ace. Have you talked to Nick Westin, next hardstand down?"

Schumacher grimaced. "That little guy? Doesn't look like much."

"Don't let looks fool you." Adler tugged on his flight helmet and buckled it under his chin. "Best pilot in this outfit. Best man in this outfit. He already made ace in the Pacific."

Irresistible bait to a newsman. "He did? Thanks for the tip." Schumacher jogged to his jeep.

Adler turned back to his kit bag.

The three men in his ground crew stood by the P-51's tail, gaping at him.

Beck cracked a smile. "Who'd you kill?"

Adler groaned and yanked out his backpack parachute.

"Yeah." Moskowitz, the armorer, clasped his hands before his chest. "Please tell me it was a big shootout in front of the saloon, with all the ladies crying in the windows."

"I'm not a wanted man." Adler wiggled into the parachute harness. "I'm just not on speaking terms with my folks. That's all."

"Too bad." Flores nudged Moskowitz. "Wouldn't that be something, knowing a real-life outlaw?"

Adler pulled the straps up between his legs and clipped them to the harness. "The only outlaws in these here parts are the Nazis, and if y'all want to see any shootouts, stop flapping your gums and help me get this bird in the sky."

"Yes, sir." Moskowitz snapped the most sarcastic salute ever.

Adler gestured to *Eagle*. "How's my girl?"

"She's in top shape." Beck headed to the nose to start the visual check, and he faced Adler.

The searching compassion in Beck's eyes made Adler hold his breath. He might have told Nick everything. He might have told Violet some things. But that didn't mean he wanted to tell everyone everything.

17

Violet stood by the window in the Aeroclub lounge and read the list of activities, careful to be concise for the men. The group had flown a five-hour mission, which made a long day for everyone.

She glanced over the top of her paper. This wasn't like the meetings she'd led in Salina. Instead of well-bred ladies in hats, two dozen young men in leather jackets faced her, sprawled over couches and chairs.

Adler sat with his ankle over his knee, his elbow hooked over the sofa back, studying the men he'd helped gather. Some pilots, but mostly enlisted men. He'd said it should never look as if officers were running the show, so he'd encouraged key enlisted men to do the main recruiting.

No doubt he would make an excellent businessman one day.

He gave her an encouraging little smile.

For a second, Violet thought she'd lost her place. But she'd only reached the end of the list. "Those are the activities we have planned for March. Now I'd like to plan an Easter party for the children. Colonel Spicer loves the idea."

"Spicer got shot down today," one of the pilots said.

Violet gasped.

"He bailed out over water," Adler said. "Pugh saw his dinghy inflate. He'll be fine."

"Chuck Yeager bailed out too."

"Can you imagine Spicer and Yeager together in prison camp?" Adler's friend Luis Camacho laughed. "The Nazis will beg us to take them back."

The men joked about the trouble the pilots would cause, but Violet couldn't catch her breath. The group had lost about a dozen pilots, but Colonel Spicer was the first she'd known personally. Such a vibrant man with his mustache and pipe and gung ho attitude.

"Miss Lindstrom?" Adler said over the laughter. "Tell us about the party."

The party, yes. She pulled herself taller and smiled at the men, who quieted again. "First, I'd like to have an egg hunt."

A redheaded sergeant raised his hand. "I can *procure* some eggs for you."

His friends hooted and slapped him on the back.

Violet tipped part of a smile to him. "Please procure them through proper channels."

A blond pilot raised his hand—Theo was his name. "I've made friends with the folks at a farm down the road. They have chickens. I'll see what I can do."

"Thank you. One per child would be plenty." Violet patted a box. "The children can paint their eggs. I have paints and brushes donated by the teachers at the school where I taught. We'll have the girls bring their Sunday hats to decorate. They can make flowers from the tissue paper my friends sent. Also, Miss Clark's mother is donating fabric scraps from her shop."

"Thanks, Millie." Tom Griffith sent her a big grin.

Millie blushed and hugged the big canvas bag she used to bring donations. The girl and her mother had barely been scraping by before Millie began working at the Aeroclub.

What a joy to help a needy family. "Yes, thank you, Miss Clark. For the boys, we can organize games like Duck, Duck, Goose."

"What about candy?" Griff asked.

Nick Westin leaned his elbows on his knees. "Why don't we encourage our buddies to pick up a few extra candy bars at the PX over the next month? With the lot of us . . ."

"That would be wonderful." Violet scribbled the idea down.

"What about music?" A skinny olive-complexioned man pointed with his thumb toward the music room. "Now that you've got instruments, some of us are putting together a band."

As much as Violet enjoyed swing music, this was a children's party. "How about . . . could you play children's songs, but with swing?"

"Say, that'd be swell." The musician snapped his fingers and belted out a syncopated version of "Mary Had a Little Lamb."

"Wonderful, wonderful." Violet's pencil could barely keep up. This was so much fun.

Guilt clamped around her heart. Service was supposed to be sacrificial, not fun. Great-Aunt Violet had warned her about becoming cozy and complacent in the Red Cross.

Regardless, she was here for the duration of the war and had to make the best of it. If she had fun in the process, so be it.

Violet had the makings of an excellent party. "Thank you, gentlemen. I know you've had a long and hard day, so I appreciate your participation. We ladies will take care of the planning. I mostly need your help to set up and take down, and at the party. And please encourage your friends to come. Thank you."

The men extracted themselves from chairs and called out good-byes while Violet called out more thanks.

Adler approached. He looked too good with his jacket unzipped and his necktie tucked into the front placket of his shirt. "Great idea for the band. The men will have fun with that."

"Thank you." She could already see the children's bright little faces. How they adored these high-spirited men with their slang and swagger.

"You received your instruments?" He glanced out the door, his eyes intent.

"On Friday. The music room now lives up to its name." Should she ask? "Would you like to see?"

"Yes, ma'am."

Violet led him across the hall. Why had she given in to that impulse? Spending time with him only fed her infatuation, but they had diverging dreams.

And Adler was still in love with Oralee, even though she'd been gone for three years. However, that faithfulness only increased his appeal.

"Here we are." The profusion of instruments made the yellow walls even sunnier. A piano, a drum set, a box of sheet music, and a stash of instrument cases. "Some of the men in the band brought instruments from home, and some are borrowing ours."

Adler squatted, opened a case, and pulled out a trumpet.

Violet sat on the piano bench with her back to the keys. "Do you play?"

He fingered the three valves in a practiced manner, but his expression drifted far away.

Holding her breath, she watched. Waited.

Before long, he plopped onto his backside, leaned back against the wall, and dangled the trumpet between his knees. "Not for"—he let out a dry laugh—"three years. That night."

The night his fiancée died? "Is that so?"

He frowned at his fingering. "We had a party for Wyatt's college graduation, big Mexican barbecue. Wyatt on the guitar, Clay on the violin, me on the trumpet. The Gringo Mariachis, we called ourselves."

"Because you aren't Mexican?"

"Well, Clay's half-Mexican. After my mother died birthing

me, Daddy married again. Marrying Mama was the best decision Daddy ever made, and he's made plenty."

She studied his wistful expression. "You were all close once?"

His lips clamped together. "Wyatt and I—we struggled together, like Jacob and Esau—but we got along for the most part. But Clay and I were inseparable. Then I ruined it all. They'll never forgive me."

Violet's chest crushed at the thought. "You know that for sure?"

Adler shifted his jaw. "Clay told me flat out he'd never forgive me. And Wyatt? Oralee's death was an accident, but I blamed him and tried to kill him. He had to leave town for a few days to save his hide, for heaven's sake. How do you forgive that?"

What a mess. "You don't blame him anymore. I can see that."

"Of course not. He'd never hurt Oralee, never hurt anyone. It's not in his nature."

"Do you think he blames himself?"

Adler arched one eyebrow. "Why would he? He did the right thing. I was the one pushing Oralee to cross that footbridge. He said she didn't have to. If she'd listened to him, she'd still be alive."

"Does he know you don't blame him?" Violet crossed her ankles under the piano bench. "I'd think it'd mean a lot to him to know you've forgiven him, that you're sorry for—for trying to kill him."

Adler's eyebrows bunched together. "I ran away from home that night. He—he couldn't know."

"And your parents? Surely they want to hear—"

"No. Trust me, they never want to hear from me again." He pushed up to squatting and set the trumpet back in its case. But he lingered and stroked the silver instrument.

Words stirred inside her, and she released them. "Would you like to borrow the trumpet?"

One sharp shake of his head. "The valves stick."

"Oh!" She darted across the room to a little case on the floor. "This has a bunch of vials and things to care for the instruments. Here we are—valve oil."

Adler stared at the vial, then at her. "You have a cure for everything, don't you?"

She laughed. "Only for the valves. Sorry."

He took the oil. "Don't suppose this would work on my family, do you?"

Violet smiled down at him. "No, but apologies are remarkably effective at greasing squeaky relationships."

Adler stashed the vial in the case and slammed it shut. "You're naïve, you know that, right?"

Was that an insult or a tease? "I suppose so."

He picked up the case, frowned at her just a bit, and then gave her a brotherly pat on the shoulder on his way out. "Don't let anyone ever change that."

She stared after him. He was the most perplexing man. And the most fascinating.

18

Nothing to see but white and blue.

Adler squirmed in his cockpit seat, rolled his shoulders, and glanced at his wristwatch. Well past noon. Past the rendezvous time.

The B-17 and B-24 bombers were flying a dogleg route, up the North Sea, then down past Hamburg to hit Berlin. The 357th Fighter Group had flown in a straight line to the rendezvous point northwest of Berlin to cover the bombers over the target and on withdrawal.

If they were anywhere near Berlin.

Adler puffed a breath into his oxygen mask. No sign of the bombers. No sign of the Luftwaffe. Clouds coated Germany with a generous helping of whipped cream.

Thirty-three Mustangs spread out over the sky, five hundred feet apart. Shortly after takeoff, fifteen pilots had turned back for Leiston with mechanical problems, including Lt. Col. Donald Graham, the new group commanding officer. That left Maj. Tommy Hayes, one of the squadron commanders, in the lead.

With the undercast obscuring landmarks, the leaders had to

121

navigate by dead reckoning—time and compass heading. Were they off course? If so, by how much?

Adler practiced trumpet fingering on the control stick. Lightly. Kept his mind sharp.

Late last night he'd gone to the far reaches of the airfield to play. He was rusty, but he was surprised how fast the trumpet came back to him.

How fast the memories came back, tumbling from the bell of the instrument. Wyatt's graduation party. The humid heat infused with the smell of barbecue, Oralee sitting on the grass in her yellow dress and engagement ring, beaming at him as he played. Just for her.

Where were those bombers? Where was Berlin? The radio silence prickled his nerves.

Adler fingered "Ciribiribin," the hardest song he knew. Like it or not, the trumpet was as likely to summon Violet's face as Oralee's.

How she'd sat on that piano bench, her pretty head tipped to one side, her soft questions tunneling deep.

Almost three years of refusing to think about his sins meant he hadn't thought through the consequences. But it was just like Wyatt to blame himself for Oralee's death. The responsible brother, the serious one. And he lived in Kerrville, where he had to see Oralee's parents and the hill where she'd fallen.

Adler started to cuss and stopped himself. He ought to pray instead. "Lord, tell Wyatt he isn't at fault."

He snapped his vision around the bright sky. He had a hunch it wasn't God's job to tell Wyatt. It was Adler's.

He pounded his fist on his thigh. "Lord, how could I do that? I can't write home. Daddy . . . Mama . . ."

Last time he'd seen them was from down on the floor of the garage. Mama—sweet Mama—with a shotgun to Clay's chest to hold him back. Ellen screaming and crying, hiding under the truck. Daddy, averting his eyes, tossing Adler's clothes on top of him, a wad of cash, the key, telling him to get out of his sight.

The pain thrust a fist into his chest, dug claws into his heart, and mauled it.

He let it. He'd avoided the pain, but now he needed to feel.

"Where is Berlin, OBee?"

Adler startled at the break in radio silence. That was Tommy Hayes, talking to another squadron commander, Capt. William O'Brien.

"I think Berlin is behind us," OBee said.

Behind? Adler cranked his head around as if the city would poke its head out of the clouds and wave.

The P-51s entered a 180-degree turn, weaving over each other in a practiced maneuver, reversing the position of each flight. Now Nick was ahead of Adler to his left.

Not once had Adler left his leader's side since that day, but Shapiro still didn't trust him. Not that Adler blamed the man.

"Bombers at nine o'clock," someone called on the radio.

There they were, coming out of a bank of clouds, a passel of B-17s with squares on their bell-shaped tails—the 3rd Bombardment Division. The 357th was supposed to rendezvous with the B-24s of the 2nd Division, but they'd guard any bombers in sight.

"Bogeys! Two o'clock!"

Adrenaline frolicked in Adler's veins. Lots of enemy fighters, dozens, maybe a hundred, on an intercept course with the bombers.

"Let's fight," Hayes called. "Drop tanks."

Adler's thumb was already on the button on top of the control stick, and the empty fuel tanks fell away from beneath his wings. He tucked in close to Nick's side.

The Mustangs curved around to approach the Germans from the rear. Mostly two-engine fighters, Messerschmitt Me 110s, with some single-engine Me 109s and Focke-Wulf Fw 190s flying top cover.

Each flight of four P-51s picked out targets, Hayes's top squadron heading for the single-engine fighters.

One group of Me 110s turned to meet the Americans head-on, and two flights of P-51s peeled off to engage. Nick continued toward the main body of the enemy, which aimed for the bombers.

"Not on our watch, you don't." If only Adler's glare carried bullets, he'd have shot down a dozen already.

"Yellow flight, break," Nick called, giving Riggs and Theo permission to hunt on their own.

Riggs broke to the left, diving after a pair of fighters, and Nick broke to the right.

Adler had anticipated the move, and he stayed in position. His eyes entered into his attack pattern, watching *Santa's Sleigh* and the sky, especially the rear, freeing Nick to concentrate on the enemy.

Occasionally, Adler let his gaze slide to the Me 110s. If Nick overshot, Adler had to be ready to follow up. He might have felt sorry for the enemy if they hadn't been fighting for Hitler. The Me 110 was good against bombers but was too heavy and slow to tangle with the Mustang.

Nick skidded from side to side, letting each enemy pilot think he'd be the target, urging him to abandon the attack on the bombers and escape.

Two of them went into a split-S, and Nick let them pass underneath. Adler eyed them in case they came back from behind.

"Come on, Nicky," Adler muttered. "Now's the time."

Nick couldn't have heard him, but *Santa's Sleigh* tipped to the left and screamed down to a pair of Messerschmitts.

"Hoo-ey!" Adler rolled down after him, close enough to assist but far enough to let his buddy maneuver.

Nick slipped in on the tail of the fighter on the right, and bullets zipped from his four guns. Flashes sprinkled the length of one wing, bullets sparking on metal.

"Good shooting." Adler's finger groped for the trigger on his stick, but he eased it away. Not today. Maybe not ever, but that was all right.

Smoke streamed from the right engine of the Messerschmitt, then yellow flames.

Nick stopped shooting, but he stayed on the enemy's tail as he dove for the deck. A dark urge in Adler wanted Nick to finish him off, but Adler pushed back against the darkness. Their mission was to protect the bombers and to destroy aircraft. Nick avoided killing, and Adler admired that about him.

G-forces built, pressing on his insides. Down through the clouds they went, and Adler stretched his eyes wide in the murk. The clouds grew patchy, then cleared to reveal the gray grid of a city beneath.

Not a good place to be. Cities were guarded by heavy antiaircraft batteries. But where was Nick?

He leveled off his dive and swung his gaze around, panic stealing his breath. How could he have lost him? They'd only been in the clouds a few seconds.

"Where are you? Where are you?" No use calling Nick on the radio. His leader was too busy to shepherd Adler.

A flaming Messerschmitt burst through the clouds with Nick behind him.

"Thank you." Adler wheeled around to join him. The German must have leveled off in the clouds to try to shake the American.

It was too late. Flames consumed the right wing. A figure tumbled out of the Messerschmitt, then another, their parachutes puffing open above them.

"Yellow two, let's go upstairs," Nick called.

"Roger." Adler followed him.

As the clouds thinned, a full-blown battle came into view, what the men called a "rat race." All around, fighters zipped, circled, dove, chased, bullets flashing, flames spouting, parachutes billowing.

Chatter peppered the radio waves—"Got him!" "Five o'clock, on your tail." "That's two for me." "Take him."

No way to tell who was winning, but it sounded good, looked good. Only brown German parachutes in sight.

Something darkened the rearview mirror Beck had welded to *Eagle*'s canopy. "Yellow one, four o'clock."

"Let's go." Nick dove a bit, then nosed straight up.

Adler mimicked his actions. Nick was doing an Immelmann turn to reverse direction and gain altitude and advantage.

At the top of the loop, hanging upside down, Adler slowly rolled *Eagle* to upright, his feet on the rudder pedals and his hands on the stick and throttle, all working in harmony.

Now their would-be attacker was below them at ten o'clock.

Before the German could react, Nick went into a steep diving turn. His bullets stitched a line down the center of the Messerschmitt's fuselage.

Adler whistled. And he thought he had a good deflection shot. "That's why you're an ace, buddy."

The fighter slid onto one wing, then tumbled slowly. The pilot must have been injured or killed. Adler winced, but if that Messerschmitt had continued on course, it could have shot down a B-17 and killed ten men.

"Chalk one up for Riggs." That was Riggs's voice.

"Two for Westin," Adler said. Thank goodness Nick was still ahead. "Some fine shooting."

"How about you, yellow two?" A taunt twisted Riggs's voice. "Gun barrels still taped up nice and neat?"

"Enough," Nick said, his voice low and weary. "Everyone did his job."

They certainly had. The rat race cleared up as quickly as it had started. P-51s speckled the sky, and a thin line of B-24 Liberators headed west in the distance.

"Yellow flight, let's escort those birds home," Nick said.

Adler entered a smooth, wide turn with the men of his flight. His shirt felt clammy under his leather jacket, and his breath huffed into the oxygen mask from the exertion of the battle, of maneuvering the controls. He never noticed it in the thick of things, only after the fact.

They'd have to wait until they returned to Leiston to find out how the group had done. How many victories. How many losses. From Adler's limited perspective, the battle had been lopsided in favor of the Americans.

And he still had only one victory. His gut twisted one direction, then the other. Guilt for how he'd obtained that victory. Frustration that he hadn't scored since.

He squirmed to undo the twisting. He'd done his job, just as Nick said.

Then a smile built. Nick had gotten two more victories, bringing his total to three. Soon he'd be a double ace, first in the Pacific and now in Europe. Adler had played a role by keeping the ace safe. Being second wasn't always bad.

Maybe that was what Jesus meant when he said the last would be first. Making peace with his role, embracing the purpose, seeing the good in it.

Steeliness formed out of that peace. Adler was a wingman. Well then, he'd be the best wingman ever.

19

Kitty searched the cabinet. "We're out of tea already?"

"I tell you, Miss Kelly, our Yanks have learned to fancy tea." Millie Clark carried a tray out to a jeep.

Had they? Violet exchanged a glance with Kitty. She never seemed to serve much tea.

Mr. Tate insisted food expenses were higher at Leiston than at other Aeroclubs. If there was a thief, how could Violet figure out who it was?

"Miss Lindstrom?" Millie came back inside and played with a strand of her light brown hair. "Do you think . . . after I make this delivery to the hangar, might I stay at the dance?"

Violet smiled at her. "Tom Griffith?"

She chewed on one bright red lip. "Yes, ma'am."

The girl might be only sixteen, but Griff was only nineteen. And he was sweet. After he saw Millie spill an urn of coffee while making a delivery by pushcart, he'd helped the Red Cross procure jeeps from the base motor pool. "Of course, you may. This is our last run. We don't have anything else to do until the parties are over."

"Oh, thank you." Millie hopped in place. "I can't wait. And I promise, Griff and I will bring everything back."

Kitty carried a tray out the side door. "Come on, Millie, let's take these to the enlisted men. I plan to do some dancing too. We all should." She tossed a wink to Violet.

Violet had no such plans, and she waved off Kitty and Millie.

Rosalind Weaver held a tray of donuts. "To the officers?"

"Yes." Violet took a box of sugar and milk to the other jeep and climbed into the driver's seat beside Rosalind. She drove slowly, the not-quite-full moon shedding light on the blacked-out road. "I'm sorry you have to work late tonight."

"I don't mind." Rosalind held back her ginger hair. "It's a special day for the boys."

"It is." The men of the 357th were celebrating one month of combat and fifty-nine victories. Just three days earlier, they'd shot down twenty enemy fighters over Berlin without losing a single P-51. The men were elated.

"I—I'm so thankful for this job." Rosalind's brow furrowed. "My husband's pension is barely enough to live on, even with little Charlie and I staying with my mum. And when the war's over, the men will come home and take back their jobs."

"Oh dear." Violet turned left. In addition, the Red Cross would leave. What would widows like Rosalind do if they couldn't find work? "I wish—"

"Everything's tickety-boo." Rosalind sent her a smile. "I'm saving what I earn here so I can take a secretarial class after the war. We'll make do."

"I know you will. You're smart and hardworking."

"Oh, go on with you." Rosalind flapped a hand at her.

Violet parked the jeep in front of the hangar and smoothed her hair.

Lord . . . She didn't know whether to pray that she'd see Adler or that she wouldn't. With the heavy pace of missions, she missed him. But she didn't want her crush to get even crushier.

Violet and Rosalind carried the food through the hangar doors into a swirl of light and music. The new base band, the Buzz Boys, blasted out "Stompin' at the Savoy." The hangar was packed with several hundred officers and local women, dancing and talking and laughing. Finding Adler would be impossible anyway.

The crowd parted for Violet and Rosalind, and men plucked donuts from the tray as she passed. She laughed and pretended to scold them.

Violet set her tray on top of an empty one on the table.

"Well, hello there. I haven't had the pleasure of meeting you." An officer bowed to Rosalind. He was one of Adler's friends, with curly black hair and a mischievous smile. "I'm Tony Rosario."

Rosalind gave him a nervous nod and rearranged trays on the table. "I'm Rosalind Weaver."

"Rosalind, huh? Ever go by Rosie?"

Violet edged to the side to replenish the sugar, keeping Rosalind in sight.

"No, just Rosalind."

"Thank goodness, because I do go by Rosie." He leaned his hip against the table. "When we get married, it'd be confusing if we both had the same nickname."

Rosalind's hazel eyes flew open. "I—I have a little boy at home."

The pilot snapped to standing. "I beg your pardon, ma'am. I'd never—believe me, I'm not the kind of man to flirt with a married woman."

Violet's heart softened. What a gentleman.

"It's all right, Lieutenant." Rosalind held up one hand. "You did nothing wrong. My husband was killed at El Alamein."

Tony's head slumped forward. "I—I'm sorry, ma'am. This war—it's so hard on women."

"I'd say it's dreadfully hard on men." Rosalind turned back to the donuts.

"If it's not too much to ask, ma'am . . . may I have this dance?"

Rosalind didn't look up, and her shoulders tensed.

"Excuse me, sir. We'll be just a second." Violet smiled at the lieutenant, grabbed Rosalind's arm, and pulled her out of earshot. "If you don't want to dance, you can blame me and say you're working tonight. But if you want to, you have my permission."

Rosalind sneaked a glance over her shoulder at the pilot. "He's very kind, but I'm supposed to be helping you."

"Nonsense. Part of your job is to be a hostess. Dancing is allowed, even encouraged."

"Thank you." A smile twitched around, and Rosalind turned back to Tony.

Violet couldn't help but laugh. If those two did end up married, the woman would be Rosalind Rosario.

"Did you mean that?" A deep and familiar voice toyed with her insides.

She faced Adler. "Hi there."

He had a strange look on his face—serious and almost hesitant. "Did you mean what you said about dancing being part of your job? If so, I'd like to ask you to dance."

Violet couldn't imagine a worse idea. He was already too attractive standing two feet away in his smart olive drab dress uniform. But to be in his arms? She gestured to the table. "The empty trays—I have to take them to the Aeroclub." Although not until the end of the evening.

One blink, and his face stiffened. "That's okay. I understand."

Realization slapped her. "How long has it been . . . since you last danced?"

He looked out over the dance floor. His lips parted, then closed. His eyes fluttered shut.

"Not since . . . ?" She squeezed out the words.

He shook his head.

Everything inside ached for him. The poor man had been mourning Oralee for three years. To ask another woman to dance was an enormous step.

She clutched his arm. "Adler? I'd be honored."

His gaze slid back to her, he nodded, and he led her to the dance floor.

The band played "Deep Purple." Violet winced at the romantic tune, but Adler's healing was too important.

In an open spot, Adler turned without looking at her and took her into his arms.

Violet forced herself to breathe evenly, as if she wasn't falling apart inside. He was so close, and his hand was so strong, his arm perfect around her waist, his shoulder firm beneath her hand, his cheek tantalizingly near, and warmth filled the gap between them.

She prayed for him as they danced, as the notes of "Deep Purple" floated around her. Such a heartbreaking song, all about true love, long lost.

This had to be difficult for Adler. He loved Oralee so, missed her so. He was all alone in this world, and Violet found herself closing the gap.

But she eased back. She couldn't heal him. Only God could, and she mustn't interfere with the process.

The band shifted keys and played "Blue Moon," one of Violet's favorites.

Adler widened the space without letting go, and he met her gaze. "They're working their way through the rainbow. First purple, now blue."

Violet smiled. He looked relaxed and content, not anguished. "What's next? 'Green Eyes'?"

That grin of his was lethal at close range. "Then 'The Yellow Rose of Texas.'"

She let out a mock sigh. "Fine. Leave me with orange."

He chuckled, then glanced toward the refreshment table. "Listen, I wouldn't mind another dance, but I won't keep you from your work."

The perfect escape, but how could she resist "Blue Moon"?

"It seems silly to make two more runs to the Aeroclub. I can take everything back after the party is over."

"Good." Adler gathered her closer again. "I'd forgotten how much I liked dancing."

"Me too."

"You?" He pulled back to look her in the eye.

"When you're six feet tall, it's hard to find dance partners."

"I'd think . . ." He shrugged and turned her in a circle. "Well, I'm different."

In many wonderful ways. "And Dennis wasn't much of a dancer."

"Dennis?" Those eyes met hers again, as blue as that moon.

"My former fiancé. I haven't told you about him, have I?"

His eyes widened, and he shook his head. "You were engaged too?"

"In college. We both wanted to be missionaries. Then his roommate's father offered him a job, and he took it. Only a few months before graduation, before our wedding."

"He broke your engagement?" Adler's mouth thinned.

"No, I did. He'd changed and drifted away from the mission society. All he could talk about was his friend's money and car and how nice they were. Then he accepted the job offer. I couldn't marry someone who no longer shared my dream."

Adler's hand tightened around hers, and he glanced away. "Yeah, I reckon not."

"I—to tell the truth, what really broke my heart was not being able to serve overseas."

"No great love then?"

"No." She swallowed the embarrassment. She'd hoped they'd fall in love, but they hadn't. "We were friends and worked well together, but we were never in love."

"But y'all—y'all wanted to walk the same path in life." There was an odd note in his voice.

She saw a question in his eyes. What was more important? The path or love? And she saw a deeper question underneath.

She hated the answer. With Dennis, she'd been willing to sacrifice love for the path. But she couldn't sacrifice the path for love. She wouldn't.

Not even for a man like Adler.

Before tonight, her feelings for him seemed like a silly crush, but not now. Not with him so near, touching her, breathing the same air, looking at her the way he was.

She tore her gaze away over his shoulder. "We did want the same path. Until we didn't."

The beat of the music changed and quickened—"Jumpin' at the Woodside."

"Now, that's what I'm talking about." Adler broke into an energetic swing dance.

Violet laughed and followed his moves, swinging away from him, to him, spinning under his arm and into his arms, right against his chest, no gap, no distance.

Then he spun her away again, joy in his eyes, new and delightful, summoning even more joy inside her.

For tonight, she'd let herself have fun in his company, in his arms, in the dream. Tomorrow, she'd wake up.

Unless . . . *Oh, Lord, please change his heart.*

20

Bill Beckenbauer screwed the cowling panel in place over *Texas Eagle*'s Merlin engine. "What kind of idiot used faulty engine mount bolts?"

Standing beside Beck, Adler poked a little screw-like Dzus fastener through a hole in the panel, twisted it until it engaged with the coil under the panel, then gave it a turn with a screwdriver. "Don't look at me. This was after my time in Inglewood."

Recently, all four bolts had failed on a 354th Fighter Group Mustang. The engine assembly had broken away in flight, and the pilot had been killed. Now the Army Air Force had grounded all P-51s to replace the engine mount bolts.

Thank goodness Beck had given in to Adler's sweet talk and let him assist. Reminded Adler of his youth helping the truckers and of his year at North American. Felt good to change from slick officer's duds into grease-stained coveralls and a mechanic's ball cap.

Adler filled his pocket with more fasteners. "You ever want to do more than this?"

"More? Than being crew chief? Nah." He held out his hand for a refill. "My fool brother keeps trying to put me in charge of some

135

big repair depot, but I don't want it. Paperwork and requisitions and nonsense. Nope, give me one plane, one pilot."

Adler gave the mechanic a handful of Dzus fasteners. In the distance, a few Merlins puttered as ground crews put them through their paces. A couple of seagulls squawked at each other as they flew overhead. A chilly wind ruffled the hem of his coveralls. And a question burned its way out. "Ever bother you, being second to your brother?"

Beck looked back over his shoulder, a streak of grease down his nose and one graying eyebrow cocked at Adler. "Second? You have crazy notions, kid."

Adler's mouth hung open due to the foot jammed in it.

Beck fitted another cowling panel in place. "My brother never could have gotten in the air without me, and neither can you."

"I know that, sir. I know that full well." Adler screwed the top corner of the panel into place. But the question still smoldered. All his life the quest to be first had driven him, both to good and to evil. Why did that urge still churn? He controlled it in combat, but he still wanted to make ace.

"I wanted to be a pilot."

"Hmm?" Adler said.

"In the Great War." Beck studied his screwdriver, the wooden handle smooth and dark with age. "I washed out, but I stayed in the Air Service. I wanted to serve my country, I wanted to be close to planes, and I wanted to be with my brother. That's why I became Johnny's mechanic. Discovered I had a knack. Johnny never once turned back with mechanical problems."

"Neither have I, sir."

"Don't you forget it, kid. When it comes down to it, both Johnny and I do something we're good at, something we love. And"—he pointed the screwdriver at Adler—"not once has anyone ever shot at me."

Adler laughed. "There's something to be said for that."

Beck circled around the nose.

Adler followed with the bucket of Dzus fasteners, then helped Beck replace a panel on the other side of the fuselage.

"Do you have a brother?" Beck asked.

"Two of them."

"From your tone of voice, you don't get along."

Adler pulled a fastener from his pocket. "We used to. As fine as brothers do, I reckon."

"Used to? This have anything to do with why you don't want your name in the paper?"

Maybe he shouldn't have come out here after all. "I can't go home again, and I'd rather they didn't know where I was."

"What on earth did you do?"

Adler's shoulders squirmed. "Let's just say I hurt everyone in my family and then some."

Beck whistled and shook his head. "Ever tell them you're sorry?"

For the second time in a short span, someone asked a question he hadn't considered in almost three years. For the second time that afternoon, Adler's mouth hung open.

With firm twists, Beck fastened the panel shut. "I don't know how they do things in Texas. But where I come from, if you do something wrong, you own up to it and apologize."

That sliced even deeper than Violet's suggestion. Because Beck was absolutely right.

Beck leaned to the side, looked past Adler, and waved. "Well, hello there."

A jeep parked in front of *Eagle*'s nose, and Violet Lindstrom stepped out.

Boy, did she look pretty in her gray-blue skirt and jacket and cap. Not as pretty as she'd looked in his arms though, with her cheeks flushed from dancing. Holding her so close, he could see gold and green radiating in the blue of her eyes.

"Good afternoon, gentlemen." She leaned into the backseat of the jeep and bustled about. "We heard what you were doing today, how hard you're working to get the planes back in the air, not even taking breaks. So we're bringing out snacks—coffee, sandwiches, and donuts."

She carried a tray to them with a bright smile that didn't hold even a hint of recognition.

Greasy coveralls were a great disguise if he ever needed one. "Howdy, Violet."

She stopped and stared. "Adler?"

He flicked his chin toward the jeep. "They let just about anyone drive a jeep nowadays, huh?"

Her smile shifted.

Uh-oh. She wasn't used to being ribbed like one of the fellows. He gave her his most dazzling grin and took a sandwich.

Violet's eyes narrowed, and she turned to Beck. "They let just about anyone wear that uniform nowadays, huh?"

Beck and Adler cracked up, and Beck slapped him on the back. "She's got you pegged."

Pegged right through the heart, and he gnawed off a bite of sandwich.

Beck pointed his thumb at Adler. "You know these glamour boys. Sometimes they want to play dress up, and we humor them."

Adler swallowed the bite and a snappy comeback. "Violet, this is Technical Sergeant Bill Beckenbauer, my crew chief. Beck, this is Miss Violet Lindstrom."

"Pleasure to meet you," Violet said.

"The pleasure's mine." Beck clapped Adler on the shoulder. "In all honesty, this kid knows his way around a wrench and a P-51."

"I'd better, since I used to build them." He took another bite and savored how it fell into his empty belly.

"Build them?" Violet frowned. "P-51s?"

"Never told you that?" He smiled. After all, she hadn't told him she'd been engaged. "Worked the assembly line at North American Aviation in my year of exile. After I left home and before I enlisted."

Violet considered him, her eyes soft but appraising.

Adler considered his sandwich, ate it.

"Say, Miss Lindstrom . . ." Beck dipped his donut in his mug of coffee. "Doesn't the Red Cross help connect servicemen and their families?"

"Oh yes. That's a very important job we do."

"Great." Beck pointed his donut at Adler. "Make this oaf write home."

Adler almost choked.

"I've tried." Violet put on a cute little pout. "But he's a mule-headed oaf."

Adler coughed and hit his chest with his fist. "Everyone take a shot at me, why don't you?"

"Listen, miss. You bat those pretty eyes at him, and he might break."

Those pretty eyes turned his way—a bit shy, a bit mischievous, a bit . . . flirtatious. "I could try flattery."

For the third time, his mouth flopped open. Only the knowledge that his mouth was full of chicken salad made him close it. Why had he told her his Achilles' heel? "You wouldn't."

The mischief disappeared. "I'll save that for a last resort, but you really should write home."

"Y'all have made your opinion quite clear on that matter." So had Nick.

"Oh!" She darted back to the jeep, set down the tray, and bustled around some more. "I have stationery. We always carry some. Now you have no excuse. How many sheets would you like?"

Adler's head swung back and forth. "A whole ream of paper wouldn't be enough."

She tossed a sympathetic smile over her shoulder and then closed one eye as if sizing him up. "How about three?"

"Sure. No, wait. I didn't say I would."

"But you should." She brought over the stationery. "Think how much better you'll feel. And they'll finally have the chance to forgive you. Give them that chance."

He'd never thought of it that way before, and he couldn't stop staring at her.

She lifted his arm and slipped the stationery into his hand. "If you won't do it for yourself, do it for them. I know you love them."

Adler fought the bending, but he was losing under the warmth of that hand. "If I write home, will y'all stop haranguing me and calling me a mule-headed oaf?"

Her eyes shone. "I promise."

"I'll stop calling you mule-headed," Beck said, "but I stand by oaf."

Adler shrugged. "Fair enough."

Violet squeezed his wrist.

Everything in him wanted to pull her close and thank her for believing in him, for sweet-talking the sweet-talker. But that wouldn't be wise. What if she fell for him and disobeyed God to be with him? He'd already led one woman into temptation, and he refused to do so again.

He spun away to the plane, stationery in hand. "All right, Red Cross, you did your job. Now let us do ours."

Beck grunted. "Oaf."

Adler glanced behind him, but Violet smiled as if he were anything but an oaf.

He was in deep, deep trouble.

That night, Adler sat on the dirt floor of the crew shack by the flight line, hunched over Red Cross stationery that was lying on a crate of spark plugs.

What could he write? "Howdy, folks. How are you doing? How's Paxton Trucking?"

He tossed aside the ball cap and ran his hand through his hair. "Lord, I don't know what to say. I only know I've got to tell them I'm sorry."

Maybe that was it. He uncapped his pen.

Dear Daddy, Mama, and Wyatt,

I am so sorry. How else could I start this letter? After what I've done, the only thing to say is I am deeply sorry.

For almost three years, I refused to think about my past because it hurt like blazes. But now I can't stop thinking about it. Yes, it hurts. Not like a stab in the heart, but like a dislocated shoulder being wrenched back into place. It had to feel worse before it could feel better. I'd been living with that dislocation for years, which made the wrenching all the more painful and all the more necessary.

About a month ago, I asked God to do that wrenching. I asked him to forgive me and to save me, and he did. Miracle of miracles.

Now I'm asking you to forgive me. Not because I expect you to do so, not in the least, but because you deserve to know how sorry I am.

This first part is to Wyatt. When Oralee died, I turned my anger on you, which wasn't fair or right. Sure, I was angry at you for interfering, but mostly I was angry because you were right and I was wrong and Oralee paid the price.

You stood up for Oralee and protected her, as I should have done. Wyatt, please know I never really blamed you for her death. I'm the only one at fault.

I am so sorry and ashamed that I tried to kill you. How can a man forgive his brother for attempted murder? I don't know, and I don't expect you to. I wish you all the best at Paxton Trucking. You're a fine man, and I know you're doing a great job.

Daddy and Mama, I didn't address Clay because I know he isn't in Texas. I saw him on the troopship, although I made sure he didn't see me.

As for what happened that night in the garage, I don't even know where to start apologizing. I was so angry, and there was Ellen with a bottle of medicinal whiskey from her daddy. I have no excuse. I gave in to every base instinct and did the worst thing I've ever done.

Instead of being grateful to Clay for stopping me from murdering Wyatt, I betrayed him and stole the woman he loved. I will always be ashamed of what I did, ashamed that you all saw me in my depravity, that I drove Clay to try to kill me, and that my mother had to pull a gun on him to save my wretched life.

That's one reason I'm writing. That night you all saw a drunken, vengeful, lecherous traitor. I'll never be able to erase that image from your heads any more than I can erase it from mine. But please be assured that my remorse runs deep.

However, my sins don't stop with my family. What I did to Ellen was vile and wrong. I took advantage of her and destroyed her future with Clay. Then I fled and left you all with the wreckage—with Wyatt fearing for his life, Clay betrayed, Ellen ruined, and with the knowledge that your middle son is a rat.

On top of it, you never got your truck back. I drove to California and sold it to get food, clothes, and a room. I'll enclose a check with this letter.

In case you wonder what I've been doing, I worked at North American Aviation in California for a year. Then I decided it wasn't right for me to be safe in a factory with a war on. So I enlisted in the Army Air Forces, and they made me a P-51 fighter pilot. I'm based on the same island as Clay.

I don't know why Clay is in the Army and not in college,

but I pray he's all right. Let me know if you think I should write him. He deserves an apology, but I'll let you decide if a letter from me would make things better or worse.

Listen to me with all this talk about "letting me know," as if I were ordering you to write me back. I certainly don't expect a reply.

I'm writing because, as a wise man reminded me today, when you do something wrong, you own up to it and apologize.

I'm also writing because I love you and respect you. My disgusting sins don't reflect how you raised me. You are the best parents a man could hope for. Your examples of faith, strength, and integrity have always been there, and now I'm finally becoming the man you wanted me to be. At least I hope I am.

Somehow I know—I feel it in my bones—that you've never stopped praying for me. That may be the only contact we'll ever have again, and I'm fine with that. Please keep praying for me, and know that I'm now praying for you as well. I'll never stop.

All my love,
Adler

With a groan, Adler capped his pen. Then he flopped onto his back on the dirt floor, staring at the lightbulb dangling from the ceiling.

He'd never felt so depleted and drained.

Yet he'd never felt so right.

21

Kitty pulled a tray of donuts out of the jeep. "He's here."

Violet set a coffeepot on the table on the grass. "Who?"

"Adler, you ninny. He's pitching."

"Oh?" She wasn't good at feigning innocence. "I wonder if he's any good."

In a meadow near the communal site, a dozen airmen were playing baseball with children from town.

Now that spring was near, the children loitered after school. When the weather was fair, they let the kids in to play.

Adler stood in the center of the makeshift baseball diamond, ball and glove held to his chest, his gaze drilling down the batter—that awful Riggs. Nick played catcher.

"Get him, Adler," she muttered.

He coiled up for the pitch, one leg high. As soon as the ball left his hand, it thumped in Nick's glove. Riggs swung at nothing but air.

Violet grinned. "I'll say he's good."

"Three strikes and you're out," Nick said.

Riggs cussed.

"Watch your language." Nick tossed the ball to Adler. "The children. The ladies."

Adler's gaze swept the field and landed on her. He smiled and waved.

She waved too, her heart bouncing like a loose ground ball.

Kitty leaned close. "See? He likes you."

"As a friend," she whispered. "And that's how I like him."

"You're a horrible liar."

Violet scrunched up her nose. Only half of what she'd said was a lie.

A boy came up to bat, Sylvia Haywood's son, Jimmy, swaggering like one of the pilots. Cpl. Tom Griffith helped Jimmy with his stance.

How could a child hit one of Adler's pitches? Violet straightened rows of donuts, her eyes on the game.

Adler wound up—and the ball meandered from his hand to the plate. Jimmy swung, connected, whooped, and ran.

The ball hopped to Adler. He scooped it up, bobbled it, tossed it to first—too short—and Jimmy touched first base.

Oh, Adler was very good indeed.

"The next load, Violet?" Kitty called.

"Oh yes." She dashed over.

"For heaven's sake, stop pretending you don't have a crush on him."

"Stop it." She picked up the box of cocoa and sugar. "He's a businessman, and I'm a missionary."

Kitty brushed a brown curl out of her face. "I'm not telling you to marry the man. Just have a fling."

"A fling!" Violet almost dropped the box.

Kitty clucked her tongue. "You make it sound dirty. Didn't you ever have a summer romance?"

"Well, yes." Her neighbor's grandson, and it had been a fine little romance. "But I'm not fifteen anymore."

"And he won't be here forever. Didn't you hear? The men finish their tours after they've flown three hundred hours of combat. They think that'll be the middle of summer for the original pilots."

"Crazy idea." Violet marched to the table.

"It'd be good for you to have some fun. That Dennis sounds like a fuddy-duddy."

Violet set out the tin of cocoa. It wouldn't be good if they fell in love and then had to break up to walk separate paths.

Out on the field, the players changed sides, the inning over.

"Hiya, fellas!" Kitty waved. "May I play?"

"Sure, Miss Kelly," Tom Griffith said. "Be on our team."

"No fair!" Jimmy cried. "If we have to have a woman, the other team does too."

Adler swung a mischievous grin to Violet and beckoned with one finger.

Oh dear, no. She shook her head.

He sauntered over, swinging a bat up to rest on his shoulder. "Come on, Miss Lindstrom. I could teach you to play."

She could envision his arms coming around her from behind, his hands over hers on the bat, his breath in her ear. She wanted to say she needed his help, but she couldn't lie—again. "I'm actually pretty good at baseball."

One eyebrow lifted. "Why do you sound embarrassed?"

"It isn't—well, it isn't very feminine to be good at sports."

Adler grunted and shrugged. "So you're tall, you're athletic, and you prefer Zane to Jane. Not all men consider that unattractive." His gaze cut away.

How could she breathe? He found her attractive. She forced air into her lungs. "All right, but it's been years, so—"

"Great. You're up." He laid the bat in her hands.

Oh dear, indeed. At home plate she took her stance, feeling rusty and awkward. But with Riggs pitching, suddenly she wanted to hit a home run.

He waved the outfielders in closer.

Now she wanted it even more.

Riggs eyed her, wound up, and pitched. The ball was too low, especially for her, but she wanted it.

Violet dipped low and felt a satisfying smack.

Riggs cussed and ducked, and Violet dropped the bat and ran. The skirt made running tricky, but thank goodness the Red Cross had issued low-heeled oxfords.

The ball bounced into the outfield, and Violet rounded first. Cheering rose, topped by Adler's loud "Hoo-ey!"

Kitty chased down the ball and tossed it, but too high. The boy on second darted away to catch it, and Violet planted her foot on the base. Then she smiled at the boy. "Good catch, George."

A little boy of about six came to the plate with Nick helping him.

"Don't be a jerk, Riggs," Violet muttered.

To her shock, he wasn't. He threw a soft, easy pitch, but the child swung and missed. Three times.

Then eight-year-old Harry Blythe came to bat. On the second pitch, he connected.

Riggs fielded it. Instead of turning to first, he turned to her.

She stayed put and smiled at him.

Too late to stop Harry, Riggs faced home and spat on the ground.

"Please don't spit, Lieutenant," Kitty called out. "You'll teach the children bad manners."

Violet stifled a giggle and exchanged a grin with Kitty.

Adler came to the plate, batting anchor, of course. He took his sweet time with his routine, adjusting his rolled-up khaki sleeves, tapping his bat on the plate, and tipping his crush cap farther back on his head.

His ease with the bat, his prowess at pitching, and the thickness of his arms said he'd be a solid hitter. Riggs would be wise to walk him.

Violet had a hunch Riggs's pride wouldn't allow that.

Sure enough, he threw straight down the center, fast enough to challenge most hitters. But not Adler.

He swung in a swift, smooth arc, and the ball sailed into left field.

The kids screamed with glee.

Kitty cupped her hand to her mouth. "Fling, Violet! Fling!"

She glared down her friend and ran. She could have walked, but she didn't care to insult Riggs.

After she crossed home plate, she turned to congratulate Harry, who was panting and glowing.

Then came Adler with a big grin, his chin ducked modestly. Not gloating, just enjoying the moment. She tacked good sportsmanship onto his long list of virtues.

"Miss Lindstrom?" Harry reached into his pocket. "I brought you a gift."

"A gift? How sweet." She put her arm around his little shoulders and guided him to the dugout area.

"Here." He handed her a tea bag, his eyes diverted and his cheeks flushed.

"Why, thank you, Harry." She loved how children gave from the heart. Then she noticed the tag—Lipton Tea Company, Hoboken, New Jersey. "Um, Harry, where did you get this?"

"Mum's tea cozy." His gray-blue eyes widened. "I asked. I promise."

She forced a smile so she wouldn't disparage his gift. How had Mrs. Blythe obtained American tea? She didn't volunteer at the Aeroclub. But then, English stores did carry American Lend-Lease food. If the tea was indeed stolen, how could Violet track it? She wasn't a detective.

She slipped the tea bag into her pocket and sat on the grass, her legs tucked to one side.

Adler plopped down beside her. "You've played before."

She smiled at the distraction from her problems—and at him. "So have you."

He draped his forearms over his bent knees. "High school and at the University of Texas before I dropped out."

"I'd say you're good, but you already know it. I wouldn't want to flatter you."

Adler chuckled and nudged her with his elbow. "By the way, you can stop haranguing me. Yesterday I mailed my letter home."

"You did? I'm so happy. You won't regret it. They'll be so glad to hear from you."

He snorted. "I doubt it, but now you and Nick and Beck can get off my back."

All that gruff talk concealed a soft heart. And one corner of his mouth puckered in such a vulnerable way, she longed to kiss it.

Thank goodness the lineup advanced, so Violet had a reason to scoot away.

Adler scooted too. "Speaking of home, any news from Kansas?"

Violet joined in the applause around her, although she had no idea what had happened. "I received three letters this week— what a treasure. My sister Alma told me she's expecting her third child. I wish I could be there when the baby's born, but at least Mom can help. And my brother Karl is doing well as a fireman—Dad's the fire chief. And Nels—he's the youngest— he's determined to enlist. Dad doesn't want him to, but Nels is nineteen now."

"You're still homesick, aren't you?" Adler's eyes were soft but discerning.

A sigh leached out. "Horribly so. It's hard to think of them going about their lives when I'm not there. I can't watch my nieces and nephews grow up. But it's more of an ache now rather than a sharp pain."

"I understand." He plucked a blade of grass. "Suppose your great-aunt gets homesick?"

"I doubt it. Kenya's her home, and she has Great-Uncle Gus, so she isn't alone."

"Have you heard from her?"

"That was one of the letters." A smile wiggled at the memory of the contents. "She's doing well. Kenya hasn't been affected much by the war, other than sending men to fight for Britain. Great-Aunt Violet has much to say about that."

"A woman of strong words, huh? I wondered how she convinced a homebody to become a missionary."

That was the second time he'd asked about that. Was he asking for personal reasons? But he only twirled the blade of grass in his fingers.

More cheering, and an airman came pounding across home plate.

Violet shrugged and scooted down in the lineup. "She can be convincing, but in the long run, I want to be a missionary because I love the Lord. He gave up everything for me, so I should be willing to give up everything I love for him."

"For the first time I understand that. I—" His voice roughened, and he shook his head. "I can't ever pay him back."

"Aren't you glad we don't have to?" She coiled her fingers into the grass so she wouldn't reach for his arm. "But the fact that you want to is good. It means you love him and want to please him."

He flicked half a smile. "Do I have to go to Kenya to please him?"

She tilted her head and made a face as if thinking deeply. "Brazil would do in a pinch."

Adler laughed. "I doubt Great-Aunt Violet would agree."

"No, she wouldn't. She is not pleased with my assignment to the Aeroclub."

"Because you're not working with poor, sick, crippled refugee orphans?"

"Worse." She leaned closer and used a stage whisper. "I'm working with pilots. Avoid them, she says. They're full of charm and full of themselves."

"Wise woman. Listen to her."

Violet expected a playful grin, but Adler fixed his gaze on the game.

"Good try, Colin." He applauded, then got to his feet and offered Violet his hand. "Inning's over. What position do you play?"

"I'm good at running and fielding. Put me in the outfield." She took his hand and felt his strength as he helped her up.

She wasn't so sure she wanted to avoid pilots. At least not this one.

22

Texas Eagle screamed toward the earth.

"Come on, darlin', you can do it." With his hand steady on the throttle, Adler tightened his muscles against the building g-forces.

Almost straight below him—ahead of him in the steep dive—Nick plunged after a single-engine Messerschmitt Me 109. Machine-gun fire lit on the edge of the German's wing.

The snowy landscape drew closer. Both pilots hoped the other would lose control and barrel into the ground, but the pilot who pulled up first would surely lose.

At two hundred feet, the German pulled out level, with *Santa's Sleigh* right behind him. Adler drew back the stick, and the change in g-forces slammed him back in his seat. He grunted and leveled off.

Sparks flew along the enemy's fuselage, then the fighter plowed through the snow.

"Get out. Get out," Nick said as he overran his victim. "Yellow two, did he get out?"

A dark figure stumbled across the field as his aircraft burst into flame.

"Yellow leader, he's out." Adler swooped up to avoid the debris. "Careful, buddy. That mercy could get you killed someday."

"A risk I'll take." Nick climbed toward the clouds, the bombers, and the rest of the fighter group.

Adler slipped into position, never letting up his scan for enemy aircraft, even at this altitude. He pushed the microphone button. "One 109 destroyed by Westin."

"Yellow three here. Just blew up a 110. How about you, yellow two?" Riggs never gave up.

"Yellow two, don't mind him," Nick said. "He's jealous you got two home runs and a grand slam off of him yesterday."

Adler grinned. That had felt good indeed, especially with Violet watching.

"Ah, that's just a game," Riggs said. "This is real life."

"Yellow flight, cut the chatter." Morty Shapiro's voice sliced the radio waves.

"Roger," Nick said.

Adler braced himself against the sting. Riggs was right. The only place Adler had ever been first was on the baseball diamond. Not in anything that mattered.

"Davis just made ace!" someone called.

"Warren got three. He made ace too."

That made Glen Davis and Jack Warren the first aces in the 357th.

"Good for them," Adler said. "Good for them," he repeated so he'd mean it.

At this rate, Adler would never join their ranks. The invasion of Nazi-occupied Europe was coming soon, in May if rumors held true. After D-day, the war was sure to wind down quickly. If not, Adler's tour would end in a few months.

Besides, the Luftwaffe seemed to be in decline. Sometimes the fighters came up in force, but they didn't oppose most missions. They appeared to be conserving aircraft, pilots, and oil.

The bomber crewmen might appreciate fewer German fighters, but the American fighter pilots didn't. Especially those who wanted to make ace.

"Lord, help me, I still do." Adler followed Nick up through the clouds.

Part of him wanted to make ace for personal glory, but something new in him only wanted to give back, to help the Allied cause and save lives by ending the war.

And his air cargo company. ACES was a great name, but he had to earn it to claim it. If not, he'd have to find a new name. He needed the company. Even if his family forgave him, he could never work at Paxton Trucking. He wasn't even sure he wanted to make a visit.

To see Daddy and Mama averting their eyes? Wyatt and Clay keeping their distance? To see Oralee's parents? Ellen Hill?

Adler hauled in a heated breath as he broke out of the clouds and linked with Nick. No sign of other aircraft.

What if his whole air shipping idea was a dud? What could he do with his life? Follow Violet to Africa? The only appealing part was Violet herself.

Those long legs as she ran the bases. The ferocious way she hit that line drive, nearly decapitating Willard Riggs. The sweet way she praised the children. How she accepted his teasing and teased him right back. She made him feel first. Better than first.

But Adler could barely wrap his mind around the fact that he was forgiven. To become a missionary? He couldn't see that. Of course, he really couldn't see Violet doing that either. He pictured her as someone's wife, a mama, a teacher, a community leader.

Adler studied flashes in the distance. "Lord, if you can make her a missionary, maybe you can make me—" He barked out a laugh. Too ridiculous to put in words.

"Blue three!" Shapiro cried. "He's on your tail."

Blue three? That was Stan Mulroney, and Adler squinted at those flashes.

"I know," Mulroney said in a tight voice. "I need a little more throttle."

"Break!" Shapiro said. "Break now."

Adler gritted his teeth. Just like Mulroney, always too cautious.

"A little more—" A horrendous shriek tore the airwaves.

An orange fireball tumbled down the sky.

Adler couldn't breathe, couldn't stop staring as a man burnt to death before his eyes.

"Lord in heaven," Nick said.

"Oh, Lord." The only prayer he could imagine was for God to end it soon, end the man's misery.

The shrieks stopped. Maybe Mulroney had lifted his thumb from the microphone button. Maybe God had answered Adler's prayer.

"Take that, you lousy Hun." Shapiro's voice was ragged and angry, and another fireball lit up the sky.

Mulroney's revenge. But it didn't bring the man back.

Adler pried his lungs open, and his breathing resumed. Maybe he should worry less about what to do after the war and more about surviving the war.

Yet the dream of life afterward . . . that pulled him through.

With hands on hips and nostrils full of paint fumes, Violet admired the men's handiwork.

The day before, Eighth Fighter Command had ordered each fighter group to paint distinctive colors and patterns on the noses of their planes. The 357th had been assigned a red-and-yellow checkerboard design, and Violet had asked the men to paint a band of the same pattern over the snack bar and around the arched walls at each end of the dining area.

It looked swell.

"Say, Miss Lindstrom." Herb Steinberg waved her over to his table. "My wife sent a picture of our little boy. Want to see?"

"Oh yes." She passed tables where men read, chatted, and sipped coffee and cocoa. Herb sat with José Flores and Clarence Gold, and Violet rested her hand on the back of Herb's chair.

"Two years old. Can't believe it. Look how big he is."

Violet smiled at the image of a laughing, dark-haired cherub.

"Strong too, isn't he? And he has his father's good looks."

"You want to see good-looking?" Clarence slipped over a snapshot of a pretty young lady leaning against the side of a sedan.

"Beautiful," Violet said. "Both the lady and the car."

The men chuckled. Even José, which was good to see. A week ago, Violet had listened to his anguish over a Dear John letter from his sweetheart. Sometimes a man felt better talking about such things to a sisterly type than to a buddy.

She smiled. "Don't forget the party at Thorpeness tomorrow. We'll have boating on the lake and all sorts of games for the children."

The men groaned as one. Clarence tucked his girl's photo into his wallet. "Only if we don't have a mission."

"Nonsense," Violet said. "You're all ground crewmen, right? It's only three miles away, and we'll have trucks running back and forth all day. You have a break while the flyboys are away, don't you?"

"Yeah." Herb tapped his son's photo on the table. "Might be nice to play with kids, you know."

"I know." Violet strolled down the hallway, peeking into the rooms. So much wholesome fun at the Aeroclub, so much satisfying work. Ironically, her work with the children had softened her heart toward the men. Only a few were brutes, many were true gentlemen, and many were just as Adler said—rough on the outside but noble inside.

Violet paused outside the library, where several men read in peace and quiet. Only a month ago, Adler had helped her shelve those books, his knuckles bloodied, his stories spilling out, bending Violet's heart toward him.

The other day she might have joked about Great-Aunt Violet's warning, but the woman was dead serious. Not only was she afraid a dashing pilot would lead Violet astray, but she feared Violet would become too content in her work.

Her great-aunt urged her to cultivate a "holy restlessness," making the best of her current situation while longing for God's true calling. Avoid the extremes of bitter grumbling and of lazy complacency, she'd said.

Violet huffed and passed the game room, where four men whooped over their Ping-Pong game and half a dozen milled around the pool table. She didn't feel lazy.

For the first time she could remember, she disagreed with her mentor.

Serving as a missionary wasn't the only way to serve God. Wasn't Violet doing the Lord's work in the Aeroclub? If so, why should she cultivate restlessness?

She headed back for the kitchen.

Tom Griffith stepped out and grinned at her. "Hiya, Miss Lindstrom. Millie and I just returned from Banister's Grocery, put the food in the icebox."

"Thanks." Violet pushed open the kitchen door.

Sylvia Haywood was hacking up a chicken, and Millie was humming and cracking eggs into a bowl.

"Hi, Millie. Griff said you unloaded the groceries. Did you log the delivery?"

"Log?" Millie's face drooped. "I forgot."

"Millie!" Sylvia frowned at her. "I told you twice."

Violet grimaced and picked up the log she'd started that week. "Please tell me you checked the delivery against the invoice."

"I think Griff did. Don't worry. Mr. Banister is a good sort. He'd never cheat you."

"That's not the point." Violet sighed. "With a thief on the loose, we have to keep careful inventory."

Millie gave her a smile too long-suffering for her tender years. "Honestly, Miss Lindstrom. That'll only tell you how much is being nicked, not who's doing the nicking."

"Regardless, please do so. Now, where's the invoice? I have to piece it together after the fact."

"I put it in your office." She smiled with too much pride in so small an accomplishment.

"Thank you." Violet left the kitchen and entered her office.

Rufus Tate stood behind the desk, examining the ledger.

"Oh! Good afternoon, Mr. Tate. I didn't see you arrive."

"Are the thefts continuing?" He flipped a page without looking up.

"Yes, sir. I'm afraid so. We're trying to keep track of how much we're losing, but we're still training the kitchen staff to fill out the logs."

"Your food budget is far higher than at the other Aeroclubs."

Violet clutched her hands together. "The thefts are foodstuffs— flour, sugar, tea, meat—"

"All rationed items." He sat in her chair and frowned at her. "Explain."

She wasn't accustomed to being interrogated, and she shifted her feet. "Since it's mostly staples, I don't think it's one of our men, unless he's selling on the black market. I'm afraid it's probably one of our workers or volunteers."

"I'm surprised to hear you say that." His voice chilled her. "Everyone knows you favor the locals over our own boys."

"Sir, that's not true." At least not anymore.

He crossed his arms over his large belly. "Someone accused you of being the thief."

"Me?" She grasped the edge of the desk.

"A noble Robin Hood, stealing from the rich spoiled Yanks

to give to the poor beleaguered English. It has a ring of truth about it."

"Sir, I couldn't." She fought for air. "Yes, I feel sorry for the English—shouldn't we?—but we *are* helping them, by giving them jobs and helping end the war. And—and all our money comes from donations back home. I could never steal from the Red Cross."

"A pretty speech." Mr. Tate slammed the ledger shut and stood. "I'm restricting your funds. You will receive the same amount as the other Aeroclubs. Stop the thefts, or you'll have to limit other activities. If this doesn't end soon, I'll have you dismissed."

Dismissed? She gripped the desk hard so she wouldn't collapse. If she were dismissed from the Red Cross, no mission board would accept her. Neither would a school board.

Mr. Tate stomped out of the office.

Violet sank into a chair and hugged her stomach. What she wouldn't give to be home right now, with Mom doing the hugging.

If her heart had been in the right place at the start, no one would have accused her.

23

THORPENESS, SUFFOLK, ENGLAND
SATURDAY, MARCH 25, 1944

A dozen boys swarmed Adler. "Let's play baseball!"

He gestured over the narrow lawn to the lake. "Not the best place, unless y'all want to feed baseballs to those swans out there."

The boys groaned.

"But it's a fine place to play catch. We can teach y'all to throw." He and some other airmen organized the kids in two parallel lines stretching away from the shoreline.

Jimmy Haywood pulled Adler's sleeve. "I want to pitch like y'all, Lieutenant Paxton."

He suppressed a smile at the boy's effort to sound like a Texan, and he squatted and held a baseball before the towhead. "First you've got to learn to throw. Accuracy first, then speed."

"Yes, sir!"

Adler plunked the ball into the boy's hand, then wandered away. The kids were too attached to him. Better to let the other men take over, men who served on the ground. One bullet could put an end to him, and he deliberately flew in the path of bullets more days than not.

He strolled along the lake. Airmen helped children into white

160

rowboats rimmed with bright colors. Even though the water in the manmade lake was less than three feet deep, the men followed Red Cross instructions and put an adult or older child in each boat.

Thorpeness had a storybook feel. Across the lake, a white windmill peeked above the trees and vacation homes, and the red "House in the Clouds" perched on top of a tall water tower. The islands in the lake had Peter Pan themes, and the kids could explore Wendy's House, the Pirate's Lair, and Smuggler's Cove, while watching out for crocodiles.

What a good thing Violet was doing. Events like this smoothed over British-American relations—which could be rough after the flyboys hit the pubs.

He sought Violet and found her. She stood by a table next to the big black clapboard boathouse with her back to the lake. Her shoulders sagged, and she wasn't watching the activities. Something was wrong.

His right knee bent, ready to take him to her, but he dug his feet into the grass. He ought to spend less time with her. Not only because he could end up like Stan Mulroney, but for countless other reasons.

"Adler! There you are." Kitty Kelly approached, one hand holding back her dark curls. "I was looking for you."

He couldn't imagine why. "Here I am."

Kitty frowned across the lawn at her friend. "I'm trying to console Violet, but—"

"Console her?" Every muscle tensed. "Why? What happened?"

"She told you about the thefts, right? Well, someone accused Violet of being the thief, and our field director seems to believe the rumor."

"Violet? A thief? That's ridiculous."

"Completely." Kitty's lips pursed. "They said she's a Robin Hood, stealing from the rich Yanks to give to the poor English.

She's afraid she'll lose her job. She won't listen to me. Maybe another voice she trusts . . ."

Violet trusted him, and he felt worthier than he had in three years. Mama's voice scolded him about his weakness for flattery, but this wasn't about his pride. Violet needed him.

He swallowed. "I'll talk to her."

"Thank you. She could use a shoulder to lean on."

That thought appealed to him too much. He propelled his feet in Violet's direction.

She gazed at the boathouse, immobile. Not normal for this woman who was always busy.

He stopped beside her. "Hi there."

Violet spun to him and raised a phony smile. "Oh, hi. Are you having a good time?"

"Kitty told me what happened."

She pressed her hand to her forehead. "She shouldn't have. Today is supposed to be fun."

"Reckon it's too late for that for you."

Quiet, she rubbed her forehead.

"Come on, let's go for a walk."

She waved her hand over the table. "I need to—"

"Everything's set up. The kids are playing and exploring. The men and the moms are watching them. Let's take a walk." He set his hand on her lower back.

Taut muscles softened under his touch. "All right."

Adler guided her along a path beside the lake, and he stuffed his hands in his trouser pockets. "Tell me all about it."

Violet spilled out a long list of missing food. She and Kitty had started keeping a log and checking it against the invoices, had designated shift supervisors to monitor the log, and had trained the staff. Locks were being installed on the cabinets, and only the supervisor would have the key.

Adler had never gotten past his general education in college, and in the family business Wyatt had been the brother gifted with bookkeeping. If only he knew more.

A pair of swans eyed him but waddled past when he didn't produce bread crumbs. "Sounds like you're doing everything you can."

"It isn't enough." Violet crossed her arms and kneaded her upper arms. "The log only tells us how much is disappearing, not who's taking it."

"It's a good start though."

Her face twisted. "If I don't find the thief soon, Mr. Tate will dismiss me. What if he files charges—"

"Hey. You haven't done anything wrong. He can't fire you based on rumor. For all we know, your accuser is the thief. In fact, that wouldn't surprise me."

She mashed her lips together. "I wouldn't be in this fix if my heart had been in the right place from the start."

He aimed an eyebrow at her. "You're not making sense."

Her face reddened. "I didn't want to come here, and Mr. Tate knows it."

"You wanted to work with kids."

"Yes. Then I thought the local people deserved help, and the airmen didn't."

"We don't."

Blue eyes stretched wide. "But you do. You risk your lives in combat every day. How many pilots have you lost?"

Over two dozen, but Adler just shrugged.

"And the men on the ground are far from their loved ones, working hard in difficult conditions. You deserve a few of the comforts of home. I know that now, but I didn't at first. I'm paying the price for my narrow-mindedness." Her face puckered up.

"Hey, now." He faced her and gripped her shoulders. Then he sucked in a breath. He'd acted as he would have with Oralee, free and easy. But she wasn't Oralee, and he needed to let go.

However, Violet's brow smoothed and her gaze steadied and plunged deep, seeking reassurance.

Adler squeezed her shoulders and made his gaze firm. "Anyone with half an eye can see your heart's in the right place. The Aeroclub looks great. The programs are a hit. The men are enjoying themselves, and so are the kids. You're friendly with all of them, and it's genuine. Everyone on base thinks the world of you, from the CO on down."

"Thank you," she whispered, and she dipped her chin, her forehead level with his mouth.

Begging for a kiss. But if he kissed her forehead, he'd pull her close and kiss her temple, her cheek. Her lips were tucked in, but he'd tease them open.

Violet raised her chin and her eyes, and she released her lips, pink and plump.

Lord, help me! He dropped his hands, stepped back, and whipped up a smile. "All better?"

A shaky laugh. "Not until the thief is caught, but thank you. I do feel better."

"Then this here cowboy's done his job." He thickened his accent and tipped his cap. "Reckon we oughta mosey on back to the fiesta, little filly?"

A smile wiggled on her lips, and she nodded and strolled back toward the boathouse.

"So, how are the plans for the Easter party?"

The smile gained strength. "Wonderful. Less than two weeks, but everything's coming together. The men donated so much candy, we had to tell them to stop or the children's teeth would rot."

As Violet related her plans, the light returned to her eyes. Too soon, they reached the main group.

"I should check the refreshments." She laid her hand on his forearm. "Thank you."

The leather of his jacket blocked the warmth of her grip, but not the soft pressure. "You're welcome."

One last smile, and she walked away.

"There you are." Nick ambled toward him. "I was looking for you."

"I haven't been this popular since college."

"Violet looked for you too?" He glanced behind him at the Red Cross worker.

"No, Kitty did. Violet's upset about the thefts at the Aeroclub, and Kitty wanted me to talk to her."

"She doesn't look upset anymore."

No, she didn't. Violet tousled a boy's hair and listened to his story.

"You two are getting close."

With his big toe, Adler poked at a rock in the grass. "Just as friends."

"Have you told her everything?"

"A lot."

"What about the girl? Your brother's—"

"No." Adler ground the rock back into the dirt.

"Why not?"

"Look at her. She's so innocent, so good. Besides, it doesn't concern her, and it's all forgiven, right?"

Nick studied the tall blonde, his mouth over to one side. "It would concern her if she became your girlfriend."

A laugh erupted. "That won't happen. We're going different directions in life."

"I think that's best. For one thing, you're still . . ." Nick returned his scrutiny to Adler. "You're raw."

Raw. Yeah, that was it.

After three years of numbness, emotions now hit his thawing nerves with increased intensity, every sensation magnified.

Grief and regret and anger at himself stung like iodine on a skinned knee.

But peace and happiness and affection refreshed like lemonade on ice.

He found Violet over the crowd, and she smiled at him, stimulating and soothing his nerves all at once.

24

LEISTON ARMY AIRFIELD
THURSDAY, APRIL 6, 1944

Millie Clark opened her large canvas bag and pulled out dozens of tiny tote bags in various colors and patterns. "My mum made these for the children to carry home their eggs and sweets."

"They're darling." Violet picked up a blue-striped bag.

"We used scraps. We didn't do anything wrong." Alarm creased Millie's young forehead.

"We know." Kitty admired a red bag. She brushed off some white powder and sniffed her fingers. "Smells like flour."

"This one smells like tea." Violet laughed. "How very British."

"I take this bag to the grocer's." Millie snatched up some bags and inspected them. "Oh dear."

Violet patted her back. "The children will be delighted."

Kitty cupped her hand over her ear. "Here they are."

The rumble of a truck engine sounded outside.

Violet opened the front door and beamed at the children climbing out of three Army trucks, the younger children accompanied by their mothers. "Welcome to our Easter party, boys and girls. Today we have special treats for you. When you come inside—littlest ones first—Miss Clark will give you a bag, and you can hunt for Easter eggs. One egg each."

The children squealed. With eggs rationed and scarce, they were a treat indeed.

Rosalind and Sylvia lined up the children, Kitty let them inside, and Violet supervised the egg hunt in the dining area. On a platform by the office, the Buzz Boys played "Pop! Goes the Weasel"—with a splat on the trombone for the "pop."

Soon about fifty children zipped around the club, laughing and calling to each other. As soon as eggs were found, Red Cross ladies showed the children to other stations.

Dozens of men helped with the activities and joked with the kids. In the lounge, kids sat on a canvas tarp and Rosalind helped them paint their eggs. In the game room, airmen and children played Ping-Pong, pool, and Duck, Duck, Goose. In the library, Millie and Sylvia helped the little girls make fabric and tissue paper flowers for their bonnets.

One brown-haired tot stuck a flower behind the ear of a mechanic, and he struck a pose like Carmen Miranda.

Violet smiled. If Mr. Tate could see the good she was doing, he'd drop his accusations. But Adler's assurances calmed her. Mr. Tate had no proof she was stealing, and now that they'd locked the cabinets and trained the girls to use the logs, the thefts had decreased.

Back in the dining area, Adler and a dozen men moved the tables and chairs that had made hiding places for the egg hunt.

Adler glanced over at her. "Around the edge of the room, Miss Lindstrom?"

"Yes, please. We'll leave the area by the bandstand open for our concert."

"I think you'll like it." His smile sparked with mischief.

Last night he'd found her at dinner and told her he had a surprise for her today. Did it have something to do with the concert?

She gave him a quizzical look, but he grabbed a couple of chairs and walked away.

That man. Still mysterious. And increasingly adorable.

After the children had enjoyed an hour of crafts and games, she and Kitty ushered them into the dining area and had them sit on the floor.

Tony Rosario stood on the bandstand with a trombone. "Good afternoon, boys and girls. We're the Buzz Boys, and we're going to play some tunes you know—please sing along—plus, some goodies from America."

They played "Mary Had a Little Lamb" and "Home on the Range." They played "Hot Cross Buns" and "I've Been Working on the Railroad." They played "Jack and Jill" and announced the next song, "Deep in the Heart of Texas."

Adler climbed onto the stage, trumpet in hand, and he shot Violet a shy smile.

Standing at the back of the crowd, she gasped. His surprise!

The piano and drums opened, and Adler joined in, his eyes closed and his trumpet raised high. He played the melody, and the brass section sounded the four "clapping" notes.

Oh, how he played. The sound was so rich, so pure, so fluid.

Violet covered her mouth, and her eyes watered. He was connecting with his past and allowing the Lord to heal him. The most beautiful thing she'd ever seen.

She was falling hard. Lately, she'd seen the attraction in his eyes as well. It had been so long since a man had looked at her like that. Dennis never had. They'd been partners, nothing more.

For years she'd felt washed-up and Amazonian. But not with Adler. Never with Adler.

His lips pursed on the trumpet. What would it be like to kiss him?

"Oh dear." She was rationalizing that fling Kitty kept promoting. Such a bad idea, and yet it wasn't. Maybe a little romance would be healthy for Adler, help him move forward.

Just last night, Kitty had told her not to pass up a fine man for a dream—a dream that might not even happen. She had a point. Convincing a mission board to send a single woman into the field might be impossible. And did she really want to go alone? For all Great-Aunt Violet's zeal, she had Great-Uncle Gus at her side.

The piano took over the song, and Adler lowered the trumpet and his head, his lips in a thin line.

Did the music take him home to Texas, to when his family was whole and his fiancée was alive? Her heart ached for him in his loneliness.

Then he raised his trumpet and belted out another verse, his fingers flying and improvising a Latin riff on the cowboy tune. His face—she'd never seen such pain and such pleasure mingled.

Her eyes misted over. If he were to want a romance with her, even a short-lived fling, how could she deny him?

The song ended, and he met her gaze over the applauding children. She pressed her hand over her heart to show him how much it meant to her.

A quick bow, and he stepped off the stage and jogged to the front door.

"Say, boys and girls . . ." Tony Rosario peered toward the door, shielding his eyes. "I heard a knock. Do we have a visitor?"

Violet and Kitty exchanged a confused look. Nick Westin was going to distribute the candy soon, but . . .

What were the men up to?

Adler swung the door open. "Look who's here!"

Then Nick hopped in. Hopped like a bunny.

The children squealed and bounced. Violet gasped and laughed, and Kitty dashed over and clutched her arm.

Nick wore one of the sheepskin-lined jackets the ground crew wore, only inside out, with the fluffy creamy side showing. He wore a leather flight helmet with floppy khaki ears, and someone had painted black whiskers and a bunny nose on his face.

As Nick hopped to the children, Adler stayed at his side, his wingman even now.

"Hello, boys and girls," Nick said in a funny voice. "If you can sit very still and be quiet as a bunny, I'll give you some candy."

The bouncing and squealing came to a sudden halt.

Nick handed out candy bars, two per child. One to enjoy at the party and one to take home.

Violet worked her way over to Adler. "I had no idea. This is absolutely wonderful."

"Didn't know if we could pull it off." He fingered one of the bunny ears. "Especially these. Finally sewed the tops of Cam's socks over flight goggles to hold them in place. We tried to use wire to make them stand up, but Cam groused that we were putting holes in his socks."

"Nick looks marvelous. And what a treat. Two surprises in one day.",

Adler shot her a sideways, lopsided grin. "That wasn't the surprise I was talking about."

"More?" She hugged his arm—she couldn't help it. "You're spoiling me."

Now his eyes shone as if she'd given *him* a candy bar. More than anything, she wanted to press a kiss to his cheek, but she released his arm and checked her watch. "When Nick is done, it's time to send the children home for dinner."

"See you later." He tipped two fingers to his forehead, then trailed after Nick.

What a delicious set of words. What could the surprise be? A gift? But she didn't need anything. Still, he'd thought of her, and that warmed her right through.

In a few minutes, Violet stepped onto the bandstand, thanked the children for coming, and wished them a happy Easter.

The staff and airmen helped the children back into the trucks. Then they cleaned up the Aeroclub so quickly, Violet and Kitty couldn't keep up with the activity.

After everything was put away, Violet headed to the kitchen to make sure preparations had started for the after-dinner crowd.

Adler met her by the snack bar. "When are you heading to the mess for supper?"

"About ten minutes."

"Great. I'll be in the back on the left. If you want your surprise, sit with me."

"What is it?" She sounded as eager as the children.

His eyes crinkled around the edges. "Not what. Who. Someone I want you to meet. See you soon."

And he left.

All the eagerness drained away. Someone he wanted her to meet?

Did he want to set her up with another man?

Violet pulled herself together and entered the kitchen. All was in order, and the supervisor had everything humming. She had no excuse to stay, so she pulled on her overcoat and walked to the mess in the dying sunlight.

Her stomach felt woozy. She'd been mistaken. The interest in Adler's eyes was the interest of a friend, and she'd let herself be swept away. Thank goodness she hadn't told him how she felt.

What sort of man had Adler picked for her? Most likely a missionary, stranded in the States by the declaration of war and drafted into the Army.

Her hand folded around Elsa the Elephant in her coat pocket. That prospect should appeal to her, but right now it didn't.

Sending up a prayer for strength and dignity, Violet entered the mess and picked up her plate of roast mutton and potatoes.

Adler sat in the back left corner, but the man facing him was small and scrawny. As if her heart could fall any lower.

Somehow she found a bright smile. "Hi, Adler."

He stood from the bench. "Violet, I'd like you to meet Floyd Miller. Floyd, this is Violet Lindstrom."

Not only was he small, but he was young, very young, with straw-colored hair and freckles on his skinny face. What was Adler thinking? "Nice to meet you, Lieutenant Miller."

"Pleasure's all mine, miss," he said in a Texas drawl even more musical than Adler's . . . and oddly familiar.

Adler motioned her around to his side of the table. "Floyd's a new pilot in my section."

"And boy, has Shapiro put me through my paces." Floyd dug into his roast potatoes.

Violet sat. Not only did his voice sound familiar, but something about his face . . .

Floyd wagged his finger at her. "You're trying to figure out where you've seen me."

Her cheeks warmed, but she nodded.

Adler nudged her with his elbow. "You know him by his screen name, Floyd Milligan."

Floyd . . . Milligan. It all made sense. Replace the crush cap with a Stetson. Replace the leather jacket with a plaid shirt and bandanna. "You—I've seen you in at least a dozen movies."

His grin was as familiar as an old friend. "I'm surprised you stayed awake through that many."

Laughter bubbled out. Floyd had always played the young sidekick, the kid the hero warned away from danger, and he was an impressive harmonica player. She clapped her hand to her chest. So many questions tumbled around, she didn't know where to start. "You know Gene Autry and Roy Rogers and Trigger."

"Honored to say I do. Not because Gene and Roy are famous, but because I've never known finer men."

Violet faced Adler and clutched his forearm, which rested on the table. Her mouth spread wide and open, but no words fell out.

He chuckled. "You're welcome."

She could only nod over and over.

Adler turned to Floyd and tilted his head her way. "Told you she likes Westerns."

Dinner flew by in a whirl of stories from the movie set. Tales of stunt failures, pranks, and mischievous horses. She hadn't had such a wonderful meal in ages or better company.

There she was, talking with a movie star, a man who knew her favorite actors. Best of all, Adler had thought of her in a personal way. And he wasn't setting her up with another man.

After dinner Floyd headed to the officers' club, and Adler walked Violet back to the Aeroclub.

She strolled along, smiling at the moonlit sky. "That was a treat. I've met someone who fed Trigger. I can't believe it."

"He's real down-to-earth too, doesn't want special treatment."

"And he gave me the best idea for our next children's party—a hoedown."

Adler laughed and bumped his shoulder against hers. "You just finished cleaning up the last party."

"I know. Time to get to work. Wouldn't it be fun? Maybe they'd let us hold it in the theater building, show one of Floyd's movies, have him play the harmonica if he's willing. We could have square dancing and serve baked beans and cornbread."

Adler humored her and listened as she rattled off ideas.

At the Aeroclub, she went down the pathway alongside the Nissen hut that led to the side entrance to her quarters. She needed to write these ideas down before her evening shift.

She squinted at the path in the dark.

"Here. Hold my arm," Adler said.

Although she did this every day, she didn't argue. "It was the best day. The party went well, and your surprises—three of them. My goodness."

He dipped his head. "I can't take credit for the bunny suit. Nick—you know they call him Santa—well, he said it was only fitting he should play the Easter Bunny."

"Either way, it was delightful. Then meeting Floyd—you know I enjoyed that."

"Reckoned you might."

She squeezed his arm. "But the trumpet—oh, Adler. You were so good, and I know how much it meant to you."

When they arrived at the side door, Adler leaned back against the wall. "It was—it was right."

She leaned back beside him, wiggling until the ridges of corrugated steel didn't poke her shoulder blades.

"Comfortable?" He gave her an amused smile.

He was so close in the moonlight, she could only nod.

Adler rested his head back and gazed through the tree branches to the moon, about three-quarters full above them. "You know, for three years I didn't think about my past because it hurt. But a whole lot of that hurt was from my sin, and I needed to feel it so I could ask God to forgive me."

Violet hadn't let go of his arm, so she gave it another squeeze, her heart full.

His jaw worked back and forth. "And some—a whole lot of that pain was from grief, and I needed to feel it so I could heal."

"I know," she said. "You've come so far."

His eyes squeezed shut. "When I buried my past, I buried the pain but I also buried the good stuff."

"Like the trumpet."

Adler rolled his head to face her, and his eyes opened. "You're the only one who knows what that meant."

"Oh." She could barely breathe in the warm glow of his eyes.

"Thank you." His voice came out throaty and deep. "Thank you for encouraging me to play again, to write home, to remember, to . . . to feel."

To think she'd helped in even a small way . . . oh, goodness.

Adler's gaze softened and drew her, and he raised his free hand and stroked her cheek. Shaky. Questioning.

She let that gaze draw her, that caress. She needed to be nearer, to touch him too.

Then his gaze shuttered. His fingers stiffened. And he jerked to standing.

All Violet knew was she couldn't allow him to flee.

She grabbed his hand and pressed it back to her cheek.

His gaze flitted, and his fingers twitched. He was wrestling again, wrestling with something deep inside.

Violet kept her gaze and her touch both firm and tender. *Don't leave. Not now. Don't leave.* The words dissolved in her mouth.

Something shifted in his eyes. Surrendered. He pulled her close, his hand in her hair and his lips on hers.

Never had she experienced such a kiss, wavering between hunger and hesitation. In the moments of hunger, she received, savoring and welcoming. In the moments of hesitation, she gave, affirming and adoring.

Far too soon, he broke away, his face crumpled up, his fingers coiled in her hair. "I—I'm sorry. I shouldn't have done that."

Out of breath from the kiss, she struggled for air. "Why not? Because of Oralee?"

He flinched. "No. Honestly, no. But we—you and I—we want different things in life."

She had no answer, but in that moment all she wanted in life was Adler Paxton.

He uncoiled his fingers from her hair. "I shouldn't have taken advantage of you. I'm no better than Riggs."

"Riggs? Oh, Adler, no. Not at all. I didn't want him to kiss me. But you? Didn't you notice? I was—I was willing."

He grimaced as if she'd slapped him. "I shouldn't have taken advantage of your willingness. Forgive me."

"There's nothing to forgive." But she was speaking to his back as he jogged to the main road. "Adler!"

He didn't stop, and she didn't follow.

Violet leaned back against the wall, and the ridges poked every bone in her back. What had just happened?

She pressed her fingers over her lips, still softened by his kiss. "Oh, Lord, what did I do?"

25

Adler let Beck help him out of the cockpit and onto the wing. After four hours in the air, his leg and back muscles didn't want to straighten. "Thanks, Beck. No mechanical problems."

"How'd it go?"

"Long, hard, good mission." Adler dropped off the wing and stretched his arms overhead, groaning from the pain and relief of it. "The B-24s demolished that aircraft factory at Brunswick. Heavy enemy attack though. A lot of bombers fell. But the Yoxford Boys got a good five victories, and no losses that I know of. Best of all, Nick made ace."

Nick strode over from his hardstand, his helmet unbuckled and a big old grin on his face.

Adler grinned back and gave him a hearty handshake. "Congratulations, ace."

Beck slid off the wing. "Every ace needs a good wingman."

"And I have the best." Nick's face sobered. "Thanks, buddy."

Adler pointed his thumb at Beck. "Every wingman needs a good crew chief, and I have the best."

Beck waved him off and strode to *Texas Eagle*'s red-and-yellow checkered nose to start his inspection.

"That was some fine shooting." Adler kicked out the kinks in his legs.

"And some fine flying." Nick laughed. "I don't know how you stayed with me in that Lufbery."

Nick had chased the Me 109 in a tight 360-degree "Lufbery Circle" for at least three minutes before the Messerschmitt loosened the turn too much. Nick got inside the curve and made a great deflection shot.

Adler headed toward squadron headquarters with Nick. His old self still wanted to be first, but his new self was thrilled for Nick. The other night with Violet showed him he needed to finish the job of killing that old self. And fast.

"Riggs made ace too," Nick said in a low voice. "Don't let him get to you."

Sure enough, Riggs ran over from his hardstand, his hand raised with five fingers splayed for his five victories.

"Congratulations, Riggs." Adler tried to mean it. After all, they were on the same team, fighting the same enemy.

Riggs fell in beside Adler. "Two confirmed victories, and two confirmed kills. The Fw 190 went up in a fireball. Kraut never had time to bail out. And the second one crash-landed, the Messerschmitt in pieces, the pilot running away. I made sure neither would fly again."

Adler's stomach clenched. "You strafed the pilot?" It wasn't forbidden, but it wasn't encouraged either.

"You bet."

Nick frowned at the pavement. "You shouldn't have done that."

"Why not?" Riggs pulled off his helmet and ran his fingers through his damp, dark hair. "If we get shot down, we're POWs at best, lynched by civilians at worst. The Germans? If they get shot down and survive, they're up in the air again the next day. It's only right."

"It's only wrong." Nick's voice was dark and hard.

Riggs snorted. "You're not my commander."

"That's not the point." Adler unfastened his parachute harness. "If we get known for strafing their pilots, they'll take their revenge—strafe us in our chutes, on the ground. You want that?"

Riggs's upper lip curled. "How many did you get today, Paxton? Stuck at one?"

"He helped me make ace," Nick said. "Just as Theo helped you."

And Riggs never gave poor Theo any credit.

Riggs raised one shoulder. "You know, Paxton, I've been thinking about your business idea. It has merit, and I'd hate to see you lose out because you're . . . losing out."

"Right kind of you," Adler said between gritted teeth.

"Maybe my old man and I could invest. I'd be the president, give the company the face it needs at the top. You could be the manager and run operations."

"No." He couldn't even add a thank-you. Second in his own company? To Willard Riggs?

"Think about it. You have the idea, but I have the money and the title of ace." He wiggled five obnoxious fingers.

In the locker room, the men turned in parachutes and life preservers. Adler sat on a bench, took off his flight boots, and put on his brown GI shoes.

Nick sat beside him. "Don't even think about taking Riggs up on that offer."

"No danger of that." Adler tied his shoes. All his life, he'd chafed at the idea of working under Wyatt. But his older brother was a good man, honest and fair and dependable.

Riggs, on the other hand, was arrogant, lecherous, murderous—Adler's old self magnified in darkest detail. At least Adler had the sense to know those traits were wrong, and he was trying to let God fix them.

"Can't wait for our forty-eight," Nick said.

"Me too." That afternoon, the men from his section were taking a forty-eight-hour pass to celebrate Easter in London.

Easter. Today was Saturday, the day Jesus lay in the grave. Adler had read the truth, how his old self was crucified with Christ and lying in that grave. That's where it deserved to be.

The men filed into the squadron pilots' room and picked up coffee and sandwiches before debriefing.

No sign of Violet, thank goodness. He hadn't seen her since that kiss.

An intelligence officer waved Nick over, and Adler sank into a leather armchair, waiting his turn.

His old self was certainly taking its sweet time dying. He couldn't believe he'd lost control with Violet, same as he had with Ellen, same as he had too many times with Oralee.

Oralee had always stopped him in time, but Ellen hadn't.

The donut tasted like cardboard in his dry mouth. With Violet, the danger wasn't only to her virtue, but to her future.

For heaven's sake, if God wanted her to be a missionary, how could Adler ask her to be anything else? And after tasting lasting love with Oralee, he didn't want anything less. He had no business starting something with Violet that he couldn't finish.

The coffee washed the donut crumbs from his mouth, leaving a bitter taste behind. He'd started it, all right.

That kiss.

Man alive. He'd shared hundreds of kisses with Oralee, but Violet's kiss reached down into his soul. Why was that?

Adler rolled his stiff shoulders. Maybe because Oralee never knew the real Adler. She knew a good old churchgoing Texas boy—cocky, yes—but good. She'd never seen him drinking and cussing and carrying on in Austin. She never knew all the church talk was phony.

But Violet knew some of his past. And she still liked him. Too much.

181

He rubbed his forehead, but he couldn't erase the memory of how that woman had kissed him. How she'd held him. How she'd refused to let him go.

Letting *her* go that night was one of the hardest things he'd ever done.

SUNDAY, APRIL 9, 1944

On Easter morning, Violet should have been rejoicing. She stepped out of the crowded theater building into a bright spring day, her head full of moving Scriptures, a rousing sermon, and her favorite hymns. But no joy.

Adler wasn't there.

She clutched her Bible to her chest and walked back to the Aeroclub. Airmen tossed Easter greetings her way, and she returned them.

Nick hadn't been at church either. The group was on a mission today—the war didn't take holidays—so maybe Adler and Nick were flying.

Her feet felt heavy on the concrete walkway. She still couldn't figure out what had happened with Adler. Why had he compared himself to Riggs? What had he meant about taking advantage of her willingness? That made no sense.

Before that he'd made too much sense, reminding her of their different paths.

She sighed. She should have let him leave when he'd wanted to. She'd pushed him into that kiss, and he hadn't been ready. In all honesty, she'd wanted that kiss for herself. She'd ignored her reservations and given in to desire.

Poor Adler had paid the price. Something had gone wrong, and it was her fault.

Violet opened the main door of the Aeroclub. They'd opened early to give the Jewish men or those who weren't religious a place to go. She'd split the girls' shifts so they could worship with their families.

Millie Clark backed out of the kitchen, her big canvas bag slung over her shoulder. She opened the gate in the snack bar and spotted Violet. "Oh, hallo, Miss Lindstrom. My—my shift is over."

"I know." She smiled at the girl's nervous expression. "No need to feel guilty."

With wide eyes, Millie edged from behind the snack bar and elbowed her bag behind her.

The girl looked as if she'd been caught with her hand in the till.

A horrible thought gripped her. The bag's strap cut into Millie's shoulder. But she used that bag to bring supplies *to* the club. Why was it full?

Millie sidled toward the entrance.

"Hi, Violet." Kitty strode down the hallway, pinning on her cap. "On my way to Mass."

Millie flinched and angled herself between the two American women.

Violet held up one hand to Kitty, urging her to wait.

"Hey there, Millie-girl. Don't tell me you're leaving me already." Jansen ambled over with his buddy, Schmidt, two of the crudest men on base, men she'd shooed away from her workers countless times.

Millie inched toward the door. "I—I need to help my mum with Easter dinner."

"Yes, gentlemen." Violet's voice came out tight. "Can't you see she's in an awful hurry?"

Kitty gave her a confused look.

"Yes. Yes, I am in a hurry." Millie's smile strained. "My mum needs me."

"Does she need what's in your bag too?" Violet said.

"My—my bag?"

"The bag you're hiding from me."

Kitty's mouth dropped open. "It was—you emptied it this morning—scraps and buttons from your mother's shop. Why is it full again?"

Millie's face reddened. "Full? It isn't full."

Jansen peeked behind her. "Looks full to me. Say, haven't you ladies had a lot of thefts around here?"

"How dare you?" Millie pulled the bag around to her front and hugged it. "These are my personal things."

Schmidt elbowed Jansen, his dark eyes hard. "I've seen dames with big purses, but that beats all. Show us, Millie."

"It—it's private." Her gaze darted toward the door.

Schmidt and Jansen stepped into her path.

Violet stretched out her hand. "May we see? You can understand why, can't you?"

Millie blinked too fast, then she opened her bag and gasped. "Flour? Sugar? Who put that in there?"

Jansen barked out a laugh. "Come off it. You mean to tell us you didn't realize your bag was twenty pounds heavier?"

A tear dribbled down Millie's cheek. "It—it's a gift for my mum. For Easter. You don't know what it's like, you Yanks with your sweets and your tea. You don't even like tea. It isn't fair."

Violet's heart settled low in her belly. "That's no excuse."

"Only once, I swear!"

Kitty pointed to the counter. "Empty your bag and leave. And don't return."

Violet pressed her hand to her belly. "So that's why you brought that bag every day."

Millie dumped out the contents, shook the bag upside down, and glared at Violet. "I thought you cared about us, but you don't. Keep this all to yourself. Be selfish. I don't care. I never want to see this place again."

The girl stormed out of the Aeroclub with her empty bag.

Violet sagged back against the counter. She'd caught the thief.

Now Mr. Tate would see her innocence and restore her budget. But she felt awful.

Kitty covered her mouth, and tears darkened her eyes. "I—I liked her. I trusted her."

Violet put her arm around her friend's shoulders. "I did too."

Then she turned her attention to men she'd neither liked nor trusted. "Thank you, gentlemen. I appreciate your help."

"Ah, it was nothing." Jansen flapped a meaty hand. "Glad you caught her."

Schmidt shook his head. "Stealing from the Red Cross? How low can you get?"

Violet offered a smile, weak but heartfelt. "Thank you."

But her mind reeled. The girl she'd longed to help had betrayed her, and the men she'd never wanted to help had defended her.

With her free hand, she gripped her spinning head. How could she be a missionary when she was blinded by prejudices?

26

"I can't believe we celebrated Easter in Westminster Abbey." Nick straightened his waist-length olive drab "Ike" jacket as the seven airmen crossed a busy London street.

Adler cranked his head in all directions, watching for traffic as he did for Messerschmitts. He hopped onto the curb just as a black taxi whizzed past, whipping a breeze against Adler's trousers. The men headed into yet another park. At least there weren't any cars or buses in parks.

"What did you think, Adler?" Nick eyed him as he had the last few days. He must have realized something was wrong, but he wasn't probing. Yet.

Adler wasn't ready to be probed. Yet. He worked up a smile. "Incredible." And it had been. The soaring ancient gray stone, the angelic choirboys, and history in every nook and cranny. If only the stained glass hadn't been carted away to safety. But German air raids had returned to London in the "Little Blitz" the past few months, so it was just as well.

"Where are we?" Luis Camacho peeked over Theo's shoulder at the map.

"Hyde Park," Theo said.

Adler, Nick, Theo, Floyd Miller—even Riggs—had attended the service at Westminster Abbey, while Cam and Rosario attended a Catholic Mass. After lunch, they'd seen the Thames, Parliament, the Horse Guards, St. James's Park, Buckingham Palace, Green Park, and the Wellington Arch. All within less than two miles.

Unbelievable.

Nick kicked a pebble on the tree-lined path. "Almost makes up for not being home."

Adler had been working so hard to keep up his spirits and not spoil his buddies' fun, he forgot his best buddy might be missing his family. He nudged Nick's shoulder. "Imagine their faces when the Easter Bunny visits."

Nick gave him a grateful smile. The men had taken a snapshot of Nick in his getup and were having it developed in the base photo lab. Soon, Nick would mail it home.

Wistfulness lowered Nick's smile. "Last Easter I was home on leave after little Gail was born. Now she's walking. I can't even picture it."

"Yeah." What would it be like? The men who were fathers missed watching their children grow and change and do things for the first time. It had to be hard on their wives too, raising kids alone and worrying about their husbands at war.

They passed a bandstand on the right and flower gardens on the left. Towering trees spanned the path, green branches against the gray sky.

"Where to next?" Floyd asked Theo. Floyd had taken Mulroney's slot in the squadron, and he fit right in. No grandstanding, and he'd informed Schumacher, the public relations officer, that he wasn't a circus sideshow but a pilot serving his country.

Theo studied the map as they walked. "There's a lake straight ahead, the Serpentine. The ladies at the Jules Club said we could rent boats."

Thank goodness Theo had been eager to get the map. Adler preferred not to interact with the workers at the American Red Cross service club. The workers in uniforms just like Violet's.

Too many couples strolled along, making moony faces at each other.

Adler looked away through the trees and across a wide lawn. Little kids chased a squirrel, an elderly couple fed pigeons, and men shouted over a cricket game. A family ambled along an approaching path—a middle-aged gentleman walking a black Scottie dog, and the man's son and daughter, both in naval uniform. Maybe they were husband and wife—no, boyfriend and girlfriend. The way the man was looking at that pretty redhead.

The young man . . . Adler glanced over his shoulder as the two paths converged.

If Adler didn't know better, he'd think the fellow was Wyatt.

He laughed at himself and peered at the lake up ahead. Ridiculous. Wyatt was no naval officer, and he certainly wasn't British.

Three young ladies sashayed past in Easter finery.

Adler's friends unleashed earsplitting whistles.

"Hiya, doll-face." Riggs swaggered toward them. "Which one of you gets the honor of taking a boat ride with me?"

"No, thank you." The brunette in the middle gave him a teasing look. "We'll find sailors. I've seen the way you blokes fly."

The men laughed and punched Riggs in the shoulder. Adler joined in and was glad to see Nick laughing too.

The girls went their way, the laughter died, and the lake appeared, covered with boats, ducks, and even swans.

"Wyatt? What's the matter?" An Englishwoman's voice floated into his ear from behind. "Wyatt?"

Adler stopped, his brain thick and slow. It couldn't be.

He turned around.

The redhead and the gentleman with the Scottie stood with their backs to him, and the naval officer strode away, his head down.

Adler's heart and lungs failed to work. He knew that walk, that build, that sandy hair.

The man's arms swung hard, flashing gold stars and two gold stripes on navy blue sleeves. An *American* naval officer.

Wyatt. Running away from Adler. Again.

His chest crushed under the weight of it. The last time Wyatt had seen him, Adler had been holding a rock over his head.

Of course he ran.

Wyatt grabbed onto a water fountain, his shoulders slumped.

Adler wheeled around. All the men were farther down the path, except Nick, who was staring at him.

Adler strode as hard as Wyatt had and motioned for Nick to join him.

"What's the matter?" Nick asked.

He caught up to the others and gripped his belly. "Say, fellas. I reckon I got a bad piece of fish. I'm heading back to the Jules Club. Nick's coming with me. See y'all later."

Cam frowned at him. "You look awful, *amigo*."

"You have no idea." Almost a dozen paths intersected at the hub, and Adler charged down one to the left, away from his friends and from Wyatt, a narrower path, more concealed, a bit curving, the foliage close to the edges.

Nick followed him. "Your stomach's fine."

No fooling that man. He waited until he was far enough away. "I saw my brother."

"Clay? Again?"

"No. My older brother, Wyatt. He—he's a naval officer. What on earth is he doing here?" He swatted a low-hanging branch.

"You're running from him?"

"He's running from me. I'm giving him the distance he wants."

"Turn around. Turn around right now."

Adler continued marching, the lake flashing to his right between trees and bushes. "He hates me. He—he's afraid of me. I tried to kill him, for heaven's sake. He doesn't want to see me, and I won't make him."

Somehow Nick's short legs matched Adler's pace. "I thought Wyatt was working for your folks."

"He is. He was. That's what he's supposed to be doing. The trucking business is vital to the war effort. He should have been deferred. Daddy needs him." That meant not one of the Paxton boys was in Kerrville.

"You haven't heard back from your folks?"

"It's only been three, four weeks." The street came into view, but Adler wasn't ready. He aimed for a bench. "What if I did this? What if my actions drove Wyatt and Clay to enlist?"

"A lot of men have—"

"You know why so many Americans are over here." Adler collapsed onto the bench, his elbows on his knees. "D-day. It's coming. Clay's a soldier. Wyatt—he's in the Navy. They're going into danger. If I put them there, my parents will never forgive me."

Nick stood in front of him. "Your brothers are grown men. They can make up their own minds."

He ripped off his cap and dug his hands into his hair, breathing hard. "Even if my parents forgive me, how can they trust me? They saw me with Ellen. They saw everything."

"You're a new man. The old man is gone."

"Is he?" Adler looked up at his friend, his hands clamped around the back of his neck. "That old man was out in full force the other night. I kissed Violet. I kissed her."

Nick's mouth scooted around, dangerously close to a smirk, and he toed a clump of grass in front of the bench. "New men kiss women. How do you think I got a baby girl?"

Adler bit off an old-man cuss. "It's not the same."

Nick ran his hand along his jaw. "I don't think I ever told you this. I kissed Peggy on our first date. She slapped me."

"She gave you a second date?"

"What can I say? She liked the kiss. She just couldn't let me get away with it so early."

So Saint Nick had a weakness. "Well, I'll be."

"Did Violet slap you?"

"I wish she had."

"Why? What did she do to you?"

"She kissed me back." He groaned.

"Most men wouldn't complain."

Adler flopped back on the bench and stretched out his legs. "Don't you see? Remember all those reasons I shouldn't get involved with her? None of those have gone away."

"Sounds like you're already involved."

"I shouldn't be. Look at me. I slept with my brother's girlfriend. I can't be trusted around women."

Nick sat on the bench. "Did you ever cheat on Oralee?"

"No, never."

"Did you—did you sleep with her?"

"No, but not for lack of trying. I pushed, but she always pushed back harder." He closed his eyes and shook his head.

"I don't know Violet well, but she seems like the kind of woman who'd push back. Trust her. More importantly, trust your new self not to push her in the first place."

Could he? He filled his cheeks with air. That drive was strong. But so was the drive to be ace, and he'd learned to control that.

Adler blew out that air. "That doesn't change the fact that she wants to be a missionary, and I want to be a businessman."

"Have you talked to her about that?"

"No. I . . . ran." Adler leaned forward and plopped his face into his hands. That was what he did whenever something went wrong.

Even today. What if he'd run to Wyatt instead of away? It could have been bad. Hot words. Cold rejection. Fists flying. By running, he'd avoided that.

But by running, he'd also missed his chance to apologize, to seek forgiveness, maybe even to reconcile.

Adler twisted his head to face his friend. "It's time I stopped running."

27

Sylvia Haywood poured oil into the donut-making machine. "Thank you for letting us keep the cabinets unlocked now. It's much more convenient."

"Only when you, as a supervisor, are in the kitchen." Violet scanned the log. Everything looked fine.

"I still can't believe Millie—" Sylvia wiped her hands on a rag. "I've known her since she was in nappies."

"I can't believe it either." At least Mr. Tate had, and he'd praised Violet and Kitty. But that praise didn't ease the pain of Millie's betrayal.

"Poor Griff. The lad's heartbroken."

"I know." Violet had feared she'd lose her close connection to the base motor pool. Many Aeroclub directors struggled to obtain jeeps and trucks. "It was sweet of him to offer to still help us. He said he refused to punish us for Millie's crimes."

"Good. I'd hate to lug donuts around by pushcart again."

"Me too." Violet headed out into the dining area. This evening the Aeroclub was buzzing. The Yoxford Boys had earned a whopping twenty-three victories over Germany that day.

Less than a week since she and Adler had parted ways, and the sense of disconnection tugged at her.

All looked well in the dining area, so she headed down the hallway to check on the recreation rooms.

A man stepped out of the library and almost bumped into her.

"There you are." Adler. He raised a casual smile as if nothing had happened between them. "Do you have time to talk?"

She gaped at him, suddenly tired of the pushing and pulling. "I'm working."

He sobered. "Half an hour. Fifteen minutes."

"I only need a few seconds to say what's on my mind." She kept her voice cool and polite, surprised at the conviction solidifying in her heart. "Every time we get close, you push me away. I—I'm done."

His cheek twitched, his eyes sad then apologetic then hardening with conviction equal to hers. "I won't do that ever again. Fifteen minutes. Please?"

She slammed her eyes shut so she wouldn't be swayed.

"Only a few fellows in the library. We could talk there."

One fellow would be too many. A walk would be private, but too romantic. "The office."

She marched around the corner, into the office, and sat behind the desk.

Adler shut the door and sat across from her. Unromantic, down to the desk between them.

Violet remained silent and expressionless. He was the one who wanted to talk.

Only he didn't. He leaned his elbows on his knees and stared at the cap in his grip. His blond hair was neatly slicked, and his jaw was tinged pink as if he'd just shaved—in the evening? He wore his dress uniform rather than his flight jacket, the tailored waist-length wool jacket accentuating the breadth of his shoulders and trimness of his torso.

Had he dressed up for her?

His jaw worked, and his distress weakened her resolve.

Violet shifted to make her chair creak and remind him his fifteen minutes was ticking.

Adler's chest puffed out, and he looked her full in the eye. "I came here to ask you to be my girlfriend."

Her breath caught.

He held up one hand. "Before you answer, we need to talk about two big things. Before that, you need to know I'm done running. I won't run from pain, and I won't run from joy."

Was that why he'd run from her? A fear of joy? Her heart stretched to him, so she dragged her gaze to Elsa on her desk, the little elephant's wood and essence springing from African soil. "It could never work. You're a businessman. I want to be a missionary."

"That's one of the two big things to discuss. You see, I'm not like most of the men here. They like to date around. But Oralee and I were together seven years. I'm not interested in a little . . ." He waved one hand around.

"Fling?" A pinprick of guilt.

"Yeah. That's fine for fellows who don't know what they're looking for. But I do."

He was looking for . . . her? Violet wrapped her arms around her stomach to hold herself together, to bind up that crumbling conviction.

Adler pointed one finger back and forth between them. "If this is going to work, God has to change one of our minds. I'm willing. Are you?"

Violet's mind spun in new and wonderful directions. "You're willing to be a missionary?"

He mashed his lips together and jerked his head to the side. "I don't want to, but I asked God to make me willing if that's what he wants."

He would do that for her? For the Lord?

Adler tossed his cap onto the desk. "Nick and I had leave in London this weekend. I told him I was too big a sinner to be a missionary. He said the Apostle Paul called himself the chief of sinners, and he was the greatest missionary in history. If God could work with Paul, he can work with me."

Violet's jaw quivered at the sacrifice he was willing to make, and she covered her mouth. "Oh, Adler."

He raised that finger again. "This would have to go both ways. You'd have to be willing to let God change your mind too. It's only fair."

Could she ask God such a thing? To make her willing to abandon the mission field? But if the Lord asked, she couldn't argue with him. She lowered her hand. "All right."

His eyebrows lifted, and his mouth parted. Then he leaned both arms on the desk and leveled a strong gaze at her. "We'd both have to promise to ask God to change one of our minds. We'd both have to promise to be willing to be the one with the changed mind. And we'd both have to promise not to try to change the other's mind."

Her vision blurred, and she groped across the desk for his hand. "I promise, I promise, I promise."

Adler gathered her hand in his, bowed his head, and groaned. "Not yet. One more big thing. The biggest. Should have done this one first." A quick kiss to her hand, then he dropped it and leaned back, his expression stark.

"What—what's the matter?"

"I promised God, promised Nick, promised myself I'd be completely honest with you. Before you make a decision, you need to know what I've done. My sins." His voice cracked.

Her hand felt cold and empty, tingling from his kiss. "You already told me. You—you tried to kill your brother."

Adler dropped his head into his hands. "There's more. There's so much more."

His distress shredded her insides. "You don't have to say anything more."

"I do." His fingers mussed up his neat combing. "You know

what I did to Wyatt, but you don't know what I did to Clay. He—
he stopped me from killing Wyatt, tackled me, pinned me down.
He saved Wyatt's life—and mine too. I would have gone to the
electric chair. I was so angry at him for spoiling my revenge. So
angry." His voice shuddered, his shoulders.

Violet had to be closer to him, had to stop him from doing this
to himself. She got up, perched on the edge of the desk beside him,
and laid her hand on his shoulder.

He shook her off. "You don't know. You don't know."

Yet she did. He had a temper. He'd taken it out on Riggs, on
Wyatt, and on Clay. Now he was taking it out on himself, and he
needed to stop.

"I have to tell you." A moan hunched his shoulders. "You need
to know."

Something writhed inside her. If it made her think less of him,
she didn't want to know. And if it increased his anguish, she
couldn't allow it.

Violet leaned forward, wrapped her arms around his neck, and
buried her face in that mussed-up hair. "I know everything I need
to know about you."

"No. No." He squirmed in her embrace.

"I do. I know all that is in your past. It isn't who you are today.
You asked God to forgive you, and he did."

Adler groaned. "Yes, but—"

"Then it's forgiven." She kissed his hair, breathing deep the
clean scent of shampoo. "If God has forgiven your sins, don't
dredge them back up."

"But you need to know."

"What more do I need to know about you?" She stroked his
soft hair, his warm, tense neck. "I know you're a fine man, brave
and strong and chivalrous and kind."

His neck muscles relaxed under her caress, but then he shook
his head. "But this . . . Violet—"

"But this is tearing you up. Please stop." She nuzzled another kiss in his hair. "Oh, Adler. Nothing you could say could change how I feel about you. Nothing."

He quieted, and she kissed his bowed head, stroked the nape of his neck, and prayed over him. Prayed he'd accept God's forgiveness. Prayed for the Lord's peace to flood his soul.

After several minutes his shoulders lifted and fell, and he straightened up, forcing her to sit up too. "So, will you be my girlfriend?"

She'd never met a man who could change moods faster than Adler Paxton. She smoothed his hair and smiled. "I think I already am."

A smile broke out, slow and breathtaking as the dawn. He set his hands on her waist and guided her down to his lap.

Violet hadn't sat on a man's lap since she'd outgrown her father's knees. "I'll squish you."

"Nonsense. This is nice."

It was, and her cheeks warmed. His legs made a sturdy seat, his arms settled around her waist in the sweetest way, and his handsome face was so near she couldn't think straight.

She rearranged her arm so it draped along his shoulder and her hand rested on his epaulette with its two silver bars.

Two? "Adler? I thought you were a lieutenant."

A chuckle puffed warm and minty on her cheek. "I was until about an hour ago. Nick gave me his captain's bars when he was promoted to major."

"Oh my goodness." She grinned at him. "What good news."

Adler's smile fell. "It's not all good news. We flew a long mission today."

"I heard. Twenty-three victories."

"And three losses. One was Morty Shapiro, my squadron commander."

"Oh no."

"I saw his chute. He should be all right. A POW, but he'll survive."

"Oh dear."

Adler squeezed her waist and gave her a reassuring smile. "Colonel Graham made Nick the new squadron commander. He's the right man."

"I agree. Good for him." She fingered the shiny silver bars. "And you?"

"Nick should have made Riggs the flight leader. He's an ace. But it turns out Shapiro—well, I'd won him over. He liked how I'd changed, how I stuck with Nick no matter what. He and Nick had been talking about promoting me." Adler wore the same modest smile he wore when he hit home runs.

"I'm so proud of you." She stroked his smooth, square jaw. He'd changed indeed, and his humility and determination moved her. "You'll do a great job."

He lifted a slight shrug. "Riggs is furious. He doesn't like Nick much, and now Nick's his commander. And I'm in charge of his flight. A double insult."

"Nonsense. You earned it, and you're the better man for the job."

One eye narrowed in a thoughtful way. "Reckon that's what Jesus meant when he said the last would be first."

Violet chuckled. "Not quite, but your hard work and strong character did pay off. You'll be an excellent leader."

"I hope so."

"I know so." She pressed a kiss to his forehead.

"Very nice," he murmured. "But this would be nicer."

He tilted up his face and captured her lips with his.

She never wanted to be released. He didn't hesitate or hunger this time, but every motion spoke of assurance. Savoring, lingering, appreciating. Nice didn't even begin to describe it.

The door creaked. A feminine gasp.

Violet sprang up straight.

Kitty stood in the doorway, gaping. Then she laughed and clapped her hands. "Hooray!" She spun away and shut the door behind her.

"Oh dear." Violet tried to stand.

Adler didn't let her, and he grinned. "She wants us together?"

Her cheeks flamed. "She . . . she wanted us to have a fling."

"A fling?" His laugh tumbled out of his mouth and into her heart. "Reckon she'll be disappointed."

"Disappointed?"

Adler set his hand behind her head and spread kisses over her cheeks, her forehead, her nose. "Darlin', this is so much more than a fling."

28

It felt good to be in front.

Adler peered in *Texas Eagle*'s rearview mirror. Floyd Miller was behind him to the right, his wingman. Willard Riggs and Theo Christopher were echeloned behind him to the left.

Farther behind, the string of B-24 Liberators faded away. The bombers had dropped a big old load on the Luftwaffe airfield at Lechfeld in southern Germany. Another group of fighters would escort them on the next relay leg while the 357th Fighter Group headed home.

Uh-oh. Where was Nick?

Adler laughed at himself. Nick was in the squadron's lead flight, where he belonged. For almost two months Adler had focused on Nick, but now he needed to focus on the enemy and trust Floyd to watch his back, while never losing his swivel-headed ways.

The P-51s reduced altitude to decrease oxygen consumption, passing puffs of cumulus clouds. Those not-so-innocent puffs could conceal Nazi fighters.

Nick said Adler would be a better leader because he'd been a wingman. He'd show proper concern for the rest of the flight.

That's why they'd passed over Riggs for the promotion. The man only thought of himself.

If Adler hadn't changed, he would have been passed over too. Nick had told Adler to lead like Jesus, putting others first.

Violet's cute little smile from when he'd misinterpreted "the last shall be first" popped into his mind. He thought he'd been put in first because he'd put himself second. That wasn't how it worked after all. He needed to keep putting himself second even when he was in first. He'd scoff if he hadn't seen how well it worked for Nick.

A patch of brown smudged the edge of a cloud beneath him, and he squinted at it. "Yellow leader here. Two bogeys at two o'clock below. I'll take the one on the right. Yellow three, take the one—"

An olive drab streak to his left—Riggs throttled up beside him and tipped into a dive, crossing below Adler.

"Watch out!" Adler yanked back on his stick to avoid a collision. "Yellow two, pull up!" he called to Floyd.

Riggs dove toward the enemy fighter on the right, Adler's target.

Adler chomped off a cuss word and aimed for the fighter on the left, but he'd lost too much speed evading Riggs. His quarry sped away.

Below him, Riggs chased a Focke-Wulf 190 with Theo lagging in the distance.

Heart thumping, Adler searched for Floyd behind him. "Yellow two, you all right?"

"Yes, sir. What on earth?"

That was what Adler wanted to know. "Yellow three, what kind of stupid stunt was that?"

"Busy now. Shooting down the enemy."

"We'll talk at base." Adler kept his voice sharp but calm, although he wanted to call Riggs every name in the book.

Adler resumed his northwesterly course, just the two of them now. His chest burned, and his fingers pulsed on the throttle and stick. Riggs wasn't just trying to get a victory for himself—that would have been fine. But he'd also meant to deprive Adler of a victory. Not fine.

Their flight could have knocked down two Fw 190s instead of one—if Riggs even succeeded. And he could have collided with Adler or Floyd, maybe tangling Theo in the mess.

He'd reprimand Riggs this evening and write him up. This wasn't a baseball game. Lives were at stake, and they had to work together.

The Allies needed air superiority to succeed on D-day. The month of May was on the horizon, and the Luftwaffe remained strong.

Now Adler had personal reasons to knock out the Luftwaffe. On D-day, Wyatt would probably be at sea and Clay on the landing beaches, both vulnerable to air attacks. Three years ago Adler had wanted to hurt his brothers, but now he wanted to protect them. They might never know what Adler was doing for them, but Adler would. God would.

He checked his instruments—altitude fifteen thousand feet, time 1602. A city appeared to the northeast bordered by a wide north–south river. Mannheim, if he'd done his math right.

At times, Adler entertained fantasies of returning to Kerrville, the whole family gathered, the Gringo Mariachis playing in harmony.

Not anymore. He'd been determined to tell Violet about Ellen, but she'd insisted on his silence. Oh boy, had she insisted. He could still feel her embrace about his head and neck, warm and soft.

The woman made good points. Sins forgiven. In his past. His old self dead and buried.

Later he'd realized he wouldn't be able to take Violet home. If she and Ellen met . . .

Adler shuddered and scanned the sky, especially toward the sun in the west.

Even if he did tell Violet, he wouldn't want the ladies to meet.

Maybe Africa wasn't a bad idea. But that was about the lousiest reason to become a missionary ever.

"Yellow three here. Scratch one Focke-Wulf," Riggs boasted on the radio.

"Yellow leader?" Theo said, his voice hard. "I can't confirm. No crash, no chute, just some smoke."

"I got it!"

Adler pushed the microphone button. "Yellow three, that's up to intelligence to decide. Then we'll talk."

"Good." Theo sounded as miffed as Adler.

He checked the engine and fuel gauges, and all looked good. Floyd's plane was the only one in sight . . . or was it?

Ahead and to the west . . . a fighter, the long silhouette of a Focke-Wulf, flying straight and level, probably returning home after attacking B-17s or B-24s, tired and low on fuel. "Yellow two, bogey at eleven o'clock, heading under that cumulus. Follow me. We'll split-S over the cloud and come in on his tail."

Adler edged *Texas Eagle* over the popcorn cloud lit up with silver and gold in the afternoon sun.

On the other side, Adler rolled *Eagle* onto her back and looped down behind the cloud, blood filling his head, then whooshing back out again.

He strained to keep the edge of the cloud in sight while checking for the enemy.

There! One o'clock, not five hundred yards ahead and only a few hundred feet below.

Leveling off from the loop, Adler gunned the throttle and swung in to attack from the tail. He'd learned from the top aces. Even though he had a knack for deflection shooting, coming in at an angle lessened the time of attack. Too much of a gamble.

A quick check behind him. He'd lost Floyd in the split-S. Swell. He'd have to watch his own tail until the kid caught up.

He closed the distance. The Fw 190 still hadn't seen him. At

150 yards, Adler lined up the German's tail in his gunsight and squeezed the trigger.

Hits sparkled along the tail fin, the elevator.

The Nazi swerved right, and Adler matched his moves, lined up again, fired another burst. Missed.

The Focke-Wulf spiraled downward, and Adler followed. Nothing could beat a Mustang in a dive, but the Germans didn't seem to have figured that out yet.

G-forces shoved Adler to the left, shoved his stomach into his throat. In the spiral a deflection shot was his only choice, so he figured out the angle, the amount of lead he needed, and fired. Only two sets of sparkles lit up the German's fuselage.

"Man alive!" His guns were jamming.

A wisp of smoke spun off the nose of the Fw 190. Adler must have hit the engine. He fired again, saw a paltry set of hits, and felt the telling yaw of the P-51.

Three of the four guns jammed. He didn't dare risk a full-blown dogfight with a single gun. But the thickening curlicue of black smoke told him the Fw 190 was sufficiently damaged not to attack anyone else today.

Adler pulled the stick toward his stomach and eased the rudder pedals to level off the turn. His vision flickered. He was graying out, and he steeled his abdominal muscles to prevent blacking out.

Texas Eagle swooped up, gaining altitude and distance from the enemy fighter. After his vision cleared, Adler swept the sky and his instruments. All clear.

Too many pilots were having problems with their guns. The P-51's thin wing made the Mustang fast, but it forced the ammunition belt to be fed to the guns at a sharp angle. The g-forces of a tight turn could kink the belts and jam the guns.

Adler checked his compass and determined his course.

"Yellow leader? I can't find you. I don't know where I am." Anxiety tinged Floyd's voice.

SARAH SUNDIN

"You're fine. Lay in a course at 310 degrees. That'll put you over the Zuider Zee in just over an hour. Can't miss it."

"Roger. I'll recognize that."

"Great. Then change your course to 270. When you cross the English coast, call Earlduke for a heading."

"Roger." The warbles vanished from his voice.

"And, kid? Next time Roy Rogers tells you to follow him, do so."

Floyd laughed. "In the movies Roy was always telling me *not* to follow him."

"Close enough. See you at home." At nine thousand feet, Adler leveled off. He unsnapped his oxygen mask on one side, flipped it away, and wiggled his face muscles.

He couldn't expect to start racking up victories on his first mission as flight leader, but he'd kind of hoped he would. Nevertheless, he'd damaged that Focke-Wulf.

At least he had a fighting chance of making ace now and securing that company title.

Then he drew in a long breath, flavored with oil and solvents and sweat. "Lord, I promised Violet I'd ask you to make me willing to be a missionary. You know I want to start my company, and you sure as shooting know I don't want to be a missionary. So if you want to change my mind, you'd better get started. Because that's a long way you have to bend me."

He tipped his head to one side, waiting for the heavenly nudge. It didn't come.

But it probably didn't work that way.

Part of him wanted to fire off another prayer for God to bend Violet's heart if he had a hankering to do so. But that felt selfish. He'd leave that between God and Violet.

A peaceful breath filled his lungs. If God wanted them together, he'd put them on the same heading.

205

29

Jimmy Haywood huffed and pushed his paper away on the table in the Aeroclub lounge. "It's too hard, Miss Lindstrom. I'm not good at maths."

Violet smiled at the English wording and slid the paper back in front of the ten-year-old. "Nonsense. If you can add, subtract, and multiply—and I know you can—you can do long division."

His blond head sagged back. "There are too many steps."

Sylvia Haywood was exasperated at her son's low marks in math and had asked Violet to help. How could she reach the boy?

The lounge bubbled with happy conversation as airmen and children painted rocks—the paint sent from Kansas and the rocks to avoid using scarce paper. With the P-51s away on a mission, the ground crewmen could help with Saturday afternoon crafts while they "sweated out" the mission.

It helped Violet sweat out Adler's absence too. When he returned, they'd take their usual walk before dinner—the appetizer, Adler called it.

She turned her attention from his very appetizing kisses to the fidgeting ten-year-old. His short pants exposed knees scuffed from many baseball games.

Too many steps? "Jimmy, you're getting very good at baseball."

His face brightened. "I fancy it even better than cricket."

Probably because the flyboys didn't frequent the cricket fields—or whatever they were called. "How did you get so good at batting? Tell me what you do."

"It's easy." He gripped his pencil like a bat. "You set up your stance—your feet, your knees, your shoulders, your bat. Then you keep your eyes on the ball, wait for the right moment, swing, and follow through." Jimmy demonstrated.

Violet stifled a smile at how his actions and words mimicked the Yanks. With a serious face, she shook her head. "That's an awful lot of steps."

Hazel eyes narrowed—he knew he'd been tricked.

Violet laughed. "Long division only has four steps, and they flow in a circle. If you can learn to bat, you can learn to divide."

She talked him through the steps again, showing him the flow. Then she wrote out four problems, each with one digit going in to five.

He moaned. "That's too long."

"No, it isn't. The same four steps, over and over, round and round. You can do it. Hit those numbers right out of the park."

That made him grin.

She patted the paper. "You work on those while I start cleaning up."

It was two o'clock. Time for Griff to drive the children home and for the ground crewmen to go to their hardstands and wait for the returning planes.

Violet assigned the older children to wash the paintbrushes in the kitchen, while the airmen helped the younger children screw lids on paint jars and the ladies wiped little fingers with a damp rag.

Herb Steinberg set the colorful rocks in a cardboard box to

send back to the village. "Say, Miss Lindstrom, you're good with kids. You ought to be a teacher."

She laughed and helped little Margie Haywood out of a smock made from one of Violet's dad's old shirts. "I am. Well, I was."

Those two years teaching third grade had been delightful. She'd loved the children and had enjoyed helping them understand new concepts.

Great-Aunt Violet had warned her not to enjoy it too much.

Her neck muscles twitched. Why had she allowed discontentment to tarnish her joy?

Violet peeked at Jimmy's work. He'd finished three of the problems, and they were correct. She squeezed his shoulders. "You did it, Jimmy. Very good. I knew you could."

He smiled up at her with even more pride than when he hit a line drive.

Tom Griffith entered the room with a tall, skinny private. "Hiya, kids! Who wants a ride in my truck?"

The children bounded to their feet, grinning and shedding smocks.

Violet scanned the room. "Excellent job cleaning up. Put your smocks in the box and then you may go home. Thank you for coming."

Griff flicked his chin in Herb's direction. "Say, Herb, could you take them out to the truck? I'll be right there."

"Sure." He carried the box of rocks over his head. "Come on, kids. Follow the leader."

"Miss Lindstrom?" Griff motioned the tall private closer. "This is Paul Harrison. He's new in the motor pool."

"Hi, Private Harrison. It's nice to meet you." She shook his hand. The young man had soft brown eyes in his long face.

"Paul was raised in China. His parents are missionaries. Miss Lindstrom here wants to be a missionary too."

Violet grinned, questions welling up inside her. This had to be a sign that the Lord would sway Adler toward missions. The timing couldn't be coincidental. "I'd love to hear your stories."

"I have the afternoon off." Paul nodded toward the emptying room. "Tell me what to do, and I'll tell stories."

"I'd love that. Why don't you fold the tarp while I clean up paint splatters?" She picked up a damp rag and bent over to look for paint that had defied the tarp. "First, tell me how you ended up in England."

Paul picked up one end of the tarp and walked it over. "When the Japanese invaded China, our mission board ordered us back to the States. My parents didn't want to go, but my youngest sister was only a baby and they were concerned for her."

"I can understand that." Violet dabbed at a yellow smear on the cement floor. Thank goodness for poster paint. The powdered paint traveled well from Kansas, mixed up with water—and wiped up with water too.

"I was drafted right after my eighteenth birthday, and here I am, fixing truck engines." Paul folded the other side of the tarp over.

"Will you return to China?"

He chuckled. "My parents will be on the first ship after the war, but I'm going to college to become an engineer. Working on engines—I like it. I want to design even better ones."

Violet frowned at a stubborn red splat. "What do your parents think about that?"

"They're happy for me, but they say they'll miss me." He shrugged as if he didn't quite believe the part about being missed.

She smiled at his back. "I'm sure they will, but I'm surprised they don't want you to follow in their footsteps."

"They said I'll be a missionary in the auto industry."

What an interesting way to think of it.

He folded the tarp into a square. "Where do you want to go, Miss Lindstrom?"

"It doesn't matter." A spot of green caught her eye, and she scrubbed at it. "My great-uncle and aunt serve in Kenya, but I'll go wherever I'm sent."

Paul flattened the tarp bundle. "You don't care where you go?"

"Wherever I'm needed."

"That's odd."

"Odd?"

He picked up a rag and knelt on the floor, squinting out the window. "My parents have always loved China and the Chinese people. Now that they're stuck in the States, they moved to San Francisco to work in the Chinese community. I've met a lot of missionaries over the years. They're all drawn to the country, the culture, the people."

A twinge in her gut. She'd met a lot of missionaries in her college mission society. Each had a strong, specific passion like that.

Paul's family loved China and the Chinese. Great-Aunt Violet loved Kenya and the Kenyans. And Violet? She loved the Lord. She loved . . . children.

"Do you see any more spots?" Paul asked. "I don't."

"Oh." Violet brought her eyes back into focus. "I don't either."

"Anything else I can do?"

"No, but thank you." She got to her feet and smiled at the young man. "I need to make sure the kitchen is ready, but please stop by the Aeroclub any time. I would love to hear your stories."

"I'll do that. Good-bye now."

Violet gathered the tarp and paint bottles into a box and stacked it on the box of smocks. She didn't like the unsettled feeling inside her.

She carried the boxes to the storage room. Why *did* she want to be a missionary if she didn't have that specific passion? She thought back to the age of ten when she'd made the decision and to her subsequent decisions.

Why? Because she loved God. Because missions seemed the noblest, the most sacrificial, the most . . . difficult.

Violet made a face as she opened the storage room. Difficult? That didn't sound quite right. That almost sounded wrong.

She set the box on a shelf and rubbed her forehead. Had God really called her to be a missionary or only to be willing to be a missionary?

With a groan, Violet shut the door. Was God swaying her heart, or were her feelings for Adler doing the swaying? What if the Lord chose her heart to change instead of his?

Maybe the Lord had something quieter for her. Less sacrificial.

Violet leaned back against the door and closed her eyes. *Lord, I promised I'd allow myself to be swayed by you. By you and you alone.*

She pushed away from the wall and headed for the kitchen. *I'm willing.*

30

At 250 yards, Adler squeezed the trigger. *Texas Eagle*'s bullets erupted the length of the Messerschmitt 110's right wing, and smoke plumed out of the right engine. Flames.

One more burst to let them know they'd had it.

The Me 110 rolled over, and two figures tumbled out.

Adler pulled up. When was the Luftwaffe going to learn to stop sending twin-engine fighters up against the Mustangs? Almost too easy to count a victory. But he'd count it. The second swastika to paint on the fuselage.

This victory would be easy for intelligence to confirm. He could still hear Willard Riggs cussing at the intelligence officer for not awarding him the victory he'd stolen from Adler. A week on restriction had only increased the man's surliness. No remorse. No apologies.

Adler sighed into his oxygen mask. *Thank you, God, for letting me learn from my mistakes.*

"Yellow leader, 109 at two o'clock below," Floyd called.

Adler spotted him. "Here we go." He shoved the stick forward and to the right, and *Eagle* dove after the single-engine fighter. A fairer match.

The Me 109 jerked and dove straight down. Adler plunged after him. Green landscape, red-roofed buildings, and one of Germany's finest aircraft spun below him. He fired, overshot.

His airspeed climbed—450 miles per hour, 460. He knew pilots who'd pushed it past 500 in a dive.

Altitude five thousand feet, four thousand. Adler fired a burst that lit up the Messerschmitt's tail assembly. Chunks of metal dinged off Adler's windscreen, and he instinctively ducked.

No cracks. Thank goodness for the extra-thick Plexiglas. Airspeed 475, altitude fifteen hundred. His eyesight grayed over.

He had no wish to black out and crash, so he pulled the stick back. After his eyesight cleared and he had enough altitude, he turned to the right.

A column of smoke rose from a clump of trees. "Yellow two?"

"No chute. He flew straight into the ground."

Adler blew out a long breath. He'd probably shot off the elevators on the tail, making it impossible for the German to pull up.

He hated to see a man die, but that man could have gone on to strafe the fleet and landing beaches on D-day.

After he got his bearings, Adler climbed toward where he'd last seen the stream of B-17 Flying Fortresses. The bombers had targeted aircraft factories in Erding. Better to keep enemy aircraft from hitting the sky in the first place.

Depending on the weather, the Eighth Air Force hit transportation targets in France some days and aircraft and oil industries in Germany on other days.

A speck ahead of him—another Me 110, flying perpendicular to his course, slow and steady. Something jumped in his chest. Easy pickings. Wouldn't it be something if he could get another two victories today and make ace?

The jumping calmed. Or he could lead from second and teach

Floyd. The pilot had gained in skill and confidence, and it was time for him to take the next step.

"Yellow two, one o'clock. See him? That maneuver we planned."

"Roger." Floyd got in place, close behind Adler to the left.

Adler made a diving turn to get on the German's tail. They were only at twenty-five hundred feet with the Me 110 at about one thousand feet. At such a low altitude, the enemy had no room to maneuver.

Adler closed the distance, out of the sun, a perfect attack. After he got within 300 yards, he would wheel off to the right, distracting the German pilot and letting Floyd swoop in.

He dove into position—500 yards, 400.

"He's mine!" Willard Riggs's voice sounded on the radio, angry and strident.

"Yellow leader!" Floyd shouted. "Watch out!"

A flash of olive drab over his canopy. Riggs! Diving on the same target!

"Yellow two, break!" Adler gave *Eagle* full right rudder to skid out of Riggs's path, then right stick to turn away, careful to keep his nose up.

Orange light blinded him, filled the canopy. A boom overrode his own engine noises. A shock wave buffeted *Eagle*'s wings. Debris pelleted his fuselage.

Adler fought his controls. "Floyd! Riggs!"

He cranked his head around. A jumbled ball of flame and smoke plummeted to earth. "Floyd! Riggs!"

"I—I'm hit." Floyd's P-51 remained airborne. "Debris. My wing."

Adler circled. The fireball—no, two distinct fireballs—splattered in a green field, flames and smoke twisting around the wreckage. Two planes.

"Oh, dear God. Riggs," Adler breathed.

"He—he—he—"

"Floyd! How's your plane? Can you fly?"

"He—he—he—"

He was dead. Riggs was dead, and the reality slammed Adler in the chest. For the sake of the intelligence officer's stupid reports, he snapped a picture with his gun camera to document Riggs's last victory and what it had cost him.

Adler couldn't think about it now. He had to get his flight home. No sign of Theo—Riggs must have shaken him off before the attack. "Floyd, your plane. How bad is it?"

"I—I don't know."

Adler came alongside Floyd's Mustang. The right wing was mangled but intact. No damage on the fuselage. "Test your controls."

Floyd nosed the plane up and down—elevators fine. It yawed right and left—rudder fine. "The ailerons. They're not responding."

"Use your rudder for turns. You're going to be fine. We're going home now, and I'll be your wingman."

Adler set a course for Leiston, his stomach twisted into a knot. This was the first loss that had really hit Floyd. He'd barely met Shapiro before the squadron commander had taken to his parachute. But he'd shared a hut with Riggs.

Now Riggs was dead.

Adler's head swung back and forth. This was harder than Mulroney's death. He'd never liked Riggs and their competition had been fierce, but he'd never wished the man dead.

Such a useless death. That Messerschmitt would have fallen to Floyd's guns, to Adler's if Floyd had failed. Riggs dove in for his own glory and to spite Adler. For nothing.

"Lord, have mercy on his soul."

Adler scanned the sky, clear except for wispy cirrus clouds high above. Riggs's death would be hard on Violet too. She had such a tender heart.

One of the many things he loved about her.

No doubt he'd fallen in love, hard and fast. Their walks were the highlight of each day as they strolled down country lanes, telling stories, laughing, and kissing. Knowing a jeep or a farmer's wagon could pass at any time made him behave himself.

Signs of a dogfight, far to the north. Looked like the Yoxford Boys would chalk up a high number of victories again today.

Now Adler had three. Two more to make ace.

His company idea seemed more realistic. He'd pored over an atlas the other day. Violet's hometown of Salina had a good-sized population and flat terrain and was near roads and railroads.

The perfect hub for an air shipping company.

Close to her family. Far from his.

To be fair, he'd also pored over a book about Africa. He'd love to visit someday. But to live there? To be a preacher?

"I couldn't handle that." Then he frowned. His new self was like a brand-new airplane model. He was still testing the controls and the engines. He didn't know its full capabilities yet.

Maybe his new self could handle more than he thought.

31

Violet turned a page in her hoedown notebook. "May 31, less than a month away. I can't wait."

Sitting next to her on the couch in the library, Kitty checked her clipboard. "I'm making progress on the food. I've ordered the beans and bacon through Banister's Grocery in Leiston, and Red Cross Headquarters is trying to procure cornmeal and molasses."

Violet made notes. "The theater building is booked, the men are asking around to see if anyone is a square dance caller, the Buzz Boys are practicing, and Floyd Milligan—I mean, Floyd Miller—agreed to play his harmonica. The Special Services Officer submitted a request for one of his movies."

Kitty nibbled on the end of her pencil. "Make sure we have an alternate movie."

"In case they can't find one?"

"In case . . . well, Floyd's a pilot." Her brown eyes stretched wide. "I'm sorry. I shouldn't have said that."

Violet sketched a border around the page. "No, you're right. It's a dangerous job. Your . . . your brother."

"Mm-hmm." Kitty's voice sounded strangled. She rarely talked about her pilot brother, but she never dated any of the pilots either.

Violet made a note to ask for a second film. The death of Willard Riggs had pressed the dangers home—and shaken her.

Never once had she thought a kind thought about the man. And worse, she'd never spoken a kind word to him. A good missionary would have been more concerned with his soul than his behavior. Now he was gone.

"Violet?" Kitty clasped her hand. "Adler seems indestructible."

She forced a smile. All these vigorous young men did, but over a third of the original pilots had been shot down.

Her gaze darted to the clock. The late afternoon was the hardest, wondering if he'd flown, if he'd survived.

"I told you to have a fling." Kitty raised half a smile. "I didn't tell you to fall madly in love."

"I'm not . . ."

Kitty gave her a comical look.

"All right, maybe a little," Violet whispered. But it was too early, and Adler hadn't said anything yet. She turned a page. "Decorations. We have money in the budget."

"I hope so."

"What?"

Kitty's mouth scooted to one side. "Rosalind told me we lost another sack of sugar."

"But Millie's gone!"

"I know, but since then the girls have gotten lazy with the logs. I'm not sure if it was theft or just poor accounting. We need to return to keeping strict logs and locking the cabinets. In the meantime, I see no need to tell Mr. Tate."

Violet stroked the nubby brown upholstery. She didn't want that nightmare to recur.

"Howdy, ladies." Adler stood in the library door in his flight jacket and khaki trousers, holding a slip of paper and scratching his head. "This here note on the office door says, 'The Red Cross director and staff assistant are in the library if you need help.'"

Violet went to him, joy chasing away every worry. "You look like a man in need of help."

"Desperately." He set his hands on her waist, pulled her near, and gave her a little kiss. "Much better. Ready for our walk?"

"A few more minutes. We're planning the hoedown."

Adler ambled to the couch, tipped his cap to Kitty, picked up Violet's notebook, and flapped it shut. "Looks like you're done to me."

That grin of his. She couldn't resist smiling back, but . . . "A few more minutes. We were just about to discuss decorations."

"No, ma'am. You're done." He headed for the door.

She blocked his path, but he lifted the notebook high.

Laughter bubbled up, and she tried to grab her notebook. He only had half an inch of height on her, but she couldn't reach. "If it weren't for those gorilla arms of yours . . ."

He wrapped one of those arms around her. "All the better to hold you with, my dear." He smacked a kiss on her nose, spun away, and strode down the hall, notebook aloft.

"Have fun, you two," Kitty called.

"You're no help." Violet wrinkled her nose at her girlfriend, then chased her boyfriend. Despite her teasing, she loved seeing him so happy. "Ad—Captain Paxton, you're awful."

"Awfully in need of a walk." He tossed the notebook on the desk, grasped Violet by the shoulders, and marched her backward out the office door. "The only thing on your calendar right now is me."

That spark in his eyes . . . oh, how she wanted to kiss him. But not in the dining area in front of all the men. "Sweet-talker."

They strolled out of the Aeroclub and out of the communal site, then up their favorite lane. A brilliant blue sky arched above, and the trees along the path rustled in a gentle breeze.

Violet slipped her hand in Adler's. "Did you fly today?"

"Sure did. The group flew two missions, and I flew one. I like these tactical fighter-bomber missions."

Violet had heard the men refer to the Transportation Plan, designed to demolish roads, bridges, and railroads in Nazi-occupied territory before the invasion.

"Dropped a couple of bombs on some railroad track, then strafed a bunch of trucks and trains. They don't count as victories, but it's important."

"Isolating the beaches."

He shot her a smile. "Someone's hanging around with pilots too much."

Violet leaned into his shoulder. "Whose fault is that?"

"All mine." He looped his arm around her waist. "D-day's coming soon. No secret there. If we keep this up, Hitler won't be able to move his tanks or troops into battle."

"Don't your missions show him where we're landing?"

"They could. That's why we bomb and strafe all along the coast. I don't know where we're landing either. But I like strafing—anything to keep the Germans away from my brothers and the rest of our boys."

The question perched on her tongue, but if he'd heard from home he would have told her. The poor man. A month and a half had passed since he'd mailed the letter. *Lord, please let them forgive him.*

Adler's brow puckered. "I was hoping I could write to my brothers before D-day."

"I know, sweetheart." She pressed a kiss to his cheek, relishing the masculine roughness.

"There's so much I want to say to them. I don't just need to apologize for that night." He kicked at a weed growing through the pavement. "But for a lifetime."

Violet squeezed his waist. She'd certainly had her squabbles with Alma, Karl, and Nels.

"Something in me always bristled at being second-born. Daddy said I was like Jacob, born grabbing at my older brother's heel. Daddy always liked that about me, liked my ambition."

"I gather you're more like him than Wyatt is."

"Spitting image." Adler cracked half a smile, then sobered. "That only fueled my resentment. I loved everything about Paxton Trucking. Everything. Wyatt only liked working on the books, never seemed excited about running the company someday. Seemed to me as if Wyatt despised his birthright, just like Esau."

Violet studied his handsome profile in the afternoon sun, his mouth bowed in a slight frown, not the frown of a bitter man but of a man reevaluating his life, a man determined to make things right.

She snuggled closer. "I love that you want to apologize to your brothers and be reconciled."

He stopped and squinted down the lane in both directions, then he grinned and backed her against a tree. "Know what I love?"

Her breath halted from his sudden change in mood and in reckless hope, but it was too early for him to declare love. And mischief danced over his features. She knew what he loved. "Kisses."

"Why, thank you. Right kind of you to offer." Now his lips did the dancing, caressing hers.

Sometimes it didn't seem quite proper, the way he held her, his body pressed to hers from lips to knees. But thick layers of leather and wool separated them, and never once had his hands strayed. And the connection between them felt good and right. Intimate, but respectful.

Adler eased back from the kiss. "There's more."

More what? More kisses? But his eyebrows pinched together in a serious way.

He rested one forearm on the trunk above her head. "I love how you've been honest with me about your wrestling—about becoming a missionary."

"Of course."

"No, not of course. You know I'm a sweet-talker. I could—the old Adler would have used that against you and tried to change your mind."

Violet ran a finger along his strong jawline. "You promised not to."

"You trust me." Bewilderment swam in his eyes. "Oralee—she loved me, but she didn't completely trust me. That was wise."

She ran her fingers into his hair. "I have the new Adler. You're a good man."

He winced and glanced away.

"You are." With one hand to his cheek, she turned his face to hers. "A very good man."

His cheek twitched under her thumb. "Not good enough for you."

Her love for him ached inside, begging to be voiced, to assure him, but he had to say it first. She wouldn't steal that from him.

Instead she infused all that love into her smile. "That's my decision to make. You're more than good enough. Far more."

Her words felt insufficient, so she kissed him. Maybe someday she could convince him.

32

Sitting in the squadron pilots' room, Adler caught Violet's eye and held up one hand to ask her to wait for him.

With a warm gaze, she nodded, and then she toted a tray out the door.

Adler reviewed his encounter report from the day's mission to make sure it was complete and accurate. Then he signed it and slid it to the squadron intelligence officer.

He scanned the form. "Looks good. We'll type it up, check it against the gun camera footage, and turn it in to Fighter Command."

"Thank you, sir." Adler stood and stretched again. He was the last pilot remaining in the room after the debriefing.

The refreshment table was empty, so he stepped outside where Violet and Tom Griffith were loading a jeep. "Miss Lindstrom, y'all need to take that back to the Aeroclub, right?"

She brushed her hair off her cheek, revealing a sweet smile. "Griff offered to take it back. Then you and I can still have a walk before dinner."

"Thanks, Corporal."

223

"Sure thing, Captain." Griff hopped into the jeep.

After he left, Adler took Violet's hand and led her down to the perimeter track and away from the base.

"We've never gone this way before," she said.

"I want to show you something." His voice clamped at the end, and he coughed to cover. He was taking a big step today.

Violet glanced up, where a few pillow clouds floated in the sky. "You had a long mission."

"Longest ever." His voice loosened at the topic. "And I mean ever. We flew 1470 miles round trip, the longest combat mission by any single-engine aircraft ever."

"Oh my goodness."

"It'll be all over the news tomorrow. We flew to Poznan, Poland."

"Poland!"

He grinned at how big her blue eyes could get. "Yes, ma'am. Reckon the sight of American fighters so far east made the Nazis quake in their jackboots."

"Fourteen hundred . . . in one day." Violet shook her pretty head.

"This is how we did it." He pointed to a stack of bullet-shaped auxiliary fuel tanks. "Our new drop tanks, made out of a paper-plastic composition. They weigh next to nothing, but each holds 108 gallons."

"Incredible. And there's your *Eagle*. Such a beautiful plane."

"Not as beautiful as my girl." He winked at her, then checked out his bird. The ground crew must have finished their work, and José Flores had already completed his paintwork. Adler pointed to the fourth swastika on the fuselage below his cockpit. "Paint's still wet."

"Four victories!" She hugged his arm. "One more and you're an ace."

"We'll see." With one finger he traced the white lettering for his plane's name. "I thought being leader meant being first. But Nick—and Jesus—are showing me how to make myself second even when I'm in the lead. Three men follow me, look up to me, and depend on me. I have to teach them, protect them, and encourage them. And I like it. I like it a lot."

Violet kissed his cheek. "I'm so proud of you."

His heart slammed into his chin, but it was time. She'd been his girlfriend for a month now, and he was certain. "Something else to show you." He led her around the plane's red-and-yellow nose to the eagle painting on the other side of the fuselage. At Adler's request, Flores had painted a violet in the eagle's grasp.

She covered her mouth. "Oh, Adler."

He circled his arm around her waist. "It's too late to name my bird after my girl but never too late to include you."

"I—I'm honored. I love it." She rested her head on his shoulder.

Adler cleared his sticky throat. "And I love my Violet."

She raised her head, her eyes wide and glistening and wondrous.

"I love you." His voice roughened, and he swallowed again. "Very much. I don't care if it's too early. I have to say it."

With a sudden laugh, she faced him, flung her arms around his neck, and planted a kiss on his lips. "I love you too. I'm madly in love with you."

Adler blinked and searched her face, but only joy and love shone out. Yes, love. More than anything, he wanted to sink into history's longest kiss ever, but not yet.

"I've got more to say." He backed out of her embrace and unzipped his flight jacket. "I want you to know no one will ever stand between us, even from the past." With stiff fingers, he unpinned the yellow scrap from inside his breast pocket.

"All—all right."

"This was Oralee's." He fingered the smooth cotton, as sunny as Oralee's smile. "It's from the dress she wore that day. It tore when she fell."

"Sweetheart." Violet's voice choked. "You—you keep it close to your heart."

"I won't let her memory come between us." His fingers tightened on the scrap, the familiar frayed edges, the three white daisies, the sound of Oralee's scream, silenced. "It's time to let this go. To let her go."

"Oh no, no, no." Violet slipped the fabric from his grip, tucked it back into his pocket, and fumbled with the safety pin. "You loved her. And your deep love for her—that's one of the reasons I fell in love with you. You're faithful, constant."

"Violet . . ." He studied the tears dribbling down her cheeks, the eyelashes darkened and flickering. "You shouldn't."

"Nonsense. You've opened your heart again and let me in. That's more than I ever dreamed." She fastened the pin, sniffled, and wiped her cheeks with her fingers. "Oh dear."

Adler tugged his handkerchief from the pocket in his flight coveralls and dried her cheeks, cradling the back of her head. He didn't trust his voice, so he pressed her head to his shoulder and held her tight.

Most men were lucky to have the love of one good woman in their lives. He'd had two.

Adler slammed his eyes shut, one hand buried in Violet's soft hair. He wasn't lucky. He was blessed. The Lord had made him a new man and had given him a new start and even a new love.

He might never be forgiven by his family and might never be welcomed home. But he wouldn't be alone. His future lay with Violet, even if he didn't know which way that future led.

Adler pulled in a deep breath of fresh spring air, and he kissed Violet's temple. "Ready for dinner?"

She laughed. "Dinner?"

"Man's got to eat, and so does woman."

Her mouth bent in a little smile. "True."

"Besides, I want to talk to you, and that's better done side-by-side than face-to-face. Or this happens." He kissed her, and the sweetness of her melted the steel of his resolve. "Over and over it'll happen."

He fell into another kiss, wrapping her close, savoring their love.

She gripped his shoulders and pushed away, chuckling. "I thought you wanted dinner."

"You taste better." He stretched toward her.

Violet spun out of his embrace and scooped up his hand. "Given the quality of the food in the mess, that isn't saying much. But we do have to eat."

His stomach rumbled, betraying him by agreeing with her. "Fine." He sounded like a whiny toddler.

She laughed and led him to the perimeter track. "You said you wanted to talk, so talk."

Adler drew in another warm breath to clear his mind. "I've worked out two plans."

"Plans?"

He marched toward the control tower, not looking at her. "I did some research, and I came up with two plans I could live with. Now to find out if you can live with them."

"Plans for us?" Her voice wavered.

He couldn't look at her now. "First idea—the easiest because it's my original plan."

"ACES?"

"Yes, in Salina, Kansas."

Violet stopped.

He tugged on her hand. "Side by side, young lady. I read up on Salina. Flat and open, perfect for an airfield and warehouses. In fact, the Army Air Forces has an airfield there. It's pretty much smack-dab in the middle of the country, with access to railroads and roads. An ideal site for a shipping hub. You'd be close to your family. You could teach if you want, or volunteer, and raise our twenty-nine kids."

A laugh burst out. "Twenty-nine?"

He winked at her. "The number's open for negotiation."

"Kansas." She leaned into his arm. "It sounds wonderful."

Adler nudged her away. "Not yet, you don't. Here's the second idea. This was harder for me. I can't see myself preaching. I'm a businessman and a pilot. I love moving freight. So last week I sat down with the chaplain and told him all that."

"You did?" She leaned into him again.

This time he let her stay. "He had an idea. Seems a lot of missionaries are isolated. It's hard for them to get supplies, hard to get medicines in an emergency. I could buy a plane and radios to communicate with the missionaries. Then I could ship supplies to them, even fly them around. If someone's sick, I could fly them to a city with a hospital."

"What a brilliant idea."

"Not mine, but I agree. I can see myself doing it and enjoying it. And you could stay put and teach the local kids about reading, writing, 'rithmetic, and Jesus. While raising our twenty-nine kids, of course."

Violet's gaze darted about, as if she were painting the picture in her mind. "You'd be away a lot, but you'd be doing such great good. You'd do that for me?"

He bumped her with his shoulder. "For God."

She laughed and ducked her chin. "Of course."

"And for you." He drew her back to his side. "Definitely for you."

33

Leiston, England
Wednesday, May 17, 1944

Mr. Banister loaded a large sack of beans into the back of the jeep.

Violet tried not to stare at the grocer's truncated fingertips and the mottled pink scars that covered his hands. Perhaps he'd suffered a war injury. "Thank you, Mr. Banister."

"You're welcome." He headed back into the store for the bacon.

Violet smiled at Sylvia Haywood as they followed him. "Just wait until you taste American baked beans."

Tom Griffith had driven Kitty down to Ipswich to pick up molasses and cornmeal at the Red Cross service club there, so Violet was making the weekly run to Banister's.

"Only two weeks until the hoedown." Sylvia adjusted her hat over her blonde hair. "Jimmy and Margie speak of nothing else. Jimmy keeps trying to talk like that cowboy of yours."

"He does have the cutest accent." Each twang in his deep voice resounded in her heart.

Mr. Banister slapped two large paper-wrapped bundles onto the counter. "Do you have your ration books?"

"Yes, sir." But Sylvia had to help Violet with the books and the money. Pounds and crowns and half-pennies—they made her head spin.

A young woman with pinned-up brown curls took the cash without a glance or a smile.

So Violet turned her smile to the grocer. "This is for the big party we're holding for the children on May 31. Do you have children, Mr. Banister?"

The cashier speared her with a glare. "They will not attend."

Violet sucked in a breath as sharp as the woman's voice. How could she respond?

"Hazel." Mr. Banister frowned at the cashier. Then he handed Violet the stamped ration books. "Thank you for your purchase. I'll load the bacon for you."

"Thank you." Cheeks burning, she followed the pale-haired man outside where the air was fresh and cool.

After the grocer set the bacon in the jeep, Violet and Sylvia climbed in.

Violet put the jeep in gear and drove out of town. "That woman certainly doesn't like Americans."

Sylvia clamped a hand over her hat. "Don't you know who she is?"

"I've never met her."

"That's Hazel Banister. Hazel *Clark* Banister. She's Millie's oldest sister. She's furious that we fired Millie."

"Oh dear." Violet's mind spun ugly patterns as she drove down the street with its sweet buildings of colorful clapboard and brick. Millie. Mrs. Banister. Mr. Banister. "You don't suppose Mr. Banister is a black marketer, selling the goods Millie stole?"

Sylvia pursed her lips. "I wondered that myself. Since the Yanks came to town, Banister's is always well stocked."

"What?" Violet whipped her gaze to Sylvia, then back to the road. "Why didn't you tell me?"

Sylvia shrugged. "It doesn't fit. Black marketers don't stamp your ration book, and they sell at high prices and only to their poshest customers. Believe me, we women know who sells under the counter, and Mr. Banister doesn't. Besides, nothing has changed at the store since we let Millie go."

"I'm glad to hear that." The road curved around Buckle's Wood, and Violet's thoughts curved too. Hazel Banister had never volunteered at the Aeroclub, so she couldn't be stealing. Perhaps the food shortages were easing, now that the tide had turned in the Battle of the Atlantic, allowing more cargo ships to cross from the US.

Violet turned left.

Sylvia squealed and grabbed the steering wheel. "Wrong side! You're on the wrong side of the road."

Heart pattering, Violet straightened out onto the left side. Then she gave Sylvia a mischievous smile. "On the contrary, I was on the *right* side."

"You Yanks." Sylvia patted her chest. "Griff will have your head if you don't return this jeep in one piece."

Violet laughed at the thought of the cheerful corporal yielding an executioner's axe.

She turned right onto the main road leading onto the base. There hadn't been signs of a mission today, only a few motors running up and a few takeoffs, probably training flights for the replacement pilots who were constantly arriving.

She steeled herself against the reason those new pilots were necessary.

The jeep passed bicycles and Nissen huts and waving airmen. Violet waved back. Her afternoon would be quieter without deliveries for mission debriefings.

Best of all, she'd have more time with Adler. On nonflying days he often had coffee in the Aeroclub, chatting with his ground crew, reading magazines, and sneaking Violet fond looks and words.

Her chest warmed, lifting a smile. She loved having him near while she worked, knowing he enjoyed being near her as well.

Since he'd declared his love, the idea of a future with him seemed delightfully inevitable. Her heart leaned toward his Kansas plan. Was Great-Aunt Violet right? Had Violet been led astray by a handsome pilot?

She turned onto the road into the communal site. As handsome and persuasive as Adler could be, that wasn't the case. If anything, he talked more about his missionary plan.

Something else was happening inside her. Ever since her conversation with Paul Harrison, she'd examined her call to the mission field. If it was even a call. She'd chosen missions because she loved the Lord and wanted to do something big and sacrificial for him.

But another notion niggled at her. Had she chosen missions so she'd look noble and godly, so everyone would admire her? What an awful reason to serve.

Violet pulled the jeep into the space alongside the Aeroclub. Lately she'd felt some sympathy for Dennis. Her former fiancé had never elaborated on his decision to give up missions, but perhaps it was more than simple greed. Perhaps he'd struggled with some of the same thoughts Violet struggled with.

She'd finally prayed and forgiven Dennis for his decision, for taking away her dream of going overseas right after college.

No matter what, she was glad she hadn't married the man.

Violet turned off the engine. Loud voices sounded from inside the Aeroclub.

She and Sylvia exchanged a worried look, and Violet bolted from the jeep and flung open the kitchen door.

"Twenty pounds of flour? Gone like that?" Mr. Tate stood in front of Rosalind Weaver, his jowls red and quivering, his finger in her face.

Rosalind gripped the counter behind her back, her head shaking. "I—I don't know how."

"What's happening?" Violet said as calmly as she could.

232

Mr. Tate wheeled on her. "You tell me. You accused Miss Clark of being the thief, yet food is still disappearing."

"I—I don't think so, sir." Violet opened the logbook on the counter. "A few minor discrepancies, but not like before."

"Minor?" Mr. Tate spluttered. "Mrs. Weaver lost a sack of flour last night."

"You did?" Violet said.

Rosalind shook her tear-stained face. "I haven't had time to tell you. I set it out to make donuts. They called me to the snack bar, and when I returned, it was gone."

"And a vat of oil." Mr. Tate scowled.

"Yes, sir." Rosalind covered her face. "I don't know who took it. So busy."

"Explain this." Mr. Tate snatched the logbook from Violet and flipped a page. "Mrs. Haywood checked out one hundred tea bags for the pilots after a mission—and returned none."

Sylvia twisted her hands together. "None were left, sir."

He turned on her. "You mean to tell me four dozen American pilots drank one hundred cups of tea?"

It was a ludicrous thought indeed. "I wish I could explain, but—"

"But you can't. Listen, I don't know what's going on here, but—but—" A vein throbbed on his forehead.

Violet had to stop his harassment of her staff. "Sir, could we please discuss this privately in the office?"

"Excellent idea." He marched out.

Violet rushed to keep up.

In the office, he motioned for her to sit in front of the desk, then he shut the door and paced beside her. "I don't know if you're the thief or if you're so incompetent as to hire thieving employees, but I've had enough."

Violet's mouth went dry. "Sir, I—"

"Enough." He waved a hand. "You have one month to clean

233

up this place. And I'm being more generous than I ought to be. One month, or I'll fire the lot of you—Miss Kelly, you, and the entire staff."

Violet gasped. "Please, sir. Please don't punish the ladies. They need these jobs."

Mr. Tate glared down at her. "Then I suggest you find the thief. Or confess."

Confess? Her eyes watered. He still thought she was a thief?

"One month." He slammed the door behind him.

Violet sagged back in the chair. She didn't know where to begin.

34

"Okay, ladies, let's think this through." Behind the desk in the Aeroclub office, Adler drew vertical lines down a piece of paper and labeled the columns "steps," "problems," and "solutions."

Sitting next to him, Violet and Kitty wore forlorn expressions as identical as their uniforms. Since Mr. Tate's ultimatum, the two women hadn't been able to think straight, not that Adler blamed them. It had taken several rounds with a punching bag at the base gymnasium to clear his mind. And women didn't seem to punch things. Too bad.

Adler shoved up his rolled-up shirtsleeves. "First step—ordering. How do y'all do that?"

Kitty tugged at a brown curl. "I don't think that's a problem."

"That's not the point. Let's think through the entire process. Ordering."

"I order most of our food from Banister's in Leiston, but some from Red Cross Headquarters in London."

Adler made notes. Nothing for the thief to exploit in the ordering process. No changes needed. "Next step—delivery."

"The Red Cross supplies are delivered here directly," Kitty said. "We pick up the rest at Banister's."

"Who and how?"

"I do. Corporal Griffith drives me in a truck." Kitty closed her eyes. "I used to send Millie. How could I have been so stupid?"

Violet gripped her friend's hand. "Not stupid. Trusting. And I doubt she stole from the deliveries with Griff right there."

"Back to the grocer's." Adler pointed his pen at Kitty. "You check the order versus the invoice?"

"Now I do. Then Mr. Banister and Griff and I load the truck."

"Do you check off the invoice during loading?"

Kitty frowned. "Um, no. Oh, dear. Do you think the grocer would cheat us?"

Under both "problems" and "solutions," Adler made more notes. "We're not blaming anyone. We're thinking this through. Does Griff drive you straight here, or do you make any other stops?"

"Straight here, then we unload right away."

"Who unloads?" He started a new row.

"We all do," Violet said. "Griff, Kitty, anyone in the kitchen."

Kitty nodded. "While they're unloading, I fill in the log."

Adler tapped his pen against his chin. "Do you fill it out from the invoice or do you check off each item as it's stored?"

"From the . . . the invoice." Kitty's brown eyes widened. "That's a problem, isn't it?"

"Possibly." Adler filled in the columns. "Someone could snitch food from the truck when your backs are turned, or Griff could leave supplies in the truck and cart them away."

"Oh, not Griff," Violet said.

Adler couldn't help but smile. "Too tenderhearted. Makes for good Red Cross ladies, but right now y'all have to think like hard-boiled detectives."

Violet chewed on her lower lip. "I hate to suspect anyone."

"I know." He loved that about her.

For the next half hour, he talked them through the process. It got messy, what with deliveries to ground crew and pilots' rooms and parties, as well as snack bar operations. By the end, they'd identified a few more holes and thought up ways to plug them.

With seventeen hundred men on the base and dozens of Red Cross workers and volunteers, they might never find the culprit. But they could make it harder for the snake to strike.

Kitty glanced at the clock. "I'd better make sure everything's ready for the after-dinner rush. Thank you, Adler." She grabbed her jacket from the coatrack and moved to shut the door.

"Keep it open, please." Not only did he want to protect Violet's reputation, but he needed to avoid situations where he might be tempted to push her. Because boy, was she tempting.

"Oh, dear." Violet ran her finger down the middle column. "We'll never solve this."

"Hey, now." Adler rubbed her back, aware of the warmth of her skin through her cotton blouse. "Y'all have a good plan."

She shook her head. "Kitty and I have other duties. We can't monitor every step."

"Of course not. Plug the holes we found, and we'll go from there." He moved her finger from the "problems" column to the "solutions" column. "Everything will be fine."

"And if it isn't? What if Mr. Tate fires us? The women need these jobs, and they're good workers. It isn't fair for all of them to be punished because of one dishonest person—who might not even be our employee."

"I know." He laced his fingers through hers. "We'll make sure that doesn't happen."

"Less than a month." Her features twisted. "Then we'll be sent home in disgrace. I can't bear that."

Adler understood that feeling well. But it was different for her. With his free hand, he tapped her under the chin. "If it comes to that, you go home and hold your head high. You've done nothing wrong."

"No one else will know that. No mission board or school board will accept me." She crumpled against his side. "And I'll miss you."

Boy, did he want to turn Mr. Tate into his next punching bag. Instead, he extracted his hand and put his arm around Violet's shoulder. "Hey, now. Soon as this war's over, I'm coming for you. I'll sweep you up on that white steed of mine, and we'll ride off into the sunset so you can raise our twenty-nine kids."

She lifted her head, her face awash with doubts.

He gave her a little kiss and a wink. "You can't run away from me that easily."

Violet rested her head on his shoulder. "I do love you."

"I love you too." So much it ached inside him.

A light knock on the open door. Nick stood there. "Mail came."

Adler blinked at his friend. The mail came every day, not that it mattered to him.

But the concern in Nick's expression jolted him. Was something wrong with his wife? His baby girl? "Oh no. Did you get bad news from home?"

Nick shook his head and laid an envelope on the desk.

The handwriting stabbed Adler in the chest. "My father."

"Oh, Adler." Violet clutched his hand on her shoulder.

"Would you like me to stay?" Nick asked.

Adler raised a flimsy smile. "Thanks, but I'm all right."

"I'm going to dinner, then the officers' club." Nick motioned with his thumb over his shoulder. "You know where to find me."

"Thanks, buddy."

"Would you like privacy?" Violet said after he left.

Every muscle wanted to flee from that letter, but he had to take on whatever pain it might inflict before he could heal. And he had Violet. "Please stay."

He uncurled his arm from around her and picked up the envelope, the first contact he'd had with his family for almost three years. His fingers barely worked, but he opened the letter and pulled out several sheets of stationery.

Something small fluttered to the floor, and Violet picked it up. "What a cutie-pie. Who's this?"

Adler stared at a studio photograph of a little boy with white-blond hair and laughing eyes. He took it and flipped it over. "Timothy Paxton, age 2."

"Is one of your brothers married?"

"No . . ." But three years had passed, and shame slapped him. "Actually, I don't know. It couldn't be Clay. With his dark coloring, he could never have a towhead like this."

"Wyatt? Is he blond?"

"Yeah. Must be." But if Wyatt was married, what was he doing flirting with an English redhead? That wasn't like him.

Adler slipped the picture into his breast pocket and unfolded the letter, his gut twining. He scooted his chair to the side and faced Violet.

She turned her chair too, set her hands on his knees, and bowed her head.

Praying for him.

Love for her swelled inside. God could get him through this alone, but he was glad God had given him Violet too.

A prayer of his own, and he dove in.

Dear Adler,

I can't begin to tell you how relieved your mama and I were to receive your letter. You were right when you said we never stopped praying for you. But you were mistaken to think we couldn't forgive you. We already have.

However, seeing the depth of your remorse confirms our faith in you, and we're pleased to hear of your salvation.

If this tragedy and sin turned you to God, it wasn't all for naught.

We will always love you, and you're always welcome here.

"They—" Adler wet his dry lips. "They forgave me."

Violet looked up, her face luminous. "I knew they would."

Such beautiful innocence. He gave her a wry smile and waved the stationery. "Still two pages to go."

We apologize for delaying our reply. A lot has happened since that night, and some of it isn't ours to tell. It took three weeks of talking to God, each other, and the preacher to decide how much to tell you and when.

Even though we know this letter will cause more pain and regret, we felt it best to tell you everything that concerns you. In your letter you said facing your sins was like wrenching a dislocated shoulder back into place. Well, now it's time to fix your other shoulder.

You assumed Wyatt was in Kerrville. However, he also ran away that night and never contacted us. About a month ago we finally heard from him. God answered our prayers to hear from both our prodigals.

Like you, Wyatt seems to be doing well. Like you, he joined up. He's an officer in the Navy, serving on the same island as you. I'll enclose his address at the end. He wants to hear from you.

Adler rested the letter in his lap. "It was Wyatt in London. He—he wants to hear from me."

"What great news."

Was it? He'd driven his brother to run away for three years! So afraid he hadn't even written home. Did Wyatt want Adler to write—or was Daddy doing a little manipulation?

Daddy hadn't seen how Wyatt had run from him in Hyde Park. And there was a whole lot of letter remaining.

> *Clay is indeed overseas with you. Financial troubles kept him from going to college. Just as well, because with you and Wyatt gone, we needed him at Paxton Trucking. Last February the military ended draft deferments for men twenty-two and younger, and the Army took him. He volunteered for the Rangers, and we're proud of what he's doing.*
>
> *We urge you to write Clay as well. It'll do you both good.*

"It was Clay on the *Queen Elizabeth*." Adler noted the difference—Clay hadn't asked Adler to write. "He's an Army Ranger. But he was supposed to become a doctor."

"That isn't your fault, is it?"

Adler frowned at the words. As much as he wanted to take on that blame, he couldn't. "No. Something about financial troubles." But that didn't make sense. Clay had saved up, and he was too focused on his goal to squander his savings.

> *As for what happened that night in the garage, we're glad to hear that you're sorry, that you've repented, and that God's forgiven you.*
>
> *But even when our sins are forgiven by God and man, consequences remain.*
>
> *It goes without saying that Clay broke up with Ellen. We didn't see her for four months. Then in October, she showed up on our doorstep. Her parents had kicked her out and moved out of state.*
>
> *Ellen was carrying your child.*

Not a wrenched shoulder. Not a stab in the heart. A millstone crushing his chest, grinding down, forbidding all breath.

His . . . child? The little boy. The picture burned against his chest.

The crushing spread to his head and ground his future to dust. His plans. Violet.

Her head bowed, her voice murmuring in prayer, her heart unaware that one sentence had changed her life as well.

He ripped his gaze from the woman he loved to the words he hated.

Of course we took her in. For the sake of the baby, we urged Clay and Ellen to marry. But Clay refused to marry the girl who'd betrayed and humiliated him, and Ellen insisted on waiting for you to return. Turns out she never loved Clay. She said she'd always loved you and had used Clay to get close to you.

Nausea swept through his belly. Adler had to marry her. For the baby. The boy. He had to marry a woman who took advantage of Clay's sweet nature. A woman who took advantage of Adler's grief and anger and taste for whiskey.

This was the kind of wife Adler was going to get. The only kind of wife he deserved.

"Adler?" Concern lifted Violet's voice.

He couldn't bear to look her in the face.

Your son, Timothy, was born March 8, 1942, healthy and strong and kicking.

He had a son. A son. A two-year-old son. For two years, he'd had a son and he'd never even known.

Violet's voice drifted around, soft and anxious as if in another room.

Adler scooted away, freeing his knees from her touch. Never

again would she touch him, talk to him, love him. It had to be that way. For the boy. For Timothy.

I'm sad to report that Ellen was killed late that spring in a car accident, driving too fast in the rain. At least the baby was home with us at the time.

That millstone ground harder. Adler didn't want to marry her, but he didn't want her dead! He'd killed her. As good as killed her. Just like his own mother. Just like Oralee.

Why wouldn't this letter end? He couldn't take any more.

Ice crystals prickled in his veins, lining up to build a protective shell.

We're raising little Timmy, and we're happy to do so. He's a blessing in the middle of the darkest years of our lives. He's bright and mischievous and cute as the dickens. Just like you at that age.

Adler skimmed the rest. "We forgive you . . . We love you . . . Please come home . . . You're always welcome . . ." But it didn't— none of it penetrated.

He fought off the ice, shook off the crystals. He'd earned this pain. He needed to feel it.

"Adler?" Violet's voice quivered. "Please, sweetheart. Please tell me what's wrong."

His gaze swam to meet hers. So trusting, so innocent, so pure. She could never . . . She shouldn't have to . . . He refused to make her.

Somehow his crushed-up, ground-up heart managed to shatter.

Adler pushed himself to standing, dizzier and more nauseated than if he were knee-walking drunk. As he'd been that night he destroyed all those lives. Oralee. Wyatt. Clay. Ellen.

"Adler?" Tears distorted Violet's eyes.

Adler wouldn't let himself destroy her life as well.

"Once—" His voice rasped out. "Once you told me nothing I did could change how you feel about me."

"Well, yes, of—"

"I won't hold you to that. I release you from that promise."

"What? I—I don't—"

Adler dropped the letter on the desk. "Read it. Good-bye."

And he fled. For good this time. For her good.

35

"Adler!" Violet swiped her eyes clear. Yes, he was fleeing.

The news must have been awful to cause him to break that promise to her.

Panic swelled, and she snatched up the letter. No time to read. She had to catch him.

She grabbed Adler's flight jacket and cap from the coatrack—he'd need those—and burst out of the office.

There he was, striding out the main door in his khaki trousers and shirt. She followed, not caring that she ought to be wearing her cap and jacket.

Adler ran down the road and fast.

But she was fast too. She sprinted after him, past curious men on their way to dinner. It didn't matter. Adler was in pain, and she needed to be with him.

"Lord, what happened?" Had one of his parents died? What could cause such dismay?

The answers were in the letter, but she couldn't stop to read.

Adler turned between two huts. She followed him out onto the baseball diamond and toward a row of trees.

Her breath came hard, and her lungs burned. She might be fast, but she couldn't keep this pace for long.

In the outfield, grasses scratched her ankles and she stumbled a few times. But she didn't stop. He needed her. He needed her. *Lord, he needs you most of all.*

When she reached the trees, she slowed down and picked her way through the undergrowth, her chest heaving and her underarms sticky.

A khaki lump in the green—Adler folded over his knees, his head in his hands.

"Oh, Adler, sweet—"

His head jerked up, he glared at her, then he hunched over again and swatted in her direction. "Go away!" And he cussed.

She gasped from the swear words, but then her heart ached for him, for whatever he was enduring. "Adler—"

"Read it! I told you to read it. Get out of here."

She only intended to obey the first half of his command. Violet sank to her knees in the moss and leaves, laid Adler's jacket and cap beside him, and skimmed the letter.

His father was glad to hear from him, had forgiven him, was glad of his salvation. News of Wyatt—nothing distressing. News of Clay—sad, but nothing that should have Adler facedown on the ground, moaning.

He covered his bowed head with his hands. "Forgive me, Lord. Oh God, forgive me, forgive me, forgive me."

Fear gripped her. Never had she heard such an agonized prayer. She reached for him but stopped. He'd only swat her away. *Lord, help him. Help him.*

She returned to the letter. Some cryptic comments about sin having consequences and Clay breaking up with Ellen. And— "Ellen was carrying your child."

Mr. Paxton was addressing . . . Adler?

Cold seeped into her bones, and leaves prickled her shins. That didn't—it didn't make sense.

Her eyes strained for more, for an explanation, for proof that she'd misread that sentence. This Ellen had refused to marry Clay? She loved . . . Adler?

The next words slashed through her eyes. "Your son, Timothy, was born . . ."

The little boy in the picture. The cutie-pie. He wasn't Wyatt's son. He was Adler's.

A cry welled up deep in her stomach and flowed out her mouth. Adler echoed the cry, but she didn't care. Didn't care.

The rest of the words flew into her brain in random order. This Ellen . . . dead. His parents . . . raising the baby. Forgiven. Love you. Come home.

Not one word changed the truth. The awful truth.

"Who—who is Ellen?" Violet didn't recognize her own voice.

Adler groaned, his hands fisted in his hair. "She was Clay's girlfriend."

Another cry gushed out. "And you . . . with her?"

"Yes! I *slept* with her. I slept with my brother's girlfriend."

Grief and fury and revulsion whirled into a disgusting mess in her stomach. "How could you?"

"I wanted to tell you. I meant to. You told me not to, but I shouldn't have listened to you. I should have told you." He pounded his fist into the ground.

"That day? In my office? This?" If he'd told her then, she never would have gotten involved with him. Never.

"When Oralee died. That night. I was so angry. Angry at Wyatt. Angry at Clay for stopping me."

"And you . . . ?" Her stomach curled up on itself.

"I should have told you." Adler clenched grass in his fists. "Dr. Hill—Ellen's father—he gave me a pill to calm me down. I refused it. I wanted to chase down Wyatt. Daddy locked the truck, wouldn't give me the key, so I went to the garage to pick the lock. Only I failed. Then Ellen showed up with a bottle of whiskey. She said her daddy said I needed it."

"I—I don't want to hear this." Violet tried to fold the letter, but her fingers wouldn't cooperate and her vision clouded.

"Listen! All of it." Grass ripped away from the earth. "I got drunk. I got falling-down drunk, and—"

"I know what you did." She flung the letter at him, and the pages fluttered down over his crumpled body.

"Mama must have sent Clay to check on me. He found us, tried to kill me. I don't blame him. He should have. He could have. I was too drunk to fight back."

Violet struggled to her feet, desperate to escape.

"My parents must have heard the ruckus. It's all a blur, but next thing Mama's holding Clay off with a shotgun and Daddy's telling me to get out of his sight. I drove all the way to the Pacific Ocean."

Violet stared down at the man huddled on the ground, a man she thought she knew. "Who—who *are* you?"

Adler just moaned, transforming before her eyes.

From protector to destroyer.

From chivalrous gentleman to heartless rogue.

From saint to the worst imaginable sinner.

Violet clutched her writhing belly. "I thought—I thought you were a good man."

"I'm not!" He glared at her, his face twisted into something monstrous and unrecognizable. "I'm a sinner. I'm a stinking, rotten, wretched sinner."

Once again, a man had dashed her dreams.

Her mind flew back to the conversation they'd had on the *Queen Elizabeth*, to something Adler had said. She repeated it. "Boys destroy."

"Yes. Yes." He slashed his arm in her direction. "Now go away. For your own good. Get out of here!"

Violet backed away, stumbling out of the woods. This time, it was her turn to flee.

36

Skimming the deck, Adler kept the silver waters of the Baltic to his right as he zigged and zagged over the railroad.

His flight had already strafed one German locomotive and was now bearing down on the city of Stralsund to the north.

The intense, repetitive work of flying a challenging mission helped numb him. He needed the numbness today. For the mission. Then he'd let the pain back in.

Last night the pain had done its work as Adler beat the ground and cried out for forgiveness. Until a voice silenced him. Not out loud, but not in his head either.

You already asked for forgiveness. I already gave it.

Way back in February, God had forgiven his sins, long before Adler knew the full consequences. Already forgiven. *All* forgiven.

Peace and fatigue had settled down in equal measure, and Adler had brushed himself off and collapsed into his cot long past midnight.

Green fields and slate-roofed buildings raced beneath him, and he scanned for the Luftwaffe and enemy trains.

Thank goodness Nick had let him fly. Adler's sweet-talking

ways had bypassed Nick's scrutinizing ways. A smiling "My parents forgave me" had done the trick. After the mission, he'd tell Nick every last detail and show him the photograph hidden in his breast pocket.

Numb. He shook himself and guided his flight in a sweeping right turn over the tracks.

Today was the first coordinated "Chattanooga" mission against Nazi rail, named after the popular song "Chattanooga Choo Choo." Six hundred fighters of the Ninth Air Force were hitting tracks in France while six hundred fighters of the Eighth Air Force concentrated on Germany. Each group had been assigned a square fifty miles by fifty miles, and at eleven o'clock sharp they struck as one.

The biggest preinvasion mission yet, and Adler had to fly. All the anger he felt at himself, he planned to unleash on trains that could transport troops and weapons to the front. Adler refused to let them reach his brothers.

Wyatt and Clay would never forgive him. Adler had driven Wyatt into hiding for three years. Three years! And Clay? Adler couldn't imagine what Clay had been through—the broken dreams, humiliation, and fury. Their parents had taken Ellen in. That meant Clay had to live in the same house as his former girlfriend, who was carrying his rotten brother's baby.

Pain convulsed his chest. The numbness wasn't working, but he had to make it work, had to concentrate on his duties. *Lord, numb me. Please.*

He curved to the left over the tracks. To the north, gray smoke trailed along the rails in orderly puffs.

A locomotive coming their way. "Yellow flight, spread out."

The men knew what to do. Theo and his new wingman climbed to the right, while Adler led Floyd up to the left. The four P-51s would work the locomotive from opposite directions until the boiler blew, then strafe the train cars.

Floyd was too close on his tail. "Yellow two, spread out."

"No, sir. I'm your wingman."

The train sped closer and closer. This was just like the Westerns when young Floyd Milligan followed the hero into danger and got himself hurt or captured. "Don't chase me to the shootout, yellow two. Back off."

No sign of antiaircraft guns on the train, but they'd have to watch out for flak cars.

Adler lowered flaps and throttled back to lower his speed and lengthen the attack, then he dove in at a twenty-degree angle to the tracks. At three hundred yards, he squeezed the trigger.

The first shots passed in front of the locomotive, and Adler guided the bullets along the length of the engine, stitching a neat line.

Then he pulled up and away to the left.

Shock waves buffeted *Texas Eagle*. Adler fought for control, obtained it. In his rearview mirror, a tower of black smoke and debris shot into the sky.

"Hoo-ey!" He'd hit the boiler on the first run.

"I'm hit!" Floyd called on the radio.

"What?" Adler wheeled his plane around. Ahead of him, a Mustang flew with half its right wing gone.

Floyd! He must have followed Adler too closely and gotten hit by debris.

No time to chastise the kid. Too late anyway. "Yellow two, you're too low to bail. Belly her in. Yellow three, strafe the train. I'll stay with two."

"Roger," Theo said.

"Okay, Floyd, head southwest, away from the tracks. We'll find a field."

"Roger." His voice sounded steady. Good, he'd keep his head on his shoulders.

Adler circled above him, talking him through the procedure. Lower speed, lower flaps, jettison the canopy, keep the nose up.

A broad field opened before them. *Lord, let this be the one.*

Floyd let his Mustang down. The plane plowed a furrow, uprooting some crop or other.

Adler held his breath.

The plane stopped, and Floyd hopped out and sprinted away from the wreckage.

"Thank you, God." Adler took a picture with his gun camera, tipped a salute to Floyd, and aimed *Eagle* back toward the flaming locomotive. "Lord, keep the kid safe."

His rib cage hardened into place. Once again, someone he cared about had gotten hurt. Anyone who got close to him ended up destroyed in some way.

Good thing Violet had escaped when she had.

Still, the memory of the shock and disgust and misery on her face slapped his bruised soul.

Fury at himself simmered to the top. It was wrong of him to have enjoyed her love for as long as he had. He should have told her about Ellen before it all started.

He was selfish. Arrogant. So intent on his own pleasure that he ignored the good of the woman he claimed to love.

Adler raced down the tracks. Brilliant arcs of light sprang from the train cars through a whirling torrent of black smoke and yellow flame. Ammunition on board.

Dozens of figures in the field gray uniforms of the German army skittered away from the tracks.

Adler cried out, long and loud, and he dove for the train, riddling the cars with bullets.

As if that train were his own stinking, sinful old body. Laughing at him. Alive. "Die! Die! Why won't you die?"

LEISTON ARMY AIRFIELD
MONDAY, MAY 22, 1944

Violet stirred her potato soup, trying to tune out the lunchtime clamor of officers. If the pilots hadn't been flying a mission, she would have eaten a sandwich at the Aeroclub again.

Kitty leaned forward over the table. "You have to eat something."

Violet took a spoonful and swallowed. "There." But her stomach recoiled.

"Please tell me what he did to you." Kitty's eyebrows peaked in concern.

"It isn't like that. He just—he isn't the man for me." She jabbed at the soup as if it were solid. To think she'd planned a life with him. To think she'd almost tossed aside her lifelong dream for a first-rate heel.

She hadn't minded that his lips had kissed Oralee. That love had a purity about it. But they'd also kissed his brother's girlfriend— the night his fiancée *died*. He'd slept with her. How many other women had there been?

Kitty directed her gaze over Violet's head. "Violet?"

She tensed. *Please don't let it be Adler.* She never wanted to see him again.

"In case you're wondering, Adler isn't here." Not Adler's voice.

Violet relaxed and turned on the bench. "Hi, Nick."

He didn't smile. "This morning Doc Barker sent him to a rest home for a week. If I'd known what was in that letter, I never would have let him fly yesterday. He put himself in danger."

Violet forced a nod, not sure how to respond. Despite what she felt about Adler, she didn't want him to get hurt.

"He isn't well." Nick's dark gaze bored into her, as if drilling for a reaction. As if he . . .

"You don't blame me, do you?" She leaned closer and used a fierce whisper. "I didn't do all those things. He did."

Nick drew back, and his eyelids drooped. Not blame. Disappointment. "Luke 18," he said, and he left.

What? She really ought to have known that Scripture reference, but she didn't.

"What was that about?" Kitty asked.

"I don't know." Apparently Adler had told Nick about the letter, but why was Nick angry with her? Because she'd left Adler that night? He'd told her to leave.

She stared down into her bowl, and the beige lumpiness nauseated her. "I—I need to go for a walk."

"Of course, sweetie. I'm covering the club this afternoon, so take as long as you need."

"Thanks."

Once outside, she drew deep breaths of cool, clear spring air to replace the fetid cigarette smoke from the mess. But the squeamishness remained.

At least Adler was away for a week, so she was free to take a walk without seeing him.

Violet headed down the walkway. Maybe she could request a transfer to another Aeroclub before he returned.

She groaned. Not until she cleared her name in the theft case. If she failed, she'd be going home in a few weeks anyway.

"If it comes to that, you go home and hold your head high. You've done nothing wrong," Adler had told her, his expression tender but firm. "Soon as this war's over, I'm coming for you."

Her chest seized. Such a sweet memory, now polluted.

She passed the Aeroclub and paused. Luke 18. She could read it as she walked.

To avoid the crowd inside, she went down the side path. Where Adler had kissed her for the first time and then fled. What had he said? "Forgive me for taking advantage of your willingness"?

Violet stifled a cry. Was that what he'd done with that Ellen? Taken advantage of her willingness? He certainly had.

"First-rate heel indeed." She marched through the side door, grabbed her Bible, and headed back outside and to the north, away from the world of Nissen huts and cocky pilots. Looking up frequently to avoid colliding with men and bicycles and jeeps, she read Luke 18.

The parable of the judge and the widow, urging the disciples to pray tenaciously.

Did Nick mean she should pray for Adler? Once her anger subsided she would, but not yet.

She crossed a side street. Two men on bicycles hooted at her, but she ignored them, in no state to teasingly scold them.

Where was she? Verse 9. "And he spake this parable unto certain which trusted in themselves that they were righteous, and despised others."

Violet gasped and stopped in her tracks.

Someone bumped her from behind. "Pardon me, miss."

"That's all right." She stared at the verse. Was Nick saying she trusted her own righteousness and despised Adler? But this was the parable of the Pharisee and the tax collector praying in the temple. Nick was comparing her to a Pharisee?

Ridiculous. She marched forward. The Pharisees loved rules more than they loved the Lord. Jesus reserved his harshest criticisms for the Pharisees. "Woe unto you!" he'd said to them seven times in a row.

"Excuse me, miss." Three airmen edged past her on the walkway.

"I'm sorry." Perhaps she should find someplace more isolated. She turned between two buildings and ambled across a field.

The chapter was long. Nick must have meant a different section.

She skimmed the familiar parable, then read it again . . . for the first time.

"The Pharisee stood and prayed thus with himself, God, I thank thee, that I am not as other men are, extortioners, unjust, adulterers, or even as this publican. I fast twice in the week, I give tithes of all that I possess. And the publican, standing afar off, would not lift up so much as his eyes unto heaven, but smote upon his breast, saying, God be merciful to me a sinner."

Violet fought for breath. "Oh no. Lord, it *is* me."

How often had she looked down at the men for their drunkenness, profanity, and immorality? How often had she taken pride in her wholesome ways, her willingness to sacrifice to serve in Africa, even in England?

"Oh, Lord. Adler—he's the publican, the tax collector." With her free hand, she gripped her stomach. She'd seen him, facedown in the fallen leaves, crying out, "Forgive me! Forgive me!"

Gritting her teeth, she read verse 14. "I tell you, this man went down to his house justified rather than the other: for every one that exalteth himself shall be abased; and he that humbleth himself shall be exalted."

So similar to "the last shall be first, and the first last." Adler had humbled himself, as a wingman, as a leader, and before the Lord. And what had Violet done? Exalted herself.

Her eyes burned. "Oh no, Lord. What have I done?"

She wiped her eyes on her sleeve and charged forward in the grass and in the chapter. Was there more for her? The story of the disciples keeping the little children from Jesus? The least of her problems. The story of the rich young ruler? Definitely not a problem.

But verse 19 snagged her. "And Jesus said unto him, Why callest thou me good? none is good, save one, that is, God."

"Oh no. Oh no." Violet's head sagged low. That night she'd snapped at Adler, "I thought you were a good man."

Violet tripped and caught herself. A line of trees stood not ten feet away. The same place she'd followed Adler that night. Where she'd judged him and rejected him for not being good. Except no one was good but God. Not even Violet Lindstrom.

Especially not Violet Lindstrom.

She stepped into the grove, same as she had that evening, and she fell to her knees, same as she had that evening.

A sob gulped out. "I am—I'm a Pharisee. The seven woes are for me."

Where were they? The book of Matthew, toward the end. There—chapter 23.

She dove in, braking at verse 5. "But all their works they do for to be seen of men."

"That's me," she moaned, and she couldn't bear it. Wasn't that the real reason she wanted to be a missionary? The reason she'd come to England rather than volunteering quietly in Kansas? To be admired?

Each verse pummeled her. Then verse 12. "And whosoever shall exalt himself shall be abased; and he that shall humble himself shall be exalted." Again! God pounding it in her smug, self-righteous ears.

Then came the woes. "Woe unto you, scribes and Pharisees, hypocrites!"

Seven times Jesus pronounced woe upon the Pharisees, upon Violet. For caring more about rules than about showing people the way to the Lord. For caring more about the outward appearance of righteousness than about true inner righteousness of the heart.

"'Even so ye also outwardly appear righteous unto men, but within ye are full of hypocrisy and iniquity.'" Violet read verse 28 out loud, her voice broken and rough. "I'm a hypocrite. I am."

She collapsed over her knees. "Oh, Lord, I'm a sinner too." In her self-righteousness, she'd judged others for their sins, failing to see her own.

Because self-righteousness was indeed a sin. A vile sin.

"Forgive me. Forgive me, Lord. I'm a sinner. I'm a stinking, rotten, wretched sinner." Same as Adler. Worse than Adler.

At least Adler knew his actions were wrong. She'd seen her actions as right.

Instead of coming alongside him as a fellow sinner, she'd stood above him and looked down on him.

"Oh, Lord." A fresh wave of misery swamped her. "He needed me that night. He needed me."

Hadn't she said those very words as she'd run after him?

Instead, she'd failed him. When he needed compassion, she'd dished out condemnation.

He'd been broken, repentant, grieving before the Lord. She should have ignored his demand for her to leave and stayed with him, prayed over him, and shown him mercy.

He was so new to his faith. What if . . . ?

"Oh, Lord, no. Please no." Her fingers slipped over her damp face. "Please don't let my sin drive him away from you."

37

At Moulsford Manor, the war was set aside. Adler sat in a wicker chair on the lawn as half a dozen officers played croquet and another half dozen rowed on the Thames, splashing each other with their oars.

Behind him stood a four-hundred-year-old country house, all stately white with rosebushes and ivy, taken over by the Eighth Air Force as a rest home for airmen.

At Moulsford, civilian trousers and shirts and sweater vests were provided, with uniforms worn only at dinner. Rest, recreation, and plenty of good food let the men forget their worries.

"Captain Paxton, would you like more coffee?" Miss Flaherty, one of the American Red Cross hostesses, held a coffeepot. She wore a uniform like Violet's.

At least most of the men could forget their worries. Adler lifted his cup. "Yes, please, ma'am."

She topped off his cup, black curls fluttering in the breeze. "I'm surprised you aren't playing croquet."

Adler had spent two full days playing croquet and tennis and

259

rowing on the Thames. Two days of hard physical activity while his mind settled into new truths and new plans.

Now he was ready. He waved to the stationery on the table. "I've got letters to write."

Miss Flaherty nodded, gazing down to the Thames, not even thirty feet away.

Adler stared at the letter from his father on the table, wrinkled and soiled, with ink smeared in several spots. Violet's tears, most likely, and a new bolt of pain shot through him. It would take a long time to get over her.

Miss Flaherty shifted her feet in their Red Cross oxfords. "We don't host many fighter pilots here. Mostly bomber crewmen."

"Doesn't surprise me. They've got to fly in a straight line through the flak and fighters and take it. But we can fight back. That makes all the difference."

She looked down at him, the question all over her round face . . . *So why are you here?*

"Family problems." He gave a quick shake of his head to silence further questions.

"We have people here you can talk to."

"Thanks. I've done my share of talking. Now I need to get to writing." He picked up the pen.

Miss Flaherty took the hint and left.

Adler had told Nick everything, even let him read the letter. He'd told the chaplain everything. He'd prayed and prayed and prayed. No more putting this off.

Wyatt's letter would be the easiest.

Dear Wyatt,

There's only one way to start this letter—I'm sorry. I'm sorry I blamed you for Oralee's death, and I'm deeply sorry that I tried to kill you. Every day I thank the Lord that he used Clay to stop me.

The real reason I was angry was because you were right and I was wrong. You fought for Oralee, while I only fought to get my own way. Since I knew how you felt about her, I used that against you to avoid facing my grief and guilt. Deep inside I knew I was responsible for her death.

I understand why you ran away from me—although you didn't need to stay away for three years. You see, I ran away from home that night too. I don't know how much Daddy and Mama told you, but I worked in California for a year, then joined the Army Air Forces and became a P-51 pilot.

That last bit won't surprise you. I know you saw me in the park on Easter, because I saw you run away from me. Instead of chasing you and apologizing and taking my punishment, I ran in the opposite direction.

But I'm not running anymore.

Trying to kill your own brother seems unforgivable. You have every right not to trust me ever again. I can only tell you I regret what I did.

I'm also sorry for competing with you all my life, pushing you and trying to be first. God put me second for a reason, and he keeps putting me second. I've made peace with that, and I even embrace it.

Since we're on the same island, I'd like to meet with you if you're willing. I'll even let you take a couple of shots at me. I miss you more than I ever thought possible. Now I realize how much I've always loved my older brother and looked up to you.

Please know I'm praying for you, especially as things heat up over here.

Adler signed his name and looked up, blinking as a cloud scooted aside and revealed the sun. He addressed Wyatt's letter and pulled out more stationery. The letter to Clay would be the most painful.

Dear Clay,

I reckon you don't want to hear from me, but you deserve to know how sorry I am. This letter isn't for my sake, to lighten my load, but for your sake, so you know I recognize the sinfulness of my actions against you and how deeply I regret them.

First, I never thanked you for stopping me from killing Wyatt. You were brave and right, and you bore the brunt of my anger to save his life. For that, I'm eternally thankful. I had no right to get angry at you, and I apologize.

As for what I did in the garage, I take full responsibility. I refuse to blame my grief, the whiskey, or Ellen. I despise how I betrayed you, stole from you, took advantage of her, and gave in to my basest instincts.

I certainly don't blame you for trying to kill me. Many times I wished you'd succeeded. But even that wish was selfish, a way to avoid facing what I'd done.

Three months ago I came to terms with God, and now I'm taking responsibility for my sins and their consequences.

By now, you probably know I wrote home. A few days ago, I received Daddy's reply and learned the extent of those consequences. Timmy's birth. Ellen's death. So many lives altered, and it rips me up inside—as it should.

To cap it off, I left you and Daddy and Mama and Ellen to bear those consequences alone. I can't imagine what you've been through, Clay. You were there as the events unfolded, dealing with rumors and speculation while watching your former girlfriend bear your no-good brother's baby.

Even more pain heaped on your shoulders, and the thought sickens and grieves me. I was also sad to hear you didn't go to college. If I played any role, I apologize for that as well.

Daddy and Mama probably told you, but I ran away to

California, where I worked for a year before joining the Army Air Forces and becoming a P-51 pilot.

On my way overseas, I saw you on the troopship. As always, I ran. But no more. You have my address. I'm willing to face you in person or by letter and to take whatever you want to dish out.

I know the reason you're on this island. Please know that on that day, I'll be praying for you and doing my best to shoot up the enemy so he can't come near you.

Despite what I did that night, I've always loved you. I miss you and the friendship we enjoyed. One of my deepest regrets is destroying that forever. Knowing now what my sins have cost you, I won't insult you by asking your forgiveness.

But please take comfort in knowing your actions that night were right and honorable—and that your older brother respects and appreciates who you are and what you've done.

Adler groaned as he stuffed the letter into an envelope. Lousy attempt at an apology, but it was all he had.

He was squeezed out inside, but he had one more letter to write. Home.

Adler stood and stretched. In a way, the next letter would be the most difficult. But he'd write it for his parents' sake and for Timmy's.

He pulled the photo from his pocket. His throat contracted at the sight of the little boy perched on a stool. Chubby cheeks, laughing eyes, slicked blond hair with one wisp sticking up in back, pudgy hands resting on pudgy bare knees.

Cute as the dickens, indeed.

Adler walked beside the hedge, stretching his legs and his mind. "My son. My son."

Poor kid. His mama had died, just as Adler's mother had died. But Adler always had his daddy. Unlike Timmy. "Thank you, Lord, that my parents are raising him and loving him."

Beside him, the Thames flowed, slow and deliberate on its set course. Adler's future no longer had little tributaries of possible plans. Only one channel.

After the war, he'd go home and raise his son. The boy deserved to have a father, even one like him. And they'd live in Kerrville. Adler was a stranger to Timmy. How could he rip the child from the only people he knew and loved?

That meant Adler had to humble himself and live with shame and stigma and rumors. In that small town he'd always be the man who slept with his brother's girl and didn't do right by her. Now the beautiful daughter of the beloved town doctor was dead.

The people of Kerrville would always see Adler's new self as a veneer tacked on top of his old self. And he'd have to bear it.

As for his career, it was in Wyatt's hands. If Wyatt agreed, Adler would be thrilled to work under his older brother. He'd always wanted to work at Paxton Trucking, and he no longer minded second place.

If Wyatt didn't want to work with him, Adler would have to find other work. He couldn't start ACES in Kerrville—it would look as if he were trying to steal business from his family. But who would hire him?

Adler walked to the water's edge, his shoes sinking into the mud. He needed a job to support his son. Because he'd be raising him alone.

No decent woman in town would marry him, and it wouldn't be fair to drag an outsider into his shame. For half a second, he imagined Violet living in a community that would never fully accept her and that would always whisper about her husband.

He marched up the bank toward the table. *Thank you, God. Thank you for letting her leave. I love her too much to do that to her.*

Adler's chest caved in, and he braced himself on the chair. Violet would be the last woman he ever loved.

38

The hoedown was even better than Violet had hoped, but it required every bit of Red Cross training and God's strength to serve up a cheerful "Howdy, pardner" with each plate of baked beans and cornbread.

Adler was back at Leiston. And he was at the party.

She'd been shocked to see him helping wrestle hay bales from a truck into the theater building and even more shocked when he'd stayed for the party.

But wasn't it just like Adler to keep his commitment to help, despite how she'd treated him?

Around the building, children and airmen ate cowboy grub while perched on hay bales. The Buzz Boys had corralled banjo and harmonica players, and cowboy tunes frolicked in the air.

One of the men in the weather detachment was a square dance caller, and dozens of men and children promenaded and do-si-doed and swung their partners high and low.

Far across the room, Adler stood chatting with his friends, his back to Violet, of course, wearing his waist-length Ike jacket and khaki trousers.

The aching cold of separation and the knowledge that it was all her fault made her shudder.

"Hallo, Miss Lindstrom." Little Harry Blythe held out his plate.

"Howdy, Harry." Violet ladled a generous helping of beans onto his plate.

He grinned and straightened the red bandanna around his neck. Violet had told her mother about the party, and Mom had recruited the women of Salina to sew up hundreds of bandannas, enough for each child—and invitations had been sent to all the surrounding villages. They even had enough for the Red Cross staff and many of the Yoxford Boys.

No one followed Harry in line. Violet checked her watch. In a few minutes they'd show *Song of Texas*, a movie without Floyd Milligan in the cast.

If it were possible, Violet's heart sank even lower. She prayed Floyd was safe in a POW camp. There were horrible rumors that German civilians were now encouraged to lynch downed pilots who had strafed civilian trains. The Americans had strafed military trains, but would the Germans care?

Jimmy Haywood stood before her—again.

She gave him a teasing smile. "More, pardner?"

"Yes, ma'am. My mum said someone nicked half the bacon for the beans, but they taste mighty fine to this here cowboy."

"Thank you." No matter what she did, the thefts continued. And this past week, she'd been too distraught to pay attention to the situation.

The hoedown would be her last hurrah. In two weeks, she and Kitty and all these ladies would be out of work. If nothing had changed in one week, Violet and Kitty had decided to inform the women so they could look for new jobs.

She had no idea where Mr. Tate would find new workers, considering how they'd scoured the area for the current staff.

"Miss Lindstrom?" Jimmy frowned at her.

"I'm sorry." She served a large portion of beans and cornbread. "You must be going through a growth spurt."

"This isn't for me. My mum said I mustn't be greedy. This is for Captain Paxton."

Like a punch to the gut, and Violet gripped the table.

Jimmy raced across the room to Adler and handed him the plate. From behind, Violet could see his cheek jut out in a smile.

Everything in her longed to run to him, blurt out her apologies, and beg his forgiveness, beg him to take her back. But he deserved an apology less public and far less melodramatic.

"Today, Lord," she murmured. "Please give me an opportunity."

Jimmy was talking, and Adler squatted in front of him, now angled so she could see his profile. He looked pale, and his smile looked as stiff as hers felt.

What must he have been through the past week? The stunning news from home, the loss of Floyd Miller, and Violet's self-righteous rejection. What a tremendous load to carry.

A tiny boy toddled up to Jimmy and tugged on his school jacket. Jimmy gave him a soft elbow, probably shooing away an annoying cousin or neighbor.

But Adler turned to the youngster and mouthed, "Howdy." Violet could practically hear him over the music and laughter and stomping feet.

Jimmy kept talking, probably explaining away the little blond boy, all of two or three.

Adler's face changed. He wasn't talking, wasn't smiling, wasn't looking at Jimmy. Only at the towheaded child.

So much like little Timothy, and Violet gasped.

The plate of cornbread and beans—Adler set it on the ground, never taking his intense gaze off the tot. Then his face buckled, and he clutched the child in a fierce embrace.

Violet clapped her hand over her mouth. Only God was good,

but Adler Paxton was the best sort of man and she loved him more than ever.

The music stopped, the dancers applauded, and the room silenced.

Adler released the child and gave him an off-kilter grin. "That's how we say howdy in Texas."

The little one giggled and hugged Jimmy's legs hard, making the older boy laugh.

Adler tipped the boys a salute and strode for the exit, leaving his plate of cornbread and beans on the floor.

Now! Violet had to catch him now.

"Come along, cowboys and cowgirls," the square dance caller said. "We've got a mighty special treat for y'all today—Roy Rogers himself on the silver screen in *Song of Texas*."

Yes, now! With the movie playing, Violet had no duties for almost an hour.

She tossed dish towels over the food and dashed after Adler. *Lord, let this be the last time I have to chase this man.*

Once outside, she blinked in the bright sunshine. Adler trudged down the walkway, his shoulders rounded, his hands in his trouser pockets.

Violet came up behind him. "Adler?"

He jerked up straight and sucked in a loud breath. Then he slowly turned to her, lowering his head and not meeting her gaze. "Go ahead. Let me have it. I know—I should have told you everything from the start. I'm sorry about that. Sorry I put you through all this."

Oh no. He thought she was angry at him. "No, no. You tried to tell me. You tried, and I wouldn't let you."

"That's no excuse."

The street in the communal site was deserted—everyone was on duty or at the hoedown—but Violet still needed to avoid melodrama. She drew in a slow breath. "I didn't come to demand an apology but to give one."

"You?" Blue eyes flicked up to her, then away. "You have nothing to apologize for."

"I do." Her hands waved in ridiculous little circles, so she gripped them together. "I need to apologize for my self-righteousness, for looking down on you and judging you."

He ground a dirt clod into the cement with his toe. "You had good reason."

"No. No, I didn't." A lump clogged her throat. "Those sins are in your past. They aren't who you are today. Who am I to condemn you when God's forgiven you?"

Adler raised one hand before his downturned face. "It's all right. I understand."

"No, it's not all right." Her voice hopped over the lump. "I looked down on your sins, when I didn't even recognize my own. Self-righteousness is a sin, a horrible sin, because you hold yourself above others. I—I'm a wretched, lowdown sinner. I had no right—"

"Stop." He knifed his hand across the air between them. "Don't do this."

"But I need to. I failed you. You'd received devastating news, and I rejected you. You needed compassion, and I judged you. You needed comfort, and I abandoned you. Please, please forgive me."

The bill of Adler's cap concealed his expression, but not the tensing and releasing and tensing of his neck muscles.

Violet held back her breath and her tears, begging God for the same mercy she'd withheld.

Adler sighed, glanced up to her and away, and clasped his hand to the back of his neck. "Honestly, there's nothing to forgive. But thank you. I do forgive you."

"Oh, thank you." She edged one foot toward him, longing to embrace him, to be embraced.

He stepped back and tilted his chin down the road. "I ought to mosey. Thanks again."

Watching his retreating back, Violet wrapped her empty arms around her stomach. Adler had forgiven her, but she'd lost his love.

What was it his father had said in that letter? Even when our sins are forgiven by God and man, consequences remain?

It applied to her too. Somehow she'd have to bear it.

39

Tony Rosario flung his arms across the wing of the Mustang and kissed it. "Leave him, baby, and come to me. I'll treat you right. Custom paint job, extra-rich fuel, and all the spark plugs your heart desires."

Adler laughed along with his friends. "She belongs to Tommy Hayes, and there's nothing you can do about it."

Rosie stood, his fingertips splayed on the wing edge. "Ain't fair, I tell you. She's the most beautiful thing I've ever seen."

"Is that so?" Nick said. "Don't let Rosalind hear you talking that way."

A sheepish smile, and Rosie tucked his hands in his pockets.

But Adler knew how he felt. The day before, the 357th Fighter Group had received its first and only P-51D model, and every pilot salivated over her.

Even sleeker than the B model, she boasted a bubble canopy, giving the pilot unrestricted vision all around and above. She had six machine guns instead of four, with the ammunition belt feed straightened to eliminate the jamming problem.

"More are coming," Nick said. "Be patient."

Theo Christopher ran his hand down a propeller blade. "Guess we old veterans will get first crack at them."

Luis Camacho slapped Theo on the back. "Never thought I'd see the day when we'd call you old."

Not old, but the war had made a man out of him, especially since Willard Riggs died.

Theo stepped back with a far-off look. "Less than four months of combat, and look at us."

"Yeah." Adler led the way to squadron headquarters. They'd been through a lot together. Dozens of the Yoxford Boys had been lost in combat, some killed and some captured, with Stan Mulroney, Morty Shapiro, Riggs, and Floyd Miller shot down in Adler's section. One bright spot in May was the return of Chuck Yeager to Leiston. With help from the French Resistance, the pilot had evaded capture and sneaked over the Pyrenees into neutral Spain.

"Hey, what happened to *El Mesteño*?" Cam pointed over to his hardstand.

Adler stared at Cam's P-51, which wore black-and-white stripes. "That's not a horse. That's a zebra."

The men jogged over, and the smell of fresh paint hit Adler's nostrils. Wide bands of black and white circled each wing and the fuselage between the canopy and the tail.

"What is this? A practical joke?" Cam marched around his bird, but his ground crew wasn't present.

Across the perimeter track Bill Beckenbauer knelt on *Texas Eagle*'s wing with a paint can beside him, and José Flores swiped black paint up and down the fuselage.

"My plane too, boys." Adler strode over to his hardstand. "What's up, Beck?"

"Painting." He didn't even look up.

"I can see that."

"Good. Sharp eyesight is vital for a fighter pilot."

"Beck."

The crew chief gave him a grin. "You know as much as I do, kid. We received orders to paint stripes, so I'm painting stripes. I'm sure you can figure out why."

Adler and Nick and Theo and Cam and Rosie looked at one another.

"Recognition," Nick said.

Cam fingered the taped muzzle of one of *Eagle*'s machine guns. "So our own men don't shoot us down."

"Those sailor boys are trigger happy." Rosie mimed firing a gun into the air.

D-day. Adler stroked the red-and-yellow checkered nose of his steed. "Tomorrow."

"If not tomorrow," Theo said, "soon."

Everyone knew it was coming. Late in May, the Eighth Air Force had issued an order for officers to carry pistols and enlisted men to carry carbines at all times. Some thought the Nazis might respond to the invasion by dropping paratroopers in England.

Now D-day was here.

What would the day hold? Adler kept stroking the plane's nose as if soothing a jittery horse. The Allies had achieved air superiority at last, and the RAF and US Eighth and Ninth Air Forces had pounded Luftwaffe airfields, but would it be enough? Once the Germans knew the invasion was happening, they'd chuck every plane in their arsenal into the battle.

They would strafe Allied troops and bomb Allied ships.

Not if Adler could help it.

Cam pointed with his thumb toward the communal site. "Looks like we'll have a busy day tomorrow. I'm going to grab lunch and take a nap."

"Sounds good to me," Rosie said, and he and Theo followed Cam.

Adler's hand drifted down over the artwork on the nose of the eagle with the US flag and the Texas flag on its wings.

The violet in its grasp.

His neck muscles tightened. Maybe he'd ask Beck and Flores to paint over the purple flower while they were at it.

But that seemed spiteful. And incorrect. Violet still held his heart.

"She hasn't forgiven you, huh?" Nick's voice was soft.

Yet it hit Adler hard. "No, she has."

"Have you forgiven her?"

Adler grunted. "Nothing to forgive. She apologized, so I told her I forgave her. But I never blamed her for reacting like that."

"Adler . . ." Amazing how well the man could scold.

"I'm not beating myself up. I'm just saying it was a lot for her to swallow all at once, and a nasty mouthful at that. You have to admit."

One corner of Nick's mouth puckered. "Think you'll get back together?"

Adler shook his head hard. "I have nothing to offer her. Poor job prospects, another woman's child to raise, and I'll be an outcast in town."

Nick's dark eyes narrowed in that thoughtful way of his. "Not many women would be willing to take that on."

"Nope." And he wouldn't ask her to. She deserved better.

"Well, you're willing to take it on." Nick gave Adler's arm a light punch. "I'm proud of you."

"For my son. For Timmy."

"You're going to be a great dad."

Beck sat on the wing, his legs dangling. "Seen the picture of his boy? Don't know how a man with that ugly mug can have such a cute kid."

Adler laughed. He hadn't told many of the men yet, but the more he talked about Timmy, the more real he seemed. "Still can't believe I'm a father. I can't wait to meet him."

Beck swung his feet. "Just wait. Kids have a way of grabbing you and not letting go."

Adler leaned his shoulder against the fuselage. "Did I tell you

I'm writing him letters? I sent that picture you took of *Eagle* and me after I got my fourth victory. Figured he needs more than my high school graduation picture."

Beck ran his hand over the four swastikas under the cockpit. "We'll take another picture when you make ace."

"Any day now," Nick said.

Adler shrugged. All that mattered to him now was doing his job well.

Nick crossed his arms. "I'm sure it means a lot to him to know his daddy loves him."

All he had was one small photo. "How can I love him already?"

Beck and Nick laughed together, two fathers welcoming a third into their fraternity.

Adler tried to imagine this little person who looked like him. What did his voice sound like? His laugh?

It would just be the two of them after the war. And Daddy and Mama. Things would be strained at first, but his parents would welcome him. Not just because of Timmy, but because of who they were.

With Daddy, Mama, and Jesus in his corner, Adler could handle anything.

Violet fanned the magazines into an attractive arc on the table in the Aeroclub lounge, but what did it matter? Mr. Tate was due to arrive at one o'clock, any minute now.

He'd review the logs and pronounce judgment. One more week, maybe two, but their fates were sealed. The thefts continued, random and sporadic, and Violet had no idea who the thief could be. For all she knew, there could be several.

Adler's suggestions to plug the holes—Violet winced at the memory of the day they'd made those plans—his suggestions had helped, but supplies still disappeared.

Today after Mr. Tate left, Kitty and Violet would tell the staff so they could look for new jobs.

Violet forced in a deep breath against the heaviness in her chest and found a smile for the four airmen chatting in the lounge. For far too long, she hadn't wanted to be at this place. Now she didn't want to leave.

She crossed the hall to the music room with its sunny yellow paint and the memory of Adler rediscovering his love for the trumpet and his need for family.

To keep busy, Violet stacked sheet music and set it on the shelf. Adler was right not to take her back. Forgiving someone and trusting that person again were two separate things.

But it still ached. Accepting your fate and being content with it were also two separate things.

The public address system blared in the dining area. Violet tried to head that direction, but all the men came out of the recreation rooms and clogged the hallway.

"What did they say?" someone asked.

"Excuse me, please." Violet weaved through the crowd and into the dining area.

Kitty almost ran into her. "Now we know why Tate isn't here."

"I couldn't hear. What happened?"

"They closed the base. No one can enter. We have a reprieve." Kitty wrinkled her nose. "But it also means no one can leave—not even the civilian workers."

"Our girls . . ."

A dozen workers and volunteers streamed toward them, concern on each face.

"We can't go home?" Sylvia clutched her apron. "My children need me."

"They can't keep us here." Mabel Smith's eyes flashed. "We're British subjects."

Edna Foster groaned and lowered her head into her hands. "My husband. I can't spend the night here. What'll he think?"

"I need to ring my mum." Young Ann Brewer twisted a towel in her hands.

"Everything will be all right." Kitty held up her hands. "I'm afraid you can't go home, and phone calls and messages are forbidden, but we'll take care of you."

Plans spun into Violet's head. The dorm room had never been used, since Violet and Kitty had never persuaded any of the touring shows to veer so far from London. "The dorm room sleeps eight. We'll get cots for the rest of you."

Rosalind hugged Edna's shoulders. "We can sleep tops to tails if need be. Everything will be tickety-boo."

"It sure will." Kitty grinned at the ladies. "It'll be fun. A pajama party."

"Without pajamas, but we'll carry on." Sylvia smoothed her apron. "You heard the gent—they'll let us eat at the mess and buy soap at the PX. Won't that be lovely?"

"Does the PX have . . . ?" Ann stepped right up to Violet and Kitty, her face crimson, her voice a whisper. "Do they sell . . . it's my . . . my time."

The poor girl. Violet patted her shoulder. "No, they don't," she whispered back. "But Miss Kelly and I have plenty. Our mothers mail the supplies to us. You can tell your friends."

"Looks like we have extra duties today." Kitty tapped Violet's arm. "I'll scrape up more cots and bedding. Why don't you take the ladies to the PX?"

"In shifts." They still had to staff the Aeroclub. "Did they say why the base is closed? Security has been tight lately, but—"

"Not a word. Something big is happening." Kitty held Violet's gaze, her brown eyes solemn and knowing.

Something so big they couldn't let one word leak to the outside. Violet swallowed hard. "I think we might be very busy tomorrow."

40

Luis Camacho showed his ID card to the MP at the entrance to the group briefing room. "Did you hear what OBee said this afternoon?"

"No, what?" Adler showed his card and put on a cheerful face for Doc Barker, the group flight surgeon, who eyed him closely. This was no day to be pulled for signs of combat fatigue.

Cam slipped his wallet into his back pocket. "When he landed, someone told him we had a briefing at eleven o'clock. He said, 'We get to sleep in.'"

Adler laughed with the rest of the men. He didn't blame William O'Brien for the error. Who would have expected a briefing at eleven o'clock at night?

In the back of the Nissen hut, he and his friends gathered by a window with its blackout curtains drawn. Nick stood in the front of the room, chatting with the two other squadron commanders.

"A night mission. We've never done that before." Adler inspected the dozens of men in the smoke-filled room. How many were good at flying on instruments?

"This is it, I know it," Rosie said.

"Me too," Cam said. "If we're going to invade, we'll do so at first light. They'll need fighters overhead."

Which meant taking off at night. Which also meant the ships were already streaming across the Channel.

Without a doubt, Clay was on one of those ships. The Rangers were commandos trained for special assaults like this. Was Wyatt at sea, or was he a staff officer safely in London?

Maybe Wyatt and Clay had been able to meet. They had nothing to keep them apart and mutual betrayal by Adler to unite them.

Adler huffed out a breath. He'd repented of his sins and apologized to both brothers. He refused to let shame weigh him down.

"Let's grab seats." He led the men down the aisle of the Nissen hut, and they sat in the second row of folding wooden chairs. The curtain was still drawn over the map on the arched wall at the end of the room. Wooden aircraft models hung from the ceiling, but Adler had the silhouettes memorized by now.

"Attention!" someone shouted from the back of the room.

Adler shot to his feet with the rest of the pilots.

The group commanding officer, Col. Donald Graham, strode down the aisle. Only a year older than Adler, but Graham had done a fine job.

"Be seated, please, gentlemen."

Adler sat, crossing his ankle over his knee. Silence hovered in the room, tense and eager.

Graham held a brown envelope, his expression serious. "Under the command of General Eisenhower, Allied naval forces, supported by strong air forces, will begin landing Allied armies this morning on the northern coast of France."

The tension exploded into murmurs. Adler glanced at Rosie and nodded. They'd guessed, and deep inside they'd known—but now it became real.

"Normandy." As the curtain was opened, Graham pointed to the map, decorated with more blue and red ribbons than ever. "Our troops will land on five beaches between Cherbourg and Le Havre. Even now our paratroopers are about to set foot on French soil."

Normandy? Adler leaned forward over his knees. Everyone expected the invasion in the Pas de Calais region where the Channel was narrowest.

Graham's pointer slid from the Isle of Wight on England's southern coast down to Normandy. "This is the shipping area. P-38 Lightnings will cover the fleet."

That made sense. The Lightning's distinctive twin-boomed profile would be easy for naval gunners to recognize.

"RAF Spitfires will provide low cover over the landing beaches, with the P-47s and P-51s of the Ninth Air Force providing high cover. Heavy and medium bombers will drop their loads on the beaches right before the first wave of troops reaches shore."

He traced the blue ribbon's U-shaped pattern for the bombers' course, south to Normandy, west over the Cherbourg peninsula past the Channel Islands, then north to England.

"The P-47s and P-51s of the Eighth Air Force will patrol this area." Graham traced a larger semicircle outside the bombers' path. "P-47s to the east, P-51s to the west."

He tapped a red rectangular box just west of Guernsey assigned to the 357th Fighter Group. Two squadrons would patrol from 0425 to 0830, covering the time of the first landings, and the third squadron would arrive later to relieve them.

If Luftwaffe opposition was heavy, in the afternoon the 357th would escort heavy bomber missions. If not, the P-51s would fly dive-bombing and strafing missions behind the invasion beaches to halt German reinforcements.

"The role of the fighters is to maintain control of the air over the critical area, to isolate the battlefield, and to support the ground troops."

Adler studied the blackboards at the front of the room with takeoff times, wind information, checkpoints, and call signs, and he wrote the most important information on the back of his left hand.

The group intelligence officer, Maj. Alfred Craven, took the floor. Everyone expected heavy opposition by the Luftwaffe. With eleven thousand Allied planes in the air, the Germans would put out maximum effort. Craven also pointed out areas where flak was expected.

Then the station weather officer, Capt. Leo Miller, took his turn. No good news. Rain on takeoff and heavy overcast all the way.

Not one man grumbled. The soldiers and sailors were already out in that weather, and they needed air cover. Adler would fly in a blizzard today if he had to.

Graham returned to the front. After he had the men synchronize their watches, he encouraged them to turn in and then dismissed them.

Turn in? With takeoff at 0215, a squadron briefing before that, and the excitement of the pending missions, who could sleep?

Nick reached over the row of chairs and clasped Adler's hand. "I'm glad you'll be up there with me, buddy."

"Me too." Adler's throat thickened, and he shook Nick's hand hard. "You take care now, you hear?"

"You too."

What would Adler have done without Nick's friendship? *Lord, keep him safe.*

Why was it that the more Violet needed to sleep, the less she was able to do so?

She rolled over again on the cot in the chilly hallway. She and Kitty had given their room to four of the civilian workers and volunteers. Maybe their presence guarding the door to both bedrooms would reassure anxious parents and jealous husbands.

Violet folded the sheet over the top of the scratchy gray Army blanket and burrowed deeper under the covers. How late was it anyway? It had to be going on two o'clock. With a busy day ahead, she needed her sleep, but how could she with the constant drone of planes—and the knowledge of what that sound probably meant?

"You can't sleep either?" Kitty whispered.

"No." Violet flopped onto her back.

"Worried about Adler?"

She hadn't heard his name for several days, and it hurt. "All the men, really." If the Luftwaffe fought hard on most days, what would they do on D-day?

"You still love him, don't you?"

Violet squeezed her eyes shut against the pain of voicing the truth. "Very much."

For over two weeks, Violet had been enigmatic about what had happened with Adler, but something about the darkness, the fatigue, and the magnitude of the day loosened her tongue. "It isn't his fault. It's mine."

"What do you mean?"

She chose her words with care. "A few years ago, he did something bad. I never knew about it. That day in the office—he received a letter. He found out people were . . . hurt because of what he did. He showed me the letter."

"And you—"

"I was awful, Kitty. Just awful." She pressed the back of her hand to her forehead. "I judged him, as if I were better than he is, which I'm not—not in the least. And I rejected him and abandoned him when he needed me most. At the hoedown I apologized and he forgave me, but . . ." Her throat muscles strangled her vocal cords.

Kitty murmured in sympathy.

Violet sniffed and hauled in a breath. "He doesn't want me back."

"I'm sorry."

"Me too." If only God had chosen another way to teach her

humility and compassion, but she hadn't learned from her earlier lessons, had she?

"Look on the bright side." Kitty sounded chipper. "In about a week, you'll get to escape all this and go home."

Something about that struck Violet as ridiculously funny, and a wet giggle bubbled up. And another.

Kitty joined in.

Oh no, they were going to wake the ladies! Violet rolled over and buried her laughter in her pillow.

Muffled sounds down the hallway told her Kitty was doing the same.

In a few minutes they stilled. Violet turned onto her side, with a strange sense of cleansing and refreshment. Yes, she'd go home to an unknown future, but she'd go home a changed woman. Surely, God could find a use for her now that she had a proper view of herself and others.

"Do the planes sound different?" Kitty whispered.

They did. Louder and throatier and closer. "I want to see."

"Me too."

Violet flung off the covers, dug her feet into her oxfords, and pulled on the wool overcoat she'd draped over her cot in case she needed to use the latrine in the middle of the night.

She and Kitty headed out the side door into the cool night. Raindrops hit Violet's head, but only a drizzle.

Overhead, aircraft engines droned. RAF bombers passed over Leiston more nights than not, but this was much louder.

Violet shielded her eyes. In the inkiness above, lights flashed, muted by the overcast. "I think they're signaling each other."

"There must be hundreds. Thousands. We must have put up anything that can fly." Kitty pressed her shoulder to Violet's arm.

In the dark and the rain, Violet watched history fly above her. *Lord, give them strength and courage and victory.*

The throatier, more distinct sound that had drawn them outside

. . . it came from ground level. From the runways at Leiston. "Our boys," Violet said.

"They've never taken off at night before, have they?"

"Not that I know of." A faint green and red glow rose from that direction, the source blocked by the buildings. They must have broken the blackout to illuminate the runways for the pilots.

"It's today," Kitty murmured.

"Today."

Kitty dropped to her knees on the walkway, pulled out rosary beads, and crossed herself. *"In nómine Patris, et Fílii, et Spíritus Sancti. Amen."*

Violet didn't know the rosary, and she'd forgotten most of her high school Latin, but the ancient prayer sank into her soul, the repetitive urgency feeling right.

"Pater noster, qui es in cælis."

Violet dropped to her knees too, the concrete cold and rough and damp through the fabric of her pajamas. "Our Father which art in heaven."

Kitty peeked at Violet.

Violet dipped her head, motioning her friend back to her rosary. *"Pater noster, qui es in cælis, sanctificétur nomen tuum."*

"Our Father which art in heaven, hallowed be thy name."

"Advéniat regnum tuum. Fiat volúntas tua, sicut in cælo, et in terra."

"Thy kingdom come. Thy will be done in earth, as it is in heaven."

Violet linked arms with Kitty, linked prayers with her. Tens of thousands of men, maybe hundreds of thousands, were flying and sailing and marching into battle. They could use every prayer they could get.

41

Low on the center cockpit console, Adler flipped the fuel selector control from the left drop tank to the right. On long flights, he had to conserve fuel. First he'd drained the auxiliary tank behind his seat since it threw off the plane's center of gravity. Now he was draining the drop tanks, and soon he'd switch to the main tanks.

Not much else to do. Morning twilight brightened the wooly layer of clouds below him, chasing away the moon that had kept him company since takeoff.

His only company. Adler scanned the purple-gray sky, but not one airplane came into view, friendly or hostile. After taking off in the rain, the 357th had climbed through thick clouds in the dark with only puny wing navigation lights to guide them. Adler had lost his entire group.

Some leader he was without a single follower.

He pictured little Timothy sitting on his lap . . . "What did you do on D-day, Daddy?"

"Me?" Adler put on his deepest daddy voice. "Just stooged around all alone above the clouds all day."

He checked his watch—0545, and he tilted *Texas Eagle* into

another left-hand turn, patrolling in a rectangle somewhere over the Channel or France or South America, for all he knew. Flying by time and compass heading, with no visual landmarks, was an imprecise science.

He'd been stooging around for over two hours, and he had almost three more hours to go.

Deadly dull. If he weren't careful, dull could indeed become deadly. Letting his mind wander and lowering his guard were dangerous temptations.

Practicing the trumpet fingering for "Las Mañanitas" on the control stick kept his mind from straying toward Violet or Timmy or anything personal. He needed to stay alert for the sake of the soldiers and sailors eight thousand feet below.

"Here I am, gallant fighter pilot, singlehandedly fending off the Luftwaffe."

Where was the Luftwaffe anyway? The paratroopers had landed, the heavy bombers had started bombing at 0530, the naval bombardment was supposed to start at 0550, and the landings were scheduled in the American sector at 0630.

Surely the Germans had figured it out by now.

The sun cast a pink glow from below the horizon, enough to allow Adler to turn off the little fluorescent cockpit lights that shone on his instruments and gunsight.

He patted the gunsight. "Sorry to disappoint you, darlin'." He hated to return to Leiston with his muzzles still taped, but he had nothing to shoot.

The clock read 0555, and he made another turn. Ahead of him, the clouds thinned.

"Swell." He headed for that thinning. Maybe he could see something on the ground and get his bearings.

He got his bearings all right.

Framed by the ragged hole in the clouds, the gray ocean below teemed with ships. A big fat battleship aimed its guns to the south, and brown smoke belched out. Smaller warships heaved shells in the same direction—right over dozens of tiny landing craft. Everything aimed for the golden stretch of beach dividing gray sea and green land.

"Wow." Was Wyatt on one of those warships? Was Clay on one of those landing craft?

"Here I am, flying in circles, doing nothing." If only he could help down there. His hand tightened around the stick, longing to tilt it forward and strafe behind the beaches.

But that wasn't the plan, and that wasn't his job. He was supposed to keep the Luftwaffe at bay.

And not in this region.

Far, far from this region.

His face went cold and tingled. Anywhere but here. *Texas Eagle* looked nothing like a twin-boomed P-38 Lightning. Even with black-and-white invasion stripes, he could still be mistaken for a Messerschmitt.

Adler wheeled up above the protective layer of clouds.

The vision of that great armada didn't leave his mind. "Lord, protect those men. Protect my brothers."

LEISTON ARMY AIRFIELD

The Aeroclub kitchen had never been so busy. Sylvia fed dough into the donut-making machine, while Edna and Mabel brewed giant vats of coffee, and three ladies ran a sandwich-making assembly line.

"Great job, ladies." Kitty patted Mabel's shoulder. "We're doing our bit today, throwing coffee in Hitler's face."

Violet arranged rows of Spam sandwiches in a wire tray. In a way, that's exactly what they were doing—pouring coffee down the pilots' throats so they could fight Hitler.

She and Kitty were dressed for today's battle, wearing their new gray-blue trousers.

Violet swigged some coffee. Not a wink of sleep last night, but the airmen and sailors and soldiers probably hadn't slept either.

It was official. Just past nine thirty, the BBC had read General Eisenhower's announcement that British, Canadian, and American troops were landing in northern France.

The side door opened, admitting a swirl of cool air and Cpl. Tom Griffith. He gestured toward the airfield. "The first wave is returning. Mrs. Weaver says she needs more sandwiches in her squadron pilots' room. Lots more."

"Oh dear." Violet frowned at her tray. "This batch is spoken for. It'll be a while."

Griff flicked his chin toward the assembly line. "Say, why don't you send bread and Spam and a knife? Mrs. Weaver can make the sandwiches there. Word is, the men are taking off again as soon as they finish interrogation."

"That's a great idea." She gathered two loaves of bread and several tins of Spam, and she marked them off in the log. The log felt burdensome today, but she'd do her job to the end.

After she and Griff loaded both jeeps, Violet drove toward the runways. A few P-51s circled over the field, descending for landing, their colorful noses bright against the gray sky. At least the rain had stopped.

Not many men were out and about, and they didn't meander and chat as usual. They strode with purpose.

Checking for traffic, Violet turned onto the perimeter track toward Adler's squadron headquarters. If only she could have switched squadrons with Griff, but that would have been childish.

In the week since the hoedown, she'd only seen Adler a few times from afar in the mess. Maybe she could finish before he returned. Two of the squadrons, including Adler's, had departed around two o'clock, and the third around five o'clock.

That meant the first wave had been flying for over seven hours, surely a record. They'd be very hungry and thirsty. Adler had far more important things to think about today than her, so she'd be mature and kind if she saw him.

But she still hoped she wouldn't.

Violet pulled the jeep alongside the Nissen hut and carried in a tray of donuts. Only two pilots, plus staff officers. No Adler, thank goodness.

"Would you like some help?" one of the staff officers, Lieutenant Fenelli, asked.

"Yes, please." She set down the donuts and gave him the most sincere smile she'd felt in days. With help, she could escape even sooner.

While Lieutenant Fenelli hauled in the urn of coffee, Violet set the box of smaller items on top of the sandwich tray and carried it inside.

At the refreshment table, Adler stood, picking out a donut.

Violet stopped in her tracks, her heart straining. His hair was tousled from the flight helmet, and his scarf hung loosely over his flight jacket. How she missed him—his smile, his voice, his love.

Lieutenant Fenelli set down the urn. "Here you go, Paxton."

"Swell. Thanks." Adler filled a cup. "Can't tell you how much I need this."

He'd want sugar, and Violet was carrying it. In fact, he searched the table.

Duty overrode her heartache.

Violet set down the tray, and she poured sugar from the box into a bowl and scooted it toward him. "Here's the sugar, Captain."

Mature. Professional. She dragged her gaze up to him.

He met it, and her heart seized.

In the gorgeous blue of his gaze lay all the chivalry she'd always admired in him, but none of the affection she'd cherished.

"Thanks." He spooned sugar into his coffee and lifted the mug to her. "Appreciate it."

Then he joined Lieutenant Fenelli at a table.

"Excuse me, Miss Lindstrom." Theo Christopher stepped in front of her. "May I have a sandwich?"

Violet's hands clutched the tray. She let go and handed him a sandwich. "Of course, Lieutenant. I hope you like Spam. We'll have egg sandwiches later."

A grin spread over his weary face. "At this point, I'd eat mutton and like it. Thank you."

"You're welcome." She busied herself setting up the table properly, despite quivering hands and jumbled emotions.

How selfish to dwell for even one minute on her own heartbreak in light of what these men were enduring. For their sake, she'd hold herself together.

42

From right below the clouds, Adler followed the north-south course of the Mayenne River, matching landmarks to the reconnaissance photos he'd seen at the briefing and to the map on his lap.

Nick had let him lead the section of eight Mustangs on the squadron's second mission, and Adler didn't take the responsibility lightly. Since the Yoxford Boys hadn't spotted a single enemy aircraft during the early-morning patrols, the fighters had been dispatched in groups of eight to bomb and strafe tactical targets one hundred miles south of the beaches.

Adler aimed across a green field, cutting off a hairpin bend in the river, and he checked his watch. Right on schedule—1138.

A few miles ahead lay the town of Château-Gontier and its bridge, soon to be targeted by the two 250-pound general-purpose bombs hanging under his wings where the drop tanks usually hung.

Adler waggled his wings to signal his section. On the armament switch panel to his left, he checked that the safety switch was still set to "safe," then he shifted the bomb control handle from "locked" to "selective." He flipped switches to arm the bombs' nose and tail fuzes and made sure his gunsight was on.

"Here we go." Adler pushed the stick forward until *Eagle* went into a sixty-degree dive, lined up the bridge in his gunsight, and flipped the safety switch to "ready."

The rest of the P-51s trailed behind him single file.

With his speed climbing, he eyed the altimeter and the bridge and the river, rising before him between creamy slate-roofed buildings.

"Now." He pressed the red button on top of the control stick, and the two bombs plummeted from beneath his wings.

Adler pulled up and to the left, and now his stomach did the plummeting.

No sounds of ground fire, thank goodness, but the "tail-end Charlies" at the end of the formation took the greatest risk as German antiaircraft gunners got their bearings.

About a mile outside of town, Adler turned north. Seven P-51s fell back into formation. Hadn't lost anyone. Good. He had one complete rookie and two pilots with only a few missions under their belts.

Now that they'd unloaded their bombs, they were free to strafe as long as fuel and ammunition allowed. Adler had no desire to hurry back to Leiston.

The pilots' room. Violet. Staring at him with wide, devastated, questioning eyes, as if she wanted to talk to him. As if she wanted him back.

Adler groaned. Why would she want that? Didn't she know what was good for her?

Railroad tracks lay a few miles north. If they couldn't find trains, they could at least shoot up some track.

He had no idea how the invasion was going. After the first mission, he'd been interrogated, briefed for the second mission, and shuttled back to the hardstand. Takeoff took place less than an hour after landing. Beck and Flores and Moskowitz had done an incredible job preparing *Eagle*.

No war news. Just told to get back over the Channel and help.

So he was helping.

An artificially straight line slashed through the patchwork terrain, and Adler dove toward the railroad tracks. His men spread out behind him.

Now to find targets of opportunity. A train would be best, but he didn't see any telltale smoke.

A junction—say, not bad. With *Eagle* in a shallow dive, Adler pumped out bullets. If he could damage the switches or signaling equipment, that could delay German troop trains.

A siding, some train cars. He sprayed bullets, and debris flew off a car.

Adler gained altitude and swept the sky and his instruments. All looked good.

Where was the Luftwaffe?

Satisfaction swelled inside. All those costly and dangerous missions had earned air superiority for the Allies just when they needed it most.

Now he'd do everything he could to stop the Germans from sending reinforcements.

Adler followed the railroad tracks, strafing anything that caught his eye.

Maybe his brothers would forgive him one day. They were good men, kindhearted. For a second, he pictured the three of them in their Gringo Mariachi outfits, laughing and teasing and making music together.

But reality washed that image away. Even if they forgave him, there would always be a wedge between them, a cautious distance. They would never be close again.

His chest tightened. He wanted his family back the way it had been, but it could never be.

Adler spat bullets into another railroad switch.

Was it greedy to want more than forgiveness? Because he did. He wanted to sit down with his brothers and answer their questions and listen to their experiences, no matter how painful it might be. He wanted reconciliation.

Forgiveness without reconciliation would be like barbecue without the sauce—nourishing, but not the full savory delight.

Adler guided *Eagle* over a rise. Violet's expression flashed in his mind again, and his breath hitched.

Wasn't that what he'd given her? Forgiveness à la carte? *I forgive you. Gotta go. Thanks for the donut.*

But that was different. They couldn't reconcile. She knew that, and she knew why.

Didn't she?

A road crossed the railroad tracks up ahead, and gray German army trucks lumbered north.

With rudder and stick, Adler turned toward the convoy. Soldiers spilled out of the trucks and sprinted away. Good. Adler didn't want to kill them—he just wanted to immobilize them.

Adler opened fire, but guilt clung like an unwanted passenger on his canopy and threw off his aim.

He peeled away and circled to the end of the queue while the rest of his section strafed the convoy.

Adler had to get rid of that guilt, not by ignoring it but by confronting it. He hadn't told Violet the many reasons they couldn't reconcile, because he'd assumed she'd never want to.

Apparently his assumption was wrong. That meant he had to talk to her, offering her all the questioning and listening he was willing to give his brothers.

Adler dove at the line of trucks, most engulfed in black smoke and bright flames. He squeezed the trigger on his control stick, and each bullet hit its target.

Tomorrow he'd offer Violet the sauce along with the barbecue and show her the toxic ingredients in that sauce. Then she'd see. Then she'd understand.

And then she'd let him go.

The ground crewman waved Violet's jeep onto the perimeter track, calling out thanks for the donut and coffee.

Planes were constantly taking off and landing, in no order that she could discern. It was almost noon, and the men had been flying for ten hours already. Rumors were they'd keep flying until dark—which wouldn't come until ten o'clock with Britain's wartime double summer time.

Violet drove up the track toward the squadron headquarters where Rosalind was working today. The busyness kept her mind off Adler and off her upcoming dismissal from the Red Cross—although they lay like lead on her chest.

She parked the jeep and carried a tray of donuts into the Nissen hut.

Around the pilots' room, men snoozed on cots and dozed in armchairs, snatching a few minutes of rest before their next missions. Such a tiring but crucial day, and her heart reached out to them.

Serving others meant more to her now. At first she hadn't considered the airmen needy enough to be served. Then she'd seen them as needy and had served them, but as a lofty benefactress looking down from on high. Now she served them as equals, as fellow sinners.

"Hi, Mrs. Weaver." Violet set the tray on the table and studied Rosalind's face for signs of exhaustion. She found none. "How are you doing here?"

"Fine, but I'm out of bread and meat."

Violet frowned at the meager pile of sandwiches. Half an hour earlier, Griff had left the Aeroclub with a full load. He'd only had one stop before this, while Violet had stopped at each hardstand to serve the ground crews. What was taking him so long?

"Hiya, ladies." Griff sauntered in with a coffee urn.

"Oh, thank you." Rosalind helped him set it in place. "Bread and meat?"

"Next load." He brushed his hands together. "Just coffee this round."

Violet's frown deepened. "But I helped you load bread and meat in your jeep."

Griff chuckled and headed for the door. "That was an earlier run, not this one."

"It was only half an hour ago."

"You're mistaken." He tossed a grin over his shoulder. "Completely understandable on a day like this. Don't worry, ladies. I'll bring out sandwich fixings in a jiff."

"Thank you." After the door shut behind him, she turned to Rosalind. "When did you last receive bread and meat?"

Rosalind smoothed her apron and studied the clock on the wall. "I don't know. Oh yes, it was right after General Eisenhower's announcement on the wireless. I remember because I told Griff about it."

Two hours ago. The lead pressed heavier on her chest.

Violet wasn't mistaken. Half an hour earlier she'd loaded six loaves of bread and a dozen tins of Spam into Griff's jeep along with the coffee.

Brewed coffee wouldn't have any value on the black market, but bread and Spam would.

Her heart folded in on itself. Was that why he'd taken so long? Had he run the food into town?

No, he couldn't have. The base was closed.

Perhaps he had a stash somewhere on the base.

Violet found a smile for Rosalind. "Anything else? Do you need a break?"

"Not at all. Other than sandwiches, I'm fine."

"Good. I'll be back later." Violet headed outside into the gray day and climbed into the jeep.

Griff had always been so kind and helpful, picking up groceries in town and delivering refreshments on base. How easy it would be to pilfer.

And he'd dated Millie, the grocer's sister-in-law. Were they all working together from the start?

Violet rested her head on the steering wheel, sick and betrayed and overwhelmed.

"Why today?" Why did she have to figure it out now, when she didn't have the time, the energy, or the heart to investigate?

43

Hills and châteaux and rivers and farms flowed beneath Adler. His section had broken up after strafing the truck convoy, each pilot seeking targets of opportunity. Once again, Adler was alone.

Movement on the ground, and he descended to investigate. A farmer ran in front of his barn, waving his beret with one hand and making the V for Victory symbol with the other.

Adler grinned and put *Eagle* into a slow roll so the Frenchman could see the stars on his wings. "Won't be long, *monsieur*. The Yanks are coming. And the Redcoats too."

At least he hoped so. It was noon. How far had the Allies marched—or had the Germans driven them back into the sea?

Adler leveled off and studied the landscape for roads, railroads, or airfields to shoot up. In half an hour he'd head back to Leiston, leaving plenty of fuel in case he had the opportunity for a dogfight.

That talk with Violet would have to wait until tomorrow. In the afternoon he'd be sent up on another mission or two. Today he needed to reserve his energy for flying and fighting—not his personal life. Besides, if he talked to her when he was exhausted, who knew what stupid words might come out of his mouth?

A dark speck against the overcast—what was that?

It was moving to the southwest, and the long nose identified it as a Focke-Wulf 190.

Adler whistled. Wouldn't it be something to make ace on D-day?

He winced at his old self, but honestly, it was his job to keep the Luftwaffe out of the sky. If he made ace in the process, so be it.

Adler pulled back the control stick and adjusted his course to the northeast so he could bounce the enemy from above and behind.

Another fighter plane, above and ahead of him. A Mustang with a red-and-yellow checkered nose. Adler pushed the "A" button on the radio box and the microphone button on the throttle. "Dollar leader here."

"Dollar red four here." That was Ray Schneider, who had two whopping missions under his belt. A good pilot with the cockiness that would make him either an ace or a corpse.

"Bogey at ten o'clock," Adler said. "He's yours."

"I see him. Rog—no, he should be yours."

By all rights, the victory should be Adler's as the section leader. But that wasn't the leader he wanted to be. "You're closer. Climb into position, then dive onto his tail. I'll be your wingman."

"Roger." Schneider's voice rang with enthusiasm.

Adler gave *Eagle* more throttle and climbed to meet Schneider. "Get at least a thousand feet above him before your dive, as high as you can. He hasn't seen us, so we have time."

"Roger." Lining up on the Focke-Wulf, Schneider climbed toward the cloud base about a thousand feet above him. Suddenly he dove.

Too soon. Adler shook his head and followed. With more altitude he could have built up more speed in the dive. "Get on his tail, as close as you can, under three hundred yards is best."

"I know what I'm doing."

Had Adler sounded that cocky on his first missions? Most likely. He took up position behind Schneider and to the left, scanning the sky, ready to swoop in if Schneider overran the enemy.

"Closer . . . closer . . ." Adler muttered.

At six hundred yards, Schneider fired. And missed. And alerted the German.

The Focke-Wulf jinked right and left, and Schneider matched his moves.

"Stay on his tail, red four. Get closer."

"I am."

Adler would have rolled his eyes if they weren't otherwise occupied.

The German dove for the deck, wheeling to the north.

Adler and Schneider gained on him. No German fighter plane could match the P-51 on the deck in level flight.

The Fw 190 darted side to side but maintained his course. Over a rise, down into a gentle valley, over another rise.

Schneider shot a few bursts but missed, too impatient to set up his attack. Adler would have shot him down by now. The Luftwaffe pilot was clearly inexperienced. But so was Schneider.

"Get close, get his tail right in your sights, fire short bursts."

"I heard you," Schneider snapped.

And the kid was going to hear more from him back at Leiston.

Adler checked his instruments, the gauges, the clock, the compass. The German was headed straight north, right toward the invasion beaches. At their current speed, only about fifteen minutes away.

He pulled up over a grove of trees. With each minute it became more important to shoot down the Nazi before he could strafe Allied troops. But with each minute the danger of Germans on the ground shooting down Adler or Schneider increased too.

"Red four, two more minutes, then we're breaking off the attack."

"I can get him. I know I can."

"Two minutes."

Over another rise, and a flat broad space opened before them.

"An airfield," Schneider said. "He's going home, and he led us right to it. We can get in some good strafing."

Adler smelled a rat. "He's leading us into a trap. Those flak guns will be ready for us. Break off."

"Nah, I'll get him before he sounds the alarm." He fired a burst. Too low.

"Break off, red four." Adler's hand tightened on the throttle. "Head west."

"I almost . . . I got him." Another burst, far to the right.

On the airfield, two Fw 190s raced down the runway aiming southeast. They'd been alerted, all right, and they were coming up to fight.

Adler pressed the microphone button. "Red four, stay with the bogey. I'll fend off the other two."

No time to set up a good attack. He peeled off to the right, coming in at a thirty-degree angle to the leading Fw 190. "Lord, let my deflection shot work. Please."

The first Fw 190 was airborne, folding up its landing gear, and the second Fw 190 took off right after it.

Adler squinted into his gunsight, calculated the amount of lead, and opened fire. Bullets winked down the length of the fighter plane.

In flames, it cartwheeled to the side, collided with the second airplane, and they spun together, leaving a fiery trail of debris along the runway.

"Two! Two in one," Ray Schneider said. "That gives you six. You're an ace!"

He was. And two men had died. Adler yanked the stick back and to the left, his stomach taut and queasy.

Flashes of light on the ground. The Germans fired at him.

Too low for acrobatics, Adler gave *Eagle* full throttle and high-tailed it away from that airfield.

A knocking sound. From the nose toward the cockpit.

Adler ducked and drew up his feet by instinct, then put head and feet back where they belonged.

No holes in him. How about *Eagle*?

More altitude, more distance, and he checked the gauges. Everything was steady. He'd been hit, but the bullets must have missed the important equipment.

"Thank you, Lord." A single bullet to the radiator or coolant system would mean the difference between landing in England and crashing in France.

Adler searched the skies. "Red four? Where's your bogey?"

"Lost him. I think he went south. But that airfield will be out of commission for hours."

The engine temperature nudged higher, and Adler frowned. Had his coolant system been hit after all?

But then he was still climbing hard at a low speed after the strafing attack. That could strain the engine. "Time to head home. I'm leveling off."

"Roger. I'll stay with you."

Adler didn't like the note of concern in Schneider's voice. The man might be a rookie, but he had a better view of *Eagle*'s beak than Adler did.

He leveled off and headed northwest. "Lord, get me home."

LEISTON ARMY AIRFIELD

Violet skimmed the logs in the Aeroclub kitchen, but exhaustion, grief, and self-doubt muddied her thinking. So many supplies had been sent out this morning, and she was in no state to decipher the mess.

At least the Aeroclub was almost empty. Occasionally, men would grab coffee and a sandwich, but no one had time to lounge and chat and read.

"Eat something, Miss Lindstrom." Mabel Smith poked a sandwich in Violet's face. "You look famished."

"Thank you." She knew better than to argue with the older woman, so she took a bite, but it stuck in her throat. She wouldn't take a second bite.

"Hiya, ladies." Griff breezed through the side door. "Now I can take a round of sandwich fixings."

Violet smiled, more from the idea that was brewing than from pleasure at seeing him. "Thank you, Griff."

She pulled out loaves and tins and marked them off in the log. *Lord, please let me be wrong about him.*

Griff loaded the goods in the jeep.

Violet grabbed some cheese from the icebox and took it out to him. "A block of cheese for each squadron. Bet the boys would like this in their sandwiches."

His face lit up. "They sure would."

So would the villagers.

"Where are you off to next, Miss Lindstrom?" He set the cheese in the backseat.

"Group headquarters and the control tower."

"Great. I'll see you later." He hopped into the jeep.

Instead of loading the other jeep, Violet marched through the kitchen, out the front door, and grabbed a bicycle from the stack leaning against the brick wall.

Griff's jeep turned down the road through the communal site. Violet waited a minute and pedaled after him, as far away as she could get without losing sight of him.

At the main road, Griff turned right.

Away from the airfield, and Violet's heart sank. "No, no, no. I don't want to be correct."

Griff made another right turn, onto the tree-lined road Violet used to stroll along with Adler.

She pedaled close to the trees to stay inconspicuous.

At a clump of trees, Griff stopped the jeep.

Violet veered off the road and peeked around a tree, her heart thumping.

Griff walked into the woods. Metal doors squeaked open. A truck. A truck was parked there.

Oh no. Violet clutched her stomach. Griff was indeed the thief.

Any relief that she would now keep her job was doused by the knowledge that she'd been deceived and betrayed.

Griff returned to the jeep, grabbed an armload of food—and looked down the road in her direction.

Violet cringed and tried to merge with the tree. Why did she have to be so tall? So very blonde?

"Who's there?" he called. "Miss Lindstrom?"

She groaned. She was bigger than Griff and she was fast, but the men had all been ordered to carry sidearms recently.

"Miss Lindstrom?" Footsteps approached.

Lord, help me. She stepped out, leaving the bike behind. She could run faster than she could ride. "Don't come any closer."

He stopped about a hundred feet away, dug his hands in his pockets, and dipped his chin. "You saw what I was doing. I'm sure you don't mind."

Violet took a few steps backward, blinking hard. "Don't mind?"

"Sure." He grinned and gestured toward town. "Everyone knows how you feel about helping the English."

"Not like this, not by selling on the black market. That's what you're doing, isn't it?"

He chuckled. "You make it sound bad, but it isn't. I sell to a local grocer, and he sells to the villagers and stamps the ration books. The people only get what their government says they're supposed to get—but never provides for them. And the grocer sells at market price. He isn't getting rich or taking advantage of the people."

Violet's jaw hardened. "And you make a profit."

Griff rubbed the back of his neck. "Actually I donate every penny back to the Red Cross. I'm not stealing. I'm just shuffling the food from the airmen to the local people. We get plenty to eat at the mess. They don't."

Violet shut her eyes, and her mind reeled. He was doing this out of kindness? Not to make a profit?

"When I saw how Millie and her family struggled, how little they had to eat . . ." His voice caught. "How could I sit back and do nothing?"

She pressed her fingertips to her temples, trying to think straight.

"See, I knew you wouldn't mind."

"I didn't say that." She swayed, and she opened her eyes so she wouldn't fall.

"But it's what you're thinking, I know it." Griff wore a satisfied smile. "You're a woman of mercy. It's why you want to be a missionary and why you joined the Red Cross—to help the needy."

"Yes, but . . ." But what was the right thing to do?

Why was she hesitating? She had to get an MP and have Griff arrested for theft. The thought filled her with a smug sense of justice.

Or was that smug feeling a sign of self-righteousness, looking down on Griff, judging him?

Her fingertips massaged her temples, but everything tumbled topsy-turvy. Hadn't she learned the hard way that God hated self-righteousness and wanted her to be merciful and compassionate? She'd failed the test with Adler. She couldn't fail again.

"I knew you'd like it." His grin grew. "No one's hurt—not the airmen, not the Red Cross. And all those little children get plenty of bread and meat and cheese, so they'll grow up strong and healthy. That's what you want, isn't it?"

Violet's head hurt, and her stomach squirmed. Compassion was best. Mercy was best. She had to choose correctly this time. She had to.

With a single nod, she retrieved her bike and turned toward the Aeroclub.

She'd be gone in a week anyway. What did it matter?

44

OVER FRANCE

The oil temperature pushed toward eighty-five degrees Celsius, the maximum.

On the panel on the left side of the cockpit, Adler toggled the coolant radiator scoop controls to make sure the scoops were open, allowing airflow to cool the engine. His last chance.

Skimming the deck, he headed straight north now, the shortest route to England even though it was the most dangerous. "Red four, turn west and go home."

"Sor—can't—hear—"

Liar. He was obviously playing with the microphone button. If Adler made it back to Leiston, Schneider would get an earful from him.

Ninety degrees. Even with the scoops wide open, the engine was still overheating. That meant his coolant system had been hit and he was losing the precious ethylene glycol that kept the engine cool enough to function.

His stomach muscles hardened. Ten minutes. At most, he had ten minutes before the engine died.

"Okay. What are my choices?" The coastline couldn't be far. If he could make it out to sea, there were plenty of ships to pick him up. If they didn't shoot him down first. His black-and-white invasion stripes served as identification, not armor.

He couldn't ditch. The big fat air scoop below the fuselage would plow into the water, causing the plane to sink in one to two seconds.

If he could keep his altitude above five hundred feet, he could bail at sea.

"Sorry, *Eagle*. We're taking a bath today." He hated to lose this plane. They'd been through a lot together, and she'd never let him down. And Beck would go into deep mourning.

Adler guided the Mustang over a wooded ridge. A blue-gray line stretched before him—the ocean. "Thank you, God."

Ninety-five degrees. "Come on, darlin'. Just a bit farther."

That stretch of sea held more ships than water. Brown-black smoke billowed from those ships. Gunfire.

Adler couldn't breathe. How could he . . . ? He couldn't drift down in a parachute in the middle of all those shells and bullets and darting boats.

But if he didn't, he'd have to crash-land—probably behind enemy lines. In a combat zone. The Germans probably wouldn't be in any mood to take prisoners.

If only he could make it to Allied territory. But where was it? How on earth could he tell where the front line was?

Pops rang out on his fuselage.

On the ground, soldiers aimed rifles at him. Germans.

Adler zigged and zagged. "Red four! Get out of here. Get above the clouds and get out of here."

"I'm staying with you."

"My engine overheated. I'm making a belly landing. Get out of here, and that's an order."

The engine temperature hit one hundred degrees, the final mark on the gauge. Adler searched the ground for a good place to land—no trees, no hills, no Germans.

Explosions and fires sprang up on the rise ahead of him. Was that the front?

"Come on, come on." Gray smoke streamed back from the nose and the engine whined in protest, but he had to keep going.

Over the rise. Bluffs ahead, then the ocean. Trees to the right, open fields to the left.

"Left it is." Adler shoved the stick to the left and gave *Eagle* left rudder.

Belly-landing procedures—he ran through them in his mind. He'd already dropped his bombs. Keep the wheels up. Keep the shoulder harness and safety belt fastened.

Coming out of the turn, Adler ripped the oxygen mask off his helmet so radio cords and the oxygen hose wouldn't tether him to the plane. He gripped the long red canopy release lever to his right, yanked it to break the safety wire, and ducked low.

The entire canopy flew off in the slipstream, and a rush of cool air buffeted his head and shoulders.

Flames and smoke licked the aircraft's nose. With the beach and bluffs to his right, he crossed a shallow ravine. A wide field stretched before him. "This is it."

Adler throttled back and lowered the flaps.

More trees coming up ahead. Green land rising beneath him.

"Lord . . ." The prayer squeezed out from deep inside him.

Adler eased the stick back to lift the nose and settle to the ground.

He hit hard, bouncing him in his seat. His forehead pounded into the crash pad in front of the gunsight. Then his body slammed back against the seat.

Adler cried out. The trees rushed toward him. "Stop! Stop!"

His nose plunged into the brush, the propeller sending branches and leaves spinning into the air, into the cockpit, whapping him in the face, scratching and poking.

The tail rode up, and Adler braced himself on the control panel. "Don't tip over. Don't."

A pause, then *Eagle* thumped to the ground, jostling Adler.

Smoke filled the cockpit. He coughed. Out. Out. He had to get out.

He groped for the safety belt, found a branch, tossed it out, found the buckle and unlatched it. He unfastened the shoulder harness and threw off the straps.

Adler tugged himself up, grasping the open edge of the cockpit. After a long mission, he usually needed Beck's help to pry him out, but now adrenaline drove him.

He vaulted over the edge onto the wing. Field to his left, brush to the right. Flames crackled through the brush.

Adler jumped off the wing and forced his stiff, shaky leg muscles to run. In about a hundred feet, he barreled into the brush. A few feet in, he collapsed to the ground, rolled onto his stomach, and lay low.

Breathing hard, he got his bearings. Bushes and trees behind him. Open field before him. Bluffs far to his left, covered with scrub.

And the noise. Booms of big guns. The rat-a-tat of machine guns. The ground trembled beneath his belly.

Where was he? German territory or Allied?

Couldn't take chances until he knew for sure. He wrestled off his backpack parachute, bright yellow life vest, and white scarf, and he shoved them under a bush. What was left? Brown helmet, brown jacket, khaki flight coveralls, brown shoes. Decent camouflage.

His gun! He might need that. He lifted his chest enough to pull his Colt .45 from the shoulder holster. The magazine was already in the receiver, thank goodness. Aiming the pistol up and away from his face, he drew the slide fully back and released it, automatically pushing the first cartridge into the chamber.

An explosion, and a wave of heat slammed into him.

Texas Eagle. Gone.

"Sorry, darlin'," he whispered. "You were the best."

About two hundred yards down the bluff, three figures in field gray rose and ran toward the burning P-51, rifles raised.

Those were not Americans or British or Canadians, and Adler melted into the ground.

Why bother? As soon as the Germans realized he wasn't in the plane, they'd come looking for him. He wouldn't be hard to find.

Part of him wanted to run out, yelling and firing his pistol until they shot him dead.

Part of him wanted to wave his white scarf and surrender. At which point they'd shoot him dead.

Adler lowered his sore forehead to his crossed arms.

He was going to die. And soon.

Instead of grief or panic, a soft sense of peace floated through him.

His parents would mourn, but they might be secretly relieved to avoid the shame and turmoil Adler would have brought back to Kerrville.

His brothers? They wouldn't rejoice, but they probably wouldn't miss him either.

His son? Timmy hadn't even met him, and he had loving grandparents to raise him. He'd grow up proud of his father, who died heroically on D-day.

And Violet? It was over anyway.

Voices called out in German, loud and strident, probably ordering him to surrender. Not that Adler would know. The only German word he knew was *Gesundheit*.

Death would come soon. What would it be like? A minute of extraordinary pain, and then release. He'd be with Jesus. With Oralee.

He smiled, his lips brushing against damp leaves. After he transferred his pistol to his left hand, Adler burrowed his right hand inside his flight jacket and into his pocket to the familiar cotton scrap.

Usually when he felt it, he saw terror on Oralee's face and heard her scream as she fell.

But now he saw her leaning her pretty head on his shoulder, twisting to face him with her luminous brown eyes. And he heard her laughter, her warm, lyrical voice.

Harsh German words, not far away, brush breaking.

It wouldn't be long now. He closed his fingers around his pocket. *See you soon, darlin'.*

LEISTON ARMY AIRFIELD

Violet pedaled down the road, her wheels and her stomach both wobbling.

It was worth it. Sacrificing her career, even her reputation, was worth it to help the English people. And choosing mercy was right. It had to be.

So why did it feel wrong?

Was she so accustomed to being a self-righteous Pharisee that mercy felt wrong?

"Griff isn't hurting anyone," she repeated.

Except for Violet and Kitty and the workers who would lose their jobs.

"No." With so few eligible women in the region, Mr. Tate would have to hire them right back. Perhaps Violet could take the fall and allow Kitty to keep her job.

"Watch out, Miss Lindstrom!"

An officer held up one hand, his other arm in a sling.

She braked and planted her feet on the ground, glad she was wearing trousers. "I'm sorry. I wasn't watching where I was going."

He laughed, his face wide and friendly and pockmarked with acne. A pilot—Lt. Clement O'Dell. "That's all right. Today we're all kind of mixed up."

Violet tried to smile. "It's a hard day for you."

Lieutenant O'Dell lifted a leather satchel. "Not me. With my wing in a sling, they have me carting papers. Doesn't seem right. All those men fighting and dying, and I can't do a thing to help."

Violet's heart careened from her problems to the men's. "Nonsense, Lieutenant. How many missions have you flown? You've done your part. Because of those missions, today will be a success. Besides, the paperwork does need to be done."

He gave her half a smile. "Red Cross improving morale again."

"Thank you." But her mouth quivered.

"I mean it." His brows met in the middle. "I suppose you ladies don't hear much other than 'Thanks for the coffee,' but it means a lot to us, what you do. It's hard over here, watching our buddies die, having to kill or be killed. Can't tell you how much it means to get a donut and a smile. It's a touch of home."

She worked up a better smile. "Thank you, Lieutenant."

He tipped his cap and continued on his way.

Violet stood at an intersection. Men strode along, working together to defeat Nazi tyranny and free the world.

Her chest caved in. Hadn't she realized long ago that the airmen deserved help just as much as the locals did?

The American people donated to the Red Cross so that their boys would receive that touch of home. When Griff diverted food, he was stealing from the airmen and the donors.

She slammed her eyes shut and forced her mind to do math. Griff said the Red Cross wasn't hurt. But if they purchased food from Banister's at market price and Griff sold it back to Banister's at wholesale, Griff would donate the wholesale cost to the Red Cross. So the Red Cross was indeed losing money.

That assumed Griff was actually donating his profits. She had no proof, only his word.

Violet gripped the handlebars, feeling woozy. She was judging him, when she was supposed to be merciful.

Something jolted inside her. Did mercy mean allowing sin to

continue? Would it be merciful to allow Nazi Germany to continue enslaving and murdering?

"Of course not," she whispered. "Lord, what's the answer?"

Jesus—Jesus was always the answer. Jesus didn't condemn sinners, but he never condoned sin either.

Mercy and righteousness, perfectly blended. Neither excluded the other.

Violet's eyelids drifted open. The world righted itself, and the wooziness melted away.

Griff might have had noble motives, but stealing was a crime, and it needed to stop.

She scanned the road for the white helmet and armband of the military police, then she flagged down an officer. "Quick! Sir? Where can I find an MP?"

45

Over the crackling flames, the sound of the Germans' voices drew nearer.

Surrender was another way to put himself last, and he had to embrace it.

He could extract his silk scarf from under the bush to use as a white flag.

Stroking the cotton scrap one last time, his fingers bumped over the safety pin. He could still see Violet fastening that pin, tears in her eyes. *"Your deep love for her—that's one of the reasons I fell in love with you."*

"I love you too, Violet," he mouthed. He'd planned to have that long talk with her, but now he never would. She'd think he didn't care for her, that he'd rejected her for judging him.

Not true. Adler gritted his teeth, and his fingertips met the stiffness of his son's photograph.

His little son. He stifled a groan. Death was just another way to run, wasn't it?

Violet deserved the full truth, Timmy deserved a real father rather than a paper hero, and Wyatt and Clay deserved a chance either to forgive him or to beat him to a pulp.

Those things could only happen if he lived. And the best way to live would be to fight. *Lord, if I die today, I want to die fighting, not giving up.*

Adler freed his hand from his pocket and transferred the pistol back into his right hand. He refused to hide anymore—from his shame, from his feelings, or from the Nazis.

He lifted his chin just enough to see. The three Germans—one about twenty feet away and coming closer, one standing guard near *Texas Eagle*'s flaming tail, and the other out of sight, probably searching on the far side of the plane.

Adler raised his Colt so it aimed about chest high. He had seven bullets. As soon as the first German discovered him, Adler would shoot him.

Then he'd jump to his feet, fire twice at the soldier standing guard, dash around the tail, fire two more shots at the third soldier, and race for the bluff. He didn't know if Allied soldiers waited on the beach below, but his chances had to be better down there than up here.

A series of booms rattled the ground. A whistling, roaring sound, and a giant fist punched into the cliff. Adler bounced into the air, fell flat, and almost dropped his gun.

He scrambled to get his knees under him.

Those had to be naval guns, and they were close.

The German by *Eagle*'s tail got back up to his feet, shouted to his comrades, and beckoned across the field. All three ran back where they'd come from—to their gun battery? An underground shelter?

Didn't matter. Now was his chance.

Another salvo rammed the bluff, tossing chunks of earth and concrete skyward.

Now!

"Lord, help me." Pistol in hand, Adler bolted to his feet and sprinted across the field, past *Eagle*, toward the bluff.

With all the noise, he'd never know if someone was shooting at him until he fell.

A dip in the brush at the bluff's edge. A path? A ravine?

Hunkered low, he burst over the top of the bluff and scrabbled down on the other side.

A shallow ravine, a rough footpath, and he kept scrabbling down. A beach lay below, crammed with smoke and equipment and men in olive drab.

Breath huffing, feet slipping beneath him, branches scratching his shins, shells exploding to his left.

He stumbled and rounded a curve in the path. A bullet zinged past his arm.

Adler barged into the brush, pistol high, heart whacking his rib cage.

"Come out with your hands up, Kraut," a man cried.

An American. His breath tumbled out. *Thank you, God.*

"Hendee hoke!"

Was that supposed to be German? "I'm an American, an American! Capt. Adler Paxton, US 357th Fighter Group."

The barrel of an M1 rifle poked in his face. "You're going the wrong way, Tex."

Adler crawled out of the brush to find a line of GIs lying flat on the path, rifles pointing at him. Just to be safe, he set down his pistol and raised his hands. "I'm an American. A pilot."

"A pilot?" The closest GI peered out from under his steel helmet. "Aren't you on the wrong side of those clouds?"

"No kidding." Adler picked up his pistol, never taking his eyes off the soldiers. "That's my P-51 burning up on the bluff. I've got to get back to England."

The first GI glanced back to the second. "Hear that? Says he's a pilot."

"Looks like a private in the infantry to me." The second fellow called down the hill. "Hey, Perkins, pass up your rifle. Flyboy here needs it. All he's got is his pretty officer's pistol."

Adler outranked them all, but a quick assessment told him not to argue. A lot of gunfire and explosions on the beach and at sea, and the Americans were headed inland, not back to England.

Early that morning, patrolling over the fleet, hadn't he wished he could have come down to help? This wasn't what he'd had in mind.

"Here." The first GI thrust an M1 rifle at Adler. "It's got a full clip, eight rounds. Perkins don't need it no more. Lost his foot to a mine back there on the slope. Know how to use it?"

Adler inspected the wooden stock and steel barrel. "Point and shoot?"

"Good enough. Follow us." He knifed his hand uphill. "Navy destroyer shot up the gun battery at the top of the draw to our right. We're going to take it from behind."

Adler hadn't even seen that gun position. "There are at least three Germans—a machine-gun nest maybe—on the top of the bluff about two hundred yards to the left."

"Thanks." He hurried up the path, hunched over.

Adler flipped his pistol's safety into place and returned the weapon to its holster.

Ten soldiers eyed him as they passed. Some gave him a smile or a joke, some gave him barely a glance, their eyes vacant or terrified or determined. Their uniforms were soaked, ripped, streaked with sand, splattered with blood. And they stank—some odd chemical smell from their uniforms, plus the stench of vomit and other bodily functions.

Gripping the rifle, Adler fell into the column toward the end. What on earth had these men seen on the beach? What had they gone through? What were they about to go through?

Adler made his way up the path, careful to keep his head down and his rifle off the ground. "Which unit is this?"

The man in front of him snorted. "Which unit *isn't* it? We're all with the 16th Infantry, I think, but the companies are mixed up. Lost half our men down there, all our officers. Sarge up there's in command."

Half their men? Adler thought the 357th had taken hard losses.

At the top of the ridge, the sergeant made arm motions to the right and left, then he charged over and to the right.

Adler followed the pack, sweat on his upper lip and warm in his armpits. *What on earth am I doing here?*

At the top, the GIs peeled off right and left. Adler followed the guy in front of him to the right and raised his rifle to his shoulder as the others were doing.

Texas Eagle lay smoking in the distance, nose buried in the burning brush. The soldiers ignored her and dashed toward chunks of concrete in the brush closer to the bluff, shouting, "Hendee hoke!"

Figures in field gray emerged from the wreckage and raised their rifles to shoot.

Before Adler could even find the trigger, shots rang out, and the Germans fell, crying out.

Adler gasped.

A GI tossed a hand grenade into the battery. An explosion, a rumble, more cries. Two Americans jumped in. More shots.

Behind him, still more shots.

Adler swung his rifle around, his breath chuffing. One American lay writhing on the ground—and three Germans sprawled lifeless. The fellows who had searched for him.

A squeeze of grief. He almost felt as if he knew them. Of course, he'd planned to shoot them too.

"All clear!" someone shouted from the machine-gun nest.

"All clear!" the sergeant yelled from the battery.

Adler lowered the rifle. His hands shook. He'd been fighting for months. He'd seen friends die, and he'd killed in aerial combat. But nothing like this.

LEISTON ARMY AIRFIELD

Sylvia Haywood scrubbed a tray in the sink. "I can't believe it was Griff. Such a nice bloke."

"I know. We all trusted him." Violet leaned back against the icebox, her legs aching from the long day and her head aching from the ordeal with Griff.

The MPs had found him loading the last of the Red Cross goods into the truck and had arrested him. They'd discovered a hidden compartment Griff had built in the floor of the truck. When he picked up groceries at Banister's, he stashed away a portion of the food—then sold it right back to Banister's.

After the base was opened again, the MPs would work with the local authorities to decide if Mr. Banister needed to be charged as well. Mr. Tate would soon learn the truth, and all the ladies would keep their jobs.

With a sigh of relief and sadness, Violet pushed away from the icebox and made plans for the evening. The 357th had finished flying for the day, and men filtered into the Aeroclub to unwind and reflect. The latest BBC announcement said the landings were successful and the Allies had driven several miles into France in some places, but details were sparse.

Ann Brewer entered the kitchen with empty trays, and the young girl grinned at Violet. "There she is! Our own Miss Marple." Then she blanched. "You're younger, of course. Much younger."

Violet chuckled, the first she'd laughed all day. "That's all right, Ann. I know what you mean."

"What I meant to say—you're my heroine."

While she hated to burst enthusiastic young bubbles, Violet didn't deserve praise. "Thank you, but you would have done the same thing."

And probably without dithering as Violet had.

She headed out into the dining area. Why had she fallen for Griff's self-serving justifications for even a single moment? It didn't matter that she was exhausted, overwhelmed, and brokenhearted. *Lord, forgive me.*

The front door opened, and Nick Westin headed her direction.

Violet gave him a tired smile. "Good evening, Major."

"Good evening." He looked even more exhausted than she felt. "Do you have a minute?"

"For you? Absolutely."

Nick led her to the library, which was deserted.

Violet chewed on her lower lip. She'd already thanked him profusely for directing her to Luke 18. Did he have more to say?

Nick sat in an armchair, his expression serious and drawn. Hesitant and concerned.

Violet's heart dropped, her legs buckled, and she sank into the couch. "Oh no. Adler?"

The concern deepened. "His plane didn't return from our second mission."

Didn't return? What did that mean? She shook her head as if she could settle all the thoughts into better positions and sort out the ones she didn't like. But she didn't like any of them.

"He was strafing an airfield, flying wingman to a rookie." His face reddened and twisted, and he clenched his hands together. "Isn't that just like him?"

Strafing an airfield . . . she could picture him in his plane, shooting up German airplanes. Alive, whole, grinning. She couldn't— wouldn't—picture him any other way.

"He shot down two Focke-Wulfs, protecting Schneider. He made ace, by the way."

Ace? That didn't matter. The only thing that mattered was Adler's life. She crossed her arms over her chest, gripping her shoulders.

"He took some damage, couldn't make it back to base. He made a belly landing in France. The plane was—it was on fire. Schneider saw an explosion. We—we don't know if Adler got out."

Violet's breath hopped around, out of control. He had to have gotten out. He had to.

Nick's head swung back and forth, slow and heavy. "Even if he did—it was in the invasion area. Don't know if it was Allied territory or German."

It was Allied territory. Of course it was. It had to be.

Nick's eyes turned dark and bleak. "I helped Schneider fill out the Missing Air Crew Report. That's everything we know. But Violet . . . it doesn't look good. You need to be prepared."

Violet moistened her tongue. "When will we know?"

Nick's cheeks puffed full of air. "Depends. If he survived and evaded capture, we could know in a day or two. If he was taken prisoner, it could be weeks. But if . . ."

If he was dead, how long until they found his body?

Violet's stomach crumpled in, and she stifled a moan. She didn't care if he never looked at her again. She just wanted him to live.

"I wanted you to hear it from me. I know you two—I know you still care for him."

Sweet Nick, thinking of her on a day like this. Her heart reached out to him. "You care for him too."

Nick ducked his chin, and his cheek muscles worked. "I've lost a lot of friends in this war, but this . . ." His voice broke.

"Oh, Nick."

He stood, raised one hand to stop the sympathy, gave her a close-lipped smile, and headed for the door. "I'll keep you informed."

"Thank you." She pressed her fingers over her mouth and shut her eyes.

Adler couldn't be dead. God wouldn't let him die now. His parents had forgiven him, but his brothers hadn't, not that she knew. And he had a little boy who needed to know his daddy.

A sob gulped up, trapped in her throat. But how many men had died today—sons missing their parents, brothers estranged from loved ones, fathers who hadn't met their babies?

"Oh, Lord." Adler's great need to survive was no guarantee that he'd done so. "Lord, please let him live."

46

NORMANDY

With the M1 rifle slung over his shoulder and someone else's steel helmet on his head, Adler trudged along the beach. Omaha Beach, the GIs called it.

The sun was falling and the tide was rising, but the day seemed unending.

A whistle overhead, and he hit the ground. German artillery—by now, he could tell the difference. His reaction was pure reflex. Not even a bump in his heart rate anymore.

Adler pressed up next to the tall grasses at the bottom of the bluff, his belly flat against the small stones and his rifle away from damaging dirt and sand.

Tank and naval fire blasted overhead, concussion waves pulling on his helmet and uniform. Noise or no noise, he could fall asleep right there.

He'd tagged along with his ragtag platoon all afternoon and into the evening. They'd cleared out machine-gun nests and sniper positions and ruined buildings in the town of Colleville-sur-Mer. After reinforcements arrived, Adler had found an officer and received permission to head to the beach and hitch a ride home.

But right now, he only wanted to sleep. When was the last time he'd slept? Back at Leiston in another lifetime. After the briefing, he'd dozed a bit before takeoff. Since then he'd flown two long missions and played tin soldier. It didn't seem real.

But his aching muscles felt real. The stinging scratches on his legs from crawling through the brush. The throbbing bump on his forehead. The burning pain in his left arm from the bullet the GIs had fired at him on the slope—he hadn't realized he'd been hit until an hour later. Just a scratch, the medic said. Keep fighting, the sergeant said. And Private Paxton obeyed.

The shelling died away, but Adler lay still as the dark fog of fatigue did its work.

Then his stomach rumbled, low and hollow. He hadn't eaten since before his last mission. Coffee and a donut. From Violet.

He tightened his abdomen, silencing the rumble but not the frustration. He needed to see her, to explain, to tell her good-bye. He couldn't do that napping on the beach.

Adler pushed himself to standing. He was supposed to find a beachmaster, so he searched for a man carrying a handie-talkie radio.

He picked his way down the crowded beach. He'd never seen such carnage in his life. The gray waters teemed with ships and boats. Some chugged in to shore. Some chugged away. Too many tilted at awkward angles, broken, half-sunk, smoking, burning.

Huge silver barrage balloons floated on cables above the fleet to keep the Luftwaffe from strafing.

The corner of Adler's mouth twitched—almost a smile. From what he'd heard, not one enemy aircraft had reached Omaha Beach. He hadn't seen the Luftwaffe since he'd strafed that airfield, and the only aircraft overhead were American Lightnings and British Spitfires.

Adler needed to get back up in the sky.

He passed a flaming tank. Hot, heavy, acrid smoke billowed around, and he covered his mouth and nose. Dozens of wrecked landing craft, tanks, and bulldozers littered the sands. German beach obstacles were strewn around as if a giant had abandoned his game of jacks. Coils of German barbed wire and American detonating wire made crazy deadly loops.

And the human wreckage. Smaller. More gut-wrenching.

Twisted rifles. Blasted helmets. A tiny Bible, the pages fluttering in the wind.

And the bodies. So many bodies. Lined up in neat rows.

Adler averted his eyes from them, but he didn't avert his eyes from the wounded. Lying down, bandaged and bleeding, as medics hung plasma bottles from rifles poked into the sand.

The smell of burning oil and gunpowder and blood and death filled his nostrils and his soul. If this was what had happened when the Allied air forces kept the Luftwaffe away, what would have happened if they hadn't?

Just past the aid station, a man stood with a radio. His helmet bore a gray band and a red arc identifying him as a member of a naval beach battalion.

Adler approached him. "Excuse me, sir. Are you a beachmaster?"

"Yeah." Deep-set eyes looked him up and down.

Adler had to look strange in his leather flight jacket, ripped coveralls, and a steel helmet. "I was told to talk to you. I'm a fighter pilot. My P-51 crashed on that bluff, and I need to get back to England."

"To England? Why, of course." He raised the radio to his beefy cheek. "Hey, Ralph. Send in my private yacht. Got a flyboy here who needs a lift. Make it snappy."

A comedian. Swell. Adler lifted an eyebrow and half a smile.

"Listen, brother." The beachmaster pointed at a giant lumbering ship just offshore. "Soon as we beach that LST, we're unloading her tanks and loading her up with the wounded. Which one of these fellows do you want to wait so you can take his place?"

"I . . . That's not what I meant. But I don't do any good over here. If y'all get me back to England, I can fly. I can fight. I can keep the Germans from strafing these boys, these ships."

The beachmaster jerked his chin to the side. "End of the line, brother."

Last place again. Adler's stomach rumbled. "Say, do you know where I could get some grub?"

"Why, yes. There's a charming little café in town. The escargot is *magnifique*." He kissed his fingertips. "Tell them Pierre sent you."

If they gave out medals for sarcasm, this fellow would earn the Silver Star.

Adler tipped him a little salute and departed. At the far edge of the group of wounded, he plopped down on the pebbly beach next to a man in blue trousers, a helmet with a gray band, and an olive drab pullover jacket with "USCG" stamped on the chest. He didn't look wounded either. "This the end of the line?"

"Guess so." The Coastguardsman's angular face broke into a smile. "A pilot? How'd you end up down here?"

"Ran into some flak and crash-landed about noon. Since then, I've been playing infantryman." Adler rested his M1 across his lap. It felt like part of his body now.

"Everyone's an infantryman today." He flicked his chin toward the ocean. "I'm a coxswain. My Higgins boat got blasted by a German shell in the first wave. Only two or three of us survived. So I grabbed a rifle and started shooting."

Adler didn't have to ask where he'd found a rifle. "Trying to get back out to sea?"

"Yep."

"And I'm trying to get back into the air." Adler rolled his sore shoulders. "Neither of us does much good over here."

"Speak for yourself." He raised a crooked grin. "I killed three Germans today."

Adler had killed two in a machine-gun nest, plus the two pilots at that airfield, but it felt wrong to boast about such things. "We still need to get back."

Leiston seemed a world away. Back at the airfield, dinner would be long over, and the men would be enjoying smokes, drinks, and tall tales at the officers' club.

Schneider would have submitted his Missing Air Crew Report, and Adler would officially be classified as Missing in Action.

Did they think he was dead? Or did they think he had a chance? How much had Schneider seen?

Either way, the men would be concerned, especially Nick.

And Violet . . .

His gaze stretched north toward her. She'd worry. She was too tenderhearted not to.

If only he could get a message across the Channel.

The beachmaster would be more than happy to oblige. Adler actually chuckled.

"What's so funny, flyboy?"

"Paxton—my name's Adler Paxton." He stuck out his hand. "Looks like we'll be here awhile. We can sit around and knit . . ."

"Mike Weber." The Coastguardsman shook his hand. "Let's make ourselves useful."

LEISTON ARMY AIRFIELD
WEDNESDAY, JUNE 7, 1944

In the dim light from her desk lamp, Violet reviewed her letter to Great-Aunt Violet. The tone had to be just right—firm, decided, and respectful.

> *I will always be thankful for how you encouraged this homebody to serve the Lord, to think of the world beyond Kansas, and to have the strength and courage to consider following in your footsteps.*

However, my time in England has made it clear that my place is in the classroom and at home. I'm not taking a "lesser" path, but the right path for me, the path God wants for me.

Now I realize God never actually asked me to be a missionary, but he only asked if I was willing to be a missionary. Do I love him enough to give up all I love to serve him? Yes, I do, but that's not what he's asked of me.

My decision may disappoint you, but please know I'm at complete peace and that I can't wait to serve the Lord as a teacher in Salina, Kansas.

Violet signed the letter and addressed the envelope. She'd mail it in the morning.

She leaned back in her chair, heaviness weighing on her.

Kitty was already softly snoring. On the evening of D-day, the Red Cross workers had been allowed to return home, and Violet and Kitty had reclaimed their room. Violet had barely slept last night, burdened by worry for Adler and guilt over how she'd wavered with Griff. Tonight she needed to sleep.

She stroked the first letter she'd written that evening, to her parents. Soon they would read it, sitting on the porch as Dad's pipe smoke perfumed the summer air. Maybe Alma and Karl would be there with their families, laughing and telling stories while the children played. Nels was already away at an Army training camp.

Violet's face crumpled. If only she were home. Mom would hug her and tell her Adler couldn't possibly be dead. Would that be a lie? Violet didn't care. She needed to hear it and believe it.

No news about him had arrived today, but the beaches were chaotic. Adler had a life to live—a good life—and she refused to give up hope.

She rubbed her eyelids, but her worries still overpowered her fatigue. Even at midnight. The room pressed in, and restlessness rattled her legs.

Violet slipped her coat over her uniform and stepped outside. In the cool air, a full moon lent the overcast a silvery tinge. She leaned back against the arched corrugated steel, same as she had the night Adler first kissed her. Most people wouldn't consider it a romantic location for a first kiss, but Violet did.

"Lord, please bring him home alive. Thank you for allowing me the privilege of loving him, even for such a short time. He was—he was good for me."

Had she been good for him too? Maybe, up until the very end.

"Lord, please let him live. Let him raise his little boy. Bring him a woman someday, a better woman, to love him. He deserves a long and happy life."

The sound of aircraft engines built. It never ended, and she'd grown to like the noise.

But a single plane? This low? This late?

Violet turned south toward the sound. Silhouetted against the sky, a plane drew near. Two engines and a shape she'd never seen, almost bulbous on top. What was that?

Loud, stuttering noises. Pink lines of fire leaped up to the plane.

Violet cried out and crouched beside the hut. A German airplane, and the antiaircraft gunners on the base were shooting at it.

The engine noises changed. The airplane turned into view, aiming right for the communal site!

Everything in her wanted to run, but she had no time to reach the air raid shelter. So she stayed put. Paralyzed.

The antiaircraft guns kept up their loud protest, but new gunfire erupted, from the enemy aircraft. Chunks of earth sprang up from the baseball field, then the plane roared overhead.

Violet screamed—she couldn't help it—and gunfire pounded through the communal site.

Then it was gone. Over.

Kitty stumbled outside in her pajamas, wide-eyed. "What was that?"

"An air raid. They hit the communal site." Time to switch from victim to Red Cross worker. "Get your coat and shoes. Let's go!"

Violet dashed back inside, down the dark hallway, and into the kitchen, where she grabbed the first aid kit and flashlight.

She flung open the front door. Men were running toward the enlisted men's mess, so Violet joined them.

"It was an Me 410," a man yelled. Then he called it unprintable names.

"Nah, I only saw one engine. A 109, I swear it."

Violet didn't know and didn't care what kind of plane it was. She only cared about the injured. "Please, Lord, keep the men safe."

"Was anyone in the mess?" a man asked.

"I just left," someone said. "Lots of fellows in there. We've been working all day, you know."

The door to the mess stood open, and Violet stepped inside. The lights were out.

"Get it off me!" a man shouted. "Get it off!"

Violet shone the flashlight around. Tables were tipped over. Men were standing, squatting, curled up on the floor, calling out to each other.

"May I have your attention, please?" Violet shouted, using her most authoritative teacher voice. "If you're not hurt, please be quiet. If you need assistance, please speak up."

"I'm trapped! I'm hurt!"

Violet swung her flashlight across the mess. A man lay on the floor with a table on his legs. A bunch of men ran over and lifted the table off of him.

Violet illuminated the helpers and recognized Adler's crew chief, Bill Beckenbauer. "Sergeant, thank goodness it's you. Please assess the situation and see how many wounded we have, organize the men. I'll tend to this man's wounds."

"Yes, ma'am." He set his hand on her shoulder and opened his mouth, then closed it, his eyelids fluttering.

He was worried about Adler too, and she gave him a flimsy smile. "Go."

Beck left.

Violet knelt beside the injured man. "Where does it hurt?"

"My legs. But I don't think it's that bad, now that the table's off."

"Let me see. Would you hold the flashlight for me, please?" She handed it to him, then shoved up his trouser legs. A cut slashed across one shin, but a shallow cut. "You're right. It isn't bad at all."

"Lousy Krauts. Don't they know they're done for?"

"Apparently not. But we ran him off." Violet pulled out her supplies. "What's your name? Where do you work?"

"Marvin Chase. I work in supply."

Violet chuckled and dabbed the blood with gauze. "How many men in your department can say they've been shot at by the enemy? Maybe they'll give you the Purple Heart."

He laughed. "Wouldn't that be something? Finally got a story for the wife."

Violet cleaned his wound, swabbed it with iodine, and bandaged it.

Beck returned, with Kitty by his side. "A few nicks and scratches, nothing bad—that fellow was the worst of them."

"The doctors are here now," Kitty said. "No one was injured by gunfire, only by knocked-over tables and chairs."

"There's the damage." Beck pointed to the roof. Three big holes opened to the night sky.

Kitty laughed. "I'm glad he was a bad shot."

"Me too." Violet closed the first aid kit. When would it stop? Men shooting at each other, hurting each other, and killing each other. *Lord, please bring this war to an end.*

47

Nick shook his head at Adler. "The things you'll do to get yourself a P-51D model."

His squadron mates laughed, that high staccato laughter when great tension has been relieved.

Adler grinned at his buddies lounging in the pilots' room. It was very good to be back. "I did it for you, Nick. As squadron commander, you'll get the new bird. I'll get *Santa's Sleigh*."

Rosie put on a mock serious face. "Paxton got himself shot down out of the goodness of his heart."

Theo leaned forward in his chair with his old baby-faced eagerness. "Tell us about it."

All he wanted to do was find Violet, have that hard talk, and hit the sack. But he launched into the condensed version of his story for his friends.

How many times had he told it already?

On D-day evening and all the next day, he and Mike Weber had helped the demolition teams clear beach obstacles while sniper and artillery fire flew one direction and tank and naval fire flew the other. Hard, dangerous labor.

Both nights they'd hunkered under a half-shelter, shivering in the cold while the Luftwaffe made pathetic and cowardly attacks on the fleet of ships.

Finally on June 8, he and Mike had hitched a ride on an LST landing ship, a slow and rocky ride over the Channel.

The entire next day, Adler had been debriefed at Eighth Fighter Command, and this morning he'd taken the train to Leiston, where he'd spent the afternoon in more debriefings.

Enough. At last he finished the story, but it wouldn't be the final time.

"Good evening, gentlemen." Violet's voice behind him.

He sat bolt upright. His heart seized.

Nick stood with a strange smile. "Good evening, Miss Lindstrom."

"I brought the refreshments for the squadron party, just as you asked, Major." Her voice had a strained cheery tone.

Adler gripped the armrests. He wasn't ready. He'd planned to compose his speech on the walk to the Aeroclub, but now would have to do.

Cam flicked Nick on the arm. "Squadron party? You never said anything—"

"Shut up, Cam." Rosie nodded toward Adler.

He'd been set up. But what did it matter? He had to talk to her anyway.

Adler pushed himself to standing, straightened his Ike jacket, and turned around.

Violet arranged sandwiches, her head bent, blonde curls framing that lovely face. If only he could kiss her and tell her he loved her and wanted to be with her forever. But that wouldn't be fair to her.

He cleared his throat. "Howdy, Violet."

She snapped up straight, her eyes huge. "You—you're alive." Her voice choked.

Of course, he was alive. Why didn't she know yet?

Violet darted around the table, then stopped short and clapped both hands over her mouth, her face buckling. As if she'd wanted to embrace him—then remembered everything that had happened.

Everything that had happened kept his feet cemented to the floor.

"I thought . . . I thought." She swayed, then she gave her head a little shake, slipped behind the table, and fussed with the food. "I'm so thankful you survived."

For crying out loud. The woman had thought he was dead. Adler glared over his shoulder. "Nick! Why didn't you tell her?"

Nick rocked back and forth on his feet, wearing that stupid grin. "I didn't find out until you arrived. I've been kind of busy since."

"Now I know why you're having a party. I'm so glad. So glad." Violet's voice warbled, and she shuffled sandwiches with her head low. Not low enough to conceal her red cheeks.

Why did she still care for him? If only she didn't. Everything would have been a lot easier. "Violet, if it isn't too much to ask, I need to talk to you."

She stilled, her hands hovering over the tray. "All—all right."

"Say, Adler?" Nick gestured with his thumb to the front door. "We moved a couch outside, under those trees to the right of the building. So you can have some privacy. A gift from Santa."

Adler gaped at him. Not only had Nick set him up, but he'd put a whole lot of work into it.

He returned his attention to Violet. "Come on. Let's go outside."

"All right." She headed for the door with her head high, but her gait wobbled.

Adler scooted past her to open the door, passing his buddies.

Nick's grin grew. Theo gave him the thumbs-up. Cam made a kissy face. And Rosie pressed both hands over his heart, batted his eyelashes, and heaved a dramatic sigh.

"See y'all later. Enjoy your *party*." Adler injected the last word with a dose of sarcasm worthy of his beachmaster pal.

He swung open the door and followed Violet to the trees. A

black leather couch sat in the underbrush, and Violet sat down, her hands over her mouth and her eyes closed.

Adler stood in front of her and plunged his hands into the pockets of his khaki trousers. Where should he start? He had so much to say, and he had to say it right.

Violet took deep breaths as if pulling herself together. "They said you crash-landed in Normandy. How did you—how did you get back?"

Adler groaned and toed the trunk of a tree. Not the time for that. "Long story. But I had a lot of time to think lately. I realized I didn't explain myself when you apologized to me after the hoedown. You probably don't think I actually forgave you."

"Why would you?" She thumped her hands down into her lap. "I was horrible."

"No, don't do this. I never blamed you." He whapped the tree with the back of his hand. "I mean, that letter upset *me*, and I already knew a lot of it. You—it was all new to you."

"But I shouldn't have—"

"Don't." He fixed a strong gaze on her. "It's all forgiven. I mean it."

The resistance flowed out of her expression and her posture. "And I forgive you too—although you did nothing to wrong me. I don't hold anything against you, and I don't think less of you. Not at all."

His shoulders squirmed, wanting to shake it off but knowing he shouldn't. "Well, thank you."

Then she sat taller and raised her chin. "And I never stopped loving you."

His chest collapsed from the impact of words he both craved and feared. It had taken courage for her to be honest, and it would take courage for Adler to be just as honest. "I never stopped loving you either, but—"

"Oh, Adler!"

"No." He had to stop the joy from spreading on her face. "That doesn't mean we can be together."

"Why not?" Wrinkles raced across her forehead. "I don't care about your past. I don't."

Adler sighed and squatted in front of her. "But you should care about my future. I have nothing to offer you."

Her lips curved in the sweetest smile. "But you do. You're a fine man."

He couldn't let flattery sway him. Time to leap in. "I have a son, and I'm going to raise him."

"Of course."

She obviously hadn't thought this through. "I can't ask you to raise another woman's child."

Blue eyes narrowed at him. "Why not? Isn't that what your mother did?"

"It isn't the same. Every time you'd look at him, you'd see . . ." He winced.

Those eyes turned fierce. "I'd see the image of the man I love and an unfortunate young woman. But most of all I'd see a little boy who needs a mother."

Adler lowered his head and clenched his hands between his knees, the tension straining the stitches on his arm. She'd do that? Of course she would, but that was only one piece of the puzzle. He cleared his throat and raised his head. "I'm raising him in Kerrville. My folks are the only family he knows. I can't rip him away from them."

"Of course not."

Didn't she see yet? "That means I won't be a missionary."

"I won't either."

"Violet!"

She shook her head with her eyes closed. "Another long story, but I already made that decision and it has nothing to do with you."

"But I can't even offer you Kansas. I'm going to Texas. It's a long way from your home."

She blinked. "All right."

Why couldn't she see the problems? "I might not be able to find a job. Daddy would take me back at Paxton Trucking, but I refuse to ask him. I'll ask Wyatt. The company will be his one day, and it should be his decision. He may not want to work with me, and I accept that."

"What about ACES?"

"Not in Kerrville. Folks would think I was competing with Paxton Trucking. I won't do that."

Another blink. "All right."

"Don't you see? I might not find a job."

"I don't see why not." She frowned at him. "You're smart and hardworking and personable."

Her innocence was so lovable and so maddening.

A cramp shot through his legs, so he sat on the couch facing Violet, one knee up on the cushion to separate them. "It's not that simple. In Kerrville everyone knows everyone else's business. They all know I got my brother's girlfriend pregnant and skipped town. Now she's dead. Who'll hire me?"

"I doubt it'll be that bad." She twisted to face him and leaned her shoulder against the sofa back. "Don't forget, I'm a teacher. I could find a job."

Everything in him bristled at the thought of a wife supporting him, but it was better than starving. And that wasn't the point. "The point is, I refuse to drag you into the mess of my life."

Her mouth tightened. "Shouldn't that be my choice?"

"Yes. That's why I'm trying to make you see how bad it'll be. My family—I doubt we'll ever be happy and close again. There'll be tension, maybe outright antagonism."

"I'm sure it'll be fine in time. Different, but fine."

Stubborn woman. He draped his elbow over the back of the

sofa. "I'll be a pariah in town. Think about it. No matter how upstanding a life I live, they'll always see me as I was. At best, I'll be politely tolerated. At worst, I'll be shunned. Don't you see?"

Violet lowered her chin and fell silent for a moment. "That will be very difficult for you."

A sigh rushed out. Finally, she saw.

"It sounds as if you could use someone by your side, someone who loves you and believes in you." She raised her chin again, and her eyes glowed with determined love.

"Violet!" He slapped the sofa back. "I refuse to drag you into that."

"Adler Paxton!" She slapped the cushion between them. "I was willing to go to Africa and live in a hut with wild beasts breathing down my neck. Don't you think I can handle some snubbing?"

Adler's jaw fell open. There was that gumption he'd fallen in love with, and he could feel himself weakening. He rested his forehead in his hand. "Violet . . . it's more than the snubbing. It's everything, all the stuff I just told you about, all together. I love you too much to do that."

"I love you too. When you love someone, you're willing to make sacrifices for him."

He didn't deserve love like that. He didn't. But he wanted it more than anything.

"And when you love someone . . ." Her voice cracked. "You don't run away from her."

He lowered his hand and met her gaze, now vulnerable and . . . lost.

In half a second, he scooted beside her, took her in his arms, and kissed her, over and over. Lips and cheeks and nose and forehead and lips again. "My Violet. My darlin' Violet."

"Don't make me cry." She clutched him close. "Please don't. I'm tired of crying."

So he kissed her full on the mouth, slow and long and honest.

This was what their love was meant to be all along—two sinners, repentant, forgiving, sacrificing, willing to face an uncertain future together.

Violet's lips twitched under his, and she laughed. "I thought they were going to give us privacy."

Privacy? What?

Then the sounds of cheering and applause hit his ears. The men he used to call friends, whooping and making smooching noises over by the Nissen hut.

Adler glared at them through the trees. "I don't know whether to beat up the lot of them or buy them a round of drinks."

She giggled and kissed his cheek. "I know which they'd prefer."

He turned a smile to her. She'd said that with humor, without a trace of judgment. How he loved her. "Tell you what. We've got a whole herd of Mustangs at this here ranch. Let's you and I squeeze into a cockpit, and we'll ride off into that there sunset."

Violet stood and offered her hand and a cute little smile. "My sweet-talking cowboy."

48

"We're excited about the activities we have planned for the rest of the summer." Violet handed typed sheets to both Rufus Tate and Col. Donald Graham. "Social, recreational, and intellectual pursuits."

"The usual activities and weekly dances, of course." Kitty smiled from her spot on the sofa in the Aeroclub lounge. "We're adding a Ping-Pong tournament, a chess tournament, and a darts tournament."

"A lecture series?" Colonel Graham tapped the paper. "That sounds interesting."

"Doesn't it?" Kitty almost bounced in her seat. "One of the staff officers is a zoology professor, and many of the men have fascinating backgrounds and knowledge to share."

Including Paul Harrison, who was scheduled to give a lecture about China. "We're thrilled about this."

"The hoedown was a big hit," the colonel said. "Are you planning another party?"

Violet looked at Kitty and laughed. "We thought about holding a

Fourth of July party, but we decided it wouldn't be proper to celebrate our independence *from* the British *with* the British."

Both men laughed.

"So we'll have a Fourth of July party for our men, and a party with the children at the end of the summer. Four times a year sounds right."

Kitty nodded. "Some of the townspeople are concerned that we'll spoil the children, so we need to keep that in mind. We won't be here forever."

"Not for long, the way things are going," Colonel Graham said.

The Allied forces in Normandy had consolidated all five beaches and were steadily advancing inland. But Berlin lay many miles away.

The colonel smiled at Violet and Kitty. "You ladies have your work cut out for you."

"They'll come through." Mr. Tate stood and tugged his vest down over his belly. "Best Aeroclub in England, I always say."

Violet avoided Kitty's gaze, or she'd break down laughing.

But she wouldn't complain. They'd worked long and hard, and the results were wonderful—a homey club, plenty of stimulating activities, and good relations with the British, even after the arrests of Mr. Banister and Griff. The fact that the thefts had been a joint American-English venture helped stop finger-pointing.

The two men thanked the ladies and departed.

Kitty scowled, puffed out her belly, and tugged her jacket down. "Best Aeroclub in England, I always say."

Violet laughed and linked arms with her friend, and they strolled down the hallway. Mr. Tate's praise of the ladies' work was as close to an apology as they'd get. Somehow it still satisfied.

In each room men chatted, read, and enjoyed wholesome fun. By boosting morale, she and Kitty were playing a small but vital role in ending the war, and she couldn't be happier.

Adler walked in the front door.

Oh yes, she could be happier.

But the sunny smile he'd constantly worn since their reconciliation was gone.

Violet released Kitty's arm and met him in front of the snack bar. His face was pale and drawn. They'd flown a mission today—was it a bad one? "Sweetheart, what's wrong?"

He held up an envelope. "From Wyatt."

"You haven't opened it."

Adler flipped it over in his hands. "I can face Nazis in the air and on the ground, but I can't face my own brother."

After what the last letter had contained, Violet didn't blame him. She reached for his left arm, but the patched area of his flight jacket reminded her of the bullet that had gashed the leather and his skin. She rubbed his right arm instead.

Haggardness dimmed his eyes. "I want you to read it first."

To screen it for him. She took the envelope. Kitty was in the kitchen, so she led Adler into the office and shut the door.

"People might talk. Leave the door open, please."

"Not today." She leaned back against the closed door. "I'm blocking your escape route."

He cracked a smile. "You may be tall, but I can still toss you over my shoulder."

That might be fun to try someday. "I don't mind you running as long as you take me with you."

Adler plunked himself in a chair, stretched out his long legs, and poked her toes with his. "The letter."

She opened the envelope. What was Wyatt like, this man who might someday be her brother-in-law? *Please, Lord. Let him have a soft and merciful heart.*

She pulled out two sheets of stationery. Well, he certainly had a lot to say.

Dear Adler,
   I'm sure you're surprised to hear from me, but I pray you'll

read this and consider what I have to say. I need to apologize and ask your forgiveness.

Sounds like you and I finally wrote home about the same time. Mama gave me your address and begged me to write you. She said you're a fighter pilot. I'm a naval officer based on the same island. Looks like all three of us are preparing for the same operation. On Easter Sunday, I believe I saw you in the park. I couldn't face you then, but I choose to do so now.

I can't begin to tell you how sorry I am about Oralee. Although her death was an accident and there was no malice in my actions, my role wasn't completely innocent. We have a long history of competition, you and I, and I resented how my younger brother bested me in everything. But Oralee rightfully chose you over me. You two were meant to be together, and I was wrong to let jealousy take root.

When she didn't want to cross that bridge and you kept coaxing her, all that resentment boiled up. My pride started that argument. My anger made Oralee cross the bridge just to stop our fighting. And my jealousy led her to refuse my help even as she teetered on the edge.

So no, I didn't kill her in the eyes of God or the law, but my actions did lead to her death. Even though the Lord has forgiven me, I will always live with the regret that her life ended far too early and that your life together never began.

Please know I am deeply sorry for the grief I caused you. If you should choose to forgive me, I'll be forever grateful. But if you don't, I'll understand.

I've never blamed you for wanting to kill me that day, and I forgave you for that long ago. How can I do otherwise when I recognize the depth of my own sins against you and Clay and while I accept Jesus's astounding mercy?

As this war heats up, only God knows what will happen to us. I can't head into battle without telling you everything in my heart. As much as we competed and fought, I miss you. I miss how you challenged me. I miss your sunny spirit, your passionate drive, and how you inspire people to do their best. You're a good man, and I admire you, respect you, and love you. I'm a better man for having you as my brother.

I pray we can be reconciled and can meet again. I'm enclosing my address, and I hope you write me. Whatever you have to say, I can take it. Even if we're never reconciled, please know I'll pray for you all the days of my life.

> *Your brother,*
> *Wyatt*

While she read, Adler paced. And he perched on the desk, and he paced, and he inspected the pictures, and he paced. "How long is that letter anyway?"

Violet drew in a rough breath and blinked away the moisture in her eyes. "It's all good news. He wrote this before D-day. He loves you, he forgives you, and he wants you to forgive him."

"Me?" Adler's upper lip curled. "Forgive him? What for?"

"He feels responsible for Oralee's death."

Adler thumped into the chair and groaned. "Of course he does. I told him he was responsible."

"They released the mail after D-day. He's probably received your letter by now." She handed him the letter. "He sounds like a very sweet man. I see the family resemblance."

"Me? Sweet?" He barked out a laugh. "Darlin', love has addled your brain."

And she didn't mind one bit. She studied his expressions as he read Wyatt's words—the regret, the concern, the grief, and the gratitude.

He sat back in the chair and flipped through the pages as if something was missing. "'My sins against you and Clay'? What's he talking about? He didn't do anything to Clay. Clay tackled me, and Wyatt skipped town."

"I don't know." Violet leaned back against the desk. "Do you want to see him?"

"Yeah, but he said he was going into battle. That means he's at sea, I reckon. All I have is his Fleet Post Office address. Who knows where he is?"

"The Red Cross does—or can find out."

"You'd do that?" He gave her the mischievous grin she adored. "What'll it cost me?"

Violet tapped her lips and smiled.

"I can pay that price." He tilted his head to the door. "But not with the door shut."

Not in the sight of every man in the Aeroclub either.

Violet opened the door, backed into the V-shaped space between the door and the wall, and beckoned with one finger.

That grin grew bigger and bigger and closer and closer, until it melded with hers.

49

Adler ambled down the London street pretending he was sightseeing and not procrastinating. Four-story buildings in white and brick stood shoulder to shoulder, neat and classy, the neighborhood's perfection marred only by vacant lots from bomb damage during the Blitz and Little Blitz.

"Come on." Violet tugged his hand. "No dillydallying."

The woman knew him too well. "Thanks for coming as my bodyguard."

Violet squeezed his hand. "Wyatt sounds eager to see you. I seriously doubt he intends to harm you."

"I should have sent camels."

She snapped her gaze to him and laughed. "Camels?"

"Remember when Jacob returned from exile, and he feared for his life? Jacob sent Esau a herd of goats and camels to appease him."

She laughed and nudged his shoulder. "Wyatt's a naval officer. What would he do with camels?"

The image did make him smile.

Violet inspected the notes in her hand. "This is the street."

Adler rounded the corner onto a side street.

Down a block or so, a man in navy blue stood on the sidewalk. Wyatt.

Adler's feet glued to the pavement.

"Adler!" Wyatt waved and ran down the street, Esau running to the brother who had wronged him. "Adler! Adler!"

"Run to him," Violet said.

Adler pried one foot free, then the other, and he walked, then jogged, then broke into a full run. "Wyatt!"

They slammed into each other, laughing, half-hugging, half-wrestling.

"You big lug." Wyatt pulled back and gripped Adler's shoulders. "Take a couple of shots at you? Why on earth would I want to do that?"

Adler grasped his brother's shoulders as well. The naval officer's dress blues looked good on him. Same warm smile, same gray-blue eyes, a bit more defined in the face. A scar slashed across his left cheek. From when Adler threw a rock at him.

He winced. "That scar. That's a good reason right there."

"Are you kidding?" Wyatt rubbed it and smiled. "I ought to thank you. Dorothy says it makes me look exciting."

"Dorothy?"

"My girlfriend, Dorothy Fairfax. This is her home. Let's go inside. I want you to meet her and her father."

"Just a second." Adler turned around.

Violet stood right behind him, her eyes glistening.

"You brought the Red Cross?" Wyatt's voice rose in disbelief.

"It's a joy to meet you. I've heard so much about you." She shook his hand. "I'm Violet Lindstrom."

"You're the one who set up the meeting." Wyatt wore a strange flat smile.

He thought Adler really had brought a bodyguard, and Adler chuckled. "Violet's my girlfriend. She runs the Aeroclub at my air base."

346

"Oh." Wyatt's smile unfroze. "Nice to meet you too. Well, come on."

He led them down a few houses. "Dorothy's a 'Wren,' an officer in the Women's Royal Naval Service. We met at naval headquarters in London working on D-day plans."

So he'd been safe on land, thank goodness. "I'm glad you were here that day."

"Hardly. I was on a destroyer bombarding Omaha Beach."

Those destroyers had come dangerously close to shore supporting the troops. "Maybe those were your shells flying over my head."

Wyatt laughed and clapped him on the back. "My aim is better than that. I hit gun batteries, not aircraft."

"And I was on the ground. I crash-landed behind Omaha and fought with the infantry. Y'all made an awful racket. Interfered with my beauty sleep."

"Well, I'll be. If I'd known you were there, I'd have lobbed a few more projectiles your way." Wyatt winked at him.

"Now, boys," Violet said in a teasing tone.

Wyatt climbed the steps to a house. "Can't tell you how good it is to see you again."

"Same here. Never . . . never thought I would."

Wyatt gave him a compassionate look and opened the door.

A middle-aged gentleman and a pretty redhead in a navy blue uniform stood inside—the people he'd seen with Wyatt on Easter.

Wyatt took off his officer's cap. "Dorothy, Mr. Fairfax, this is my brother, Capt. Adler Paxton, and his girlfriend . . ."

Poor Wyatt had never been good with names. "Violet Lindstrom."

"It is such a pleasure to meet you." Dorothy shook Adler's hand, tears in her bright blue eyes. "I've dreamed of this moment as long as I've known Wyatt."

More handshakes and greetings, then Dorothy ushered them into the sitting room, filled with luxurious dark woods and upholstered chairs.

A black Scottish terrier sat by the coffee table, eyeing Adler warily.

Wyatt scooped up the pooch. "This is Bonnie Prince Charlie, a member of His Majesty's Royal Highlanders and the scourge of the Nazi squirrels in Kensington Gardens."

Violet shook his little paw. "At least there's one war hero in the room."

Dorothy laughed. "I think you and I shall get along famously. Please have a seat and help yourself to the biscuits. Would you like some tea?"

Biscuits? Oh yeah, cookies. Adler sat on a small sofa with Violet at his side, while Wyatt and Mr. Fairfax sat in armchairs.

Dorothy poured tea into china cups with blue and pink flowers on them. "As hostess, I'm establishing one rule for today. You are not allowed to apologize to each other."

Adler shot Wyatt a look, but his older brother looked confused too. "But that's why I came."

"Nonsense." Dorothy set down the teapot and sat between her father and boyfriend. "You wrote Wyatt a lovely letter apologizing and begging forgiveness. And Wyatt, you wrote a terribly long and terribly maudlin letter cataloging every unpleasant thought, word, or action committed against your brother in the past twenty-five years. Am I right?"

Wyatt gave her a sheepish smile. "Maybe."

"Of course I'm right. So there's nothing left to say on the matter." She gave a firm nod.

"That's a wonderful idea." Violet picked out a shortbread cookie. "Just enjoy each other's company."

The old Adler was more than willing to sweep the past three years under the Fairfaxes' Oriental rug, but the new man had something to say. "I appreciate that, Miss Fairfax—"

"Dorothy. Please."

"Dorothy." He cradled the delicate cup in his hands. "But there's something I didn't put in my letter."

348

"It's all right," Wyatt said.

"No, it isn't. My anger drove you to run away. That cut you off from Daddy and Mama and Clay as well. For three years! I realized that recently, and I feel awful about it."

Wyatt's face lengthened. He turned to Dorothy, who mirrored his expression. Wyatt pressed his lips together. "Daddy and Mama didn't tell you."

"Tell me what?"

"You know why I ran away, but not why I stayed away."

"Because of me."

Wyatt fiddled with his black necktie. "I knew you'd calm down eventually. I stayed away because of what I did to Clay."

To Clay? Was that what he'd meant about 'sins against Clay'? "What happened?"

"After Oralee . . ." He took a deep breath.

Dorothy patted his arm. "Go ahead, darling."

"I ran home," he said, his voice rough. "Daddy and Mama told me to leave town for a few days, let you cool down. Then they went to fetch Dr. Hill and the sheriff. After they left, I realized I had only fifteen cents in my pocket, not enough for a train ticket. I searched the entire house for cash. Then I got to Clay's room."

"Yeah?"

"He'd just withdrawn his college money from the savings and loan. I didn't stop to calculate how much I needed. I just grabbed the envelope and ran. I went to Charleston to stay with a buddy. I meant to send back the balance, but I let my friend talk me into investing in his company. It went belly-up and I lost every penny. I've spent the last three years saving up to pay him back. It's all done now. I sent a check right before D-day."

"Every penny, plus interest." Dorothy hugged Wyatt's arm and smiled at Adler. "You know your brother."

He thought he did. Wyatt, a thief?

"Paying him back doesn't undo what I did. Clay didn't go to college because of me."

That's what Daddy meant about Clay having financial troubles. But it wasn't really Wyatt's fault. Adler's rage caused Wyatt to panic and steal. "Oh no."

"God's forgiven me, and so have our parents, but I don't know if Clay ever will."

Then a force like a full salvo of shells hit Adler in the chest, and he gasped from the pain. "Oh no. Clay was betrayed by both of us."

"You? What did you do?"

Adler hung his head. "Daddy and Mama didn't tell you either."

Violet stroked his arm. "Tell him, sweetheart."

Adler dragged his heavy gaze up to Mr. Fairfax and Dorothy. "I beg your pardon. I don't want to burden y'all with the Paxton family's darkest secrets."

"The Fairfax family has a few dark secrets of its own," Dorothy said with a rueful smile.

"And if it concerns me," Wyatt said, "it concerns them."

Adler drank in one last strengthening, encouraging look from the woman he loved, the woman who loved him in spite of all he'd done.

Then he told the story. All of it. The failed attempt to steal the truck. Ellen and the whiskey. Clay finding them. Daddy and Mama and the shotgun. Timmy's birth. Ellen's death. Adler's deep regret.

When he finished, Wyatt rubbed his hand over his mouth, his eyes wide and stark. "He—he has good reason to hate us both."

Their gazes locked. For Adler's whole life, his relationship with Wyatt had been frayed by competition and jealousy. But now unity coursed between them—brother to brother, man to man, sinner to sinner—bound by mutual regret and mutual love for the little brother they'd both betrayed.

"I wrote to him same time as I wrote you," Wyatt said. "I haven't heard back."

"Same here. Daddy said he's an Army Ranger. Reckon he fought on D-day."

"They . . . they took heavy casualties."

"I've made inquiries with the Red Cross," Violet said softly. "We'll let you know as soon as we hear anything."

"Thank you," Wyatt said.

Silence fell in the room, dark and weighty.

Mr. Fairfax harrumphed and straightened his suit jacket, a touch of amusement in his eyes. "I'm afraid you Yanks are unaware that, to the English, discussing unpleasant subjects over tea is most improper."

Wyatt raised his teacup. "That's why we drink coffee."

Dorothy giggled and covered her mouth. Then Wyatt chuckled, and Adler and Violet joined him.

To laugh with his brother again, after all they'd gone through— what a gift.

"My dear Mr. Fairfax," Wyatt said in a fake English accent. "Would you please be so kind as to inform my brother as to proper subjects to discuss over tea?"

"Business." He took a sip of tea. "Business is always an excellent topic."

"Papa is a businessman," Dorothy said.

Mr. Fairfax addressed Adler. "I understand you have a keen interest in commerce."

"I do." And now was as good a time as any to ask. "Wyatt, I want to ask if I could work for Paxton Trucking after the war."

Wyatt raised one eyebrow. "That's Daddy's decision, not mine."

"The company will be yours someday. If you don't feel comfortable working with me, I understand. You don't have to answer right away. But it's your decision."

"Actually, it isn't." He took another cookie from the plate. "I already wrote home about this. I'm an accountant. I have no interest in running the company."

"He's received another offer of employment," Mr. Fairfax said. "From me."

"We have a few bureaucratic hurdles, but if we can jump them, I'll stay here." Wyatt gathered Dorothy's hand in his.

Adler pulled himself together. "Congratulations. Wow. Living in London."

"I love it here."

Adler had a hunch the appeal ran past the city to the adoring redhead beside him. "Wow."

"The company's yours," Wyatt said with a huge grin. "You're the best man to run it, and you and I and Daddy have known it all along, even if we never said it."

Adler knew his mouth was hanging open, but he couldn't close it. He'd always wanted to run the company. That desire had fueled his jealousy and resentment and competition with his brother. That desire had destroyed too many lives. "I—I don't deserve it. I shouldn't have it."

Violet looped her arm through his. "That's why you're ready. You've learned to be the best wingman, so now you're the best type of leader and the right man to run that company. Because now you put others first."

Adler slammed his eyes shut, wrestling with God again, trying to throw the gift back into his arms. He didn't deserve this woman. He didn't deserve a future with her, in the position he'd always wanted, in the town he'd never wanted to leave.

Once again, God was winning the wrestling match, and Adler silently thanked him.

For most of his life, he thought he'd deserved all of it. God had waited to give it to him until Adler knew he deserved none of it.

50

The sun sat low in the west, warming the trees in the Victoria Tower Gardens with a golden glow and flinging glitter along the Thames. The pale gray spires of the Houses of Parliament peeked above the trees, bright against the clear sky.

Violet leaned into Adler's shoulder as they strolled. "I don't think I've ever had a more wonderful day."

"I have that effect on you."

She laughed at his roguish smile. "No, silly. Seeing you and Wyatt reunited."

They'd stayed at the Fairfax home through lunch and tea and dinner. The brothers told funny stories from their boyhood and war stories from their manhood. They were so different, yet shared the same strength and integrity and good humor.

"It was . . . more than I expected. Better than expected." Adler gazed into the distance.

"I know." She watched him in silence. He was absorbing the fullness of forgiveness and reconciliation more quickly than she'd thought he would.

Adler flashed a sudden smile at her. "I like Dorothy. She's a bundle of energy, just what Wyatt needs."

"They're darling together."

"I reckon she'll end up part of the family someday." Backing Violet up against the stone embankment beside the Thames, he wrapped his arms around her waist underneath her unbuttoned overcoat. "I reckon you will too."

Violet's breath hitched, and she dissected the pensive look in his blue eyes. They talked about their future as if it were certain, but he hadn't proposed.

He kissed her nose. "The way you keep talking about raising my son, I'd better ask you to be my wife pretty soon."

"Or your nanny."

He chuckled, his tea-scented breath puffing over her lips. "Wife. If I had a ring, I'd ask you right now."

And she'd say yes. Pure contentment raised a smile and lowered her eyelids, then she felt the gentle pressure of his forehead against hers.

"What would you say?" he murmured.

"Maybe it's my turn to be the mysterious one."

"As if you could. You're transparent, darlin', always have been. Besides, Timmy's too cute. I know you can't wait to be his mama."

She stroked his solid, wool-clad back. "You're awfully cute too."

"Cute enough to marry?"

She slid away from between the cold stone wall and the warm Adler wall and sashayed down the path, casting her most mysterious smile over her shoulder.

He grinned and jogged to catch up with her. "Not without a ring, huh?"

"You make me sound mercenary."

"Not the woman who wanted to live in a hut." He captured her hand in his, but his brow puckered. "Are you absolutely sure about not becoming a mission—"

"Yes. I told you. I wanted that for the wrong reasons."

"It's never wrong to love God and want to serve him."

"True." In her overcoat pocket, she found Elsa's familiar wooden form. "That's why I don't regret following that path. And God's brought such good out of it. If I hadn't wanted to be a missionary, I would have married someone straight out of high school. I wouldn't have gone to college, I wouldn't have become a teacher, and I wouldn't have joined the Red Cross and learned all the lessons I've learned over here. And I wouldn't have met you."

"Well then, I'm glad you misheard the Lord."

She laughed and bumped up against his side.

"As long as you're sure." Atypical uncertainty lowered his voice.

"Positive. My mission field is in Texas at your side."

"At your side. I like the sound of that." He hooked his arm around her waist.

"It's hardly original. At his side—the Red Cross motto."

"My motto too."

Violet pulled Elsa from her pocket. The little elephant's wood was worn smooth from years of loving. Two spots of white marked where Violet's youngest brother, Nels, had snapped off the tusks. Elsa had provided much comfort and inspiration.

"It's time Elsa found a new home." Violet set her on a bench that was raised on a stone platform so people could see the Thames over the embankment. "Maybe another little girl will find her and be inspired."

"Violet, no." Adler circled the bench, sat, and picked up Elsa. "She represents your dream."

"Not anymore." She strolled in front of the man she loved. "I have new dreams."

Adler poked his hand inside his Ike jacket. "Just because we have new dreams doesn't mean we forget our old ones."

"No, but . . ."

With a fierce look Adler held up a square of yellow fabric. "You didn't let me throw this away. Why?"

She sighed and joined him on the bench, loving him still more. "Because Oralee was your dream, and you need to treasure her memory. She helped make you who you are today, in her life and . . . and in her death."

Nodding and frowning, he wrapped the scrap around Elsa's neck like a bandanna and pinned it in place. "Someday Elsa will sit in our house, just like this."

"Oh, sweetheart." Violet's vision blurred.

Adler took her hand and set Elsa in her palm. "Without our dreams we never would have found each other."

And out of the rubble of those broken dreams, a new and lovely dream had risen.

Violet leaned against Adler and clutched Elsa in the valley between their shoulders, their hands, their hearts, and their dreams entwined.

★ ★ ★

Read On for an Excerpt of the Next

Story

Most men woke in a cold sweat when they dreamed of their own deaths, but not Private Clay Paxton.

Clay crawled through a foxhole with bullets zinging overhead, just like in his recurring dream. But these were American bullets fired to teach the Army Ranger recruits to keep their heads down.

"Come on, G.M.," he called to his buddy. Gene Mayer might be fast and wiry, but the Californian wilted in the Tennessee humidity.

"Right on your heels, Pax."

Clay slithered out of the foxhole and under rows of barbed wire. His wrestling training kept his movements low, controlled, and speedy, even with full gear on his back.

The volunteer to his right cussed. His rifle barrel had gotten caught in the wire.

"Back up, Holman." Clay elbowed his way through the dirt. "Try again. Head low."

Holman cussed again, but a friendly sort of cuss.

Clay cleared the wires and sprinted to the next station in the obstacle course, his respiratory rate hard but even.

He clambered up a cargo net and slapped his hand on the wooden platform that led to the rope bridge over the Elk River.

A boot slammed down.

"Watch out!" Clay yanked his hand away, and he lurched down, barely catching himself.

Bertie King sneered down at him. "No room in the Rangers for a half-breed."

If he wanted Clay to bite, he'd have to use fresher bait than that old worm.

"No room for a half-wit either, King," Gene said. "Let him up."

"What's the holdup, boys?" Sergeant Tommy Lombardi strode over. "King! Get your tail over that bridge. Paxton, Mayer, what are you waiting for?"

King stepped out onto the bridge. "Stupid wop," he muttered.

Clay puffed out a breath. Nothing stupider than insulting your sergeant.

He hefted himself onto the platform, grasped the two side ropes, and set his boot on the center rope. Angling his feet, he worked his way across.

"Why do you let him talk to you that way?" Gene asked.

Clay shook his head. Not only had he never been the brawling kind, but any fight would be considered his fault, just because his mama was Mexican. "Let's save the fighting for the battlefield."

"You have to put up with this a lot?" Gene asked, his voice low and hard.

"Not as much as you might think." Growing up, he'd had Wyatt and Adler to protect him.

Until that night two years ago when they'd stripped him of his future and cast him into a pit. Showed what they really thought of their half-breed half brother.

Pain and humiliation threatened his balance, and he hardened his chest. None of that mattered anymore. The Lord had given him the dream to show him the way out of the pit, and Clay thanked him once again.

On the far side of the river, Clay ran through the forest, hurdling logs and darting around boulders. Gene's long legs gained on him.

As soon as Clay had seen the notice at basic training about the Rangers, he'd volunteered. Styled after the British Commandos, the US Army Rangers had already seen action in North Africa. In April, the 2nd Ranger Battalion had been activated at Camp Forrest, and now Clay hoped to replace one of the original volunteers who hadn't made the cut.

Clay jogged to a dangling rope and climbed ten feet to the single rope line across the Elk. Hand over hand, Clay swung like a monkey over the green water.

An explosion to his left, and a geyser shot up and soaked him. He didn't lose his grip or his nerve.

"Do that again, boys," Gene shouted. "Feels good."

It did, and Clay laughed.

On the other side, he sprinted to a ten-foot-tall wooden fence. He worked his wet fingers into cracks and made his way up.

"They don't call me king for nothing." Bertie King straddled the fence and beat his chest like Tarzan. "You girls might as well give up, 'cause they only take the best. Me."

Clay kept climbing. Didn't King realize the Rangers wanted men who worked together?

"No stinking Jew-boys." King kicked at Sid Rubenstein's hand.

Ruby dropped to the ground, yelling and swearing.

King threw back his head and laughed.

A mistake.

He lost his balance and toppled backward. With a scream, he cartwheeled to earth and landed hard on one leg.

A crack.

Two years ago, a fall, a scream, and a crack had changed the course of Clay's life. Once again, he scrambled down to help.

Bertie King's lower right leg bent at an unnatural angle. The man cussed and struggled to sit up.

"Lie down, Bertie. Stay calm." Clay pressed on the patient's shoulders. "Medic! Gene, go get the medic."

Bertie swore at him, insulting his heritage, his paternity, and his intelligence.

"Lie still, or you'll further injure your leg." Clay unsheathed his knife and sliced the trouser leg open from knee to ankle. "Everyone, back up and give him some air. Ruby, Holman, open your first aid kits, get out the sterile dressings."

"How bad is it?" Bertie said between gritted teeth.

The blood and the angle of the leg made the diagnosis simple. "Complicated compound fracture of both the tibia and fibula—the bones in your shin." The man would need surgery, and he'd be out of the Rangers.

Clay took a sterile dressing from Ruby and opened it, careful to touch it as little as possible with his filthy hands. Right now stopping the bleeding was more important than sterility, so he pressed the dressing to the bloodiest part of the wound.

"Medics are here!" The circle of men opened up.

Two fellows ran up with a litter and medical kits. "What happened?"

Lt. Bill Taylor stood behind the medics.

Clay's heart hammered harder than it had running the course. Time to play dumb again. "King here fell off the wall. Reckon he broke his leg."

"What? You should have heard Paxton a minute ago," Holman said. "Talking about fibulas and all. He ought to be a doctor."

He winced and let the medics take his place. "Nah, I ain't smart enough. I just paid attention in first aid class, that's all. Y'all should have done the same."

"A medic then." Rubenstein pointed to the men splinting the remnants of Bertie King's leg. "Say, Lieutenant, didn't you say you need more medics in this unit?"

"Very much so." Keen eyes fixed on Clay, and Lieutenant Taylor beckoned him over.

No, no, no. Clay trudged to the officer. Medics didn't heave hand grenades into pillboxes like in his dream.

Taylor crossed muscular arms. "We need medics who can handle the physical training. You're doing well here, Paxton. You're the ideal candidate."

If the brass dug into Clay's records, they might learn he'd been top of his high school class, admitted to the University of Texas as a premedical student.

Clay sharpened his gaze. "Sir, I didn't volunteer for the Rangers to patch people up. Doesn't the Good Book say there's a time to every purpose? A time to kill, and a time to heal?"

"It certainly does."

"Well, sir, this ain't my healing time."

The lieutenant grinned. "I can't say I'm not disappointed, but I do like your fighting spirit. You're dismissed."

Clay released a long breath. He had to be more careful.

He couldn't allow the shards of his old dream to shred his new dream.

TULLAHOMA, TENNESSEE
SUNDAY, JUNE 13, 1943

Leah Jones studied the poem in her composition book as the bus jostled down the road.

> Between these lines
> Begins a tale
> Of hope, of chivalry beheld.
>
> Beguiles my soul,
> Becalms my heart,
> And here I find where I belong.

"Is *begins* too mundane?" she asked her new roommate, Darlene Bishop. "*Beget* perhaps? Or *bespoke*? No, neither is right."

"Sugar, you need to get your head out of the clouds." Darlene's Southern accent rocked in unison with the bus.

Leah scribbled more "be" words in the margin. "Librarians are supposed to have their heads in the clouds."

Darlene's bright red lips twisted. "You're working at an Army camp, sugar. These soldiers are wolves, every one of them. If you don't keep your eyes open, they'll eat you alive."

Leah laughed and smoothed the threadbare charity barrel dress that hung on her like a gunnysack. "They won't give me a second glance."

"Nonsense." Darlene's blue eyes narrowed in scrutiny. "When you get your first paycheck, I'll take you to the beauty shop and the dress shop. And makeup, but you won't need much with your dark coloring. Why, we'll smarten you right up."

Leah fingered the curl at the end of her long braid, and a thrill ran through her. Oh, to have things of her own. She still couldn't believe the boardinghouse placed only two girls in a room, and she had a bed all to herself.

"That's Gate 1." Darlene pointed out the window.

Cars and trucks and buses lined up at a booth with a sign that read "Camp Forrest." The camp had been named for Confederate General Nathan Bedford Forrest, but the pine trees framing the entrance still seemed appropriate.

"Do you know where the library is?" Darlene asked.

Leah blinked at the blonde. Darlene had worked at Camp Forrest for a year. How could she not know where the library was? "Miss Mayhew's letter said it was between the service club and the sports arena."

"The service club's a swinging spot. Here's your stop." She tapped Leah's arm. "If you need me, I'm at the PX at Avenue G and 26th."

"Thank you." Leah stuffed her book in her canvas schoolbag and squeezed past Darlene.

"Lamb to the wolves," Darlene muttered.

Leah smiled. A lamb could never have survived the orphanage.

She stepped off the bus, and pine-scented heat settled on her. A long two-story white frame building marked "Club 1" rose before her.

Leah passed groups of khaki-clad soldiers who cast sidelong glances that declared she didn't belong.

There it was. A smaller white frame building, too simple and plain for the splendors it housed. If only all libraries could be as glorious as the one in her earliest memory.

A soldier stepped out of the library, as grand as an Indian chief with his strong features and high cheekbones and a complexion even darker than her own. He slipped on a cap over shiny black hair, and his gaze landed on her.

Leah held her breath. She'd been caught staring.

He gave her the same bewildered look the other soldiers had, but then he tipped his head in a thoughtful way and descended the steps. "Pardon me, miss. Are you lost?"

Men never talked to her, and her gaze swung to the library. "Oh no. I'm found."

"I reckon you like libraries." His accent sounded more cowboy than Indian, and he had a nice deep chuckle.

"They're my greatest joy. After the Lord, of course." She didn't think she'd ever seen such dark eyes, yet they shone with warm amusement.

"Glad your priorities are straight, miss."

He obviously shared them, except . . . "You don't have a book."

He flashed a grin. "A muddy tent is no place for books. I do my reading here."

Leah wrapped her fingers around the fraying strap of her school-bag. "Maybe I'll see you again. I work here. Well, I will. Today's my first day."

"Oh." With rounded eyes, his gaze swept her up and down, but in a swift way as if he thought it rude. "Then I won't keep you, Miss . . ."

Something about him made her want to tell the whole story of her name and why it wasn't hers at all, but she merely extended her hand. "Leah Jones."

"Private Clay Paxton." He shook her hand with a grip both strong and gentle.

She said good-bye and climbed the steps. Darlene was mistaken about the men being wolves. She obviously hadn't met Clay Paxton.

Once inside, the rich familiar scent enveloped her, of ink and ideas and imagination.

A brunette stood behind a desk to Leah's right, setting books in a stack. She looked up and startled, then gave Leah a curious look. "May I help you, miss?"

"I'm Leah Jones. Are you Miss Mayhew?"

"You're . . . Leah . . . Miss Jones?" Shock and pity and restraint battled for control of her pretty features.

Leah stretched to her full five-foot-one. "Yes, ma'am. Miss Tilletson sent me. I have my papers here." She poked her hand into her schoolbag.

"No, no." Miss Mayhew blinked rapidly. "That isn't necessary. Oh my. Miss Tilletson said you came from the orphanage, but I had . . . no idea."

Shame and grief wound around Leah's heart in equal measure.

Miss Mayhew wore a trim powder blue suit. She inched closer as if afraid Leah might smell or have lice, but the orphanage had stressed cleanliness as a great virtue.

"Do you . . ." She gave Leah a sympathetic frown. "Do you have something more professional to wear? And your hair . . . could you do something? Put it up, perhaps?"

Leah's stomach curled up. "This is my best dress, ma'am. But when I get my first paycheck, I'll buy outfits and get a haircut. I promise."

Miss Mayhew's cheeks reddened, and she returned behind the desk and opened a drawer. "You won't be paid until the end of the week. That won't do."

"I'm sorry, ma'am." Her eyes stung, but years of practice kept them dry. "Miss Tilletson and the ladies from my church in Des Moines gave me money for my high school graduation last week. They were very generous. Very. They meant for me to buy clothes, but after I paid for bus and train tickets and my first month's room and board, I had nothing left."

"You're working the closing shifts." Miss Mayhew strode to her and held out a ten-dollar bill. "Tomorrow morning, go downtown and buy an outfit or two."

Leah edged back. "No, ma'am. I refuse to take charity ever again."

The librarian pursed her lips. "It isn't charity. It—it's an advance on your first paycheck."

That much money would buy a suit and blouse and shoes and a haircut too. "I promise I'll earn it. Every penny."

"I'm sure you will. I've known Miss Tilletson since library school, and she said you were smart and diligent." Miss Mayhew gazed around the room. "I would rather have hired a library school graduate. You aren't qualified to help with cataloging or research, but you should be able to serve as a circulations librarian."

Leah tucked the money into the deepest corner of her bag. "I know the Dewey Decimal System, I read all Miss Tilletson's library science books, and I plan to go to library school after I earn the tuition."

Miss Mayhew's smile twitched between pity and disbelief. "Yes. Well. Why don't you set your—bag in this drawer, and I'll show you our operations."

"Excuse me, ma'am." A tall blond soldier nodded to Miss May-hew. "My sergeant told me to read the field manual on service of the 75-millimeter howitzer. Do you have it?"

"Yes, sir." She turned back to Leah. "Have a seat, Miss Jones. I'll be right back."

"Thank you." Leah sat behind the librarian's desk and set her bag in the drawer—beside a heart-shaped cardboard box with a tag that read "To Myra. Love, John."

Her mouth watered. What would it be like to have an entire box of candy to herself?

She tipped open the lid. She just wanted a look. A smell. About half the chocolates were gone, but a dozen remained, round and glossy, with pretty swirls on top, and her fingers closed around one and slipped it into her bag.

Tonight she'd pretend her father had brought it home for her. He'd want her to have occasional treats.

But most of all, he'd want her to find her sisters.

The bookshelves called to her. If she could discover a picture or a snippet of information connected to one of her memories, then she'd know where she came from. And maybe she could find a Greek surname that sounded like her memory.

Ka-wa-los.

When her parents died, she'd only been four, too young to pronounce her name properly.

With a name and a city, she could locate the first orphanage she'd been sent to, the last place she'd seen her twin baby sisters. Every night she prayed that they were safe, that they had each other, and that one day she'd find them.

Only then would Leah belong.

Dear Reader,

When D-day is discussed, the aerial component is often over-looked. The dangerous and costly missions flown by the Royal Air Force and the US Eighth and Ninth Air Forces helped make the invasion possible by granting the Allies air superiority and by strangling German transportation to the invasion beaches. The missions flown on D-day by eleven thousand transport aircraft, bombers, and fighters greatly contributed to the success of Operation Overlord.

The 357th Fighter Group was a real unit, and the mission details were drawn from the historical record. Leiston is pronounced LAY-stin, if you're curious. The "Yoxford Boys" were famous as the first P-51 Mustang group in the US Eighth Air Force and the fighter group with the most aces (42) in the Eighth. I was honored to read the stories of the brave men who served in this prestigious unit.

Many of the real commanders, pilots, and officers of the 357th are named in this novel: Edwin Chickering, Henry Spicer, Donald Graham, Leonard "Kit" Carson, Clarence "Bud" Anderson, Tommy Hayes, Don Bochkay, Chuck Yeager (yes, the man who broke the sound barrier in 1947!), Jim Browning, Bob Becker, William O'Brien, Glen Davis, Jack Warren, John Barker, Alfred Craven, and Leo Miller. All other characters in the 357th are purely fictional.

There was indeed an American Red Cross Aeroclub at Leiston Army Airfield, run by Virginia Rado. All Red Cross personnel in this story are fictional, as are the details of the Aeroclub. But the setup and activities run by Violet and Kitty are typical.

During World War II, seven thousand Americans worked overseas for the Red Cross, operating service clubs, clubmobiles, Aeroclubs, Donut Dugouts, and many other services. Twenty-nine ARC workers lost their lives while serving. Their work aiding servicemen and providing those touches of home—including 1.6 *billion* donuts served!—were greatly appreciated.

Two "too coincidental to be real but really happened" moments occurred in the story. The 357th Fighter Group and the US 2nd Ranger Battalion actually sailed to Britain on the same ship on the same day. When I found out, I actually squealed. Also, the Luftwaffe did fly a "nuisance" air raid to Leiston on the night of June 7–8, 1944, causing minor damage and injuries in the enlisted men's mess.

I hope you enjoyed reading about D-day from the air. Please join Clay Paxton on the ground in *The Land Beneath Us* (2020) and Wyatt at sea in the first book in the series, *The Sea Before Us*, if you missed it.

If you're on Pinterest, please visit my board for *The Sky Above Us* (www.pinterest.com/sarahsundin) to see pictures of England, Normandy, Red Cross workers, P-51s, fighter pilots, and other inspiration for the story.

Acknowledgments

In writing my eleventh acknowledgments page, I run the risk of repetition. But can gratitude ever be repetitive? A writing career is a peculiar thing, and I could not write stories without the support of my family and friends. Not only do they bear with very odd writer quirks, but they also drag me out into the sun to interact with real human beings. And without sunshine and real human beings, there can be no stories.

And without my publishing team, there would be no published stories. My agent, editors, cover designers, publicists, marketing directors—I appreciate your talents and am so thankful for your support.

In this novel, several character names were "won" by readers in the pre-order campaign for *When Tides Turn*. Vicki Caruana contributed "Kitty Kelly" for her grandmother who was a volunteer during the war. I thought it a fitting name for Violet's perky Red Cross friend.

Joanna Hiemstra contributed "Theo" for her grandfather who emigrated from the Netherlands and "Christopher" for her cousin who recently passed away. She also contributed "Sylvia" for her storytelling grandmother who was a young girl during the war.

"Nick Westin"—reader friend Rachel DeFelice suggested this name several years ago. The reason she's naming a character is private (snicker). I'm so glad I found a character worthy of the name—and I admit Nick almost stole the show.

Also, thank you to writer friend Rachel McDaniel for telling me about her grandfather, Lt. Dale Karger, who was the youngest ace pilot in the 357th Fighter Group, although after the time frame of this novel. It was an honor to see video footage of him relaying how he shot down a Messerschmitt Me 262 jet fighter!

Small-world coincidences have been a lifelong occurrence for me, so I was thrilled when my friend Pauline Trummel casually mentioned her mom's cousin was an ace pilot in the 357th. She sent me scans of newspaper clippings and photos. Capt. Bob Becker was one of the original pilots, as my fictional Adler was, so of course I had to work his name in.

Extra thanks to my husband for brainstorming a pithy Texas saying with me.

And thank you to my readers! I appreciate your messages, prayers, and encouragement. Please visit me at www.sarahsundin .com to leave a message, sign up for my email newsletter, read about the history behind the story, and see pictures from my trip to England and Normandy. I hope to hear from you.

Discussion Questions

1. The aerial component of D-day is often overlooked, yet Allied airmen flew almost fifteen thousand sorties on that day. Have you heard of this aspect of D-day or of the preinvasion missions? What parts interested you?

2. The American Red Cross played a crucial role in keeping up morale for men and women in the military during World War II, both stateside and overseas. Could you see yourself working or volunteering? What areas interested you?

3. As a second-born child with a naturally ambitious personality, Adler has always striven to be first, both with his brother and as a pilot. In what ways is his ambition good? In what ways is it bad? How does he learn to temper this?

4. Violet struggles with the pain of an unfulfilled dream. Have you ever had an unfulfilled dream? How did you deal with it?

5. At the beginning of the story, Adler's philosophy is "If it hurts, don't think about it." Can this be a good self-protective mechanism? When does it go too far? What do you think

about his later realization that "the more he allowed himself to feel pain, the less it hurt"?

6. In what ways is Kitty Kelly a good friend to Violet? What traits do you like in your friends? Do you gravitate toward friends who are similar to you or who are different?

7. Nick Westin never gives up on Adler, even at his worst. Did Nick's example give you any ideas about how to deal with hurting or unbelieving friends? What approach do you like to take?

8. Violet suffers from homesickness and tries hard to overcome it. Are you a homebody? Or do you long for adventure? Or somewhere in the middle?

9. Adler clings to the scrap from Oralee's dress. How did this affect your opinion of him? What do you think of his decision to give it up for Violet—and of Violet's response? When is it good to hold on to our memories and mementos, and when is it better to let them go?

10. Likewise, Violet clings to Elsa the Elephant. What do you think of Violet's missionary dream? What's the difference between being called by God and being asked to be willing? Do you think she made the best decision at the end?

11. "The last shall be first, and the first last" (Matt. 20:16) is the theme verse for this story. How does this play out in Adler's story? In Violet's? Does this concept inspire you—or make you squirm?

12. Violet wrestles with self-righteousness, a quiet sin common in "good Christians," a sin we're often quick to spot in others but not in ourselves. How does this manifest in her thoughts and actions? How does she change? Did any of her revelations strike you?

13. When Adler learns of the full consequences of his sins, he goes through a second round of mourning, regret, and re-

pentance. In what ways is this right and good? When does it become unhealthy?

14. Adler and Violet share a love of Westerns. What hobbies or interests do you share with your loved ones? How do they make your relationships more fun?

15. Adler sees parallels between his life and the biblical story of Jacob. What similarities do you see? Are there any biblical characters you're particularly drawn to? What is it about their stories that you relate to or draw strength from?

16. If you read *The Sea Before Us*, what did you think about the continuation of Wyatt's story? From what you've heard about Clay Paxton, what might you expect in *The Land Beneath Us* (Clay's story, coming in 2020)?

Sarah Sundin is the bestselling author of *The Sea Before Us*, as well as the WAVES OF FREEDOM, the WINGS OF THE NIGHTINGALE, and the WINGS OF GLORY series. Her novels *When Tides Turn* and *Through Waters Deep* were named to Booklist's "101 Best Romance Novels of the Last 10 Years," and *Through Waters Deep* was a finalist for the 2016 Carol Award and won the INSPY Award. In 2011, Sarah received the Writer of the Year Award at the Mount Hermon Christian Writers Conference.

A graduate of UC San Francisco School of Pharmacy, she works on-call as a hospital pharmacist. During WWII, her grandfather served as a pharmacist's mate (medic) in the US Navy and her great-uncle flew with the US Eighth Air Force. Sarah and her husband have three adult children—including a sailor in the US Navy! Sarah lives in northern California, and she enjoys speaking for church, community, and writers' groups. Visit www.sarahsundin.com for more information.

Nothing but Love Could Heal the Wounds of War . . .

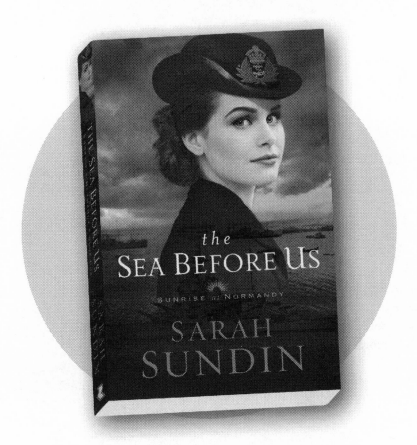

As D-day approaches, American naval officer Lt. Wyatt Paxton is teamed up with Dorothy Fairfax, a British officer. Once they piece together family and reconnaissance photos to map Normandy, will Wyatt's bombardment plans destroy what Dorothy loves most?

WAR IS COMING.

Can love carry them through the rough waters that lie ahead?

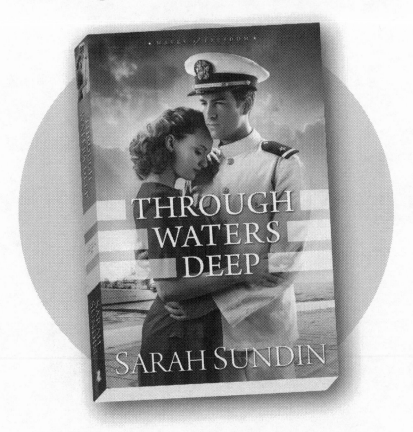

In 1941 as America teeters on the brink of World War II, Mary Stirling and Ensign Jim Avery work together to expose a saboteur. Will the dangers they encounter draw them together or tear them apart?

In a time of sacrifice, what price can one put on true love?

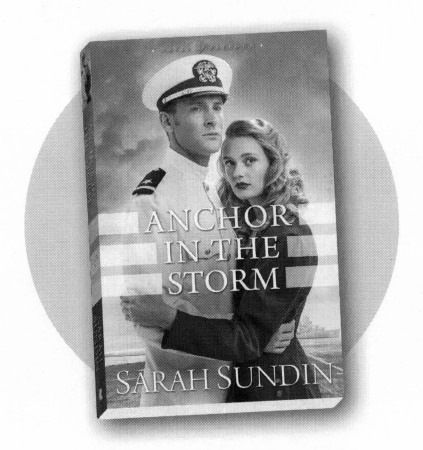

World War II pharmacist Lillian Avery is determined to ignore the attention of Ensign Archer Vandenberg, but will that change when she's forced to work with him on a dangerous case?

In a time of war, sometimes battles take place in the heart.

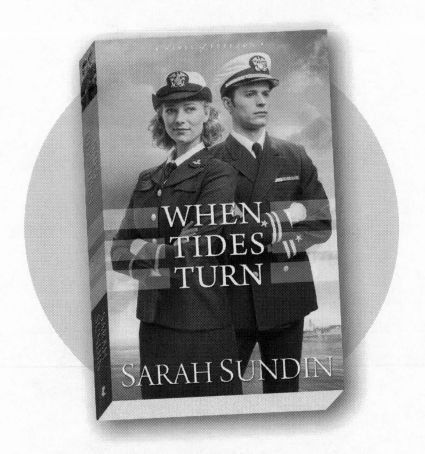

A fun-loving glamour girl. A no-nonsense naval officer. Only a war could bring them together. What happens next will change their lives.

"A gripping tale of war, intrigue, and love."

—*RT Book Reviews* on *A Memory Between Us*

"Sarah Sundin seamlessly weaves together emotion, action, and sweet romance."

—USA Today's Happy Ever After blog

GET TO KNOW

SARAH SUNDIN

To learn more about Sarah,
read her blog, or see
the inspiration behind
the stories, visit

SARAHSUNDIN.COM